Cursed with a poor sense of [          ] propensity to read, **Annie C**[          ] her childhood lost in books. [          ] [          ] Literature followed by a career in computing didn't lead directly to her perfect job—writing romance for Mills & Boon—but she has no regrets in taking the scenic route. She lives in London: a city where getting lost can be a joy.

**Susan Carlisle**'s love affair with books began when she made a bad grade in mathematics. Not allowed to watch TV until the grade had improved, she filled her time with books. Turning her love of reading into a love for writing romance, she now pens hot Medicals. She loves castles, travelling, afternoon tea, reading voraciously and hearing from her readers. Join her newsletter at SusanCarlisle.com.

Discover more at millsandboon.co.uk.

# COUNTRY FLING WITH THE CITY SURGEON

## ANNIE CLAYDON

# FALLING FOR THE TRAUMA DOC

## SUSAN CARLISLE

MILLS & BOON

First published in Great Britain 2024
by Mills & Boon, an imprint of HarperCollins*Publishers* Ltd,
1 London Bridge Street, London, SE1 9GF

www.harpercollins.co.uk

HarperCollins*Publishers* Macken House, 39/40 Mayor Street Upper, Dublin 1, D01 C9W8, Ireland

Country Fling with the City Surgeon © 2024 Annie Claydon

Falling for the Trauma Doc © 2024 Susan Carlisle

ISBN: 978-0-263-32157-9

04/24

This book contains FSC™ certified paper and other controlled sources to ensure responsible forest management.

For more information visit www.harpercollins.co.uk/green.

Printed and Bound in the UK using 100% Renewable Electricity at CPI Group (UK) Ltd, Croydon, CR0 4YY

# COUNTRY FLING WITH THE CITY SURGEON

ANNIE CLAYDON

MILLS & BOON

# CHAPTER ONE

'THIS IS JUST…lovely…' Stella Parry-Jones slowed her car, muttering to herself, before she gingerly turned into the dirt track ahead of her. There was nowhere to park on the narrow country road that led here, and it seemed that her car was going to have to take its chances with the wicked-looking thorns in the hedge to the left of the track.

But when she'd stopped at the village post office she'd been assured that this was the right way to go. And up ahead she could see a white painted house, nestling amongst a group of trees in the patchwork of fields. Since the first line of the address she'd been given was *The White House*, she'd take that as a sign she was going in the right direction.

*Physically* going in the right direction… Whether this was the right thing to be doing with a warm, clear Saturday morning was anyone's guess.

Going to see the man who'd had her job before her—that might be helpful or a big mistake. Asking for his help… Stella told herself that she had nothing to lose if Rob Franklin said *no*. She'd just drive back to London, tick this possibility off her list and she wouldn't have to think about it again. If he said *yes,* then her patient potentially had a lot to gain.

She headed down the hill, towards the house. The wide gate that led into the driveway was open and she parked next to a battered SUV, which had clearly not managed to avoid the hedge on a couple of occasions. When she got out of her own vehicle to inspect for similar damage it was caked with grime, but Stella could at least congratulate herself on arriving here without having scratched her car.

The newly painted front door had no bell but there was a heavy brass knocker, fashioned in the shape of a dragon. Hoping that the dragon wasn't a warning, she grasped it firmly by its shiny snout and rapped loudly. No answer.

She'd been told that he would be here. Maybe *'in all day'* meant something different to Rob than it did to her and he expected her to wait if he was out. She'd met the previous Deputy Head of Reconstructive Surgery at the Thames Hospital in London only once, when he'd popped in to collect some paperwork from the HR department, and attend a hand-over meeting with Stella. The meeting had been awkward in the extreme, and Phil Chamberlain, the Head of Reconstructive Surgery, had been forced to do all of the talking, while Rob Franklin had tapped his foot, nodded and drunk tea.

Phil had drawn the meeting to a close quickly, and on leaving the sum of her predecessor's advice to her had been a terse, *'Good luck with it, then.'*

Stella reminded herself that Rob Franklin had been going through a lot, back then. Phil had apologised to her, saying that he should never have allowed the meeting to go ahead because Rob was clearly having a bad day. Rob had been one of the brightest and the best, a brilliant surgeon and innovator and one of the best human beings that Phil knew, and his worried face as he ran for the lift to catch up with Rob and walk him out said more than all the rumours that had been flying around the department.

But three years was a long time. In the last year she'd seen Rob's name on several academic papers and been impressed with his clarity of thought and the bold simplicity of his solutions. When she'd floated the idea of contacting him with Phil, he'd agreed immediately and said that he would call Rob and find out if it was possible to set something up.

Stella knocked again. No answer. Phil wouldn't have let her come all this way if he'd thought there was any chance that Rob would duck out of their meeting, and Stella decided there must be a back door. She followed the paved path which ran around the house, past a well-tended kitchen garden.

A man was working in the dappled sunshine, amongst a cluster of fruit trees that lay beyond the garden. A gardener maybe, his tanned arms showed that he spent a lot of time outside. Stella opened her mouth to call out to him, but the words died in her throat.

Rob Franklin. Just the way that he moved, reaching to inspect the branches above his head, was different from when they'd last met. Since he wasn't looking her way, Stella could stare for a moment longer than she really needed to. He'd been wearing a suit when she'd seen him last, but she was sure that wouldn't have disguised these broad shoulders. And she would definitely have noticed the measured, relaxed grace with which he worked, clipping the extra fruit spurs so that those which remained would have more room to grow.

And then... It almost knocked Stella off her feet when he turned and, catching sight of her, he smiled. Taking a breath, to steady herself, she walked towards him.

'Stella?' It wasn't clear whether he recognised her or if first names were now just the way he worked. Still, the image of the man who'd looked straight through her and seemed to be waiting for any excuse to get out of the room was stronger than the one in front of her and she decided to play it safe.

'Yes. Mr Franklin?'

'No one calls me that any more. Rob, please. I'm hoping

that your visit means that you've set aside my behaviour at our first meeting.'

He remembered. And he wasn't going to skirt around any awkward truths. That suited Stella. 'Of course. Rob.'

He nodded, bending to pick up the bag of clippings at his feet. 'You found your way all right?'

'Yes, I followed the directions that Phil gave me.' They *had* been accurate, even though they hadn't involved a postal address, which had prompted her satnav to claim that the place didn't exist. The smiling woman at the post office knew exactly where The White House was—about a mile along Snakes Lane. And it was indeed on the only road which ran west from Little Beddingford village.

He nodded, walking over to a large compost bin and emptying the bag of clippings. As he strode back towards her, pulling off his gardening gloves, she could see that his hands, at least, were still those of a surgeon, well-tended and clearly carefully protected. His eyes were grey-blue, but they seemed like a welcoming sky now, instead of freezing waters, and his face had lost that hollow-cheeked look that she remembered. Whether his smile was the same... Stella couldn't come to any conclusion on that, because Rob Franklin hadn't smiled once at their last meeting.

'Come inside. I dare say you could do with a cup of tea.'

Perhaps he was referring to the drive from London. Stella hoped so because she'd been working hard to conceal her surprise. Whatever. She could do with a drink, and the hospitality didn't seem out of character with Rob Franklin version two. Or maybe the man she'd first met was version two—everyone at work said that he'd changed in the six months before Stella had arrived—and the one she saw now was the real Rob Franklin. The way he'd been before stress had got the better of him and he'd burnt out.

Stella had quite deliberately not enquired too closely into what had happened. Her eyes were firmly fixed on success and whatever the pressures, whatever else she had to give up to make this job work, she wasn't going to go the way that Rob Franklin had. Although, right now, his complicated life trajectory didn't seem to have ended up so badly—he had a vague but unmistakable aura of relaxed happiness about him.

'How are things?' He threw the question over his shoulder as he made the tea. At least this was a question she could answer.

'Good. We've strengthened our links with several other reconstructive surgery units and that increased exchange of information is proving beneficial. We've also attracted a couple of newly qualified surgeons, who are showing a lot of potential…'

He turned suddenly. That smile again. It seemed that it was frequent enough now that Stella would have to start getting used to it.

'I was referring to you. Not so much the department.'

'That *is* how I'm doing. Right now, the department's the most important thing to me, and I don't have a lot of time for anything else.' Maybe she should make that clear. Because the thought had already occurred to her that this new Rob Franklin might make a fascinating dinner date, and if by any chance he thought the same of her she wouldn't have the self-control to say no.

He nodded, walking over to the kitchen table with two mugs of tea. 'Okay. Since that makes you happy, then perhaps we'd better get straight to it. What are you here for?'

No chatting about fruit trees. No walking out into the garden with their tea to take a tour of the vegetables. That was a relief, but suddenly it seemed that Stella had missed out on something as well.

'You're the best in the business, Rob.'

He shook his head slowly. 'I *was* the best in the business. Maybe.'

'I've read your papers.' Whatever he liked to say now, his work on developing suture techniques was still right at the cutting-edge. He must know that.

'That's theory. Unless you hadn't noticed, I don't practise any more. Not surgery, anyway.'

Stella resisted the temptation to ask what he was practising, because surgery was all she was interested in. 'We've used your work as a reference for our own surgical techniques, and in one of our training programmes. I believe you've consulted with equipment manufacturers…' She paused, waiting for his reaction.

That smile again. She was beginning to wish he wouldn't do that. 'Okay. Busted.'

'Then I can get on to what I want from you. If I may.'

'Be my guest.' He leaned back in his seat, propping one ankle onto the other knee. A picture of someone relaxed enough to listen and perfectly capable of saying no. Stella leaned down, taking her best shot at this out of her bag.

'This is a patient file, so…'

'Confidential. I understand.' He reached for the file and opened it. Stella had clipped the two pictures that she really wanted him to take notice of to the inside of the front cover. The shot of Anna's right profile showed a young woman with a good bone structure and a flawless complexion. Her left profile…

'Traffic accident?' Rob's expression had darkened suddenly.

'Yes. There were a number of bones broken and we're working on prosthetics to realign the shape of her face. Her left eye was saved, but as you can see there's a scar on her brow which has contracted, so it's pulling at her eyelid. There are problems with the way that her jaw has healed, which affect her bite and the overall shape of her face, and as you can see there's heavy scarring on her cheek and around her jaw.'

'Other injuries?' Rob rightly came to the conclusion that there must have been some reason why they'd waited so long to address this.

'Yes, she had internal injuries, which were operated on straight away. She's recovered very well from them, and we can think about further surgery now. As you know, there's a great deal that we can do for her, but it's going to take a lot of planning and skill. Anna's twenty-four years old, and she has a first-class law degree…'

Rob held up his hand. 'If you were about to paint a picture for me, that's not necessary. There's a lot we can fix…'

So he hadn't turned his back on surgery quite as completely as he claimed. Rob must have seen the involuntary quirk of her lips because he shot her a reproachful glance.

'There's a lot that *you* can fix. But you can't mend people's lives.'

'I've read your guidelines on what reconstructive surgery can and can't do.' Rob couldn't deny that he'd once been a surgeon, and the guidelines he'd written for the department were an excellent reminder on how to manage patients' expectations. 'But Anna's age is a factor when considering surgery, and her intended career is too, because her confidence in making someone's case in court has been undermined by her injuries. I was also going to mention that I've met her partner and that she's very supportive of Anna. You'll be well aware that family support's a factor too.'

'And her name's Anna.' Rob's gaze hadn't left the photographs, and he was clearly struggling to take a step back from the case.

'What else do you want me to call her? If you feel something when you look at these pictures, and you want to help, then maybe that's down to you.'

And maybe her reply was a little sharp. So what? Rob had opened the door on the discussion.

'I'd be interested in knowing exactly what you mean by the word *help*.'

It was a straight question that deserved a straight answer. And Rob must know that she'd come here with a shopping list.

She started to count on her fingers. 'I want to consult with someone with a detailed knowledge of skin grafting techniques, who isn't afraid of blending new techniques with tried and tested ones. Someone who can help plan and prioritise a complex set of surgical procedures. Someone with practical theatre expertise.'

'And you don't have all of those skills yourself?' Rob shot her an innocent look, as if this was actually a question that needed answering.

'I'm looking for someone who's as good as I am, in all of those areas. You know full well that discussion and collaboration make everyone better, and this is a complicated case so I feel it's going to be a vital part of the process.'

'Anything the matter with the guy in the office next to yours? Or did you just have a yen for some fresh air and a long car journey?' Rob's lips curved in half-smile, half-challenge that set Stella's pulse racing. He knew the answer to that question as well, but he was going to make her say it.

'Phil's job is to run the department. He advises, he puts people together when he believes they can form productive working relationships and he encourages collaboration. My job is to push boundaries, knowing that he has my back.'

'And you think I can push those boundaries with you?'

Stella was becoming a little impatient now. 'That's up to

you to decide. I'll take whatever help you feel able to give me, in any of the areas I've outlined.'

Rob nodded thoughtfully. His frank manner had prompted frank responses, even though they barely knew each other. But that was good. Productive.

And…somehow intimate. The look in his grey-blue eyes made her shiver, and Stella needed to put aside the thought that she was becoming personally invested in getting Rob to agree to this. Nothing about it was personal, it was all business.

'Maybe I wish I could help and feel that I shouldn't.' He closed the file, putting it down on the kitchen table. There was something corrosive about the honesty in his eyes. Regret, over something that Stella couldn't see.

'May we talk about that?'

He seemed to be right on the edge of a *yes*. But then his phone rang and Rob apologised, taking the call. He listened for a moment, before briskly telling the person at the other end of the line that he'd *'deal with it'* and tucking his phone back into his pocket.

'I'm on call, and I have to make a visit.' He got to his feet. 'I'd like to answer your question, though, and I won't be any more than half an hour. Feel free to raid the fridge if you're hungry.'

'On call?' Stella raised an eyebrow. She was hungry, but she was a great deal more interested in what this sudden mission of Rob's was all about.

'Yes, I applied to retrain and I'm a junior doctor with the local GP's practice. I cover the village at weekends. It's not a very big place, as I'm sure you noticed during the minute and a half it took you to get from one end of the high street to the other, so I'm not called out all that often. This is just bad timing.'

'You're a *junior* doctor?' Today was turning out to be full of surprises.

He laughed suddenly. 'Yeah. Junior suits me at the moment, in lots of ways. You want to come along and try it out?'

That was an offer she couldn't refuse. 'Okay, yes, I'm interested. Who are we going to visit?'

'Emma Bradbury. Eighty years old, and lives alone. She's just been diagnosed with a heart condition and she's worried about her medication.'

# CHAPTER TWO

ROB HAD BEEN wondering about Phil's sudden emailed request for a meeting. They'd stayed in contact and spoke regularly on the phone, which was more to do with Phil's stubborn refusal to stop calling than any attempt on Rob's part to keep up with his London friends. He owed Phil big time, and that had a lot more to do with his agreement to meet Stella than anything else.

He couldn't recall her, but Phil's ill-concealed hint—'*You'll remember Stella, from the hand-over meeting*'—told him that they must have met and that she clearly remembered him. When he'd first caught sight of her, he'd realised just how far he'd come in the last three years.

The photograph on the hospital's website, which he'd consulted in preparation for her visit, was in black and white. She looked businesslike and sympathetic, which was clearly the aim of the shot. In real life, her red hair and green eyes were strikingly beautiful, and there was an honesty in her gaze that sent a tingle running down his spine. If he ever needed evidence of how messed-up he'd been when he'd left the Thames Hospital then he had it now because, however much he searched his memory, there was nothing pertaining to this fascinating, challenging woman.

It didn't help to think about the past. He'd struggled to make peace with it, and he'd come to a place where he could at least sleep at night and function during the day. Somehow, and without really considering that as one of his goals, he'd learned how to be happy.

Rob had made a lot of mistakes, let a lot of people down. Worst of all, he'd driven away the woman he'd promised to love with all his heart. He couldn't change any of that, but he could change what he did now. He'd taken one look at the photographs in the file that Stella had brought and the old excitement had taken hold. He could do something to help change Anna's life for the better...

Now he'd fallen into the trap of thinking of an anonymous patient by name. He was going to have to stop that, because getting involved opened up the possibility of further mistakes, more opportunities to let people down. Talking a few things through with Stella was an option—he was sure that she must have ideas on how best to treat her patient, and perhaps he could make a few suggestions. But there was no going back, and he had to keep this all at arm's length.

He went upstairs, quickly changing out of his gardening jeans and into a pair of chinos, which were quite respectable enough for work these days, even if they weren't quite as smart as Stella's dark blue summer dress. Picking up his medical bag from the cupboard under the stairs, he ushered her out of the front door. It was impossible to miss the look on her face as she breezed past him.

'If I wear a suit, Emma's going to think there's something really wrong with her. I don't want her to get the wrong idea.'

'And what about turning up with reinforcements?' Stella shot him a questioning look.

'I think we'll just say *friends,* shall we.' Rob thought better of the plan. 'Friends and colleagues.'

He opened the front passenger door of his car and she climbed in, leaving every nerve in his body suddenly on red alert at the subtle fragrance of her scent. As he walked around to the driver's door and started the car, he decided that, since he couldn't ignore the feeling, he had to just enjoy it and let it go.

'Anything I should know?' Stella reached for her seatbelt and the soft profile of her face prompted a sudden wave of longing.

'If she offers you cake, bear in mind that Emma makes the best coffee and walnut cake I've ever tasted.' Flippancy seemed to help with the *letting go* part of the process.

'It's good to know that this isn't a serious medical emergency.'

'It's serious. Just not an emergency yet.'

It was a seven-minute drive to Emma's cottage, and from the twitch of the net curtains she'd obviously been looking out for his car. She answered the door as soon as he pressed the bell, clearly having moved from her station behind the window to one behind the door.

'Thank you for coming, Rob. I hope I didn't interrupt anything.' Emma was looking at Stella, frank curiosity on her face.

'Rob and I were colleagues, when he used to work in London.' Stella spoke up before he got a chance to. 'I'm a doctor too, and I'm interested to see how his practice here compares with my own job. If you don't mind, that is…'

'Of course not, dear.' Emma stood back from the doorway, beckoning them both inside. 'Come and sit down. Do you have time for some tea?'

'If it's not too much trouble…' Stella smiled and Emma responded to her offer to help with the tea things by shepherding her through into the kitchen, leaving Rob to wait in the sitting room.

She was good with people. He heard the muffled sound of conversation floating through from the kitchen, and suddenly Emma laughed. She was still smiling as she led the way through into the sitting room, motioning to Stella to put the tray that she was carrying down on the table that stood in front of the sofa. It seemed that a three-minute acquaintance was enough for Stella to be allowed to pour the tea, while Emma insisted he tried a lemon drizzle cupcake.

'They're really good. I had a taste of one in the kitchen…' Emma reacted to Stella's comment by offering her another cupcake, and Rob decided that they'd done quite enough bonding and it was time to get down to the medical details.

'What can I do for you, Emma?'

'It's my medication. I had my prescription delivered from the chemist this morning and I'm not sure whether it's right or not. I called them and they said it definitely was…' Emma frowned, the worried look returning to her face. 'I'm sorry to bother you on a Saturday, but you did tell me I had to take these tablets without fail, and I'm really not sure whether they've made a mistake or not.'

'That's fine, I'd far rather you called me if you have any concerns. Let's have a look at them.' Rob reached for the bag that was sitting next to the tea tray, opening it and studying its contents.

'What did the pharmacist say when you called?'

'Just that they'd sent me the right medicine and that I wasn't to worry. But they're not the same as the ones I had last time, these are called something different. Look.' Emma got to her feet, opening a drawer in the sideboard and taking out an empty packet.

'Yes, you're quite right. Many medicines have two names, a generic name and a brand name. The medicine they've sent you has exactly the same active ingredients, it just has a different package.'

Emma's face fell. 'I didn't know that. I'm sorry…'

'It's not your fault, Emma, they should have explained that

to you. And they should be sending your medication a little earlier than this, so that you still have a few days' worth of the old ones, in case there are any mistakes or you have any queries. Since they did neither of those things, you were absolutely right in calling me to check.'

'That's good of you, Rob...' Emma was still looking a little sheepish.

'I wish more of my patients took the same notice as you do, Emma.' He glanced at Stella, and she nodded.

'Yes, some of mine could take a leaf out of your book. It's bound to worry you when you've been taking one drug and you get something that looks entirely different.'

Emma shrugged. 'I dare say they have my age on their records somewhere. They don't explain anything because they think I won't understand.'

'That's no excuse!' Stella's flash of outrage made Emma smile and Rob couldn't help following suit. Maybe the days when medicine made his heart race weren't quite as distant as he'd thought. And maybe he'd reached a place where he could deal with that.

'While I'm here, I'll just check your blood pressure and heart.' Rob reached into his bag and Emma shot him an enquiring look.

'Because you need to, or are you attempting to reassure me?'

He'd been expecting something of the sort. 'Don't you know me better than that?'

'Very well. If you'd needed to know what my blood pressure was, you would have already made an appointment with me. Since you never seem to like the word *attempt,* I'll accept your reassurances.' Emma smiled mischievously as she pulled up her sleeve and Rob wound the blood pressure cuff around her arm.

'Okay.' Rob checked the monitor. 'As expected, your blood pressure's fine and the same as it was the last time. You've been taking some gentle exercise and following the diet recommendations I gave you?'

'Yes. Do you want to see my notebook? I've been writing it all down.'

'It's okay, I trust you.' Rob turned his attention to the portable heart monitor and Emma held up her hand, ready for him to clip the sensor to her finger. Out of the corner of his eye, he saw Stella turn her gaze slightly towards the read-out, and Emma craned her neck to see it too.

He couldn't help feeling that there was an element of courtesy in the way that they both waited for his verdict; after all, they'd both seen enough of these to know what the reading meant without him telling them. Rob did his best to inject a suitable gravitas into his tone.

'That's fine. Steady as a rock. How's the reassurance coming along?'

'Very well. Thank you so much for coming, Rob.'

'It's my pleasure.' He packed up the monitors, putting them back into his bag and withdrawing the two books he'd brought with him. 'I finished the one you lent me, and I have one in return.'

'Oh! Splendid...' Emma took the books, glancing at the covers. 'I'm getting to really like these Scandinavian crime stories. They're quite different, aren't they?' Emma turned to Stella, who nodded. From the uncomprehending look in her eyes, it was clear that Stella wasn't a fan of murder mysteries. Probably not a fan of any kind of fiction—when Rob had had her job, he'd never had time for books. He'd only recently rediscovered the joy of reading for pleasure.

'I really liked the one you picked for me. The end came as quite a surprise.'

'Didn't see it coming, eh?' Emma got to her feet, examining the spines in the large bookcase in one corner of the room. 'Try this one for size.'

He took the book, stowing it away in his bag. Stella was persuaded to take some lemon drizzle cupcakes with her for later and they walked out into the sunshine, leaving Emma smiling at her front door.

'This is such a beautiful place,' Stella murmured as they drove through country lanes, back to the house.

'Yeah. I like living here.' He turned onto the dirt track, missing the hedge by mere inches. Maybe he needed to concentrate a little more on his driving, but Stella made that difficult.

When she got out of the car she hesitated, and then seemed to come to a decision. 'You're done with London, aren't you?'

The question surprised him. But when he thought about it, the answer had been there all the time. 'Yes, I am.'

'Is there anything more for us to say, then?'

This place had taken him in and nursed him back to health. More than that, it was somewhere he belonged. It would be easy to tell Stella that he'd never go back to London—that was *a* truth, if not the whole truth. He could allow her to believe that she'd done her best but that there was no shifting his resolve.

Or he could follow his instincts. Believe in the straightforward honesty between them, which seemed to have just clicked into place, without any particular effort on Rob's part. The thing about having a home, a solid base, was that it allowed him to reach out and explore whether what seemed impossible really was out of the question.

'Am I going to have to move house in order to consult with you?'

Stella smiled suddenly, and Rob knew that was what she wanted to hear. 'Absolutely not.'

'Then we have more to say.'

# CHAPTER THREE

MAYBE STELLA SHOULD remember what Phil had said to her on the way to the lift yesterday evening.

*'Don't walk away too quickly, Stella. Rob's a problem-solver and if he doesn't think he can help in the way you want him to, he'll try to work something out. He might even come up with a better solution...'*

She hadn't meant to issue Rob with an ultimatum. She'd simply meant to say that she realised now that his decision was more complicated than she'd thought. To acknowledge that asking for his help wasn't merely a matter of seeing whether he had space in his diary. He didn't just live here, he'd made an entirely different life for himself, and in the process he'd rejected the life that she had now.

The sun had moved in the sky and when they returned to Rob's kitchen light was streaming through the windows. He stowed his medical bag away under the stairs and started to go through the motions of making more tea. Stella didn't want any more tea and he probably didn't either, but it seemed to be Rob's way of giving himself time to think. He handed her a full mug, ignoring the file that still lay on the kitchen table and beckoning her outside.

They dawdled past the blackberry bushes at one end of the kitchen garden, and Rob stopped to snap off a withered shoot and throw it into the compost bin.

'We could go and see how your tomatoes are doing?' She gestured towards the ripening plants in the greenhouse. 'Or you could just tell me what I'm still doing here...'

Rob grinned suddenly. 'You're very frank.'

And she was still coming to grips with why that seemed so natural with Rob. 'It must be the country air. What's your excuse?'

'Not sure that I have one.' He began to stroll down towards the apple trees. 'Do you know why I left the Thames Hospital?'

'I don't know the details. I do know that it was a waste of a very good surgeon...'

He turned, blue steel flashing in his eyes. 'A waste? That's what you think my life is?'

'I'm sorry. I shouldn't have said that. I don't know the whole story and even if I did it's not my place to make value judgements.' She was doing it all the same. Wondering how he could reconcile throwing away all of that training and hard work, all of the dedication and expertise.

Rob pursed his lips and the thought occurred to Stella that maybe he couldn't reconcile it as well as he liked to make out. But it seemed that her apology had been accepted, and when he spoke his tone was matter-of-fact, as if he was trying to distance himself from the words.

'I thought that I could have it all. A great career, maybe some travel, a beautiful home and a family. For a while that didn't seem so difficult. My wife and I had a nice flat in London and we'd bought this place, reckoning on doing it up for weekends and holidays. I made deputy head of the department at thirty-four...' He turned towards her, the obvious question flashing in his eyes.

'Thirty-three.' Stella couldn't help rising to the bait.

He chuckled. 'I'm not going to hold that against you. How's it going?'

'It's good. I know I can't have it all. I don't have a partner or children, and I haven't got any big property development plans. But I have the one thing that I really want.'

He nodded. 'Maybe that's the answer, then. I didn't see it at the time, and I was always rushing, trying to push forward on too many different fronts. There were speaking engagements, even some talk of a possible publishing deal. Kate and I both liked to travel and we carved out some time for a few great holidays, but even then there was a lot to fit in and not much time to just sit in the sun and watch the world go by.'

Stella puffed out a breath. 'That's a lot for anyone to take on.'

'I'm not exactly idle now.' He sat down on a bench in the shade of an old oak tree that stood at the perimeter of the orchard. The scent of blossom and early summer growth hung light in the air and Stella sat down next to him, stretching her legs out in front of her.

She saw what he *hadn't* been saying, now. Anyone might feel a sense of failure if they'd left all that behind, and perhaps there was an element of trying to convince them both that the life he had now was just as rewarding, but in different ways.

'Working as a GP and publishing your research, you mean? And you've obviously done a lot here.' The outside of the house looked freshly painted, and the kitchen was obviously new.

He chuckled. 'Yeah. Sometimes I don't notice.'

He noticed. Stella didn't spend a lot of time on her surroundings, they were either practical or not practical as far as she was concerned, but this place was a carefully constructed home. Maybe Rob thought that it was a second best, something he made do with because he'd lost what he really wanted, and he expected her to judge him in the same way. That wasn't what she'd come here to do.

'It looks as if you'll get apples from some of those trees

over there.' She waved her finger towards the group of larger trees that he'd been pruning when she'd arrived.

Rob snorted with laughter. 'Yeah, okay. Don't try to pretend that you know what you're talking about. I will get some fruit, but they're pear trees.'

'Very well pruned pear trees. I'm a surgeon and I notice those things, at least!' she shot back at him, grinning. Their frank exchanges about work spilled over all too easily into the personal, and that was surprisingly delicious.

'Thank you. I'm going to take that as a compliment.' He drained his cup, setting it down on the bench beside him. 'The trouble with building a house of cards is that you remove one and it all comes crashing down. My wife, Kate, left me, which was one of the best decisions she ever made. I took on too much, and in trying to keep everything going I forgot that marriage takes time and attention too. I knew that I'd failed her, and I moved out of the flat and got a bedsit near to the hospital and spent every waking moment there. Then I started to fail at my job.'

Stella stared at him, questions bubbling in her head. Rob must know what those questions were…

'It would have been very serious if that had affected a patient.' The knowing look in his eyes told her he understood what was making her heart thump uncomfortably in her chest. 'I couldn't sleep and I was getting stress headaches. I spoke to Phil about it, and we agreed I'd take a step back from surgery for a while, and concentrate on research and staff development. But a surgeon who doesn't trust himself to operate…'

Was a failure. Stella could see what Rob was thinking, even if he couldn't say it. 'Needs some help, through a really difficult time in his life?'

Rob shrugged. 'Whatever. My initial solution was that if I ignored it all, it might go away. That clearly wasn't the right one. I found myself working even harder and getting more stressed. Then I had a psychogenic seizure.'

'I'm sorry to hear that happened to you.' Stella tried to conceal her shock; psychogenic seizures were often mistaken for epileptic seizures at first, with the same shaking, jerking and loss of consciousness, but were actually often caused by serious psychological stress.

He nodded an acknowledgement. 'It lasted for fifteen minutes. I hit the floor of my office, conscious but unable to move or stop my limbs from shaking. By the time I was able to get up again I'd already thought through every possible medical option, and none of them were good.'

Rob was sticking to the facts, but it must have been terrifying. And suddenly that frank connection between them broke, a casualty of all the things he wasn't saying.

'You were at work?'

'Yeah. In case you're wondering how I managed to get fifteen uninterrupted minutes alone during the day, I was working late.'

Stella forced a smile in response, although Rob probably knew that the joke wasn't funny. 'That explains it. Of course, seizures *can* be a result of stress...'

Rob shot her a reproachful look. 'Were you asleep when they covered that at medical school? Never assume a seizure is caused by stress unless you've checked for everything else first.'

'But you said it was psychogenic—so you *did* go and get yourself checked out.'

'Yeah. I went to a friend of mine, who runs a private clinic. They ruled out all the usual suspects—heart problems, epilepsy, substance abuse—and while the results of all the tests were coming back it happened again. The day after I was diagnosed with stress and clinical depression, I put my resignation in at the hospital.'

'But...they're recognised medical conditions, with understood treatment paths. Did you think of taking sick leave?'

She saw his lip begin to curl, and then he shook his head. 'At the time, I would have seen that as a final expression of failure. I felt that I'd lost everything, and I needed to get away and start again. I'd insisted that Kate took our London flat in the divorce settlement, reckoning that was the least I could do, and we'd kept the house because neither of us were quite sure what to do with it. I bought out her share and came down here, more as a matter of getting away from the scene of the crime than anything.'

Stella turned the corners of her mouth down. Failure wasn't a crime. Her father had often told her that pushing at the limits was all about finding out what was and wasn't possible. Why else would she have got into her car and driven down here this morning, on a mission that might well have failed?

'Would it be too much to expect that you took the usual route of counselling and medication?' Stella had a feeling that Rob had applied his own solutions to the difficulties he faced.

'Afraid so. I turned down the counselling that I was offered, and I didn't give the medication much of a chance either. As a doctor, it's not what I'd advise anyone else to do, but a complete change of scenery, somewhere I could start again and rebuild, was what worked for me. I've reached a place where I'm at peace with myself now, and I haven't had a seizure since I left London.'

'I didn't realise what I was asking of you, when I came down here. It's not that you don't want to help, is it?'

Rob shrugged. 'You didn't need to show me those photographs or tell me your patient's name. I know full well what's happened to her and what it must mean and I'd be there like a shot if I felt that there was something I could do. My hesitation is because I'm not sure that I'm the one who can help Anna.'

Should she take him at his word? Fail gracefully in her mission to gain his assistance in a way that preserved everything she already had, as her father had taught her? The feelings that Rob had awakened were just chemistry, and if the catalyst of their possible work together was removed, they'd fade quickly enough.

But she could feel that he was looking for a way to make this work. She was too. And if it *did* work then the benefits for Anna couldn't be ignored.

'Phil doesn't appear to think so.'

He let out a brusque laugh. 'I wondered when you were going to play that card...'

'I'm not playing a card, Rob. If you were entirely sure that there was nothing of any value you could add to Anna's treatment, we wouldn't be having this conversation, I'd be on my way back to London right now.' She thought she saw a slight downward quirk of his lips at the idea, and ignored it.

'I can see how coming back to work at the hospital is a big step, but we can keep things flexible. And the level of your involvement is entirely up to you, ranging from an informal consultative relationship to possible participation in Anna's surgery. If you can't do any of that, then I understand completely and there's no more to be said. But I'm really hoping that you want to keep talking and exploring possibilities.'

Simple. It made her position clear and left Rob the option of giving her a straight answer, so that they both knew where they stood. Why did that make her feel so breathless, all of a sudden?

'Okay, boss. How does here and now suit you? To explore possibilities.' The smile that hovered around his lips and the look in his eyes really weren't helping. They belonged in the realms of a delicious agreement between a man and a woman, and not a clearly thought through arrangement between two medical professionals.

Maybe Rob recognised that too, because his expression became suddenly thoughtful. That was only slightly less stirring than his smile, but Stella could deal with that if they both knew exactly what footing their relationship should be on.

'Here and now is fine with me. I don't have to be back in London at any particular time. My only condition is that you don't call me *boss*.' Rob clearly didn't have any intention of taking instructions from her in the foreseeable future.

He chuckled. 'As you wish. Any objections to lunch?'

Rob decided that a working lunch would be good. Not too much time for pleasantries, or getting to know each other too much. Despite his sudden wish to get to know Stella very well, it wasn't what he needed right now.

A ploughman's lunch, with salad and ginger beer, took only ten minutes to prepare, and relied on locally sourced ingredients to make it tasty. Stella followed him through to his office, which was when the plan of keeping this professional crumbled a little.

'Rob! You work here?' Stella was looking around her with the same expression of delight that he'd felt when his first spring here had provided the warmth for him to sit in the old orchid house, built on the side of the property, and he'd realised what it might become.

'Yep.'

Stella was looking up at the butterflies which had been disturbed by their entrance, and he couldn't help re-seeing the quiet magic through her eyes. The glazed partition which separated the conservatory area from his office space was folded back, and Stella nudged the door that led out into the garden closed.

'They'll all escape...' She grinned up at him.

'That's okay, they're not prisoners, and they escape all the time.' He nodded up towards the open vents in the glass ceiling. 'They come back again; the plants attract them. I keep the door to the house closed in the summer, so that they don't get through there.'

'You built this?'

'Renovated it. The previous owner grew orchids, but the windows were falling apart from lack of maintenance and so I had to replace them.' He put the tray that held their plates and glasses down on the desk, which together with a long work surface occupied a shaded area of his office. 'It was a big job, and I didn't get it finished until last year.'

'Doesn't it get really cold in the winter?'

'No, orchids need to be warm all year round, so it's built to keep the heat in. The back wall is attached to the house, and the side walls are both double thickness brickwork.' He gestured towards the fully glazed roof and front wall. 'This is all modern and well insulated. In fact, the main difficulty is keeping the place cool in the summertime.'

Stella nodded, gazing up at the two large fans that turned lazily over their heads, providing a comfortably cool breeze around the towering plants and shaded benches. Then another movement caught her eye. Sophie, the elderly labrador, generally spent the first couple of hours of her morning with Rob and then retreated to the peace and quiet of the conservatory to sleep, ignoring any comings and goings in the house. But she was awake and taking an interest now, and had quitted her dog basket to amble over towards them.

'Oh! You have a dog?' Stella bent down, holding out her hand and Sophie nuzzled against it.

'Sophie was a hearing dog. Her owner was an eighty-two-year-old man in very poor health and when he died his family weren't able to take Sophie. It looked as if she'd have to be put down.'

'So you gave her a home.' Stella smiled up at him. She and Sophie had clearly hit it off and Sophie was leaning against Stella, almost knocking her off-balance.

'Hey, Soph. That's enough…' He tried to guide Sophie away, but Stella glared at him as she crouched down to Sophie's height, winding her arms around the dog's neck defiantly. 'It wasn't really a decision. She didn't have anywhere else to go, so she came with me.'

'And she's putting her paws up, now that she's retired?'

'Yeah, she's nearly fourteen now. She wakes up early, has something to eat and then she and I go for a walk down to the fruit trees and back again. That's about her limit for the morning and she comes in here for some peace and quiet. Although she still sometimes gives me a nudge when the post drops through the letterbox, just for old times' sake.'

'Anyone else live here that I might need to know about?' Stella squinted at the plants in the conservatory, obviously wondering what they might conceal.

'Not as far as I'm aware. There were a pair of robins nesting in the rafters this spring, but they've gone now.'

'Hmm.' Stella got to her feet. 'Those baby birds making a racket must have been awful when you were trying to concentrate.' She shot him an amused look.

'Dreadful. We were both glad when they were gone, eh, Soph?' Rob opened his desk drawer and Sophie ambled over to him, knowing that he was about to produce the packet of dog treats. He saw the look in Stella's eyes and couldn't resist handing them over to her, so that she could make a fuss of the dog. It seemed slightly at odds with the businesslike efficiency she'd displayed earlier on.

'I can see how this place would help anyone regain their balance.'

'Not in the way you might be thinking. When I first came here to live, I just wanted to get away and didn't think too much about creature comforts. It was just before Christmas, and that was a cold winter...'

She turned her gaze on him suddenly. Stella had the knack of making a person want to talk, even if she'd asked no specific question. He was falling hook, line and sinker for it, and he didn't even *want* to put up a struggle.

'I remember.'

'Sitting things out until the summer wasn't an option. It was freezing, none of the doors closed properly, and you could feel the wind when you stood within a couple of feet of the windows, so I started to work on the place just to keep warm. Then there was a heavy fall of snow at the end of January, and I went out to help clear it in the village. That was when I first got to know Emma—she runs a scheme to help with shopping when the weather's bad, and she tapped me on the shoulder and told me that I seemed to be making good headway with the pavements and she could do with another volunteer. It wasn't really a question, more a demand.'

'She seems a resourceful woman.'

'You have no idea.' Maybe Stella did have some idea. She struck Rob as being a force to be reckoned with too. 'The thing is that it wasn't the peace and quiet of the countryside that pulled me out of the ever-decreasing circles I'd found myself caught up in. It was a set of simple challenges, which had straightforward answers.'

'You haven't talked about this before, have you?'

Along with all of her other talents, Stella was perceptive

and she read between the lines. Now suddenly seemed a very good time to back off and get things on a more professional footing, before Stella asked why he was talking about it now.

'Why don't we take another look at Anna's file?'

Stella paused, just long enough to let him know that she'd noticed the abrupt change of subject. Then she let him off the hook with a sudden smile and a quick shake of her head, in a *no matter* gesture that sent threads of golden light cascading through her beautiful hair. 'Thanks. I really appreciate it.'

Rob was beginning to feel a little less off-balance. A little less caught between the lure of returning to the one thing he'd really excelled at and his doubts about ever going back. What had happened three years ago had suddenly become very relevant to the decisions he made today, but as he and Stella worked through the file it felt as if today, and what they might do with it, was what really mattered.

'You're very thorough,' she murmured, looking at the practice suture kit that he'd taken from the cupboard, to assess the practicalities of one of the techniques they'd been discussing.

'And...?'

'You've kept yourself up-to-date with the latest techniques. You write papers. I don't suppose you have anything else up your sleeve?'

'Like what?'

Stella shrugged. 'Teaching, maybe?'

'I've thought about it. I've thought about a lot of things...' He leaned back in his seat, aware that Stella was watching him.

'I've come too far to go back now, Stella. I can only go forward. But maybe going forward includes working with you and using the skills I have to help Anna.'

He heard her catch her breath. When he looked up at her, Stella was trying to conceal a look of triumph.

'You're sure that's the right thing for you?' She had the grace to question his decision.

'No, but if it's a mistake then I dare say I'll learn something from it. And I want to make it clear that I *am* moving forward and that it'll be on my own terms.'

She allowed herself a smile. 'Mine too?'

Rob was suddenly aware of how close they were sitting. Up until now, it had just been a matter of sitting at the same desk, discussing the same things. Now it felt as if he needed to be breathing the same air as Stella if his own lungs were to work properly.

'That goes without saying, doesn't it?'

She leaned forward slightly. 'Say it anyway.'

So close. With two minds working together in such exact synchronicity, what could their bodies do…? Rob dismissed the thought quickly.

'On your terms too.' Why did that feel as if he'd just given himself to her? It was an obvious and productive grounding for any business relationship.

'Do we have a deal, then?' Stella held out her hand, looking him straight in the eye. A bargain was never really a bargain unless you looked a person in the eye, and Rob took her hand, feeling the pressure of her fingers around his. He'd expected her touch to be firm although not quite so soft, and the combination was making his blood boil.

'Yeah. We have a deal.' He let go of her hand before the heat between them became unbearable. 'Since you have what you came for, are you going to be on your way now? Or can you stay for dinner?'

She was thinking about it. And the way she turned the corners of her mouth down told him that a few unnecessary hours spent having dinner together appealed to her. In someone who displayed the level of focus that Stella did, that was a small and very satisfying miracle.

'I shouldn't really. It looks as if it's about to rain, and it'll be dark soon. I wouldn't much fancy my chances on the lane leading back up to the road...' Stella looked up as a few drops of rain splashed onto the glazed roof, as if the weather was adding its own warning to her reservations.

'You could always stay over...'

Rob bit his tongue. It was a more natural offer when you lived in an out-of-the-way place, but perhaps his wish to get to know Stella better had something to do with it too. He was sure that there was some straightforward way of saying that his suggestion was a simple matter of practicality and not a come-on...

'The spare room's pretty well stocked with anything you might need. My sister makes sure of that—she often stays when she comes to visit.' That would have to do. He'd at least managed to incorporate the keywords *spare room* and *sister*.

And it seemed that Stella had got the message. She nodded, smiling.

'Thanks for the offer. Can we take a rain check and have dinner some time when you're down in London?'

So dinner was okay and staying over was to be avoided. Now that he thought about it, that was a good decision. Friends, but not too close.

'I'd like that. I'll give Phil a call and set up a date for me to come up for a meeting, shall I?'

'Yes, that would be great.' Stella hesitated gratifyingly before she got to her feet. One more moment, surrounded by her scent. A small acknowledgement that she knew what had passed between them, and that this was more than just a professional connection.

And she was fighting it too. Rob was pretty clear about

why he felt it would be a bad idea to take things any further than a professional friendship with Stella. The guilt of tearing everything down once was bad enough, and twice would be impossible to bear. It was less obvious why someone like Stella should feel that she had to exclude everything else but work from her life.

But it was too late to think about that now. Rob watched as she gathered her things together, putting Anna's file back into her bag. He'd put himself on a road that had no clear destination today, but Rob knew that he was committed now and couldn't retrace his steps.

# CHAPTER FOUR

WHEN SHE ARRIVED at work on Monday morning, Stella was still smarting slightly from the realisation that a perfectly innocent offer of dinner and Rob's spare room for the night had taken on an unintended secondary meaning in her head. She had to get this relationship onto a purely business footing and keep it there. But there was still a forbidden thrill of excitement when Phil called her into his office to tell her that he'd just spoken with Rob on the phone, and they'd arranged a meeting for two o'clock on Friday.

'There's one thing I'd like to make clear to you, Stella. You're the boss in this relationship.'

Stella shifted uncomfortably in her seat, wishing that Phil hadn't chosen to call it a *relationship*, even if he was only referring to a collaboration at work. 'I did tell him that he wasn't to call me *boss*.'

Phil chuckled. 'I'm glad he understands who's boss, even if you don't. And now that we're considering Rob's return...' Phil had an air of someone who was choosing his words carefully. 'Don't get me wrong, I think you made a very good decision in suggesting we ask Rob back and I'm personally delighted that he's open to working with us again. But you shouldn't let him have everything his own way.'

Stella thought for a moment. 'I've promised to be flexible,

though. I think that's the right thing to do, in the circumstances, isn't it?'

'There's nothing wrong with flexibility and I completely agree with your approach. Rob's brilliant, one of the best surgeons I've ever seen, and he thinks outside the box. But he can be uncompromising at times...' Phil paused, clearly choosing his words carefully.

This conversation would be much easier if she just came clean. 'When Rob and I talked on Saturday, he told me that he'd been diagnosed with clinical depression and that he had several physical symptoms of stress when he left his job here.'

Phil nodded. 'I'm glad you had that conversation. You understand that it wouldn't have been appropriate for me to mention it if Rob hadn't done so himself.' Phil was always meticulous in protecting the confidentiality of all his staff, and everyone here appreciated that.

'Of course.'

'But now that you *do* know... He may have mentioned that I've been keeping in touch with him and I'm confident that he's fully recovered now. But he's been through a lot and my belief is that he needs a strong framework to support him while he's finding his feet.'

Stella nodded. Phil seemed to be overestimating the amount of support that Rob would need, but he knew Rob a lot better than she did.

'I can provide the framework on one level, but I'm going to need you to back it up on a day-to-day basis, Stella.'

Maybe that was what Rob had meant when he'd called her *boss*. He wanted Stella to help him, and she'd turned him down without even stopping to think.

'I can do that, Phil. I'm committed to making this work.' Not just for Anna's sake, although she was the most important person in all of this. For Rob's sake, and maybe even for hers.

Phil smiled, leaning back in his seat. 'I wouldn't have given the go-ahead for this if I hadn't been confident that both of you can make it work very well...'

Stella had been unable to stop herself from looking forward to seeing Rob again on Friday afternoon, and it was making her very nervous about the possibility that he might make a last-minute decision not to turn up. But Reception had called, saying that Rob was on his way up, and Stella joined Phil in his office, sitting down in one of the comfortable chairs around a coffee table that was used for informal meetings. They waited in silence, and Stella jumped when a brisk knock sounded at the door.

Rob had clearly been making his own preparations for the meeting. Sunglasses weren't remarkable in this weather, but perched on the top of his head they made it look as if Rob was here on a social call. His light shoes, casual trousers and shirt were perfect for a summer evening with friends. And he'd grown a beard.

Not much of a beard, admittedly, but it was a good achievement for just six days. Well-trimmed and neat, and it suited him. If Stella had to sum up the overall look, *not here permanently* was the closest she could get.

'Rob!' Phil sprang to his feet, stepping forward to shake his hand. 'It's good to see you. You're looking well.'

'Thanks. It's good to be back.' Rob didn't sound quite as enthusiastic about the prospect as Phil did, but then he'd undoubtedly just run a gamut of curious glances and murmurs behind hands, because sunglasses and the shadow of a beard weren't really much of a disguise. Probably a few appreciative stares as well, given that he was looking particularly delicious today, even if that probably hadn't been his aim.

Phil waved him towards a chair, then made for the door

to bellow for coffee. Stella was about to get to her feet, wondering whether shaking his hand was the right greeting, and Rob's sudden smile kept her in her seat. It had all the intimacy of an old friend.

'Hello again.' He sat down opposite her.

'Hello. Good journey here?' It was all that Stella could think of to say.

'Yeah. I left Sophie with Emma, they're keeping each other company for the afternoon. The fast trains into London from Hastings are pretty good.'

'Must be a little strange to be back...'

She saw his lip curl. Stella had learned what that meant at the weekend, and that Rob preferred not to bother with tact.

'Hard, you mean. Yeah, it is.'

'Right, then...' Phil interrupted the moment before Stella could reply, plumping himself down in a seat that was roughly equidistant from both of them and loosening his tie a notch. He had a way of making people feel comfortable around him, and Stella had learned that he did very little by chance. It was a gesture that was intended to bridge the gap between her smart trousers and jacket, and Rob's more casual look.

That wasn't needed. From the moment Rob had smiled, the connection was there, so strong that it was almost frightening.

'We'll get down to business, shall we?' Phil smiled at them both and Stella dragged her attention away from Rob. 'I'll be needing to know what role you feel you might take in this case, Rob.'

Nothing like cutting to the chase. Stella would like to know that too. Rob waved his hand in a gesture that intimated he wasn't too interested in roles.

'I was thinking of as and when Stella thinks I'm needed. On an informal basis.'

'Okay.' Phil gave Stella a querying look. It seemed that both he and Rob wanted her to take charge, and she didn't normally feel this flutter of uncertainty when that was required.

'Anna's case is one where we need to assess and integrate different skin repair techniques, and be prepared to apply them in new ways to provide a good result. We started to talk this through on Saturday, and I'd like to continue with those discussions and involve Rob in my planning of the surgery. Clearly Rob will need to see Anna in person, before we go too much further with either of those elements.'

Stella took a breath, wondering if either of the men was going to say anything, but neither did. So far so good, and this next part was where either Rob or Phil might have stronger opinions.

'It may well be beneficial for Rob to take some part in the surgery. What that part is depends largely on the outcome of our discussions, but also on how Rob feels about returning to surgery after a three-year break. We have some time before the date we've provisionally set for Anna's surgery, so can I suggest that we prepare for that possibility and make a joint decision on it later.'

Rob and Phil were both staring at her, and it was difficult to know what either of them was thinking. Then Phil spoke.

'I'm happy with that. What do you say, Rob?'

'Yep. Sounds good to me too.'

Phil beamed at them both. 'Right, then. And you're available on Thursdays and Fridays?'

'And every other weekend, when I'm not on call.'

'Weekends don't work for me.' Stella had thought about this and decided that she couldn't stop Rob from working weekends, but she wasn't going to facilitate it. He shot her a knowing smile, and she wondered whether she was in for a battle.

But he just shrugged. 'Okay. I can prune my fruit trees.'

Rob was too compliant. Maybe it was Phil's presence, or the

fact that he was back here at the Thames Hospital, but Stella doubted that. Something else was coming…

'Anything we haven't covered?' Phil's innocent look told Stella that he was thinking the same as her.

A flash of steel showed in Rob's eyes, even though he was still smiling. 'As you know, I had my doubts about coming back to work here, but I can see how I might contribute to this particular case, and I'd like to help. I'm happy to work on a volunteer basis.'

'Wait…' Maybe Stella had missed something that had been understood between the two men, although she couldn't imagine that Phil would agree to that. It was irregular to say the least, and possibly even prohibited under the rules that governed the hospital's medical practice. 'When you say *volunteer*…?'

Phil nodded. 'My thoughts exactly. This hospital has plenty of volunteers, but I've never had a doctor in this department volunteering their services. Are we misunderstanding you, Rob?'

'Nope. You call on doctors with particular expertise all the time. I'm an NHS employee who has all of the necessary accreditation still in place, and this is the way I want to do things. If that's okay with you.'

This sounded a lot like *take it or leave it*. And from the creases that were forming on Phil's brow, it was a deal-breaker.

'I'm going to have to speak with HR…' That was Phil's usual get-out clause when he needed some time to think about something. Rob clearly knew that too, and he got to his feet.

'I'll let you do that…'

Phil looked up at him. 'Thanks, Rob. We do need to explore the options here. Where will you be?'

'Coffee bar. The one in the main building that used to do great pastries.'

'They still do...' Phil called after him as he made for the door, turning to Stella when Rob closed it quietly behind him.

Phil frowned in annoyance. 'This is Rob all over. He knows he's throwing a spanner into the works. We need to make sure that this is done properly and I'm not going to take any short-cuts or make Rob a special case, however much he wants to do things his way.'

Stella nodded, thinking hard. They'd gone through the motions with Rob, discussing availability and what his role might be. But they hadn't talked about what really mattered: Rob's guilt, because he felt he'd let everyone down. Phil's own feelings about what had happened three years ago.

'I've got a suggestion for a possible way forward...' If Stella couldn't find a compromise, then she very much doubted that Rob or Phil would be able to.

Maybe he'd gone too far... Rob hadn't thought too much about what he was going to say to Phil at their meeting, partly because he'd spent most of this week wondering exactly what he'd let himself in for. And coming here had confirmed some of his fears. People remembered him, and three years ago they must have put two and two together and realised what had happened. He'd received only smiles and greetings, but in his mind they felt tainted with a past that he'd fought to leave behind.

It had left him off-balance. Wanting to turn and walk away, and knowing that if he did so he'd let Stella and Phil down. Maybe that was the real problem. Not letting them down today opened up a whole world of possible ways he might let them down in the future, and the idea weighed on his mind.

The coffee bar was just the same, situated in one corner of the large open-plan ground floor of the main building. There was always activity here, people walking from the entrance to the lifts, sometimes stopping for coffee or to browse the book exchange or visit the newsagent. And now that the midday rush was over there were plenty of seats, and he chose one in a corner by the window.

He'd ordered automatically, reaching into his pocket to pay while he was still absorbed in the choices that he'd already made, and those which lay ahead. Rob stared at the mug and plate in front of him. Coffee, with an extra shot to keep him alert, and a pastry as the quickest way to fill an empty stomach. That was what he'd always ordered three years ago, and he wondered whether herbal tea wouldn't be more in line with what he wanted—or maybe needed—now.

All the same, he sipped his coffee and took a bite from the pastry, the buzz of caffeine hitting him. Rob leaned back in his seat, another automatic reaction kicking in as he tried to relax before work claimed his concentration again. He made an effort to stop his fingers from tapping on the table in front of him, and tried to think about the open air and apple trees.

He was almost there—could almost see his orchard growing here in the heart of a city hospital, and feel the gentle rhythm of caring for trees instead of people—when he saw Stella walking towards him. He'd seen two sides of her on Saturday—a forthright, focused doctor, and a softer, more sensual woman, and there was no doubt which one was heading straight for him now.

Her hips had a businesslike sway to them, giving the sense that she knew exactly where she was going and was confident she'd get there. She sat down opposite him, looking at him thoughtfully for a moment. Her gaze seemed to burn into him.

'May I get you something?' Everything else seemed too hard at the moment, and Rob resorted to good manners. It was difficult to say the wrong thing when you were being scrupulously polite.

'No, thanks. I've just been drinking coffee with Phil.'

Stella's smile never quite managed to conceal her allure, despite her professional appearance. The combination of the two was tempting in the extreme, and he felt caught now, in the heat of her gaze.

'Here's how it's going to be, Rob.'

He nodded. Rob reckoned that was about all a man could do when faced with Stella at her most determined.

'I know that coming here hasn't been easy for you...'

'You understand that?' Despite her apparent ability to put herself in his shoes, he was pretty sure that she didn't appreciate the finer points of it.

'No, I don't, because I haven't been through what you have and had the guts to come back from it. I have an imagination, though.'

Good answer. And Stella didn't pull any punches. He liked that about her, because she couldn't possibly hurt him any more than he'd hurt himself, with the constant reproach and guilt. And her no-nonsense attitude made him feel better about what he was feeling now. He nodded, and felt that sudden connection between them. That was challenging too, but meeting it head-on made him feel a little stronger.

'You need an opportunity to go with the flow a little, and ease yourself back into the hospital's routine. Phil needs to run a department, and that means knowing what to expect from everyone at any given time...'

That was a pretty good summary of the situation. Rob opened his mouth to concur, and Stella silenced him with a wave of her finger. Clearly even his agreement wasn't necessary at the moment.

'So this is what I propose. For ten hours a week you're welcome here in the department, doing whatever you want to do, on a voluntary basis. You can have as much coffee as you like with whoever you like, scrub up to observe a few surgical procedures...' She waved her hand to encompass many possible options. 'Since we're a teaching hospital you can even collar a few of our students and point them in the right direction.'

That sounded like something he could live with. There was obviously more coming and Rob swallowed his agreement and confined himself to a nod.

'You lay one finger on a patient, attend a planning meeting or read a file, and you're on the clock. Phil can get HR to draw up a contract for ten hours a week, in addition to the hours you spend volunteering.'

'Two shifts a week.' Rob couldn't help noticing that Stella's own contribution to the discussions was incorporated, and that he probably wouldn't be getting any chance to add weekends to his work schedule.

'Not necessarily full shifts. We can negotiate with you over the times we need you, and you organise your volunteering however you want, that's up to you. You're in control of part of your time, but you allow us to depend on you to be there when we need you. Can you commit yourself to that?'

*Really* commit himself. Rob was under no illusions about that, because Stella's focus didn't brook any half measures. But she'd come up with a plan that allowed him to feel his way back into a challenging situation, and still have the rewards of participating in the demanding work of the department. And he reckoned that Stella would get what she wanted too.

'Are you happy with it?'

She smiled suddenly. 'I want you on my team.'

'Okay. You have a deal...' He offered his hand to shake hers.

'You're sure? This is binding, Rob.'

*Don't let me down.*

That was her meaning, but for once Stella didn't come straight out and say it. But she'd already suggested a framework where he could feel confident that he wouldn't let her down.

'As soon as we shake on it, it's set in stone.' He threw back his own challenge, and saw the spark of excitement in her face that he always felt when faced with a testing situation.

There was a touch of the playful about the way that her fingers drew back a little before meeting his. Something delicious, that made their final contact all the more meaningful. Stella shook his hand and then gave him a smile, taking her phone from her pocket and starting to type with both thumbs.

'Okay…ten hours volunteering…ten hours working. Have you thought about an hourly rate…?'

'That doesn't matter, does it?' This was all about recognising his fears over being able to fit back into a situation that had once broken him.

'No, I suppose not. I dare say HR can sort out those details…' Stella shot him a smile. 'It's not really the money, is it? As soon as Phil puts you on the payroll, all of the checks and balances and safeguarding procedures kick in. That's the real point, for both of you.'

She saw that. Rob had too, and Phil obviously had, but Stella had broken it down and made something workable out of it. She finished typing and then put her phone down on the table, picking it up again when it vibrated.

'Okay, Phil was clearly staring at his phone, waiting for my text… He says that's fine.' Her phone vibrated again in her hand. 'And… He's off to twist a few arms in the HR department and your contract should be ready for you to review by the end of the day.'

'That's great, thanks. Does that mean I can call you *boss* now?' The sudden resolution of a problem that had been bugging him all week allowed the joke.

'Not until you know me better,' Stella flashed back. '*Stella* will do for the time being.'

Rob chuckled. 'Right you are. Any chance of staying around for the rest of the afternoon? I'll pick the contract up from Phil when it's ready and sign it.'

'Absolutely. Remember Prof Maitland?'

'Of course.' Everyone knew Alma Maitland—she'd been teaching here for thirty years, and it was no surprise to Rob that she was still refusing to retire.

'Well, I just so happen to have noticed...' Stella's grin told Rob that she'd made a point of looking it up '...that she's doing a tutorial on suture techniques this afternoon. She never minds a bit of teaching assistance from anyone who happens to be at a loose end.' Stella left the suggestion hanging in the air between them.

'I'll pop in and see her, and ask whether I can sit in. Phil first, though, just to confirm my agreement to everything.'

'Yeah, that would be good.' Stella picked up her phone, typing another text. 'You feel as if you've let him down, don't you. Did you realise that he feels he's let *you* down?'

That hadn't occurred to Rob. 'Phil never let me down. He did all he could to help when I was working here, and after I left he was the only person who stayed in touch.'

'That doesn't surprise me. But how we feel about a situation isn't always a reflection of how things actually are.'

Message received, loud and clear. 'Maybe it's time for me to thank him, for all the support he's given me. Clear the air a bit.'

Stella nodded, leaving it at that. Her phone buzzed and she picked it up. 'Ah, that's Alma. She says you're to get your gorgeously rounded intellect up to her office before she has to send out a search party.'

Rob chuckled. Clearly, Alma hadn't changed. 'I don't have

her number in my phone. Could you tell her twenty minutes, after I've had a chance to see Phil.'

Stella smiled, typing a reply. 'I don't suppose you have time for something to eat before you go back home tonight?' After all of the hard questions they'd just faced, this was the one that prompted a sudden diffidence in her tone.

And it was the question that Rob had wanted to ask too. 'Six o'clock? My shout.'

'You can pay for mine and I'll pay for yours.'

It was an elegant twist on splitting the bill, but Rob was under no illusions that he'd just hit a brick wall. Stella's frankness felt very intimate at times, and she clearly cared about the people around her. But she drew a hard line between friendship and even the smallest hint of anything closer. Rob did too, but he couldn't help stumbling over it from time to time when he was in Stella's company.

'Fair enough. I'll do my best to work up a healthy appetite.'

Stella chuckled, getting to her feet and picking up her phone. Whatever was next on her agenda seemed to be beckoning. 'You haven't seen my to-do list for the afternoon. I'll be ravenous by six o'clock.'

On a Friday evening in summer, every pub and eatery on the banks of the Thames was full to bursting. Stella had given a bit of thought to the matter and decided against being squashed against a whole crowd of people she didn't know, and having to shout to make herself heard.

They'd stopped off at the new fish and chip shop by the hospital, and then walked towards the river, finding a place to sit on a set of wide steps that led down to the embankment. Spreading the bag out between them, she arranged the tub of tomato sauce and sachets of salt and vinegar on it and then opened the paper wrappings around her fish and chips.

'Mmm. Really good chips. The fish is nice too.' Rob was a little ahead of her, obviously hungry. 'If that place had been open when I worked here, I wouldn't have got so thin...'

He could make a wry joke about it now, even if it was accompanied by a downward quirk of his lips. That seemed to be a good sign.

'How was Alma's tutorial?'

Rob chuckled. 'Pretty much as you'd expect. She took a brisk hop through the theory and then threw me in at the deep end along with her students, and told them that if they were going to pass muster they needed to be able to emulate what I was about to demonstrate.'

'And how did everyone do?' Stella knew the answer to that already. Alma was notorious for making sure that no one in her tutorial group got left behind, and no doubt Rob had found himself in the shadow of that over-arching principle as well.

'It needed a few tries, but they got there. And a few of them stayed around to ask questions afterwards. It's nice to be around all of that enthusiasm again. And I'm glad to find that I can still suture with ten pairs of eyes trained on my every move.'

He seemed pleased. And he had an envelope, stowed away in the inside pocket of his jacket, which contained his copy of the contract that Phil had given him before they'd left this evening, which Rob had read through and signed straight away.

'Including Alma's?'

He nodded. 'Yeah, she was right at the front of the group, watching every move I made. If she didn't correct me, then I reckon I can't be too rusty. How was your afternoon?'

'Good. After finding a way of making you and Phil see eye to eye, a couple of surgical scar reductions were a piece of cake.'

'I'm sure they were. You're not a middle child, are you?'

'As it happens, yes. You think that makes me a mediator?'

That wasn't what Rob was asking. She knew a great deal about him, and now Rob wanted to know something about her. The thought made Stella smile.

'I wouldn't reduce it to that.' He picked up one of the sachets, opening it and then sprinkling his chips with salt. Clearly waiting to see whether Stella would respond to his invitation.

'I have an older sister and a younger brother. Chloe's married with three children, and Jamie and his wife have a little boy. They all get on very well together, and so there's not much call for mediation.'

'Nice. I like nephews and nieces, I have a few of them too. I'd show you the pictures only my fingers are getting a bit greasy.'

There was a trace of regret in his smile. It struck a chord somewhere in Stella's own heart. 'The road not travelled?'

Rob nodded. 'Yeah. There are a few of them. I never got to be a newsreader, or a sea captain either.'

'You wanted to be a newsreader?'

He shrugged. 'It was a phase. When I was eight years old, I thought that sitting behind a huge desk and knowing everything that was going on in the world must be wonderful. Then it occurred to me that it would be better to actually *see* all of the places they were talking about, and decided on sea captain. It was touch and go between that and a pilot for a while, and then I decided on surgery.'

'I only ever wanted to be a surgeon...' Suddenly Stella wished that she'd at least thought about being something else. Ballerina maybe. Or a pilot sounded like a good ambition to have for a while, and then leave behind in favour of the one you really wanted. 'My dad's a surgeon, and so I got hooked on the idea pretty early.'

'So you were pretty focused, even when you were a child.'

Stella couldn't work out whether that was a criticism or a compliment. 'There's nothing wrong with focus, is there?'

'Not a thing.' Rob turned the corners of his mouth down. 'It does tend to mess with everything else, though.'

'No one said that being a surgeon means that you can't have a life. My mum and dad wanted different things and that made them a great team. Dad wasn't around much when we were little, but we understood why and knew that he was doing important work. And Mum was always there for us.'

'So it's all a matter of finding the right person?' Rob seemed to be turning the idea over in his head.

They were straying into territory that made Stella feel uncomfortable. Rob's relationship with his ex-wife was his own business, and talking about it felt like stepping over a line that shouldn't be crossed.

'I'm no expert on marriage.'

He laughed suddenly. 'You think *I* am? I'm not looking for any answers, I'm just interested in what you think.'

'I just know that my mum and dad made things work because they'd both made their own choices about what they wanted from life, and they were each doing what they wanted to do. When I applied for medical school, Dad sat me down and told me that it wasn't going to be easy...'

'And that prepared you?' Rob raised an eyebrow.

'What do you think? I knew that studying medicine was going to take commitment, but I still had to find out what that really meant. I did that the hard way, like everyone else. I had my share of boyfriends who just walked away because I was studying when they wanted to go out. Had my heart broken...' Stella pressed her lips together. That sounded as if her whole life, every decision she'd made, had been a reaction to having been hurt.

'In my experience, young men of that age can be foolish.' Rob murmured the words quietly. It was tempting to pretend that she hadn't heard them, because they opened a door that had remained shut for some time.

But she *had* heard, and it made her feel good. Made her want things that she knew she couldn't have.

'It is what it is. I've made my choices about what I want out of life, and I focus on the things that I care about. I don't give untravelled roads too much thought.' She grinned at him. 'They're probably full of potholes, anyway.'

'I envy you your certainty.'

Stella's grip on that certainty was beginning to loosen. But a warm evening, spent with a man who was both emotionally intelligent and unsettlingly attractive, was just a passing temptation. It wasn't a reason to make any sudden, uncontrolled changes in direction.

They sat, watching the boats travel up and down the river, finishing the last of their chips. Rob screwed the wrapping paper into a ball, tossing it restlessly from one hand to the other, while Stella folded hers neatly.

'So what's on your agenda for the weekend?' he asked.

Probably best not to mention that she was thinking of popping in to work tomorrow. Stella told him about the family lunch at her parents' house on Sunday, and showed him the pictures of her nephews and nieces on her phone. Rob reciprocated with pictures of a cute little girl, whose grey-blue eyes were just as mesmerising as his, and two older boys. When questioned about his weekend, he laughed.

'The thing about gardens is that you just go out there and they tell you what needs to be done, rather than the other way around.' He looked at his watch, pulling the corners of his mouth down. 'I should get going. My train's in twenty minutes.'

Stella nodded, picking up her bag and threading the strap across her shoulder. 'Thanks for dinner.'

'Thank *you*.'

Parting was strange and awkward. It deserved some acknowledgement of the confidences they'd exchanged, but a kiss on the cheek was too intimate. A handshake too formal. But when Stella looked up into his face, Rob's smile and the look in his eyes was just right. Warm, almost tender, and above all unspoken. She turned, taking that smile with her, as she walked away.

# CHAPTER FIVE

STELLA HAD DECIDED that this was positively the last time that she would allow herself to miss Rob for the five days that he was down in Sussex. Next week she'd barely think about him. Rob had turned up at the hospital bright and early on Thursday morning, putting his head around her office door to announce his presence.

'Am I back on the clock?'

'Yes.' Stella smiled at him, pushing Anna's patient file across the desk.

Anna was due in for a consultation at half past nine, which would give Rob a chance to meet her and examine her injuries. And Stella wanted to revisit her discussions with Anna about what she wanted from her surgery, in the light of the possibilities and techniques that she and Rob had already considered.

'Does Anna have any clear idea about her own priorities?' Rob asked as Stella made a list of talking points.

'She's a little overwhelmed by it all at the moment and I'd really like to get her to see that she's in control of the process, and what she wants matters to us. Maybe if we start with your examination, and then we can bring that around to a more general discussion?' Stella didn't want to be too proscriptive about who did what, and she was happy to allow Rob to lead the session while she sat in, ready to take over if necessary.

'You know her best.' He gave her a dazzling smile. 'I don't want to step on your toes...'

Stella didn't want that either. It implied the kind of physical closeness that would make her forget about crushed toes, and think only about pulling him a little closer.

'We'll see how it goes, shall we? Work from there...' Her phone buzzed and she picked it up. 'Anna and Jess are a little early, they're here already...'

Rob was quite capable of insisting that everything went his way. But the way that he spoke with Anna and her partner, Jess, left neither of them in any doubt that his whole focus was making sure that they went Anna's way. Right from the start, he was gentle and encouraging, listening to everything that Anna said and taking careful notes. And then suddenly he swerved off script.

'How we see ourselves is entirely personal. It's inconsequential, but I have a bit of a thing about the bump on my nose...'

There wasn't anything wrong with the bump on his nose. Stella quite liked it. One slight imperfection in an otherwise perfect face. And mentioning it seemed a little tactless—until Rob shot Jess a querying glance, and Stella realised that he'd read Anna and Jess perfectly...

'The bump's fine. You could get rid of the stubble, though.' Jess was always the more forthright of the two.

'Jess!' Anna shot her partner a reproving look. 'Don't listen to her, the beard's fine. It makes you look less like a doctor.'

Rob nodded, scraping his fingers across his chin. 'Glad you think so. To be honest with you, that was why I grew it in the first place.' Anna and Jess couldn't know the reasons behind that, but the vulnerability that showed in Rob's eyes couldn't be manufactured.

And it broke the ice. Anna began to talk, and this time she

was using her own likes and dislikes as a guide. Rob answered all of her questions, giving her an honest appraisal of what could and couldn't be done.

'So…before we go can I just ask…' Jess had one more question, and Rob turned to her, grinning.

'Absolutely. Ask away.'

'Who's going to be doing Anna's surgery?'

'Ms Parry-Jones.' Rob didn't miss a beat. 'She's the senior surgeon for Anna's case and she'll be making all of the decisions with you.'

Jess and Anna looked at each other. Clearly Rob's quiet but authoritative manner had impressed them both, and they were wondering who this new person on their radar was.

'My role is technical consultant. Ms Parry-Jones has asked me to provide input on a few specialised aspects of your case, Anna, so that she can give you the best all-round care.'

'Right… Okay, thanks.' Jess seemed happy with the answer, but Stella couldn't leave it at that.

'Mr Franklin has specific expertise in the reduction of scars like the one you have on your forehead, Anna. His input is going to be particularly useful there.' Anna had mentioned that the way that the scar was pulling at her eyelid bothered her.

'That's great. Thank you so much, both of you.' Anna seemed much more confident about the process that lay ahead of her now.

Jess gathered up their coats, waiting for Anna to say her goodbyes. When the door closed behind the two women Rob turned to Stella, a reproachful smile on his face.

'You didn't need to say that.'

'Yes, I did. Anna has a right to know that she has excellent people on her team.' And Rob had a right to know that his own expertise was valued. 'Did Phil give you that job title?'

'No. I made it up on the spur of the moment. What do you think of it?'

She thought that Rob was probably trying to make a point. 'It's a little self-effacing, isn't it? You could have just said that you were a surgeon working on Anna's case.'

'I'm not wholly comfortable with that at the moment. I'll go with technical consultant for the time being.'

'And a beard.'

He shrugged. 'Opinion appears to be split on the beard. I don't suppose you'd like to exercise your casting vote?'

'No, I wouldn't. I don't suppose that all of this has anything to do with letting me know that you're not here to challenge me, does it?'

He shrugged. 'You're the one who doesn't like it when I call you *boss*. But if you'd like me to remind you that you're in charge, then I can work it into the conversation whenever I get the chance.'

Stella puffed out an exasperated breath. 'I wouldn't want to put words into your mouth. I suppose that being in charge of Anna's case doesn't extend to me asking what you're up to for the rest of the day.'

Rob gave her a delicious smile, getting to his feet. 'Right in one. Largely because I'm off the clock now, and I'm not entirely sure myself.'

Stella had been meaning to ask Rob whether he'd like to scrub up for the procedure to correct Dupuytren's contracture that she was carrying out at one o'clock. Releasing the thick bands of tissue that bent the fingers and restricted movement was a relatively straightforward process, and Stella was under no illusions that she had anything to teach him about it. But an hour in Theatre, even if he was only observing, might make Rob think a little more about including surgery in his job description. Since she couldn't find him at lunchtime, she decided that the conversation could wait.

The surgery went well, and when her patient was wheeled through to the recovery room Stella scrubbed out, flipping through the messages on her phone as she waited for the lift to take her back to her office.

'There's a facial injury in A&E?' She stopped in the open doorway of the department's admin offices, and Sadie, who always knew where everyone was at any given time, looked up from her computer screen.

'Don't worry about that one. Mr Franklin's dealing with it.'

'Okay. Thanks, Sadie.'

*Don't run. Not even if your heart's pounding and you're wondering if Rob has just broken every promise he made, and gone completely rogue...*

All the same, Stella hit the lifts at a very brisk walking pace, and was a little out of breath by the time she entered A&E. The senior doctor was standing at the admin station, and looked up from a tablet.

'Hey, Stella. No one told me that this was Visit Your Emergency Doctor Day.' Therese grinned at her.

'Sorry. No one told me either. I don't suppose you've seen Rob Franklin down here, have you?' Stella slowed down, shooting her a smile.

'I've seen everyone—Rob Franklin, Phil Chamberlain, now you. Must be a slow day for the Reconstructive Surgery department...' Therese reached over to answer the phone, mouthing an apology.

Okay. If Phil was here, then maybe she should just turn around and go back upstairs, because he would be dealing with the situation. Then she saw Phil emerging from one of the cubicles and heading towards her.

'Thanks for coming down, Stella. Rob's just going through

a few aftercare points with a patient, and I've had a call from the ward and I need to go back up there.'

'So everything's under control, then.' Now would be a very good time to go, before Rob got the impression that she was stalking him.

'Uh… Wait…' Therese had finished her conversation and was now replacing the phone back into its cradle. 'Is there any chance of one of you being able to stay? A young man's just walked in with a series of lacerations to his shoulder, which are bleeding profusely. He's with a doctor now, and we're doing scans to find out exactly what's going on, but we may be calling you to ask if you're able to come back down again any minute now.'

Phil nodded. 'I can get someone to cover for you upstairs, Stella.'

'I've just finished the Dupuytren's contracture surgery, and I need someone to look in on that patient when he's out of the recovery room. Then I have ward rounds…'

'I can take care of that. You stay here and work with Rob.' Phil didn't give any room for an answer, let alone a disagreement, and hurried away.

'You can relax.' Therese mistook Stella's look of discomfiture for lack of confidence in Rob's abilities. 'He's as good as he ever was. Better, maybe—he seems to have developed his interpersonal skills.'

Working as a GP would do that. And Therese had been here for some years, she must be in a position to see the difference. 'He's been away for a while, though.'

Therese nodded. Everyone understood the need to go carefully until they were sure that Rob's extended absence hadn't affected his performance in any way. That was for Rob's sake as well as being a safeguarding measure for their patients.

'Don't go telling me that he's better than I am…' The

thought that had been nagging at Stella slipped out. She knew Therese well enough that it wouldn't go any further than just the two of them.

'No, it's not like that.' Therese grinned. 'Apples and pears, you know?'

Stella wondered whether she should mention that she'd mistaken one of Rob's pear trees for an apple tree, and decided not to. Therese could see the differences better than most, and she worked outside the Reconstructive Surgery Unit, so had nothing to gain or lose in comparing Rob's performance with hers. *Apples and pears* was the best answer she was going to get from anyone.

'Got to go…' Therese was already on the move, leaving Stella alone by the admin station. A&E was always busy and wasting time talking about fruit, and her own private misgivings, wasn't helpful. And Stella reminded herself that losing her focus wasn't helpful either.

She should keep that thought uppermost in her mind. When she knocked and opened the door to the cubicle she'd seen Phil emerge from, focus seemed suddenly impossible.

Rob was sitting opposite the patient couch, talking to a young boy in school football kit and his mother. He'd found one of the patient leaflets and had clearly been taking the mother through aftercare for cuts and stitches, while keeping the boy amused with stick figures drawn in the margin. The first was clutching its head and Rob had covered the whole procedure, through to his own ministrations in stitching the wound.

'And you say there won't be a scar?' the mother asked, grinning at her son's delight over the final stick figure, which had a broad smile on its face and seemed to be kicking a football.

'There will be—but just a hairline. It'll be barely noticeable and David's young so it may well disappear completely in time.'

Just a glance at the stitches on the side of the boy's face was enough to tell her that Rob's estimate was correct. It had clearly been a nasty cut and the droplets of blood falling from the head of the first stick figure were probably no exaggeration. But she couldn't fault the treatment of the wound, it was exactly what she would have done. Better than she could have done, maybe. Apples and pears...

'If you see any signs of infection, you need to either go to your GP or come back here and get someone to look at it.' He handed the guidance leaflet to the mother, and the boy grabbed it from her, getting a special smile from Rob. 'And David. Less tackling with your head and more with your feet when you're playing football, eh? You're not going to score a winning goal by landing up in A&E, are you?'

David shook his head, and responded to his mother's nudged prompt. 'Thank you, Dr Rob.'

'My pleasure, David.' Rob produced another leaflet for David's mother, and she stowed it away in her handbag. Her son clearly wanted to stay here with Rob, and she practically had to drag him away, thanking Rob again and smiling at Stella as she left the cubicle.

'You've taken over nursemaid duties?' The warmth was still in Rob's face, and the twinkle of humour in his eyes was almost irresistible.

'I wouldn't say that.'

'No, you wouldn't.' He got to his feet, and suddenly his bulk seemed impressive in the small space. 'That's *my* interpretation. I was the one who was cautious about coming back, remember? The joke's on me.'

Stella wondered whether anyone who'd known Rob when he'd worked here three years ago would be surprised at finding he had become the butt of his own jokes. That was irrelevant, because the present was what mattered.

'There's a new patient with lacerations to his shoulder. They're controlling the bleeding and doing preliminary scans right now.'

Rob nodded. 'No point in going back upstairs then, if we get paged in the lift.'

'Yep...' Stella's phone beeped and she pulled it out of her pocket, looking at the message. 'Cubicle Ten.'

Moving, having something to do, clarified everything. There was no more time to appreciate his broad shoulders and the precise deftness of his hands. To think that while patients must find his touch very reassuring, she could imagine his hands provoking a far more erotic response. There was no more uncertainty over meeting Rob's gaze and she could focus now. Stella led the way to one of the larger cubicles, situated next to the trauma unit, which was equipped to handle patients who needed minor surgical interventions.

The young man lying on the bed was conscious, his gaze taking in everything that was going on around him. A nurse was dealing with a mess of bloodstained clothing and dressings and their patient's pallor, emphasised by his freckled face and shock of red hair, was another indication of blood loss. Stella remembered Therese's words—'*just walked in*'. How could anyone, let alone someone who looked so young, walk very far with these injuries?

She turned to the doctor in attendance, seeing relief in her eyes as she rapped out the details. 'This is Matthew Jarvis, he's seventeen years old. He has lacerations to his right shoulder and upper arm, and there's been significant blood loss, but we have that under control now. We've set up a live X-ray and ultrasound, and I don't see any indication that the lacerations are deep.'

'Okay, thanks.' Seventeen. That was too young, and Matthew looked like a child, surrounded by the medical equipment that was being used to scan his wounds. She turned to the live X-ray screen, studying it carefully.

'What do you think?' She'd already made her decision about what should come next, but asking Rob allowed him to make the formal diagnosis. The twitch of his lips showed that he saw exactly what she was doing, and the warmth in his face told her that he was grateful. He looked at the X-ray screen before moving on to the ultrasound, adjusting the sensors so that they could see the full extent of the long cuts on Matthew's shoulder and arm and assess their depth.

'It doesn't look as if any of the tendons or muscles have been compromised, and there's nothing in the wounds. They all look relatively shallow.' Rob turned to the lad. 'How did this happen, Matthew?'

'It's Matt.' The boy's face twisted into an expression of bravado, which only made him look even younger. 'There were some kids in the shopping precinct, playing with knives. I went to take 'em off them.'

'That's very public-spirited. What kind of knives?' Rob's face gave no indication of his thoughts.

'They were like hunting knives. A bloke came to help and he took charge of them. The kids ran away when he said he was calling the police. I didn't realise they'd cut me at first, but when I saw the blood someone brought me here.'

'They brought you in?'

'Nah, he dropped me off in the car park. He gave me a lift, but he said he had errands.'

There was something about this that didn't quite ring true. Stella had seen pretty much every kind of wound that it was possible to inflict and the ultrasound scans indicated that Matthew's injuries had been caused by something with a short blade, like a box-cutter, not a long-bladed knife. And Stella couldn't imagine that many people would drive a badly injured young man to hospital and then leave him in the car park, however many other things they had to do.

Stella glanced up at Rob and when his gaze met hers for a moment she could see her own thoughts reflected in his eyes. Matthew was lying about something, and when that something involved knives it made everyone in a hospital particularly careful.

'Okay. Thanks.' Rob turned his attention back to the screens, studying them carefully.

'What do you reckon?' Stella prompted him again.

'I think do a visual check, and then close the wounds. I don't see any evidence of other damage that would need to be repaired surgically.'

'I agree.' For all of the precision of the medical equipment around them, their own experience and the look of a wound was still a valuable part of their assessment. She picked up the patient notes, writing one word in the margin and showing it to Rob.

*Security?*

He nodded. 'My thoughts exactly. You go and speak with Therese.'

Rob's tone brooked no argument. Stella supposed that it made sense. He would stay with the duty doctor and the two nurses who were tending to Matthew, while she raised their concerns with Therese. All the same, there was a protectiveness in his manner, and he shot her a smile before he moved towards Matthew, asking whether he might take a look at his shoulder, and gently easing back the dressings from one of the wounds. The A&E doctor stepped back, out of Rob's way, as did both of the nurses, and Stella hurried from the cubicle to find Therese.

# CHAPTER SIX

WHAT MATTHEW HAD said didn't add up, and Rob had a strong feeling that something wasn't right. He and Stella didn't even need to speak about it; the guidelines about how they should deal with this kind of situation were clear. It was best to err on the side of caution and there would be no questions asked if they requested that one of the security guards who worked in A&E be stationed outside the door of the cubicle in case he was needed. With security guard Terry in place outside the door, Stella returned to the cubicle and she and Rob went ahead and treated their patient in just the same way as they would any other.

Rob had made sure that anything which might be construed as a weapon was out of Matthew's reach. The lad wasn't particularly talkative, but then the level of analgesic that had been needed before they embarked on stitching the four long gashes on his shoulder and arm was enough to make anyone a little drowsy.

This was what Rob had lived for, once upon a time. This level of challenge. It had usually been dictated by the medical difficulties involved in a particular patient's case, but although his gut feeling that something wasn't quite right here was very different, it produced the same heightened awareness. The same feeling he'd clung to when he'd been working here at the hospital three years ago.

'That's it, Matt. All done.' Stella gave Matthew a dazzling smile, telling him he'd done well. Rob had had better patients—Matthew had grumbled about the time that the stitches were taking—but he'd had worse as well. And he was back. He knew now that he'd lost none of his edge and that he'd completed the complex closure of the intersecting wounds with the same skill that he'd been able to command three years ago. Stella didn't need to tell him that, although he hoped she might later on.

'Can I go now?' Matthew sat up, wincing as he tried to use his right arm.

'Not yet.' She picked up a pair of surgical scissors. 'I need to trim some of the stitches and then we'll dress your arm and give you a sling to use for the next few days. Is there someone at home who can look after you?'

'Yeah. My mum. I should really go now—she's expecting me and she'll be worried.'

'Can you phone her? Perhaps she'll come and collect you.'

'Nah, she never answers her phone. I'll be all right.'

'Well, perhaps we can get you a taxi when we're finished here. I don't think you should go home on your own. And there's something else I want to talk to you about as well...'

Matthew's attitude so far had largely been one of irritation that everything was taking so long. Rob had been keeping a close eye on him but, although he wasn't being particularly cooperative, he hadn't shown any hostility towards them. He allowed himself to move back a little to sort through the dressings they'd need, reckoning that if Stella's smile couldn't get through to Matthew, then nothing would.

'We have a social worker attached to the hospital who's available to speak with anyone who's been involved in an incident with knives. If you'd like me to give her a call and see if she's available I can do that now.'

'No. I can't be bothered with social workers.'

'Okay. But I think we should also report this to the police. Your injuries are fairly significant, and they may want to speak with you.'

'No police.'

'It's important, Matt.' This had to be said, and Stella's tone contained no hint of a challenge. But something had made the hairs on the back of Rob's neck rise, and he turned to glance across at her.

'No police!' Matthew became suddenly aggressive, and Stella yelped in surprise as he snatched the surgical scissors from her hand, winding his arm around her neck and dragging her back against him.

'Matt. Put the scissors down.' Rob heard his own voice, calm in the face of his raging anger and his fear for Stella.

'No police. And get out of the way. I want to leave now.'

'I'm afraid I can't. Not until you put the scissors down and let my colleague go. All she's done is try to help you, Matt.'

'She wants to call the police. And I'm out of here, now.'

'Whether or not we call the police about your injuries is your choice. But if you hurt anyone here, or take one step outside this room with those scissors in your hand, then everything changes. You won't have any choices.'

It was already too late for ifs. One tear had escaped from Stella's frightened eyes and even though Rob could see that she was trying to hold herself together she was terrified. Matthew had already hurt her, but Rob had to concentrate on making him believe that he had a way out of this.

The panic button was only two steps away, but he couldn't risk it. Matthew was pressing the scissors against Stella's neck now, and she whimpered as she felt the cold steel against her skin. The outside edges of the scissors were rounded and designed not to cut, but she had no way of knowing which side of the blade she could feel.

'Put the scissors down, Matt. Let her go.'

'Then what?'

'Then I'll dress your wound and give you a sling. After that, you'll be released and you can go wherever you want.' That was a downright lie. But Rob would swear that up was down and dance on the ceiling to prove it if that got Stella away from Matthew.

'All right. Just give me the sling, I don't need anything more. And I'll go straight away.'

'Not until you let her go, Matt. That's the way it works. I can't do anything for you until you do that.'

The scissors clattered onto the floor, and suddenly Stella was in his arms. Rob's first and only instinct was to get her away from Matthew, and he pulled the door open, bundling her out of the cubicle. Terry, the security guard who'd been sitting outside the door, jumped to his feet.

Rob hadn't forgotten the procedure; it was ingrained in everyone who'd ever worked here. Standing in the doorway so that he could keep an eye on Matthew, he quickly relayed the code for an assault on a member of staff. Terry nodded, speaking quietly into his radio to alert the security centre for the building.

'Step back now, please.' Terry was one of the most amiable people it was possible to meet, but when he gestured to Rob to stand to one side and moved into the doorway, his sheer size was enough to get Matthew to sit back down on the bed, clutching his shoulder and grunting in pain.

And Rob could do the one thing he'd been aching to do, and concentrate on Stella now, knowing that the situation with Matthew was under control. She clung to him and he put his arm around her shoulders, trying to comfort her. Then he saw her hand move to her neck, her fingers searching…

'You're okay, Stella. He didn't cut you. He was pressing the blunt side of the scissors against your skin.'

'I thought…' Stella tried for a smile and failed miserably. 'Silly…'

'No, it's not silly at all. You couldn't possibly have known that. Just hold tight for a moment, we'll be out of here soon.'

He could see a ripple of concern move through the A&E staff as the alert went out. Another guard came hurrying towards them, along with one of the male doctors, and they joined Terry as he walked almost casually into the cubicle, closing the door behind them.

The work of the department carried on, doctors and nurses doing their best to preserve an atmosphere of calm and control. It felt to Rob as if he'd just woken from a bad dream, adrenaline still coursing in his veins, but nowhere to run and nothing to do.

'Rob…make sure he's all right… Don't let anyone hurt him.' Stella clutched at his arm, her fingers pressing tight.

'No one's going to hurt Matthew. They're making sure that everyone's safe, him included.' Stella knew that as well as he did, it was just the adrenaline talking.

Therese was hurrying towards them now, a look of concern on her face. 'Are you guys okay?'

'Yes.' Stella broke free of him, almost pushing him away. Her sudden air of composure was the most worrying reaction she could have displayed. 'I'm just going upstairs for a moment.'

Stella didn't wait for an answer before starting to walk towards the exit. 'She's in shock.' Therese stated the obvious. 'I'll go.'

Rob watched as Therese caught up with her, and the two

women walked together towards the double doors that led through to the A&E reception area and the lifts. He knew that Therese would look after Stella, but couldn't help wishing that he was the one at Stella's side right now.

But Stella had asked him to make sure that Matthew was all right. He was still a doctor, and there was a job here for him to finish before he went to find Stella. Rob shook his head, turning reluctantly towards the door of the cubicle.

Every moment that Rob was away from Stella felt like an age, but in truth it took little more than half an hour to hand over to the A&E doctor, then give his account of what had happened to the police. Therese arrived back in A&E, beckoning him into an empty cubicle, and closing the door behind them.

'How's Stella?'

Therese sat down in one of the chairs, and waited until Rob sat down in the other. He was pretty sure that she did that with most of her patients, there was something about sitting down together that changed the nature of a conversation.

'She's obviously shaken up. But she's okay and she'll deal with it in her own way.'

Rob nodded, taking a breath. 'Which is?'

'Well, at the moment that takes the form of sitting in her office and pretending to do some work. I made her a cup of tea and stayed with her while the police took a brief statement. Phil Chamberlain's keeping an eye on her, now.'

'So…she's on her own?'

'That's what she wanted, Rob. Give her some time to think it all through and then she might just work out that she's not to blame for all of this.'

'It's not Stella's fault. It's mine…' Rob ignored Therese's eyeroll. 'If I'd been quicker, I could have stopped him.'

'Will you listen to yourself? It's not Stella's fault and it's not yours either. We deal with people in crisis every day, and these things happen. The main thing is that no one was hurt.' Therese frowned at him and Rob puffed out a breath.

'So I'm acting like an idiot?' Rob had always liked and respected Therese, and that was what she clearly thought.

'Yes and no. Yes, because you very clearly aren't to blame, and no because with twenty/twenty hindsight it's natural to feel there's something you could have done to prevent what happened.' Therese leaned forward, clearly intent on catching his attention. 'That's why it's hospital policy to make a counsellor available to any staff members who are involved in incidents like this.'

'I don't need…' Rob stopped himself before he fell into that trap. 'I expect that's what Stella said as well.'

'Not quite. Stella finished the sentence. At least you have the wit to see that the policy's there for a reason.'

Rob leaned back in his seat. There was something about sitting down and being on the sharp end of Therese's common sense. 'I know what happens when you try to bottle things up. First-hand.'

'Yes, you do. I don't think I ever said how sorry I was about what happened to you, Rob. It's really good to see you back.'

'I didn't give anyone the chance to help me, and I really regret that. It's good to be back.' Rob knew exactly what he needed to do now. He was living, breathing proof of the way that stress could quietly build until it was a force that could destroy a person. And he was back now, and that had to mean something.

Therese nodded. 'You'll be around for a while?'

'Long enough to buy you a beer one evening…if I'm not too late in asking?' Maybe he'd burned all of his bridges three years ago, when he'd left without a word to anyone.

'You'll throw in a packet of crisps?' Therese grinned at him.

'Done.' Rob got to his feet. 'I'll catch up with you next week? There's something I need to do now.' There was no point in learning from experience if those lessons were never used.

Therese nodded. 'Yes. See you then.'

Stella sat at her desk, staring at her tea. She supposed she ought to drink it, but it was beginning to get cold.

She'd wanted to reach out to Rob, but shame and embarrassment had stopped her. She'd been such a fool. She'd known that there was something wrong with Matthew's story and she'd practically invited the situation she'd found herself in. Why hadn't she sat a little further away from him? Why hadn't she just put those darn scissors *down* before she'd mentioned the police…?

The scissors. She could still feel them, hard and cold, pressed against her neck. Not being able to tell whether this was the sharp or the blunt side of the blade, and not quite being able to believe that she had suddenly become one of the stories that came out of A&E from time to time, and there was nothing she could do to stop it.

Trying not to cry or struggle too much, because Matthew's wiry frame was surprisingly strong. Losing herself in Rob's gaze because he was her only way out of this situation. Hearing him say the only words that mattered, again and again, until Matthew heard them.

*'Put the scissors down…let my colleague go.'*

She was going to have to put all of this aside. Get it under control and go and face him. Apologise and hope that they could move on from this. Soon, but not now. Not just yet…

A knock sounded on the door. Phil, probably—he'd been chasing everyone else away and taken it on himself to check on her every now and then. Stella summoned up a smile, hoping it would sound in her voice when she called to him that everything was okay.

Too late. Rob hadn't waited and was already in the room, holding two mugs in one hand and closing the door behind him with the other. He leaned forward, pushing the cold cup of tea to one side and replacing it with one of the cups he'd brought.

'Does this have as much sugar in it as the one Therese made me?' She tried to avoid his gaze, because that reminded her of the stark intimacy that had bound them together so strongly as he'd tried to talk Matthew down.

He leaned forward and took a sip of the cold tea, grimacing at the taste. 'No. I thought you might like something a bit stronger and not quite as sweet.'

Stella nodded, tasting the hot tea. 'Thanks. That's better. How's Matthew?'

'Medically speaking, he's fine. No one's quite sure how he managed to do what he did, with those injuries and the level of painkillers he had in his system, but he's quiet now and resting under observation. He's in trouble though.'

'I don't want to press charges.' Stella had already decided that.

'That's not going to make any difference. As you know, the hospital has a zero tolerance policy over violence and this took place on their premises. But that's not Matthew's biggest problem. There's another seventeen-year-old in the A&E department at a hospital in Richmond, with the same kinds of wounds that Matthew has, only to his face and leg.'

She was beginning to think a little more clearly now. Rob's strong but not so sweet approach seemed to be working. It felt much more consoling than the blanket assurances that everything was all right and she didn't need to worry.

'Do they have anything to do with each other?'

'Yes. Apparently, there was some kind of dispute between

Matthew and this other lad, and they decided to settle it with a fight. The box-cutters were supposed to add a bit of excitement to it all rather than inflicting actual injury, but things went too far and their friends found that it's a bit more difficult to deal with cuts than it is in most action movies. Someone called their parents, which turned out to be the worst move they could have made, because it was them who left the lads at separate A&E departments, hoping they'd be treated and released before anyone worked out the connection.'

'That's…' Incredibly stupid, and at the same time it might just have worked.

'Yeah. I suppose the kids involved have some excuse, but the adults…' He shrugged. 'Apparently, they were trying to keep them out of trouble.'

'What's going to happen to them?'

Rob shook his head. 'I don't know. It's out of our hands now.'

He could speculate, couldn't he? But none of the possibilities that Stella could think of were good ones, and she wasn't sure that she wanted to hear the not so good ones.

'Have some more tea.' Rob's voice was suddenly tender and Stella felt a tear roll down her cheek. Crying in front of him was exactly what she'd been trying to avoid.

But Rob didn't seem to notice. He motioned towards her cup and Stella obediently took a sip. It did make her feel a little better, and she took another.

'Here's what's going to happen—'

'No, Rob. This was my fault. I handled the situation very badly. What's going to happen is that I'm going to apologise and do better next time.' Stella didn't want to hear anything more.

'That's how I feel. I wasn't quick enough and I didn't wrestle him to the ground before he got a chance to put a pair of scissors against your neck. The truth is that we can both find a few things we could have done better, and maybe we're right. Maybe not. We both know that we had to raise the subject of reporting Matthew's injuries to the police, that's part of our job.'

'Perhaps I should have called Terry in…?' That would have been better, now that Stella thought about it.

'Right. Terry's a lovely guy, but having a six-foot-four security guard standing over our patients really isn't the way to go, is it?' Rob leaned forward, looking at her intently. 'This is not an opinion, Stella, it's a fact. What happened was not your fault.'

He didn't sound particularly sympathetic or understanding, but Stella didn't need either of those things. She needed his certainty. His frank opinion and the harsh, consoling reality in his tone.

Stella took another sip of her tea. It felt warm and comforting, and she was feeling stronger now.

'Tackling Matthew to the floor wouldn't have worked, Rob. You did a really good job of defusing the situation and talking him down.'

She saw his hand shake a little as he raised his own cup to his lips. 'Thanks.'

'Are we done now?' Stella hoped that they were. That they could leave this behind them and move forward.

'Not even close. I know exactly what it's like when something happens and you bury it and get on with the job. It works, and so you do it again. And finally, you can't hold all of that grief and pain in one place, and the bubble bursts.'

He was talking about himself. Impassioned by his own memories and the mistakes he felt he'd made. There was no disagreeing with what he said either.

'You're telling me that we need to deal with this?'

'Yes, we do. You've been through a frightening experience, in a situation where your control was taken away from you.' Rob paused, taking a tissue from the box on her desk and handing it to her. Stella hadn't even been aware of her tears, and she rubbed at her face.

It was becoming harder and harder to hold those tears back. She could send Therese and Phil away, tell them that she was okay and just needed a little time on her own, but Rob had been there. She knew that he'd seen her terror, because his steady gaze had reached out to comfort her.

'Phil must have suggested that you go home, because that's what he suggested to me when I saw him on my way in here. So I'm going to call a taxi and take you home. You can change into your pyjamas and eat ice-cream...' He waved his hand in an *or something* gesture.

Stella managed a smile. 'And ice-cream's going to make all the difference, is it?' It had done, in several films that Stella had seen. Generally eaten with your best friend, on a sofa. At least Rob hadn't mentioned calling her best friend, which was a relief because the person she really wanted right now was him.

'Maybe, maybe not. What *is* going to make a difference is that you're going to make an appointment with the hospital counsellor, tomorrow morning. First thing.'

'Am I? Do as I say and not as I do?' Stella wrinkled her nose at him, wondering if telling him to back off was going to work. She very much doubted it, and right now backing off was the last thing that she wanted him to do.

'If you think you're getting your hands on my fruit trees as therapy, you have another think coming. And even though I'm absolutely sure that it's not going to be of any benefit to me, I might learn something I don't know. You might too.'

She puffed out a breath. 'Okay, I will if you will.'

'Good. We'll do it together. Compare notes afterwards.'

Tomorrow seemed like a very long way off at the moment, and Stella wasn't even sure how she was going to get through the evening.

'You want to get something to eat on the way home? I'm staying at my sister's in Clapham tonight—they're away at the moment but I've got keys to the house. And Emma's looking after Sophie. So I've no train to catch this evening.'

He was being careful. Having somewhere to go for the night ring-fenced their relationship and took all of the uncertainty and stress out of it. Best friends for an evening, but not lovers.

But whatever they chose to call their relationship, Rob was there for her. 'You're not going to give up on me, are you?' She tried to make a joke of it.

'No.' The look in his eyes, and that one word, meant everything.

# CHAPTER SEVEN

ROB HAD GONE into Stella's office with a very clear idea of what he wanted to say, and how he needed to bring his own experience along with him, to convince her that she needed to deal with what had happened before she moved on. Stella could take the truth and, even if he'd sounded a little harsh at times, he'd got through to her. That was really all that mattered.

Even the quiet bustle of the hospital, as they walked down to the taxi rank outside the front entrance, seemed to spook her a little. They'd decided against eating out, in favour of going straight back to her place and getting a takeaway. Stella seemed almost apologetic when she showed him into her third-floor flat. The sitting room was bright in the late afternoon sunshine, and very organised.

'One of these days I might think about getting a few ornaments to dust...' She gave a half-hearted laugh.

'It's overrated. You need a cleaner when you have as much clutter as I do.'

Stella thought for a moment. 'Your place doesn't strike me as cluttered. Unexpected, perhaps. Interesting.'

Rob's house was his refuge. The place he'd run to and made his own, so that he could venture back out again into a life that suited him better. It held all of the pain, as well as the good things, because without one he could never have built the other. Stella's place was different, like a clean sheet of paper. Wherever she kept her doubts and mistakes, it wasn't here.

'I really like your flat. It's calm.' Pale shades, mostly creams with a little blue, took on a new meaning here. There was no story of Stella's life to be discerned from it, just the feeling that now was the best and only time.

She gave him an amused look. 'You mean it doesn't have any personality?'

'There's a lot of space here for *your* personality.' He grinned at her and suddenly their gazes met. The overwhelming feeling that they could be the only two people in the world if they wanted to, had no limits here. No definitions, and none of the things that might keep them apart.

None of the externals, Rob reminded himself. They were still two very different people here, more so perhaps, because there was none of the background noise of everyday life.

He was learning more about her. Her kitchen was as immaculately tidy as the rest of the flat. She liked her curries not too hot, and washed down with the same brand of low-alcohol lager that he did. And when they repaired to the sofa in the sitting room, she didn't automatically turn on the TV and flip through the channels for something to watch. Rob had grown used to his own company during the evening, and it seemed that Stella was too. He wondered whether this might be the time to suggest ice-cream.

'You know…it's days like this that it would be nice to have someone to come home to.' She looked at him, a smile hovering around her lips. 'Thanks for being here, Rob.'

'It's my pleasure. I needed the company too.' Someone to come home to wasn't always what it was cracked up to be. When he'd been married it had more often been someone to rush home to, and then rush back out again for an evening engagement.

'My mum told me something, quite recently.' Stella was

clearly still turning the idea over in her head. 'She said that she always knew when Dad had a bad day at work, because he'd come upstairs and just sit by each of our beds for ten minutes. Watching us sleep. I never knew that.'

'I suppose you probably weren't meant to.'

Stella nodded. 'No, I'm sure we weren't. I guess that just being home, with his family, got things back into perspective for him.' She shot him a querying look.

'I wouldn't know. When Kate and I were married, time to stop and take stock didn't feature all that much. That was a large part of the problem.' He'd spoken more about his feelings to Stella, despite having only known her for a fraction of the time he'd known Kate. That was mostly his fault, but he wondered whether Stella would have let him get away with it, as Kate had.

'You surprise me.' Stella left the thought to hang in the air, not requiring an answer. But Rob wanted to give one.

'Kate and I got married as soon as I left medical school. She knew that I worked long hours, and that was never going to change, but…it was different then. We didn't give much thought to how things would work when we started to want a house in the country, and children. Or when I began to get an increasing number of opportunities at work, and ended up being sucked into all of them. Teaching, researching new techniques…you know.'

'That's what makes you so good at what you do. You just can't leave things alone.' There was a hint of humour in Stella's eyes.

'Yeah. But there's a flip side to it as well. I don't have your focus.'

'You're good at living, though. Sometimes I wonder if there isn't a bit too much clear air around me.'

Rob considered the idea. They were so alike in the challenges they'd chosen to face, and so completely different in the way that they'd solved them. Curiosity was biting chunks out of him and he couldn't resist asking...

'You never thought about getting married?'

'I did, a long time ago. It was a case of wanting too much.'

'I can identify with that.'

Stella's gaze searched his face. She wouldn't find anything new there, because Rob wasn't in the habit of swallowing down what he thought with her.

'My relationships didn't have a very long shelf life when I was studying. I'd go out with someone a few times, they'd say that they were fine with the commitment that a combination of both practical work and study take, and then suddenly they weren't. Then I met someone who didn't seem to mind that I wasn't always around because I was working.'

'It does happen.' Rob was hooked now, and there was no way he could let the subject drop before he'd heard the rest of the story. It seemed to explain all of the little inconsistences that he'd wondered about.

'As my parents have proved. I was thrilled, I thought I'd finally found my Mr Right. And he would have been, if I hadn't minded him taking my evenings at the hospital as carte blanche to go out and spread a little love around. Lust, actually...'

If he'd had Stella for one day in the year, Rob would have lived like a monk for the other three hundred and sixty-four. 'That's... You deserve a great deal more than that, Stella.'

'I thought so too. I never had any regrets about breaking up with him, but I lost the dream. The possibilities, you know?' She smiled suddenly, laying her hand on his arm. 'And my grades went down.'

The sudden contact, even through the thin fabric of his shirt, was electrifying. Rob didn't dare move, in case it deprived him of just one moment of it. 'That's unspeakable.'

'I thought so too. I came to the conclusion that I could do anything I wanted, but not everything. You know what I mean?' She tapped one finger against his arm to emphasise her point, and pure pleasure made him want to laugh out loud.

'Funnily enough, yeah.'

'I decided that the *anything* I wanted was my career. Not so much the career, the surgery. The buzz I get from changing lives.'

He knew what she meant by that as well. Stella took her hand from his arm and it felt as if she'd left a void there, which extended right down to the pit of his stomach.

'And you've never regretted it?'

'No.' She reconsidered for a moment. 'Maybe ninety-nine per cent of the time. Falling to ninety on evenings like this.'

Last week, she'd professed no interest at all in the road not travelled. Tonight, Stella was down to ninety per cent, which left him ten per cent to work with. If he could persuade her differently…

Not tonight. She was vulnerable and far too open to making decisions that she might regret later.

'Do we need ice-cream yet?' He grinned, not finding the change of subject as painful as he'd thought. He wanted, more than anything, to make Stella feel better, more comfortable in her skin after a terrifying experience.

She smiled suddenly. 'I'd say so. Ice-cream would be really nice.'

'You have some in the freezer? Or I'll order in?' He'd seen a takeaway menu for a local ice-cream parlour in the bundle that she'd produced from the kitchen drawer.

'You fancy going out to pick some up, and then bringing it back here to eat on the sofa? I could do with a walk.'

Anything she wanted. And eating it on the sofa made them best friends for the evening. 'Me too.'

They'd dawdled down to the ice-cream parlour, taken their time over their choices, and set up shop on the sofa together to eat it. It was comfortable and companionable, and Rob almost forgot about the unanswered questions that surrounded his and Stella's relationship. Where it might be going, and what it might become. Whether either or both of them could change radically enough to make anything more than a friendship work.

'Do you think that Clapham can do without you for a night? This is a sofa bed.' Stella's spoon rattled in her empty bowl and she tapped the cushion next to her, looking at her watch. It was impossible to tell whether she was saving him a journey or Stella really wanted someone here tonight.

'It'll be hard. But Clapham will manage.' Rob decided that if there was any chance that his presence might make Stella feel more secure and able to sleep, then he'd take it.

He was tired and the sofa bed was comfortable, so sleep came easily after Stella had gone to bed—but every noise woke him. A car accelerating noisily in the street outside. The slight thud of a door banging somewhere in the block of flats. And then the one his sleeping mind had been waiting for. The soft turn of the door handle in the early morning hours.

Then nothing. The doorway was dark, but he could hear her breathing. Short, staccato breaths, which could only mean one thing.

'Hey. You okay?'

'Yes. Sorry to wake you. Go back to sleep.'

No... He wasn't going to let her escape now, not when he could hear the tears that he'd been waiting for all evening in her voice.

'Why don't you come in?'

Silence. Stella was hesitating in the darkness, and Rob wondered just how far he might go to show her that he was here for her. As far as getting out of bed, or even walking to the doorway? What would happen if she'd already made her way back to her bedroom?

Then he saw her, her footsteps silent on the carpet. Moving into the glow from the streetlights that was filtering in through the curtains. He could see fabric moving around her legs, along with something wrapped around her shoulders, and she seemed smaller somehow. More fragile.

He was reminded of the small form of his niece, trailing her teddy bear and finding her way to his room in the darkness, to tell him that his house made funny noises that frightened her. He'd stayed awake for the rest of the night, guarding little Grace from her fears so that his sister and her husband could get a good night's sleep on a much-needed weekend away. As far as he could see, Stella had no teddy bear with her, but he still felt the same protectiveness. The same feeling that somehow he might keep her from harm.

'You could sit down…?' Preferably not in the chair on the other side of the room, but that was always an option if Stella preferred it.

Her shadow moved towards him and he felt a slight movement as she perched herself right on the far edge of the sofa bed. Still, she was too far away.

'Can we…just talk for a minute?'

'Of course.' Rob eased himself up a little, resting on his elbow. 'What would you like to talk about?'

He saw her shoulders move in a slight shrug. 'I'm not sure.'

'Fair enough. Maybe you could be a little more comfortable while you're thinking about it?'

She hesitated again. And then suddenly she moved, with the

kind of certainty that he usually expected from Stella. Sliding onto the bed, she lay down on top of the duvet, next to him. Rob curled his arms around her, pulling the bulk of the quilted bedspread that was wound around her shoulders down a little, so that it would cover her legs and keep her warm.

'That's nice.' She gave him the two words he needed before he could pull her a little closer, curled up against him. He could smell the scent of her hair, feel every breath she took. And then, as if she'd finally found her safe place, Stella began to cry.

'Sorry...' She extricated her hand from the bedspread, wiping her face with her fingers.

'Don't be. This is all okay. It's all good.' Rob caught his breath as he felt Stella's fingers wind around his, clinging on to him as she wept.

# CHAPTER EIGHT

AT SOME POINT they must have fallen asleep. Rob had woken more than once, and each time Stella was still in his arms, sleeping peacefully. Like a dream that refused to fade. Wanting her the way he did should have kept him awake, but tonight wasn't about that and the gentle rhythm of her breathing lulled him back to sleep again.

Finally, he woke to a loud crash, coming from the kitchen, which was right next door to the sitting room. He sat up in bed rubbing his eyes, and called out to Stella, 'Everything okay?'

Her voice drifted through the open door. 'Yes. Sorry, did I wake you?'

Rob looked at his watch. His brain had got around to processing the noise now, and it had sounded like a pile of baking tins hitting the tiled floor. Either Stella had decided to make cupcakes at seven-thirty in the morning, or this was his wake-up call. Stumbling from the bed and grabbing his clothes, he made for the bathroom.

When he joined her, she was sitting at the table, which was positioned in the window at the far end of the galley of gleaming kitchen units. Opposite her, a place was laid with freshly made toast and coffee.

'Good morning.' Her greeting seemed strangely formal, and Rob detected a hint of morning-after embarrassment. He smiled, sitting down at the table. 'Is toast all right? I haven't got anything else.'

Rob grinned. 'Toast is fine. When I'm working I usually make do with a handful of granola on the way to the car.'

'That's nice with strawberries. Probably a bit messy when you're driving, though…' Stella seemed intent on making conversation.

'Yeah. Not quite as loud as making toast either.'

She stared at him for a moment and then started to laugh. 'I suppose not. I wasn't sure whether you had an alarm clock with you.'

And she hadn't wanted to come back into the sitting room. Fair enough. Last night was…last night. Rob reached for the marmalade to spread some on his toast, and Stella got up to make herself another cup of coffee.

'I suppose…' She was staring fixedly at the machine, clearly avoiding his gaze. 'We don't have to tell a counsellor everything, do we? I mean, about last night.'

'We don't have to tell them anything. Just talk about the things you want to talk about.' It was nice that she didn't want anyone else to know. He didn't either, because it had been special. 'I wasn't going to mention it.'

'No. Neither will I.' She shrugged, picking up her coffee. 'It's not relevant…'

Maybe it was time to cut through all of the uncertainty, and tell her how he really felt. If Stella didn't feel that way then that was okay.

'Last night was one of a kind. It meant a lot to me that you wanted me here. After everything that happened yesterday.'

She smiled suddenly, coming to sit down opposite him. 'It meant a lot to me too, Rob. I couldn't sleep and…'

'Yeah. I know. I needed some company too.'

'Thank you.' Her gaze found his, in that increasingly familiar gesture that acknowledged they'd said all they needed to say.

Maybe things would have been a little less awkward if they'd simply made love last night. They might have cared less and walked away more easily and it would have gone without saying that they'd keep it to themselves. But this had been different, a kind of closeness that had nothing to do with the physical and everything to do with an emotional connection.

'I'll have to see whether the hospital counsellor is free this morning, because I'm operating today.' Stella seemed to have regained her enthusiasm for the day ahead now. Rob knew what a valuable commodity that was. All of the days when he'd woken up, filled with an obscure feeling that the future held more than he could handle, had taught him to cherish these bright mornings.

'Is that an invitation to come and watch you operate?'

She laughed. 'Do you need one, Rob?'

'It's customary.'

'In most circumstances I suppose it is. But my theatre door is always open to you.'

'In that case…what time? I'm interested in seeing what you can do.' Rob knew that was a challenge.

'Maybe *I'm* interested in what you can do.' She responded in just the way he'd thought she might. 'The team meeting's before lunch so that we can start promptly at two o'clock. Don't be late, will you, or I'll have to start without you.'

She couldn't chase his doubts away. She knew that returning was a hard process for him, and that there might be obstacles along the way. But Rob recognised in Stella the approach to the day that he'd once had. That the one and only point of obstacles was that they could be pushed out of the way.

'I'll be there.'

\* \* \*

The day had taken a turn for the better. It had started in the very early hours, when Stella had finally decided that lying in bed, allowing her thoughts to prey on her mind, wasn't a good idea. She'd wrenched herself away from the warm duvet, wondering if a glass of water might help. And somehow, she'd found her way to the sitting room door, which wasn't where she was supposed to be going at all.

But she'd been safe in Rob's arms, like a child afraid of the darkness. And that had meant something more than just the practical need to get some sleep before a busy day at work. At the time it had meant everything, and even now Stella couldn't leave it behind. It was like a dream that stubbornly refused to shrivel and die in the morning light.

Phil had already alerted the hospital counsellor, probably deciding that he'd have a battle on his hands in that respect. But when Rob returned from his session, he murmured quietly to Stella to *'Just give it a chance'*. She did, and it helped more than she'd bargained for.

Now the only thing between her and a quiet evening in, followed by an early night, was a student called Ottilie. It was the patient who occupied the place of first importance in an operating theatre, and medical students were usually right at the bottom of the pecking order, considered by many surgeons as beneath their notice. But the two procedures on Stella's schedule this afternoon were straightforward, and she had no concerns about her patients. Ottilie, on the other hand…

She had a lot of potential, and was indisputably bright and enthusiastic. Most students got over their initial nerves in Theatre and settled down, but Ottilie just seemed to get more jittery every time, constantly tripping over her own eagerness to help. She'd managed to get herself in everyone's bad books, which wasn't easy because Stella had a great team, who were generally very supportive of students.

Stella had taken her to one side and explained, as kindly as she could, that the first priority of a student in an operating theatre was to keep out of the way and do as they were told. Ottilie had apologised, promised faithfully to be better in every way in the future, and then the very next time she'd been in Theatre she'd been reduced to tears by a harsh rebuke from the head nurse.

She didn't blame Martin. An operating theatre was a high-pressure environment and it was important to get everything exactly right. And when he was trying to make the first count of all of the instruments, the last thing anyone should do was stand behind him, murmuring their own count, however quietly.

Stella had been forced to ask Ottilie to leave the theatre, and found her crying inconsolably in the locker room afterwards. She'd tried to take a firm but kind stance with her, and explained again how she needed to act in Theatre, but this afternoon was going to be Ottilie's last chance. None of the other surgeons in the department would have her in their operating theatres, and Stella was reluctantly beginning to feel the same way.

Ottilie had attended the team meeting, and as usual she'd taken copious notes. Stella could do nothing but hope for the best, and the way that everyone was ignoring Ottilie wasn't giving her much cause for optimism.

'You want me to keep an eye on Ottilie?' Everyone had filed out of the room, leaving Stella alone with Rob.

'That's not what you're here for, Rob. I've spent a lot of time explaining how she needs to act in Theatre.' Stella bit her lip. 'I don't mean to be ruthless...'

'It's exactly what you should be. It's your job not to allow anything to get in the way of the patient's welfare.' He seemed to understand the dilemma.

'I had a lot of help when I was a student. My dad sat me down and told me exactly what would be expected when I first went into Theatre. He even set up a few practice sessions at home, barking orders at me. I saw quite a different side of him.'

'And now Ottilie's failing and you don't know how to help her? That's not what *you're* here for. I, on the other hand, am a free agent.'

Stella rolled her eyes. 'Believe me, I'm quite aware of that. How on earth did you know about the difficulties with Ottilie, anyway?' He'd been here for just a few days and already he seemed to know what was going on in the unit better than she did.

'There's something to be said for knowing how everything works, and having the time to just talk to people. I'm quite enjoying it.'

'And something to be said for wanting to prove yourself?' Rob wasn't so very different from Ottilie in that respect, only he had a much better idea of how to go about things.

'That too.' He grinned at her. 'I'm clearly far too transparent.'

Stella gave in. There was no getting over Rob's way of looking at things. 'This is my final offer, then.'

'Make it a good one...'

'I won't ask you to take Ottilie on, because that's not what we invited you here for. If you could point her in the right direction, I'm sure the whole team would be massively relieved, and I'd personally be very grateful.'

Rob made a pretence of thinking about it for a moment. 'Okay, boss. Happy to comply.'

'Do *not* call me boss, Rob! Not when you're busy doing

whatever you want…' He was already on his feet, and he didn't turn. But Stella heard him chuckle as he walked out of the room.

If Stella had feared she'd been giving the young woman a hard time, then Rob was outdoing her. She suspected that he'd given Ottilie the task of arranging the theatre shoes carefully on the rack, the named ones at the top and the spares at the bottom, because no one else would have thought to do it. And when she arrived in Theatre, Ottilie was already helping lift the patient onto the operating table, backing away as soon as Rob signalled for her to do so.

So far so good. Stella looked around, checking that everyone was here and ready to start work, and suggested some music.

'Which CD would you like, Ms Parry-Jones?' Ottilie responded.

'What do you think, Sajiv?' Stella turned to the anaesthetist, who generally took charge of the choice of music.

'Number four, Ottilie.' Sajiv shot her a smile. 'Thanks.'

The operation was a delayed breast reconstruction for a woman who'd had a mastectomy six months previously. Stella noticed that Rob had positioned himself and Ottilie in the best vantage point possible, without getting in the way, quietly motioning towards the things she needed to watch. It was actually quite a relief not to have to wonder whether Ottilie was at her elbow, trying to see what she was doing.

'Retractors…' Out of the corner of her eye she saw Ottilie stiffen, clearly knowing that this was a job she could help with, but under Rob's stern gaze she didn't move. 'Rob, can you assist, please?'

He quietly came forward, taking on the job of holding the retractors as if it was the most natural thing in the world for a fully qualified surgeon to do. Ottilie stayed where she was, until Rob motioned for her to come forward and take over from him. When Stella suggested that Rob might like to close for her, he nodded, closing the wound with all the expertise she had come to expect, and giving Ottilie a running commentary on exactly what he was doing. Stella found herself watching as well, in the hope of learning something.

'I think that'll be all right. What do you reckon, Ottilie?'

Ottilie reddened. Even she knew that she wasn't supposed to pass judgement on a surgeon's work, but Rob gave her an encouraging nod.

'Flawless, Mr Franklin.'

'Yep.' Rob knew full well that his work *was* flawless. Stella had come to learn that he expected nothing less of himself. 'Think you can cut the stitches?'

Panic showed in Ottilie's eyes. This was something new, and Stella wondered whether her jumpiness and the way that she crowded everyone was due to lack of confidence. If that was the case, then Rob might be taking a risk here.

He knew that, though. He showed Ottilie exactly what he wanted done, guiding her when she hesitated. They were in danger of running a little late, but Ottilie was turning a corner, learning how to succeed, and despite the team's frustration with her it was what everyone wanted.

When Ottilie was finished, and Rob had nodded his acceptance of her work, she stood back. The team took over, an efficient machine that worked with Rob to finish on time. Stella thanked everyone, and then turned to Ottilie.

'You did well this afternoon.'

Ottilie beamed at her. 'Thank you, Ms Parry-Jones. I really appreciate your having me here.'

'Scrub out…' Rob jerked his thumb towards the swing doors leading out of the operating theatre, and Ottilie nodded, hurrying away.

'What on earth have you done to the poor girl?' Stella frowned up at him.

'I collared her and took her for lunch—we had sandwiches in the park. She had a few very interesting things to say for herself.' Rob shot her an enigmatic look and it was clear that Stella was going to have to ask if she wanted to know more.

'You're going to tell me? Or do I have to force it out of you?'

'Well, if you must know…and I'm a little upset over having to give up my people management secrets…' He grinned at her, clearly not upset at all. 'Ottilie's the first person in her family ever to go to university, let alone medical school. When she told her parents that she was going to start on a surgical training module they threw a party, telling the whole family that their daughter was going to be a surgeon.'

'Ah. The weight of expectation.'

'Yes. She's got all she needs to succeed, but she's just terrified she'll let everyone down, and that's pushing her into making mistakes. So I told her that there was only one person that she needed to impress.'

Stella folded her arms, shifting from one foot to the other, to ease the ache in her back. 'The only person she needed to impress was you, I suppose?'

'I can give her immediate feedback. Everyone else is too busy to notice that she tidied the shoe rack.'

'And classifying according to job descriptions. I did wonder who'd done that.'

'Exactly my point, Stella. Your concentration is rightly on the patient, and you don't have the time to discuss shoe racks with student doctors. I asked her to do it, she did it really well and I told her she'd done a good job.'

Stella puffed out a breath. 'So I'm the big bad wolf in all of this.' Rob opened his mouth, obviously about to deny it and she held up her hand. '*You* didn't say that. I'm saying it.'

'If you were, I'd have had my head bitten off before now. You focus on what you need to focus on, and that's what makes you a good surgeon. That doesn't put you in the wrong, you just have a different job description.'

Stella had always felt that way, but it was good to hear someone say it. Good to hear *Rob* say it, actually.

'Do you miss it?'

Rob shrugged. 'Not in the slightest. That tingling feeling I got when I stepped into the theatre is probably just my blood pressure. I ought to get that sorted.'

'I can take your blood pressure if you want me to.' She called his bluff and Rob shook his head. 'I'm thinking of coming in on Saturday to work up a plan for Anna's surgery. I meant to start on that yesterday but never managed to get that far. If you're around…?'

'I'd love to join you. But I need to be back at home. I'm on call.'

Right, then. Stella could suggest an alternative, or let it slide. Rob needed his weekends, probably more than ever since he'd started to step back into a life that had once almost broken him. But he did look genuinely disappointed.

'I could always drive down to yours. If you want me to, that is—it's probably better just to email you with my thoughts and we could discuss it next week.'

'The train's faster.' He smiled suddenly. 'I'll pick you up at the station if you text me and let me know when you're arriving…'

Had it really been just a couple of weeks? Rob felt as if he'd experienced one of those major turning points in life, where one moment could change everything.

That had never happened before. Change had always felt like a gradual process, which relied on a myriad different things. But his life felt as if it had been chopped in two—before Stella and after Stella.

It probably wasn't Stella at all. His lingering discontent with a life that didn't include the thing he'd worked so hard to achieve, the excitement at the thought of stepping into an operating theatre again.... That *had* to be it.

All the same, when he drew up at the station on Saturday morning and saw Stella waiting outside, sunglasses perched on the top of her head and wearing a sleeveless blouse with a summer skirt and flat sandals, surgery was the last thing on his mind. His world tipped, much as it had when he'd first seen her, but this time the reaction was far more dizzying.

He'd set up a table and chairs in the shade of a spreading oak tree that had been standing since before the house was built. The breeze tugged at her skirt, its fingers riffling through her hair as they worked, and when it was time for lunch he brought lemonade, sandwiches and a bowl of cherries from the kitchen. Finally, Stella sat back in her seat.

'I think...we're almost there.'

'Yep. We can run through a few simulations next week, to settle our outstanding points.' They'd disagreed over a couple of suggestions that Rob had made, both impassioned and neither willing to back down because the stakes were so high. Rob had fought for his ideas before, but it had never felt quite so delicious.

Surgery was one thing, both challenging and rewarding in equal measure, and even though it had broken him he still loved it. But Stella was quite another. She understood him and she could meet needs that he'd never even realised he had. And that all-important but indefinable thrill whenever he saw her was there too. It was just too bad that their differing lifestyles meant that they could never be happy together.

# CHAPTER NINE

THE WEEKS LEADING up to Anna's surgery were busy. Rob had immersed himself in the work of the unit, and always seemed to have a student or one of the junior doctors with him, taking copious notes of everything he said. They ran simulations, explored possibilities and did the practical work of making sure that the long surgery would be done in such a way that Rob could take over from Stella at regular intervals, to give her a chance to rest. The prosthetics they'd need to reshape Anna's shattered jaw had been made, and they were ready. Stella was excited about the possibilities and aware of everything that might go wrong in equal measure.

She and Rob faced each other across the operating table. The gallery above their heads was full, students and junior doctors pressed tightly together. Around them, the team that Stella had chosen, who had worked together for long enough to be able to anticipate most of her requests before she even voiced them. Anna had been prepped and anesthetised, and now everyone's attention was directed on them. Stella's was directed on Rob.

All she could see was his eyes, but that was enough. It was ten in the morning, and the surgery was expected to run through the whole day, and probably into the late evening. But they'd be there for each other. There for Anna, and striving for the new life that she wanted.

'Sajiv…?' She didn't need to ask for the music, she knew that Sajiv would have prepared something.

'Coming right up.' The quiet strains of an orchestra threaded through the air of anticipation. Sajiv generally started with a classical piece, moving on to something a little more modern later.

Stella felt for the exact point to start her first incision. She saw Rob's nod and took a breath, feeling the theatre nurse place the scalpel in her hand…

As soon as they'd started, all of the hopes and fears dissolved. There was just the present, and the intense concentration needed for the task at hand. One of the screens above their heads displayed their progress through the complex set of procedures, mostly for the benefit of the gallery because she and Rob been over it so many times that it was fixed very firmly in Stella's head. Every time she stepped back to stretch or check on the live X-ray screen, Rob was there, almost a part of herself who knew everything she knew, saw everything she saw.

By midday, the work on the scar on Anna's forehead had been completed and Stella took a break. A visit to the ladies' room, which she didn't really need but there was a long afternoon ahead of her. Something to eat and drink, which wasn't completely necessary either, but when they'd discussed the plan, Rob had reminded her of the need to pace herself.

By two o'clock they were ahead of schedule. At three they had to stop until Sajiv was happy that Anna's vital signs were steady again. At five, Stella stepped back from the table for a moment and realised that her back and shoulders were beyond aching.

'Take a break?' Rob murmured the words and she nodded. They weren't finished yet, but it had already been a long day and it was necessary to keep physical and mental tiredness at bay.

'Yes.' He would take over her role while she stretched her complaining muscles.

At seven o' clock in the evening came the words that everyone had been waiting for. Stella glanced around at the team, and then at Rob, who nodded his agreement to her unspoken question. The demanding and intricate work of reshaping Anna's jaw had been done, and they were ready for the next part of the procedure.

'We'll close now.'

She didn't need to tell anyone what to do. Rob was ready to take on the next part of the process, and the theatre nurse was already counting the instruments and the large pile of discarded swabs. Now wasn't the time to lose her concentration, but she could step back a little, taking on a support role in the intricate task of moving the skin flap on Anna's neck upwards and applying skin grafts where needed, ready for the wounds to be dressed and for healing to begin.

They were done just before midnight. The team who would care for Anna as she regained consciousness swung into action, and Stella stepped back from the table for the last time.

'Thanks, everyone. You all rock…' Finally, she had a moment to glance up at the gallery and she was surprised to see many of the faces who'd been there this morning. Phil Chamberlain was on his feet, and the silent applause from the gallery was mirrored in the operating theatre below, a short burst of quiet clapping that didn't often happen, but meant a great deal when it did.

*'You're the one who rocks…'*

As they scrubbed out together, Rob murmured the words and even though she was suddenly far too tired to be feeling anything, tingles ran the whole length of Stella's aching spine.

'Not so bad yourself.' She grinned at him. Stella was far too tired for grinning as well, it felt as if her face was about to tear apart under the strain.

They both knew the first thing that they had to do now. Rob bumped his arm against her shoulder in an expression of support as they walked through to the lounge, where Jess was waiting with Anna's parents. The hospital's patient support team would have told them that there would be no news during the course of the day, but all the same it looked as if they'd been here for a while, filling up the bins with coffee cups. Stella walked over to where they were sitting and waited a few moments until they were ready to hear her news.

'Jess, Mr and Mrs Leigh… I'm very pleased to tell you that Anna's surgery has gone as well as we'd hoped. She's in Recovery now, and they'll take her through to Intensive Care for the night, and probably most of tomorrow. But as soon as she's back on the ward, you'll be able to see her.'

'She's going to be all right?' Mrs Leigh asked tremulously, clutching her husband's hand.

'It's too early to give you a complete response. Anna still has a long road ahead of her.' Rob smiled encouragingly. 'But she's come through the surgery well, which is very promising, and we have reason to feel optimistic.'

Mrs Leigh burst into tears, and her husband hugged her. Jess jumped to her feet, enveloping Stella in a bear hug. That was the last thing she needed at the moment, but she didn't have the heart to pull away.

'Thank you. Thank you so much…'

'If you want to thank her, then not hugging would be a great idea.' Rob's voice sounded full of humour and understanding. Jess let her go suddenly.

'Sorry… You must be exhausted.' Exhaustion didn't really cover it, but Stella smiled, nodding. 'Thank you for everything...' Jess seemed to be looking around for someone else to hug, but made do with grabbing Rob's hand and shaking it.

'Why don't you go home and try to get some sleep? You won't be able to see her tonight, but I promise you that Anna's in very good hands and that she's being well cared for,' Stella suggested and Jess shook her head.

'I just... I know it's crazy but I just feel that I want to stay as close as I can...' Jess pursed her lips. 'They will tell me, won't they? How she's doing?'

'Yes, they will. You're Anna's partner and she signed a form, nominating you and her parents as her joint next of kin. You have a right to ask and be answered.' That hadn't always been the case and, after a day spent waiting around with nothing to do but worry, Jess had probably forgotten that this had all been dealt with.

'Then...' Jess turned to Anna's parents. 'Why don't you both go home and get some sleep? I can catch some shut-eye on the couch here, and I promise I'll call you straight away with anything.'

Jess was clearly determined to stay, and Mrs and Mrs Leigh both looked very tired.

'That's a good idea.' Rob turned to Anna's parents. 'There's nothing you can do here, and the best thing you can do for Anna now is to pace yourselves and be ready for when she wakes up. She's going to need you then.'

'He's right, Jo.' Mr Leigh squeezed his wife's hand. 'Why don't you come with us, Jess? You don't want to be here all on your own.'

Jess shook her head miserably.

'We'll get someone to find Jess a bed in one of the family rooms. She can get some sleep, and she'll be woken if there's any news to pass on to you,' Rob suggested.

'That sounds great, thank you.' Jess smiled at him, clearly

beginning to feel that she might be able to sleep now. In an effort to stay on her own feet, Stella reminded herself that this fatigue was a good thing, a result of her allowing herself to relax because things were going well.

Handshakes were exchanged, and there were more thank-yous than Stella could register. She followed Rob out of the waiting room and into the corridor, too weary to take much notice of anything until Rob stopped suddenly.

'Ottilie!'

Stella turned to see Ottilie, standing behind the open door of the waiting room. It had concealed her presence while they were talking to Anna's family, and Ottilie was pressing her body against the wall now, clearly hoping that it might open up and swallow her.

'Sorry...' Ottilie backed away, clearly hoping to make her escape in the opposite direction, but Rob called her back.

'Anything we need to know?' Rob fixed her with a look that seemed designed to break down anyone's defences. Stella certainly couldn't resist it.

'Sorry. No. I wanted to see how you handled this part...' She turned to Stella. 'I was watching whenever I had some free time today. I think you're amazing.'

'And very tired,' Rob chided her gently. 'Are you thinking about how much you have ahead of you?'

He'd got it exactly right and Ottilie reddened. 'I don't think I'll ever be able to do what you do, Ms Parry-Jones.'

'You may not be able to do it now, and you probably can't see far enough ahead to believe you'll ever make it. You'll just have to take it from me that you're going in the right direction, even if you do feel that you're travelling blind.'

Ottilie nodded. Rob had clearly said something of the sort to her before, and was reinforcing that message.

'Go home, and get some sleep. If you want to follow up on

this patient then you can do it tomorrow, and you can leave your write-up of all your observations in my pigeonhole. I look forward to reading it.' Rob's tone was firm but kindly, and Ottilie looked up at him with thinly disguised hero-worship.

'Thank you. I'm on it…' Ottilie turned and hurried away, and Rob called after her.

'Sleep first.'

'You think she knows she's headed for the medical imaging suite?' Stella murmured to him.

'Probably not. She might wait around the corner until the coast's clear to come back this way again.' Rob chuckled. 'She's worth the effort, you know. I think she'll make a great surgeon if she just stops worrying about the future and concentrates on the present. I've been looking through some of the write-ups she's done on the surgeries she's attended and she's good.'

'You've been helping her?'

'Yeah. I think she's got a lot of potential, and that she's just going through a bit of a rough patch. Once she stops thinking about whether she's doing the right thing or not, she's surprisingly thoughtful and assured. She's very bright, and she was used to being the best kid in the class at school. Then she came to university and found herself among a load of other bright and ambitious young people. It takes a bit of getting used to.'

'And you know this how?' Perhaps Rob had taken a course in psychology in his spare time, during the last three years.

'I live in a village. Seven hundred and ninety-nine people… in a few days we're expecting it to be a round eight hundred. And I'm a GP, remember? When they're awake, patients have a habit of telling you things.' Rob smiled down at her. 'Ottilie's quite right, of course. You *are* amazing.'

Stella nudged his arm with her elbow. 'Don't underestimate your own part in this.'

A night spent curled up in his arms had brought them closer, and today had brought them closer still. In different ways, perhaps, but it all came down to trust. The kind of trust that had made her feel safe when every shadow held a young lad with a pair of scissors in his hand was the same kind of trust that allowed her to move back from a patient, knowing that she was leaving them in good hands. It had helped Rob and Stella to work together seamlessly, and give Anna their best.

If she took his arm, held on to him as tightly as she wanted to, she was sure that Rob would respond. But the thought that Ottilie might decide that the medical imaging suite wasn't on the way to anywhere that she wanted to go and suddenly appear behind them made Stella think better of the idea. She'd seen enough in Rob's eyes today to know that if she touched him now she wouldn't let him go.

'Are you going to get some sleep yourself, now?' His raised eyebrow told Stella that he knew full well she wouldn't.

'I may go and shut my eyes for ten minutes in my office. I want to be around to see Anna get settled in the ICU. How about you? You're not going back to Sussex at this time of night, are you?'

'No, I've taken myself off the on-call rota for the weekend. I thought that I'd stick around for a little while too, and then go back to my sister's place and tip myself onto the couch in an effort not to wake anyone.'

'There's always Phil's office couch, he won't mind if you crash out on it for a couple of hours.' If curling up with him on the smaller couch in her office was out of the question, at least they'd be in the same building.

'Sounds blissful.' He stopped outside the lifts, stabbing at the call button with his finger, and the doors to one of the cars opened obligingly.

They were alone in the lift for probably less than a min-

ute. But it felt a great deal longer, because Rob was a man
who made good use of his time. Catching her hand in his, he
raised it to within an inch of his lips, his eyes suddenly dark
and searching. When Stella gave a small nod, he planted a
kiss on her fingers.

'Rob, I…' Too late. The lift doors were opening and they
were back in a world where, even at this hour, there would be
someone around to see whatever passed between them.

And now anything that did pass between them would be all
about loss and regret. They'd see each other again—there was
still a lot left to do for Anna—and Rob had become so much
a part of the department now that he had a lot of loose ends
to tie up before he could leave. But they wouldn't be battling
together, against each other and against all the odds. They'd
changed each other's lives and now everything was going to
be focused on moving on.

'I know…'

Of course he did; he'd been there too. It was almost a relief not to have to put it into words, because there was nothing that Stella could say which would reflect the way she felt.

# CHAPTER TEN

ROB HAD STAYED in London until Sunday afternoon, catching a few hours' sleep on Friday night, before going with Stella to see how Anna was early the following morning. He'd gone to his sister's house on Saturday evening, knowing that it was a very poor idea to take Stella up on the offer of her sofa bed for the night. It wasn't very likely that he would stay in his bed, and Stella in hers, after the closeness of the last couple of days.

Before he left the hospital on Sunday afternoon, ready to get a good night's sleep before going to work on Monday morning, there were a few moments for a goodbye. Only that goodbye had already been said, in unplanned, stolen moments in a lift. He'd already felt the loss, and it seemed as if they were just going through the motions.

'I'll see you.' She smiled up at him.

'Yeah. Around.' He grinned back at her.

'Around where?' Stella did like to keep things as predictable as possible and in a sudden urge to see whether she might compromise with him, he decided not to set a date.

'I know where you are. You know where I am. Probably at a time when we least expect it.'

'You mean I'm not going to get the chance to prepare for it?'

'Absolutely not. Just take my word that it'll happen...'

* * *

As the week wore on Rob became more annoyed with himself, as he didn't like making empty promises. He'd given his word to Stella in the heat of the moment, and it had seemed the right thing to say at the time, but with each day that passed it felt more and more like a mistake. Stella was beautiful, perfect just as she was, but he'd let a lot of people down—Kate, his colleagues at the hospital... Rob might be determined not to do the same to Stella, but he had a lot of previous in that respect.

And they were so very different. He loved the country, the slow pace of a small village where he knew each of his patients personally and was liable to bump into any one of them whenever he went to buy a paper or post a letter. Stella thrived on the fast pace and pressures of surgery in the heart of the city. He might miss that, but Rob wasn't sure how he could ever make it his whole life again.

She'd promised to email him with news of Anna, and Stella had kept her word. Short intimate messages, which really should have had kisses at the bottom but didn't. He'd replied in kind, alluding to the photographs and reports that she'd enclosed, and wondering whether this was the beginning of the end. Whether Stella had realised that it would be hard to maintain a relationship in the present, when neither of them had any clear idea of what they wanted for the future, and was letting him down gently.

He spent Thursday and Friday digging a ditch. It wasn't an entirely necessary ditch, more a precaution against unusually heavy rain in the autumn, but the repetitive, tiring nature of the work helped him to keep his mind away from what-ifs. By Saturday, the trench was a lot longer and deeper than any stretch of the imagination required, and he resorted to weeding the kitchen garden.

When he heard a car drawing up outside the house he didn't take off his muddy boots to go inside and answer the door. Whoever it was would know that he'd probably be working in the garden. Parcels would be left on the doorstep and visitors would come and find him. He heard footsteps on the path around the house and something about them made him turn suddenly.

Stella. Dressed in jeans and a brightly coloured summer top, and looking as delicious as a long, cool glass of lemonade. His mouth suddenly felt very dry.

'To what do I owe this pleasure?' Rob managed to summon up the words, and add a smile to them.

'Not expecting me?'

He hadn't expected this. Stella was his dream of a woman, but the way she looked right now was beyond even his wildest dreams. He couldn't see any difference from the way she usually looked, although he always liked her more casual weekend outfits better than her monochrome work attire. Maybe it was a week spent wondering whether he'd ever see her again that made her red hair seem so fiery in the sunshine.

'If I had been I'd have answered the door. And planted up hanging baskets to welcome you.'

'That would have been very nice. If I'd heard you were up in town on one of your days off, and could drop round for dinner, I'd have gone for flaming torches on my doorstep...'

Stella's taste for the dramatic. There was no question about it now. She'd taken the next step, and he'd responded. They would be seeing things through, wherever it led them. Not yet, though, because she'd opened the leather bag that was tucked under her arm, and taken out an envelope. She held it out towards him, and Rob caught sight of the hospital's logo in one corner.

'What's this?'

'It's something that Phil came up with. I agreed that it was a great idea, and said that I'd bring his proposal down to you at the weekend.'

Rob took off his gardening gloves and dropped them onto the ground. Luckily, his oldest jeans and shirts were in the wash, after having come in close contact with the ditch, and he had a relatively respectable shirt on today. Without the gloves, he looked relatively clean and tidy—other than his boots, which were still on his feet and caked with soil.

He opened the envelope and drew out a wad of paper, skimming the letter from Phil, which was paperclipped to a larger document underneath. 'He wants me to *what*...?'

'It's... I don't know what you'd call it. Staff development in partnership with the teaching arm of the hospital. Mentoring, maybe. You have a lot of skills and knowledge, and you have a way of thinking around things that...' Stella shrugged. 'It's only for a day a week, and perhaps some work from home via email or video-conferencing. But you might enjoy it.'

Rob smiled. He could see which way this was going. 'And it might tempt me to come back? Because I'm wasting all my valuable training, working here as a GP?' The idea hurt, because he knew he'd disappointed everyone—the people who'd supported him in his career, and the teachers who'd inspired him.

'No... Well, yes. I'll admit that I think it's a waste that you have so much skill and talent and you're not using it. But I understand now why you had to stop, because it was eating you up. I told Phil that he shouldn't expect you to come back full-time unless you were absolutely ready, because if this isn't right for you then *that's* the real waste. It's your decision, and I'm not here to persuade you either way.'

'It's tempting. I'll admit that.' Stella's honesty had made

it even more tempting. 'One thing, though. Is my email suddenly not working?'

Her smile told him that there was nothing wrong with his email. 'I don't know. You'd be a better judge of that than I am.'

That was all he needed to hear. And now there was no going back. He took one step forward, his shadow falling across her face. He was already lost in her gaze when she reached up, putting her arms around his neck.

It was one hell of a kiss. The kind of kiss that might bring him to his knees if it lasted too long, but which made him feel stronger than he had in a long while. She was soft and sweet-smelling in his arms, and yet Stella was strong enough to kick down the barriers that lay between them.

'I never thought it would be *this* nice.' Stella's lips seemed redder, her eyes brighter.

'You underestimated me?' Rob raised an eyebrow.

'No. It seems that my imagination's not as good as I thought it was.' She moved against him, kissing him again. One more unimaginably beautiful kiss.

'Maybe we should go inside. Talk…' Rob knew exactly where this was leading and he couldn't stop it. But he wanted Stella to be sure.

'I think that's a very good idea.'

This was all that Stella had dreamed about but hadn't dared to hope for. She knew that she and Rob were friends, and that they had a connection, but that didn't mean that they should be lovers. For the first time in her life, she was going into a relationship without knowing where it would lead, and she was actually okay with that. Okay with the idea that Rob had the power to turn her life upside down, because she trusted him enough to know that he wouldn't.

He stepped out of his boots and into the kitchen before

quickly making for the sink and soaping his hands, automatically beginning to clean each finger in a process that would take another ten minutes to complete.

'You're taking time to think about this?' Stella wound her arms around his waist, laying her head on his back.

'I want you to be sure.' He abandoned the scrubbing and turned the tap off, twisting around to face her. 'Really sure. Because I don't know how this is going to work out.'

'That's my line, isn't it? Always wanting to predict the end before I commit to the beginning. Perhaps I'll just steal yours, and tell you that I want this beginning. And that I trust you enough to take it without knowing the end.'

His face darkened suddenly. 'I'm not entirely convinced that you should trust me…'

She picked up the towel by the sink, carefully drying his hands. In the heat of his gaze, even that small intimacy felt a lot like foreplay. 'Too late, Rob. There's nothing you can do about that.'

She kissed his lips, feeling his arms gently embracing her. This was just delicious. There was passion there, she could feel it in the tension of his body, but Rob was clearly determined not to rush.

'How are we going to take this?' His kisses trailed across her jawline, towards her ear.

'Any way you want it…'

She felt the pressure of his touch reduce suddenly. She liked the way he hesitated. It showed that he understood the challenge she'd just thrown him.

'Sorry to interrupt the moment. But you're going to have to explain exactly what you mean by that.'

'I know what I like. Finding out what you like might add a few things to that list.'

He got it now. She wasn't inviting him to take, she wanted

him to give. And his body supplied the answer she wanted, clearly aroused at the thought.

'And of course you're more than capable of telling me to stop if my fantasies don't happen to coincide with yours.'

Oh! Fantasies! Rob really *did* know how to do this, perhaps better than she did. The thought of getting acquainted with all of his fantasies, and being able to show him hers, was beyond allure. Beyond the sharp pull of arousal, and moving into something that was deeper and wilder.

'In a hot minute.'

'Make that thirty seconds…' His smile made her tremble, because suddenly Stella had no idea what Rob was going to do next.

He backed her against the worktop, lifting her up onto it. She tugged at his shirt and he let her pull it over his head, but when her fingers went for the waistband of his jeans he brushed them away, pushing her knees apart so that he could stand close and pull her against him. She felt his arm around her, supporting her back, his other hand caressing her neck. Suddenly Stella knew exactly what he wanted. He wanted to bring her to fever pitch, and he wanted to do it slowly.

She wound her arms around his neck, feeling the warmth of his skin under her fingers. The smooth contours of bone and muscle. His scent. One by one, he was slowly undoing the small buttons on her blouse, and it was driving her crazy.

'Look at me.' There was no hint of command in his voice, but when she met his gaze she was caught, unable to get away. He planted soft kisses onto her lips as he slowly eased her out of her blouse, and she shivered at the touch of his fingers on her skin.

'You…' He'd found the thin, silky material of her bra and she gasped at the caress of his fingers. 'You could…'

'Take it off? Yeah, I could. Now or later?'

He made *later* seem like a sensual delight that was worth waiting for and really didn't need to be hurried. 'Later's good.'

His fingers skimmed her breast and Rob's mouth curved in a smile when she gasped. Gently gripping her arms, he pushed her hands behind her, winding his fingers loosely around her wrists. His light grip would have allowed her to escape in a second. He wanted her to stay put of her own volition and wait to find out what he was going to do. The thought made her shiver with desire.

Rob kissed her shoulders, running the fingers of his free hand lightly along the lacy edging of her bra. Touching, kissing her skin, everywhere but where she really wanted him to go. She pressed her lips together, determined not to beg, trembling at his every touch. Rob seemed intent on watching, enjoying every part of the arousal that was running through her body. *Later* had been a very good decision…

By the time they'd got upstairs and finished stripping off their clothes, Stella was so lost in him that she could barely notice anything else. Still he couldn't be persuaded to rush. He pressed a condom from the drawer of the bedside cabinet into her hand. It was there for her to use any time she wanted, and Stella wondered just how long she'd be able to hold out.

Minutes, hours—this was too all-consuming to even register the passing of time. They were both so aroused that it seemed impossible that they could wait any longer, but this slow dance was so exquisite that it always seemed to hold a few minutes more of enjoyment.

'Rob…' Finally, she grabbed his hand, moving it down between her legs, feeling his fingers caress her most sensitive places.

'Like this?' He trailed kisses across her breasts.

'Yes! Yes, just like that…' The orgasm hit her like a bolt of lightning, tearing its way through her. Rob stayed with her, making sure that it lasted, and then gently bringing her back down again. He knew just what to do, and had a rare talent for keeping the momentum going without forcing the pace too much.

'How do you know how to do that?' Stella smiled at him lazily, feeling her desire for him retreat and then slowly start to build again, like the insistent rise and fall of an incoming tide.

'You give yourself away.' He brushed his lips against the spot where a pulse beat in her neck. Then he slid his fingers gently back inside her, pressing in just the right spot to make her gasp. 'You're so generous in your reactions.'

And Rob was a man who took enough care to watch for those reactions. She pressed the condom into his hand. 'Now you have to give something of yours to me.'

He smiled, leaning away from her for a moment to roll the condom into place. When he eased inside her she could feel that their long foreplay had been just as stimulating for him as it had for her. He moved slowly at first, finding out how their bodies worked together and what gave them both the most pleasure.

'Rob!' Stella choked out his name as he slid one hand beneath her hips, lifting them a little so that he could go deeper. His eyes darkened and his sudden, sharp gasp told her that they'd just got it exactly right.

And then it got better. She could feel his body, burning up against hers, his movements more and more assertive as blind passion began to take hold. Stella squeezed the muscles that cradled him, and a low groan escaped his lips. Once more and her own orgasm came hard and fast, her body arching beneath his to savour every moment of it. Then Rob let out a cry and she held him tight as his body stiffened and convulsed.

There were no words for this. He cradled her in his arms

and she felt her heart beating wildly against his. Slowly, their bodies started to wind back down again, and he rolled away from her for a moment before curling his limbs around hers.

'Are you...all right?' It felt as if they'd both spun together into a different world, one where they might have to tread carefully for a while. But Rob's low chuckle reassured her.

'I've been way better than just *all right* for a while. I think I've reached a completely different plane now. You?'

'You took me right there with you, Rob.'

Rob had thought about what being with Stella might be like, but his imagination couldn't possibly have stretched to anything like this. She liked the same things that he did. Instead of snuggling together under the covers and letting their bodies relax into sleep, she wanted to continue their voyage of exploration. Now it was relaxed and contemplative, her fingers gently tracing the route of all the primary muscles in his shoulders and arms, where previously she'd gripped them so tight that he was sure there must be some evidence on his skin. He liked that too. That she hadn't left him exactly as she'd found him.

He'd expected that she would be bold, because that was how Stella was in everything else. But he hadn't expected quite this kind of assertiveness. It had challenged him to take charge because she had to know how much he wanted to please her. It had left him in no doubt that he *had* pleased her.

When the warmth of their bodies had started to cool, he'd risen from the bed, taking her on his lap in the large wicker chair that stood by the window and wrapping them round with the quilt that hung across its back.

'Do I get to call you *boss* now?' He kissed her forehead.

'Only here. And only if I get to call you boss too...'

Rob chuckled. 'You have a deal.'

She looked up at him questioningly. 'Do I? Is there any time limit on that?'

One of them was bound to say it, sooner or later. Was there a way forward for them?

'Sussex isn't so far from London. Neither of us is going to have to move house.'

Stella moved against him, planting a kiss on his cheek. 'Moving house would be easy.'

They'd tumbled into this, driven only by the certain knowledge that they wanted to be together. And now reality was beginning to bite.

'We've done this before. Started something and agreed to find out where it leads. We have different lives, different aims, but there's no reason why we can't travel together and see where it takes us.'

'I'd like that…' Stella hesitated. Something was on her mind, and Rob could guess what it was.

'If you're not here, that doesn't mean that I'm not still committed to you, Stella. That's non-negotiable.' He'd never treat her the way she'd been treated in the past.

She smiled suddenly, her gaze searching his face. 'For someone who's afraid of messing up, you make a very good job of *not* messing up.'

'That's good to know.' He kissed her to seal the deal. 'Whatever comes next…'

'We'll handle it. Let's concentrate on today now, eh?'


Rob had thought that Stella had given him everything, but now there was more. They'd found a tomorrow that they could both live with, and that meant they truly had today. They could trade fantasies—there was none of the tentative worry that something might shock, because he knew that Stella was capable of a simple *yes* or *no*. Right now, he could believe that she was capable of anything that she set her mind on doing, and the thought that she'd set her mind on him was the ultimate turn-on.

'You like to watch, don't you?' She planted a kiss on his cheek. 'I like you watching me.'

That was sorted, then. One more thing to look forward to. 'Don't stop there.'

'I notice that you have a mirror over there…' She freed one hand from the folds of the quilt, pointing towards the antique cheval mirror that stood in the corner of the room. It didn't get much use, but it had caught Rob's eye and he'd bought it at a local auction and cleaned the wooden frame.

'Which can be moved to the location of your choice.'

'I noticed that too. Or we could always swap places.'

The thought of watching Stella climb on top of him, and what she might do with him when she did, was almost too much to bear. She smiled, moving gently against him, which only made it more difficult to resist gathering her up right now and taking her back to the bed.

'So soon?' she teased him.

'It's been hours. Are you telling me that you're done with me already?'

'Not a chance.' Her fingers brushed against his erection, and Rob caught his breath. 'Impressive.'

'Really? You know all the right things to say to a guy. Or are you just very easy to please?' It was the first time that anyone had chosen to describe him as impressive, and maybe that was because this was the first time that Rob had let himself simply go with the flow, unhampered by his own expectations and goals.

'I'm only speaking as I find.' She kissed him, her mouth sweet and inviting. When he cupped her breast with his hand, Stella looked up at him, her eyes full of desire.

'How are we going to take this…?' The mischievous glint in her eyes told him that she wanted to turn the tables on him now.

'Any way you want it, sweetheart…'

# CHAPTER ELEVEN

THEY'D BEEN MAKING love for a good part of the morning and most of the afternoon. Stella could have stayed here all evening as well, but they had to eat.

Rob had chuckled when she'd asked him for a hanger so that she could fold her clothes neatly over it in the bathroom, where the mist from the shower would deal with the creases. She'd defiantly snatched up the shirt he'd been wearing and put it on, hoping that he wouldn't take another clean one from the closet, because a physique like Rob's could stand a little more inspection and she wasn't quite ready to leave the hours they'd spent together behind. He'd pulled on his jeans and a T-shirt, which was a good enough compromise since she could still trace every muscle through the thin fabric. They'd padded barefoot down to the kitchen to raid the fridge.

'Shall I put a couple of these part-cooked baguettes into the oven?' Stella inspected the packaging.

'Yeah, good idea. There's ham and cheese in there somewhere to go with them...'

'Somewhere' was about right. Stella began to sort the contents of his fridge into some kind of order and he looked up from the papers she'd brought this morning, which had caught his attention almost as soon as they'd entered the kitchen.

'Hey! Don't mess up my system!'

'There's a system?' She frowned at him.

'Yeah. I buy a load of stuff and I put it into the fridge on the right-hand side. Then what I don't eat gets pushed to the left the next time I go shopping.'

'Okay.' Stella inspected some of the sell-by dates, which backed up his claim. 'Sorry. I see how it works now. Get on with your reading.'

'Tidy up a bit if you absolutely have to, as long as you keep the right/left thing going.' He grinned at her and started to read again, his finger poised beneath each line to focus his concentration. Stella decided that since he'd opened the door to the idea, he could hardly object if she threw away the half carton of milk hidden at the back on the left. There was a full carton on the right, and she'd use that one for their coffee.

She took a quiche from the left-hand side of the fridge, along with ham and cheese and all of the salad items she could find, putting them on the table. By the time the oven had heated and the bread was ready, Rob had finished reading and was ready to eat.

'You know that it's not going to stay like that, don't you?' He nodded towards the closed door of the fridge.

'Yes, I know. You'll have to ask me back some time, so I can do it again.'

His gaze suddenly held all of the warmth of their time together upstairs. 'Any time you like. My fridge door is always open to you.'

They ate in silence for a while, their makeshift meal seeming like a feast because, however messy Rob's fridge was, he clearly bought local produce whenever he could, which was fresh and tasty. When her plate was empty and she was helping herself to seconds, Stella could no longer ignore the elephant in the room.

'What do you think about the job? First impressions, I mean...'

Rob nodded. 'It's tempting. To be honest, it's just what I've been looking for—a chance to take a step back on my own terms.'

'Maybe you shouldn't see it as a step back. It's a step forward into a place you've been before.'

'Yeah. Good thought. How do you feel about it? My working within the department.'

'You should make your own decision about this, Rob. What's best for you.'

He thought for a moment. 'Is there anything you need to tell me? Was this your idea, and Phil's just signed off on it?'

Time to come clean. It was a reasonable question, even if Stella wished he hadn't thought to ask it.

'I… This is all Phil's idea, although of course I knew about it. Telling him I could deliver the documents by hand was just an excuse. Would you have turned up on my doorstep with the suggestion that we had sex?'

Rob chuckled. 'I probably would have made you read through a draft of my latest paper, and then bored you to tears with possible amendments before I worked up the nerve to mention it. Although, to be honest, I probably wouldn't have come at all. I know how much your work means to you, and how focused you are. You might not want to add a complication like me.'

The thought had occurred to her. But Stella had come because she wanted to. 'You're not a complication, Rob. You're far more…' she waved her hand, trying to find the right word '…far more complicated than that.'

He laughed. 'I'm glad you feel I'm more than just an ordinary complication. You're more complicated than a mere set of labels too.' He leaned back in his seat, clearly considering the matter, and Stella got to her feet, walking over to the coffee machine. They were going around in circles, and maybe they both needed to step back a bit and straighten things out.

'Here's the bottom line…' The second cup was filling before he spoke again, and when she turned Rob had the same look on his face that she'd seen when he was defining issues to do with Anna's case. If he was half as good at this as he was at surgery, then they were home free.

'I've learned to my cost that I can't have everything. You know that focusing on the area of your life that you most want is what works for you.'

'Yes. That's fair.'

'They're both good coping strategies. But neither of them is a universal truth, and they're not going to work if we use them as an excuse to keep us from the other things we want in life. We just have to respect each other's boundaries. I used to do your job, so I know exactly how to respect yours.'

'I want to be with you, Rob. Very much.'

He got to his feet, enveloping her in a hug. 'And I want to be with you. This is not too much to ask of life—people do manage to have jobs and relationships at the same time. It's not so easy when you have a job that's as all-consuming as yours, but we can make it easy. No recriminations over spending too much time at work…'

'You've had those too?' Stella twisted her mouth down.

'Yep. And maybe being involved in each other's professional lives, however much we keep that at arm's length from the personal, is going to be of some benefit. I'm proud of the work we did together on Anna's case, and Phil does mention that there's a potential for more of that kind of consultancy.'

Stella hadn't realised that Phil had included that as well—it must have been a last-minute revision after he'd spoken about the idea to Stella.

'I'm proud of it too. I'd like to think we could do it again some time.'

'What do you say, then? How *do* you feel about working with me?'

She'd thought that ducking the question, putting it to the back of her mind, was the right answer. Now Stella had a different response. She reached up, laying her fingers on the side of his face.

'I think it's a great opportunity for both of us. And that we can have a lot of fun compromising with each other.'

Who'd have thought that running away to a house in the country, and having sex for most of the weekend with the most gorgeous man she'd ever seen, would improve her work performance on Monday morning? But somehow the little niggles seemed less niggling than usual, and everything Stella touched seemed to go remarkably well. At lunchtime, Phil rapped on her door and blustered in, smiling.

'Just had a call from Rob. He says he's taking the job. He wants to add a few things to the scope of work, of course, but that's no particular surprise. He's signed the contracts and he'll be posting them back today.'

'That's great.' Phil didn't need to know that Rob had signed the contracts yesterday, leaning them on her back. Then she'd felt the pen against her skin and she'd screamed in mock outrage, scattering the papers and snatching the pen from him. Pinning him down on the bed, she'd signed her own name between his shoulder blades, only to find when she looked in the mirror that, instead of his name, her skin bore a couple of entwined love hearts.

Phil was still rattling out the details, most of which Stella had already discussed with Rob. '… He'll be coming in on Thursday. I told him that it was unlikely we'd get the paperwork back by then, but he didn't seem too bothered about being paid on time...'

'No, I guess not. Phil, I asked him to mention...'

'About the two of you? Yes, he did.' Phil had a habit of delaying his reaction to anything until he'd heard people out. Clearly, he was waiting to see what else Stella had to say.

'Is that okay with you?'

'It's none of my business unless it affects your work, and you're both professional enough not to allow that to happen.' Phil smiled. 'Anything else?'

'No. Thanks, Phil, I really appreciate it.'

'It couldn't happen to two nicer people. I know that Rob's had his issues, but he's one of the best people I know. And if you ever want to chat—off the record—you know that I'm partial to a glass of orange juice at lunchtime.'

Stella nodded. Everyone knew that if they saw Phil drinking orange juice with another member of staff in the pub at lunchtime it was best to give them a wide berth, because Phil would be listening and dispensing a little wisdom. That was what made him such a good boss. The unit was personally loyal to him as well as professionally loyal, and Stella had always tried to follow his example with her own team.

'I'll bear that in mind. Rob's one of the best people I know too. As well as being a very gifted surgeon.'

'No arguments there. It's good to have him back here on a more regular basis.' Phil breezed out of the room, clearly happy that he'd achieved whatever he'd set out to do.


'Miss me?' Rob appeared in her office at eight-thirty on Thursday morning.

'No.' Stella laughed at his expression of dismay. 'How can I miss you when I'm still tingling?'

'Good point. I had a set of small and completely painless bruises to comfort me in your absence.'

'You did? I wasn't aware of having bruised you.'

'As I said, they were small and painless.' He rubbed his arm and Stella vaguely remembered clinging on to it for dear life at one point. 'I would have barely noticed them if they hadn't been something I felt sentimentally attached to.'

'Right. Think you're over them now, or do I need to take a look?'

'You were the one that brought tingling up. Want me to take a look at that?'

Touché. 'We'll neither of us take a look at anything. I shouldn't have even mentioned it since we're at work.'

Rob grinned, sitting down in the seat opposite her desk. 'I'm not at work yet. I don't start until nine in the morning.'

'Sadly, I am. What can I do for you, Mr Franklin?' Stella shot him her most professional smile, which didn't seem to faze him in the slightest.

'Rob, please. I think first names are okay between colleagues. I hear that Anna's coming in this morning.'

'I have an appointment with her at eleven. I've mentioned it to Phil, as he was hoping to spend some time with you before lunch, and I reckoned you'd want to check up on Anna as well.'

'Thanks. Would you mind if Ottilie sits in on that? She wrote a cracking report on the surgery, and she's hoping it'll count towards her marks for this part of her course.'

'I've already asked her to get me the results of Anna's scans and X-rays, and told her that if Anna's okay with her staying it's fine with me. Ottilie's still a bit rough around the edges, but she's turning out to be really helpful to everyone in Theatre, and I thought she might like to follow through with Anna.'

'Perfect. I'll just go home now, shall I? Since you appear to have organised everything.'

'Don't you dare. I think Phil's got something up his sleeve that he needs some help with. We're a surgeon down this week.'

Rob grinned broadly. He was never happier than when he was on the move, and busy suited him. 'I'll get out of your hair, then. See you later.'

Ottilie knocked on her door at a quarter to eleven sharp, proffering a tablet with all of the information that Stella needed. She flipped through the X-rays, thinking aloud for Ottilie's benefit. 'The real test is when we see her face, nothing replaces that. But from here I can see that the implants are beginning to knit well and I'm hopeful. We need to be very honest about our prognosis, but at the same time we can obviously give Anna the encouragement she needs. She's been through a lot to get this far.'

Ottilie nodded.

'I want you to have these X-rays ready for me or Mr Franklin to refer to during the consultation, but don't show them to Anna or any members of the family unless I tell you to. Anna's usually interested to see scans and X-rays, but we have to be sensitive to her needs on this particular day. I want you to be responsible for making sure that the information's there when we need it, but that the screen's off when we don't.'

'Thank you. I'll do that, Ms Parry-Jones.'

'Good. You haven't seen Mr Franklin around anywhere, have you?'

'I think he's in with Mr Chamberlain.' Ottilie had clearly made sure that she had an answer for everything. 'Would you like me to knock?'

'Yes, get him along to Procedure Room Three when you find him, will you? I'm going to see how Anna's doing...'

The nurse had already administered an analgesic, removed the outer bandages and moistened the inner pad to make sure that it could be removed without traumatising the area of the grafts. It was an uncomfortable process, but Jess was there, holding Anna's hand and talking to her.

'Hey there, Jess. How are you feeling today, Anna?'

'A bit scared. Today's the day, isn't it.' Anna's speech was slurred by emotion as well as the fact that her jaw was still very tender.

It was an important day. Not the only day... 'This is a long process, Anna. We'll be able to see a little more today, because the swelling's gone down now, but you've still got quite a bit of healing to do.'

'It's going to be difficult to see at first. But we can take the docs' word for it and use our imaginations,' Jess chimed in. 'I know you're scared, though. I am too.'

'We're going to wait until the dressing's moist enough and... Ah, here's Mr Franklin.' The door had opened and Rob appeared, closely followed by Ottilie, who sat down on a chair in the corner.

Anna waved her hand, unable to move her head to see Rob properly, but Jess got to her feet and made straight for Ottilie. The two young women exchanged a few words and Ottilie seemed to be trying to persuade Jess to go back to sit with Anna, clutching the tablet against her chest so that Jess would have no chance of seeing it.

Rob turned. 'Is there a problem?'

'No...' Ottilie waved Jess away again.

'There's no problem at all.' Jess could always be relied upon to make her feelings known. 'Ottilie found us and brought us sandwiches and coffee when Anna was in the operating theatre. Then some soup later on, and she stayed and chatted with Anna's dad about his crossword—he couldn't concentrate on it but he wouldn't put it down and I'm no good with cryptic clues. I never got the chance to thank her—'

'I didn't say anything. About how the operation was going.' Ottilie interrupted Jess, reddening furiously and clearly worried that Rob might think she'd done something wrong. There were lots of reasons why information about patients was carefully controlled, and Stella hoped that Ottilie hadn't given in to the temptation to give Anna's family an incomplete and possibly incorrect assessment of how Anna's surgery was progressing.

Jess could see that something was up. 'Was it wrong of me to ask how Anna was doing? I'm sorry, but the waiting was really getting to me…'

Rob stepped in. 'Please don't stop asking questions, Jess. I'd be heartbroken.' Anna's shoulders were shaking with laughter now, and she gave Rob's retort a thumbs-up.

'Well, Ottilie couldn't give me an answer anyway. She said that she knew it was hard but we had to wait, because the only people who could tell us what we needed to know were the surgeons who were operating. But that's beside the point. What I *really* wanted to tell Ottilie was that I was so busy worrying about Anna that I never gave her the money for the food she brought us.'

Rob nodded, clearly happy with the situation. 'That was a very kind gesture, Ottilie, thank you.'

'I went to the hospital kitchen and they gave me some leftovers; it didn't cost me anything.' Ottilie smiled at Jess. 'I didn't think you'd remember me.'

Rob raised his eyebrows, obviously thinking the same as Stella. Ottilie still had a lot to learn. She'd gone out of her way to try and comfort Jess and Anna's parents on one of the worst days of their lives. Of course Jess remembered her kindness.

But they couldn't keep Anna waiting any longer. 'There'll be plenty of time to talk later on. Are you ready to start now,

Anna?' Stella received a thumbs-up in reply, and turned towards the basin to wash her hands.

Peeling the dressings back from Anna's face and neck had to be done carefully, and then there was the matter of how to concentrate on what she saw, without creating an awkward silence that would leave Anna wondering what was happening. Rob made that a lot easier, stationing himself where Anna could see him and murmuring words of encouragement, while Stella got on with inspecting the healing skin grafts and checking Anna's jaw was aligned properly.

Now it was just a matter of resisting the temptation to punch the air and hug Anna, and give her a more professional assessment.

'I'm really pleased with your progress, Anna. You're healing well and the shape of your jaw is much better now.'

Anna gave an emphatic thumbs-up, slurring out a few words. 'I want to see.'

'Okay. That's fine. Now, remember that the skin's looking very discoloured still, that's to be expected, and it's an indication that there's a good blood supply to the grafts. Your jaw is still a little swollen, so don't expect any miracles just yet.'

Anna nodded. 'Let me see.'

Rob carefully raised the head of the couch, bringing Anna up into a sitting position. Stella signalled to Ottilie to fetch the mirror from the cupboard and hold it up for Anna. She grinned, knowing that this was a special privilege.

There was silence for a moment, everyone waiting as Anna stared at her reflection. Stella gave her a little time to take everything in, and then began to carefully explain.

'You see here, the shape of your jaw on the left side matches the right. As I said, the skin grafts are discoloured—'

Anna waved her away. She understood. Her eyes filled

with tears, and Stella quickly wiped her left eye so that they shouldn't fall onto her cheek.

'I look like me.'

Battered, bruised and swollen, and with a lot of healing ahead of her. But Anna was right. Something about the shape of her face did suggest the young woman that Stella had seen in the photographs from before the accident, which Jess and her parents had provided.

'Beautiful. You look beautiful, sweetheart.' Tears were streaming down Jess's face and Rob reached for a box of tissues.

Stella couldn't help shooting a secret grin in his direction. This was the moment. The one that made the long hours of preparation and the careful, painstaking work all worth it. And Rob saw that too, he understood. He knew that if she worked at weekends, or late into the evening, this was the result she was reaching for. All of the broken relationships, the partners who hadn't understood why she had to focus so fiercely on her work... They didn't matter any more because Rob was here, sharing this moment with her.

Stella had quickly taken some photographs for the file, and Anna had passed her phone over to Ottilie, so that she could take some of her and Jess together. Then Stella had re-dressed Anna's face for the last time. The next time she came to see her, Stella expected that the grafts would be healed enough not to need any protection. Jess had said her thankyous once again, and she'd left Rob and Ottilie to take Anna and Jess through to the unit's patient lounge, where Anna would be able to sit for a while until she was ready to go home.

She didn't see him again until the evening. Rob had texted her, saying he'd meet her at a nearby café, and she found him sitting outside, under a flapping sunshade in the large paved area which overlooked the banks of the river. The last of the rush-hour commuters were snaking their way along the pavement below, their heads turned down, and Rob was watching the boats. Stella usually went straight home after work, but this seemed a better way to spend her time than crushed up against a gazillion people in an underground train.

'How was your afternoon?' She sat down and Rob signalled to the waitress, catching her attention to order another cup of coffee for himself, and tea for Stella.

'Good.' He grinned. 'Terrifying.'

'How so?'

'You reckon you have the knack of thinking aloud when you have a student in tow?' She nodded. 'Yeah, so did I. It's a bit different when you have thirty of them, all staring at you, and no patient to concentrate on. It's like being in a tank of piranhas.'

Stella laughed. 'Don't exaggerate. They're not going to eat you.'

'Maybe not. But I had to keep my wits about me; they're quite capable of sucking me dry for information. You remember what it was like when you were a student? They used to call it a keenness to learn.'

'And did they?'

'You'd have been proud of the way I fought back. Yeah, they learned. I took in a bag of bananas…'

Stella chuckled. She remembered carefully stitching the skin of a banana when she'd been a student. 'Don't they have any artificial skin pads in the stock cupboard?'

'Yep. But I'll let them have them when they get it perfect on a banana. They're on student grants, so they're much cheaper to practice at home with, and you can eat the banana afterwards so…' He waved his hand. 'You know. Magnesium, Potassium, Vitamin B6…'

'So they'll be well nourished and clamouring to try out their perfect stitching by the time they're allowed into Theatre. Thanks a lot, Rob.'

'I've added that to my lesson plans. I'll bark out orders and they have to read my mind, run around and keep out of each other's way. It's going to be a non-compulsory session.'

'Is anyone going to turn up?' Non-compulsory sessions were traditionally a bit more interesting than learning how not to bump into people, even if that was a very necessary skill.

'We'll see. I had a video-conferencing session with Phil and the head of the teaching faculty during the week. Phil's exact words were *"Good luck with it".'*

'I can't believe you don't know what he means by that.' The waitress had arrived with their drinks, and Stella took a sip of her tea. Sitting down with a cup of tea after work always helped her to switch off for whatever remained of the evening, and doing it here, with Rob, instead of at home on her own, was far more effective.

'We'll see. I'm taking the unspoken *It's never going to work* part as a challenge.' Rob was still smiling, but there was a flash of grey-blue steel in his eyes.

'Well…good luck with it, then.' Stella grinned at him, swallowing down the temptation to ask why Rob hadn't found the time to video-conference with *her.* That was new. Her partners' absences from a relationship had generally been something of a relief, because they'd diverted attention from her own.

'So…lecturing. What else?'

'I filled in with a couple of short procedures in Theatre since we're understaffed, attended a planning meeting and did Phil's ward rounds for him while he was in Theatre.'

'So you took it easy since it's your first day.' It was no particular surprise that Rob had hit the ground running. He probably reckoned it was just a brisk jogging pace.

'Are we going to talk about ears?' He was on to the next thing now.

'Anna's ear, you mean? No, not right now. Maybe never. At the moment she's content with her ear the way it is. She's already had enough surgery to last most people a lifetime, and there may well be a few more corrective procedures ahead of her.' This was new too. Usually, Stella was quite ruthless about separating her work from her leisure time, but she could trust that Rob's reaction wouldn't be incomprehension or mild horror at the details.

'Your restraint is commendable. It's a pretty straightforward earlobe repair.'

'And it's *her* earlobe. I'm not going to encourage her either way.'

'You're right, of course. It's exactly what I'd do, but I wouldn't be able to help a bit of private frustration over not getting things as perfect as I could for her.' He frowned suddenly, taking a sip of his coffee. 'I might have caught myself out there. I was reckoning that I wouldn't fall into that trap again this time.'

'Would you have even seen it before?' Stella was seeing her own life a little more clearly since she'd met Rob.

'Nah, probably not. There's a lot of mental energy involved in making every aspect of your life perfect. Not a lot of time for anything else.' He thought for a moment. 'Jess sees Anna as perfect already.'

'No, she doesn't. Jess doesn't need perfect because she sees Anna as beautiful. That's different.' Stella had spent more time with Anna and Jess and got to know them better than Rob did.

'Yeah. That's an interesting point.' He was tracing his finger around the handle of his cup, and there was obviously something more bothering him.

'What?'

'It's just… Are you okay? Really okay, I mean. We're turning each other's lives upside down… I'm chipping away at your focus…'

That wasn't arrogance on Rob's part; they both knew the impact they'd had on each other. Keeping everything else secondary to her job had always worked for Stella, and Rob *was* challenging that at the moment. His guilt over wanting to have everything, and then finding that was the most destructive thing possible, made him unsure too.

'I'm okay. It's new territory for me, but you're a surgeon. You understand the focus.'

He nodded, clearly reassured. 'What do you say we skip the nice meal at a little restaurant I happen to know? The champagne and strawberries and a surprise red rose in the taxi home…'

'Champagne and strawberries would have been lovely, and the rose is a really nice touch. But it is a weeknight. What do you have in mind?'

He moved his hand across the table, his fingers meeting hers. The slight pressure of his thumb was a lot more intoxicating than mere champagne. 'Get the tube back to your flat. Feel our skin touch.'

'That sounds beautiful, Rob.'

The word *beautiful* wasn't lost on him. He laughed, signalling to the waitress for the bill.

# CHAPTER TWELVE

THERE HAD BEEN a beginning, but he and Stella had no defined aims, no particular point where they needed to end up. It was a new experience for Rob, but he was thriving on it.

He'd decided that a date—a proper date where they dressed up a bit and went somewhere—was his next step. He'd booked some theatre tickets, a long-running West End thriller, and bought a suit with him when he came down to London the following week. A pre-theatre meal was going to be a rush, as Stella never got away from work on time on a Friday evening, but he reckoned that a post-theatre meal would work, and that since he wasn't on call on Saturday they'd be able to sleep in as long as they wanted.

'You scrub up *very* well, Rob.' He'd showered and changed at work, so that he could arrive at her place in a taxi to pick her up. She met him on the front doorstep of her block of flats, promptly taking his breath away.

The classic little black dress took on a whole new meaning when Stella wore it, because her red hair and green eyes gave all the intensity of colour and the subtlety of shade that was needed. She took his arm and he led her down the steps outside the building.

'You look absolutely stunning. I'm beginning to wish that I'd been there to watch you dress.' He murmured the words into her ear before they got into the taxi.

'Thank you.'

Rob waited for the expected comment about him being there to watch her undress but it never came. Stella seemed a little subdued, but maybe she was just tired. Perhaps Rob should have waited for tickets on Saturday evening instead, but this was the play they both wanted to see, and Friday tickets had been the only ones that were available. She checked her phone in the theatre foyer, typing a text and then nodding silently when the reply pinged back.

The play was great. Witty and suspenseful, with beautiful costumes and sets. The interval came round too soon, leaving the audience to chatter about the cliff-hanger they'd been faced with as they left their seats. Stella's hand disappeared into her handbag as they walked towards the crowded bar, and she seemed to be trying to surreptitiously switch her phone on.

'Stop right there.' He caught her arm, guiding her to a less busy spot, and Stella snatched her hand from her bag guiltily. 'What's up?'

'Nothing… Nothing at all. Theo Vasilis is looking after a patient of mine and he said he'd text me if there was any news.' She pulled her phone out of her bag, switching it on and showing it to him. 'Look. No news. Let's see if we can elbow our way across to the bar, shall we?'

'You want to call him?'

Yeah. She did. Rob could tell because he'd been right there in her shoes, many times.

'No, it's fine. Theo will be looking after her. I never have any worries about patients of mine who are in his care. We both spoke with her husband after the operation and I handed over all the notes…'

'Okay. Why are you so keen to follow up on this patient?' He glanced over at the bar. 'We're not going to get served at the moment, so you may as well indulge my curiosity.'

'Young woman with a cyst on her neck, Aarya. She'd had it for a little while and was going to get it removed, but then she found out she was pregnant and decided to wait until after she'd had the baby. She came back in for the surgery today— the cyst was quite large and it needed a general anaesthetic.'

'And...'

'The anaesthetist had a little trouble stabilising her, just as I was about to close. I stopped and made sure that she was all right, then we finished up. She came round from the anaesthetic with no problems at all.'

No surgery went entirely smoothly, because they were dealing with people and a delicate balance of many different factors. Stella had done everything correctly and according to the book. Rob knew all of that, but he also knew that had he been in Stella's place, he would have wanted to stick around for a while as well.

He took her arm, propelling her through the foyer and out of the theatre. Then a golden taxi drew up alongside them, its 'For Hire' sign alight. Rob hesitated, wondering whether he was witnessing a miracle, and then realised that it was one of the taxis that had been resprayed to celebrate the Queen's Golden Jubilee, and that finding an empty taxi so quickly on a Friday evening was just exceptionally good luck. He signalled to the driver and opened the door, ushering Stella firmly inside.

'The Thames Hospital, please,' he said firmly, and the driver pulled away from the pavement.

'Rob, there's no need. We can turn round now and catch the second half of the play.' She was protesting loudly and the taxi driver slowed, clearly wondering whether he was about to be asked to perform a U-turn.

'It's okay.' Rob caught the driver's attention. 'If she kills me, just take her to the nearest police station.'

Stella laughed suddenly and the taxi driver chuckled. 'Right you are, mate.' The taxi sped up again, making for the hospital.

'Don't give me that look.' Stella had stopped protesting out loud now. 'I can't count the number of evenings that I've raced home in the nick of time, and spent a whole evening somewhere worrying about a patient. Trying to put on a show of enjoying myself, when I'd really rather be at the hospital. Kate would be shooting me reproachful looks, and I'd be feeling guilty about not being able to be in two places at once. I don't want to be on either side of that again, not with you.'

Stella pressed her lips together. 'I know that she'll be all right.'

'Of course she's all right. But we're all human—something happens and a patient suddenly pushes all of your buttons and you want to stick around. The same way we stuck around for Anna when there wasn't really anything more we could do for her.'

She nodded. 'I suppose so. Aarya brought her new baby with her when she came in for the pre-op examination, and she was just gorgeous. And her husband was clearly worried about her when we went to find him afterwards. I just wanted to make everything go well for them all, I suppose. I'm so sorry, Rob.'

'You've already made everything go well. And you don't need to apologise to me. I'm a doctor, remember? I said that I didn't want to put myself in between you and your work, and this was exactly what I meant. That we're both free to enjoy our time together because we're not being torn in two all the time.'

Stella leaned over and kissed him on the cheek, the caress of her fingers making him shiver. Maybe Rob had overreacted a bit, but he'd made Stella smile again.

And maybe he hadn't been quite as unreliable as Kate had

liked to make out. She'd known what she was getting when she'd married him, and the things that Rob had been working so hard for were things she'd wanted too. He'd never reproached her for anything, and he wouldn't now, even in the privacy of his own mind—but there *had* been a breakdown in communication between them.

Stella insisted on paying for the taxi, giving the driver a broad grin, and laughing when he joked about his relief that there had been no deaths in the back of his taxi. They walked into the hospital side by side, ignoring whatever whispers and second glances followed them, and made their way up to Stella's office.

She took off her watch and bracelet and put on her doctor's white coat, more to disguise the dress than anything else. Rob took off his jacket and tie and rolled up his sleeves. They made their way down to the post-operative suite and Stella beckoned to a young doctor, who came hurrying over.

'We were just passing.' That probably didn't fool anyone, but it saved face. 'How's Aarya been?'

'Fine. I had a nurse sitting with her but she wasn't needed. We let her husband in for a few minutes and he's gone home now. I think she's still awake if you want to check in on her.'

'Thanks, Theo. I really appreciate it.'

Theo chuckled, nodding. In Rob's experience, most surgeons just breezed into post-operative wards without bothering to check in with anyone, and Stella's courtesy had clearly earned Theo's respect.

It took a moment for his eyes to adjust to the subdued lighting in the cubicle, but when they did he could see that Aarya was awake. Stella approached her bedside, a smile on her face.

'How are you doing? Your neck's a bit stiff, I imagine.' There was a large dressing on the side of Aarya's neck.

'I'm fine. They gave me some tablets and it doesn't hurt.'

'That's good.' Stella sat down by the bed. 'Everything else okay?'

'Yes, I saw Dipak. I told him to go home now.' Aarya turned the corners of her mouth down.

'I bet you're missing your baby.'

'It's the first time I've been away from her. Do you think Dipak will be able to bring her into the ward tomorrow?'

'I'll ask for you. You may have to go out into the visitors room to see her, but the staff here will organise everything. And you'll be going home to her soon. The best thing you can do now is get some sleep and feel better in the morning...'

Rob slipped out of the room, taking the patient notes with him, so that he could flip through them and report back to Stella. She appeared through the curtains ten minutes later, shooting him a reproachful look as she took the notes out of his hand and went back to replace them at the end of the bed.

'Everything okay?'

'Yes, she's sleeping now. Are her notes okay?' Stella just couldn't resist asking.

'Absolutely fine. Nothing to worry about.'

Stella signalled a goodbye to Theo on the way out, and they walked back up to her office. Taking off her white coat, she picked up her handbag from the desk while Rob rolled down his sleeves and put on his tie. They were ready for date night part two.

'Thank you, Rob.' Stella put her arms around his neck, kissing him. 'I really appreciate this. And I'm sorry we missed out on finding out who did it...'

'It's my pleasure. We'll go again another time and catch the end of the play, and as for tonight—we're in time for our dinner reservation.'

She kissed him again. This was turning into a perfect date

because they'd done everything they both needed to, and done it together. Suddenly, Stella stepped back from him. 'I smell of soap, don't I?'

'Yes, you do.' He pulled her back towards him, kissing her for one last time before he pulled on his jacket. 'Don't you know by now that I *love* the smell of soap...'

# CHAPTER THIRTEEN

THERE HAD BEEN nine perfect weekends, spent at Rob's house in Sussex. Sunny days, hot sultry nights and Rob to share them with. Stella sometimes needed to bring some work with her, but they would sit down together in the conservatory office and he'd work on his teaching plans or research notes, while she logged in to the secure hospital network and reviewed patient files and answered emails. It was companionable and easy, Sophie sleeping in her basket under the cool greenery and only waking up if a butterfly got too close to her nose.

It was a lot easier to finish work when Rob was around as well. There was none of that clinging worry that usually came when she closed her laptop on a Saturday afternoon, because there were farm shops to visit and then the local supermarket. Saturday evenings were for cooking and eating, often in the garden as the sun went down. On Sundays they'd go exploring. Rob had visited surprisingly few places of interest in the area, and so they could discover them together.

And shot through all of it was the excitement of his kiss. The brush of his fingers on her bare arm, the feeling of lazy delight when she woke in the morning, knowing that they wouldn't be getting up until Rob's slow caress had put the finishing touches to a night where desire dictated everything. Curling up with him afterwards, until the sun made it impossible for them to stay in bed any longer.

This weekend, though, there was no work before they could relax and play. Rob was already loading up his car when she arrived, and Stella took the sparkly silver envelope from the glove compartment.

She kissed him, and then batted away his questions about what she'd been up to this week, and gave him the envelope. Rob opened it, reading the card inside, and a broad grin spread across his face.

'That's really nice.'

'Isn't it? I got a card too, only my envelope's pink.'

Ottilie had done well in her end of term assessments and had sent them gorgeous thank you notes. They'd expected that, because Rob had written a glowing report on her practical work, but her case studies and other academic work had attracted top marks as well.

Rob nodded with satisfaction. 'She deserves it.'

'Yes, I told her that. And I said that we were looking forward to working with her again.'

'That's great. I'm going to put this on the mantelpiece right now...'

Rob disappeared into the house, while Stella regarded the collection of seemingly unrelated items in the boot of his car. He was still smiling when he re-joined her.

'Have you got room for three more boxes?'

'Three? Where did you get three boxes of books from?'

'I put an empty box on the table in the hallway of my block of flats, with a note saying that any unwanted books would be appreciated, and that they were being sold in aid of an adult literacy scheme. The first box filled in under a day and I had to go down to the corner shop and ask if they had another.'

'Nice one.' Rob walked with her to her car, and she opened the boot. He pulled the packing tape off one of the boxes and started to poke around amongst the contents. 'This is really good... I haven't read this one.'

'Put it back.' Stella tapped the back of his hand with her fingers. 'If you want it, you'll have to pay for it like everyone else.'

Rob dropped the book back into the box, propping it on top of one of the other boxes and ferrying them to his own car. Stella brought the last box, which had to go on the back seat because there was no room for it in the boot.

'Do you really need those pieces of wood for a village fete?'

'Might do. There weren't enough tables to go round and I built a stall for Emma, along with a board at the back for her to pin up her notices about the literacy scheme. She might want a few alterations. I said I'd pick her up on the way, she's got a few more boxes of books as well.'

'Okay, I'll go in the back with the boxes, and Emma can go in the front seat.' Stella looked around. 'Where's Sophie?'

'Ah... I'm going to need her basket as well. She'll want a snooze. Maybe I should go and get the roof rack.'

They finally managed to get everything into the car and set off for the village, stopping along the way to pick up Emma. When they arrived at the large grassy area behind the church it was bustling with activity. Emma's stall turned out to be a stoutly built affair, with a brightly painted sign and plenty of room for the leaflets and posters she'd brought along with her.

'I didn't know that you were involved with an adult literacy scheme, Emma.' Emma had sorted the books according to what she thought they would all fetch, and Stella was busy writing the prices inside the front covers.

'Oh, yes. I have been for years. I used to be a teacher, you know. Still am, I suppose. You never quite stop doing something you love.'

'I suppose that's okay if you're a teacher. I can't see myself having a stall at a village fete doing scar reduction.'

Emma chuckled. 'That would be something new. Rob seems to be finding a use for his talents.'

Stella looked across to where Rob was safely out of earshot, patching up one of the old tables with some of the wooden lathes he'd brought. That wasn't quite the same thing, but it seemed to involve the concentration and care that surgery took, even if the tools weren't the same.

'He was in a very bad state when he first came here,' Emma mused, almost to herself. 'It was months before any of us even saw him.'

Stella nodded. 'Yes, I know.' Emma was clearly fond of Rob and she was a shrewd judge of human nature. This wasn't idle gossip, and it must have been obvious that Rob wasn't well when he'd first arrived here.

'I'm glad he's found you. It's about time he started to go back out in the world again.' Emma had opened Rob's box of books and was sorting them into piles for Stella to price up. 'What's this one? *Crypto...*'

Stella glanced up at the book. 'Cryptotia. It's where the ear doesn't develop properly. I'm not sure that anyone's going to be much interested in that, he might have put it in there by mistake.'

'We'll put that to one side then, you never know when it might come in handy. How much should we sell this one for? It's already been read at least twice, because Rob lent it to me.'

'A pound. You're obviously both careful with your books because it looks almost new. And look at the price on the back. I bet someone would give a pound for it.'

'I was thinking twenty-five pence.' Emma thought for a moment. 'But you're right, someone will give a pound and it's all for a good cause. Perhaps you should price all of the twenty-five pence ones as fifty pence instead. If I see someone who I know can't afford much, I can always give them a discount, can't I?'

Emma knew practically everyone in the village, and had probably taught many of them. And she'd welcomed Stella here, always stopping to say hello and talk for a while when they bumped into each other in the shop or the main street, which happened quite often because Emma went shopping every day, around the same time that Rob usually walked down to get his paper.

'How *was* Rob when he first came here?' It felt wrong somehow to ask, but Emma was as protective of Rob as she felt. And she couldn't help herself.

Emma laid the books she was sorting down in her lap. 'He was in an awful state. So thin, and when I found him shovelling snow in the high street he jumped nearly a mile when I tapped him on the shoulder. Burned out, I'd say. He did what he was told but he wouldn't take the initiative with anything.'

Stella had known all this, but Emma's description brought it all home far more clearly.

'He told me you set him to work, getting people's shopping.'

'Well, yes, I did. We had plenty of volunteers, we always do, but I thought it might do him a bit of good. Something that he could get his teeth into and succeed with. In my experience, failure can eat into a person and it's not too difficult in those circumstances to blame yourself for everything.'

'You never said you were a detective.' Stella wondered what Emma thought of her, but decided she probably wouldn't say.

Emma laughed. 'All schoolteachers need to be detectives. You have thirty faces in front of you, and not very long to decide what makes each one of them tick. Rob Franklin wasn't all that hard to work out.'

Maybe not, if you were as perceptive as Emma. The inside

of an operating theatre *did* teach you a bit about human nature, but not in quite the same way.

'You're very kind, Emma.'

Emma waved the comment away, although Stella could see that it pleased her. 'It's nice to see two people making a fresh start.'

Two people? Stella supposed that she was making a fresh start of sorts, but hers didn't involve the long road that Rob had travelled. She must have shown her surprise, because Emma shot her a knowing look.

'Come here. You've left the price tag on your dress, right at the back of your neck. It's such a pretty dress and it quite spoils it. I'll cut it out for you…'

Rob had finished shoring up a few tables, and was now carrying the sunshades out of the storeroom at the back of the church hall. Deciding that Emma could probably do with one of them, he walked over to where she and Stella were arranging books on the stall. There was clearly a bit of discussion going on, and he imagined that neither of them was about to give way on exactly how they should classify them.

'Shall I fix your sunshade, Emma?'

'Thank you, Rob. The sun is getting a little hot. I could do with a cool drink.'

'I'll go and fetch you one when I've finished.' Rob hauled the heavy base into place, and started to fix the sunshade onto the curved support.

'I've got one of your books here, Rob. I'm not sure that we'll have much of a call for books on cryptotia this afternoon.' Emma enunciated the medical term carefully.

He glanced at Stella, and she avoided his gaze. Clearly, she wasn't going to take any part in this conversation.

'No, probably not. I don't know how that got in there; it was in my recycling pile.' Emma raised her eyebrows. 'It's a little out of date. Things change pretty quickly.'

'If it's out of date, Rob, it's not going to be much use to anyone,' Emma rebuked him gently and waved the book at him. Stella came to his rescue, grabbing the book while he finished adjusting the sunshade.

'How's that?'

'Very nice. Thank you. I'm going to need all of my wits about me this afternoon, because Stella and I have decided that we're going to drive a hard bargain with our customers. We've priced everything at more than fifty pence.'

So Stella was on Emma's team now, was she? That was pretty much par for the course and Stella didn't seem to mind. Rob didn't either; it was nice to see her getting to know people here.

'Good call. Most people can afford fifty pence.'

'Emma's going to give me a nudge if she sees anyone who can't. We'll give them a discount. But we want to make as much money as we can, because it's such a good cause and the scheme needs to buy more teaching materials.' Stella grinned at him.

So, presumably, if he wanted to see Stella at all today he was going to have to help out on the bookstall. Emma had probably already thought of that.

'What would you like to drink? Some orangeade, or tea?'

'Actually, I think I'll go inside, Rob. We have a couple of hours before things start in earnest, and I wouldn't mind a quiet cup of tea and a nap in the church lounge before I leap into the fray.'

He watched as Emma walked across the grass, towards the church.

'Emma's really kind, isn't she?' Stella murmured.

'Yeah. Smarter than most as well...' Rob turned, suddenly

aware of a commotion coming from the refreshment tent. One of the women who'd been cutting cakes and sandwiches appeared, making a beeline for him, and he walked towards her.

'Anything the matter, Cathy?'

'Yes, Janice has cut herself. You couldn't come and have a look at it, could you? It probably needs a bandage or something.'

'No problem, my medical bag's in my car.' Rob always kept it with him when he was on call.

'I'll fetch it for you.' Stella nudged him and he gave her the car keys.

Janice had been one of his first patients when he'd started work as a GP here, a young woman expecting her first child. Her little boy was sitting on one of the women's laps at the far end of the refreshment tent, and Rob realised he knew the names of all of the children in the makeshift crèche. It occurred to him to wonder for a moment whether the difference between his two jobs—his two lifestyles—was as apparent to Stella as it was to him right now.

He sat down opposite Janice, giving her a smile. She had a pad of kitchen towel wound tightly around her thumb, and from the look of her apron the wound had been bleeding freely.

'Hi, Janice. How are you doing?'

'If I let go, it just starts to bleed again.'

'Okay, just keep hold of it for a moment. Do you feel dizzy or sick?'

Janice shook her head. 'No, it was a bit of a shock, but I feel okay.'

Stella must have hurried to catch him up, because he heard her voice behind him and the buzz of the zip on his medical bag. He turned and she held out a wipe for him to disinfect his hands and then a pair of surgical gloves. Perfect, seamless synchronicity, as if one world had intruded on another for a moment and the sounds and smells of the operating theatre were about to overwhelm the sound of children playing and the scent of newly baked cake on a warm Saturday afternoon. Rob peeled back the kitchen towel, hastily reapplying pressure when blood started to drip from the wound.

'Bit more pressure, I think…'

He checked the wound again quickly to make sure that there was nothing in it, and Stella passed him a wad of gauze. He applied more pressure, raising Janice's hand above her head.

'You're pretty well kitted out,' Stella murmured as they waited.

'Yeah, you'd be surprised how many cuts I see. It saves everyone's time to do this myself, rather than send someone down to the small injuries clinic if they need a couple of stitches.'

After ten minutes, the bleeding still hadn't stopped. Cathy unlocked the church kitchen and Stella wiped the table down with disinfectant, before opening the wound care pack and laying the dressings out on a sterile sheet, while Rob cleaned the wound and checked again whether there was anything in it. The two stitches and applying a sterile dressing took less time than it did for him to write down the wound care instructions for Janice.

'Give the surgery a call on Monday and make an appointment with me for the following Monday to take out the stiches. In the meantime, keep the wound covered with the dressings I've given you and if there are any of the indications of infection that I've listed out, give me a call straight away.'

'Thank you. Can I go back and help with the refreshments?'

'I'd give that a rest for today. You've done your share, go and enjoy the fete.'

They cleared up the mess, dropping it all into a plastic bag.

Stella's shoulders were shaking with laughter. 'Overkill or what, eh? Two surgeons for a couple of stitches.'

Rob shrugged. 'No such thing as having too many surgeons. Anyway, I'm a GP here.'

She looked up at him. 'You're still a surgeon, Rob. You've proved that beyond any shadow of a doubt.'

It seemed important to her that he should classify himself that way. Rob could understand that; she'd worked hard for the title and she had a right to be proud of it.

'I…don't really feel as if I am.'

'I think that Anna might beg to differ. I certainly would. And so would your students.'

'It's different. I know a lot about surgery, and I still have the skills. I'm not sure that I could do it every day, like you do.'

She seemed deflated suddenly, sitting down with a bump on one of the kitchen chairs. 'What is this?'

Rob sat down next to her. 'There's a lot I can do. I can pass on my knowledge, I can help plan and execute surgeries. That's a lot more than I felt I could do three months ago, and I have you to thank—'

'No. You have *yourself* to thank,' Stella interrupted him.

'Whatever. I told you when we first started that I wasn't sure I had it in me any more to be able to work full-time as a surgeon, and I'm still not sure.'

He could practically see the cogs whirring in her brain. He wanted to reach out and touch her face, do something to change the subject to a lighter topic, but experience told him that once Stella took hold of something, she didn't let go that easily.

'You think that you let people down? Still?'

'I *did* let people down. I allowed myself to get to a place where I just couldn't function. I couldn't pull myself to-gether…'

She brought her hand down onto the table with such a bang

that they both jumped. 'Don't you dare! You were diagnosed as suffering from stress and clinical depression, and no one can be expected to just pull themselves together in those circumstances. If you ever said that to one of your patients, you'd be in real trouble. So don't say it to yourself.'

'Hey. Are you giving me a hard time?'

'Yes, I am. Because you give me a hard time when you think I'm doing something wrong. I wish you could see how far you've come in the last few months, and know that you can go a lot further.'

'I see it. And I hear what you're saying, Stella. Maybe you should just keep wearing me down.' Like cool water flowing across obstinate rock. If Stella stayed with him, then maybe one day he'd start to believe that he could take the risk of moving forward without letting her down.

'Is that a challenge?' She shot him a mischievous look.

'Yeah. Please do take it as one.' He leaned forward, planting a kiss onto her lips. That made him feel a lot better, because Stella's lips could chase away all of his fears and insecurities.

'I'm not going to forget all about this just because you're kissing me...'

'No?' He kissed her again. 'You're sure about that?' He knew one way to make them both forget about everything. But they had a fete to attend before they'd be alone.

She gave a mock sigh. 'All right. We're just going to have to agree to differ for the time being then.'

'And in the meantime I bet I can sell more books than you...'

'Really?' She drew back from him, folding her arms. 'You think so?'

'I've read a few of them. When did you last have the time to sit down and read a book, cover to cover? Medical books don't count.'

'So I'll just read the blurb on the back and say it sounds interesting. How does Emma do it?'

'We're not even in Emma's league. Last year people were just picking up a couple of books, giving her a note and telling her to keep the change. Everyone knows it's for a good cause. You, on the other hand... I reckon I can beat you.'

'I'll be interested in watching you try.' She got to her feet, plumping herself back down on his knee and kissing him. 'I'll be pulling out all the stops, Rob.'

Fair enough. That was all Rob needed. The future could look after itself, as long as she was here for him today.

# CHAPTER FOURTEEN

IN HER MORE uncertain moments Stella had wondered whether all of the happiness of the last weeks had been an illusion, capable of disappearing in a puff of smoke. Maybe it had, because after three months of bliss, this last week had been excruciating. Horrible, uncertain…every other word that could be applied to a complete disaster.

Stella hadn't seen Rob; he'd been away at a medical conference to brush up on his networking and bring him up-to-date on some new developments in surgical techniques. That, at least, had taken the pressure off a bit.

Or loaded the pressure on, because this should be the one time when she really needed him. It *was* that time, even if Stella was struggling against the realisation.

She was due to drive down to Sussex on Saturday evening. By then the uncertainty of the situation was resolved. But she was still dealing with the fallout, with all of the solutions that had occurred to her, and mostly with the one that she knew she would have taken.

He was out in the garden, obviously unable to resist pulling up a few weeds that had appeared during the last week. Rob's face brightened when he saw her, and he pulled off his gardening gloves and enveloped her in a hug.

'I've really missed you.' She could feel his body against hers, and it was tempting to allow herself to just fall into that pleasure. Tell herself that everything was all right, and that there was no reason why they shouldn't resume their dangerous journey into the unknown.

'Are you okay? You look tired.' He knew immediately that something was bothering her.

'I haven't been sleeping.'

'Work?' He put his arm around her shoulders as they walked towards the back door and into the kitchen.

'No, I...' Stella sat down miserably. She'd spent most of drive convincing herself that she didn't need to tell Rob about something that might have happened but hadn't. But she'd been ducking the issue, because she knew exactly what her reaction would have been if it had.

He walked over to the kettle, making her a cup of tea and setting it down on the table, next to her elbow. Then he turned one of the kitchen chairs to face her and sat down.

'Come on. Spit it out.'

'It's nothing, Rob, really. My period started this morning.'

He nodded. That one piece of information told him everything, but it was impossible to gauge his reaction. Surprise, maybe. Concern, but that didn't say much because she couldn't divine what he was actually concerned about.

'How late were you?'

'A week. That doesn't sound like much, but I can normally set my watch by when my period arrives.'

'We've been careful.'

That had been her own first reaction. Disbelief. Counting through the number of times they'd been together and trying to work out where there might have been a slip.

'I know. Accidents happen and nothing's one hundred percent.'

'Not this time, though.' At least he wasn't laughing with relief. That was something.

'No, not this time.'

'You want to talk about it?' His fingers found hers and he squeezed her hand. This was all that she could want from a partner in these circumstances. He was concerned, and he seemed shaken by the news. But he was obviously waiting to find out how she felt and address that first.

'No.'

'Okay. Later, maybe…' Rob stood up, looking around the room, clearly trying to find something that urgently needed to be done. Then he sat back down again. 'You're sure?'

She needed to say this now. He wanted to hear how she felt and she wanted to tell him. She reached out to him, taking his hand.

'What is it you need to say to me, Stella? I can see something's bothering you and I'd like to know what it is.'

That was nice. Rob was being really nice about this, which was only making things worse. But she knew Rob well enough to wonder whether his own fears might kick in and he'd stop being quite so understanding when he found out what was on her mind. But she couldn't keep this from him, whatever the consequences.

'When I first thought I might be pregnant, I panicked. I kept telling myself that I couldn't be, but… I couldn't help thinking about the idea. What I might do, if I was…'

'Did you decide?' Rob was clearly trying to keep his composure, but she knew that fixed look on his face. He was struggling with something and when his hand went to his mouth it stayed there, as if to guard against words he might regret later.

'I decided that, whatever happened, if I was pregnant then I'd keep the baby. I really *wanted* the baby…'

Rob didn't hide the relief that showed in his face. Her first instinct was to kick him, for even thinking that she might have decided to end something so precious, but she could see where that was coming from. They'd never talked about it, and every woman weighed up that choice differently.

'You did a test?'

'Yes, I finally worked up the courage to do it yesterday, and the kit said I wasn't pregnant. Then my period started this morning.'

'I'm so sorry, Stella. Even if you were never pregnant, you thought you were and that's a loss...' He shifted forward, putting his arms around her.

She could leave it at that. Accept that all of last week's worried uncertainty was over now. Understand that Rob's embrace, his care for her and everything they meant to one another *was* real. But that wasn't the point. It wasn't what had shaken her so badly.

'Rob, I... What would have happened? If I had been pregnant.'

'You wouldn't have done it on your own, if that's what's worrying you. I would have been with you all the way.'

That was what any woman faced with an unexpected pregnancy wanted to hear, wasn't it? It was what any woman wanted to hear full stop—that the man she loved wouldn't walk away when things got tough. She'd come to rely on Rob and to trust him, but Stella knew that he sometimes didn't trust himself.

'Does it frighten you, Rob?'

'Why should it?' He answered just a little too quickly. 'A baby's something special. The *most* special thing that could ever happen...'

'Someone who relies on you completely. I'd have to rely on you too.' Stella wasn't afraid of that, but she knew that Rob was. He still carried a lot of guilt over what he saw as letting others in his life down.

His face darkened. 'You're thinking that I can't step up and be a good father?'

'No, I'm not. I trust you, Rob. The question is whether you trust yourself.'

He couldn't answer that. Rob shook his head, clearly backing away from those thoughts.

'It doesn't matter now, Stella.' He spoke gently. 'You thought that you were pregnant, and that stirred up a lot of different feelings. I can understand that. But you aren't and we can move forward from that.'

Could they? Stella would have loved to be able to agree with him, to tell him that things between them could go on just as they had. But she'd got a glimpse of the future, and it was one that neither of them was ready for.

'It's not what either of us had planned, is it?' They hadn't planned anything. They'd lived for the day, knowing that their different lifestyles made it impossible for them to think ahead. But it had all worked too well, and Stella had fallen in love with him. Dared to dream that a future together might be a solution, when in fact it stood at the very heart of the problem.

'No. We could be more careful, maybe?'

'How? We've been careful, and we're both doctors so we both know pretty much everything there is to know about contraception. And that's not really the point. The point is that whatever we do together, we have to be able to take the consequences.'

He shook his head. 'There's always a solution, to any problem. It may not seem obvious at the time…'

'The solution *is* the problem, Rob.'

They'd somehow managed to put this aside, deciding to sleep on it and see how they felt in the morning. It was a relief when Stella agreed to his suggestion that they go out to eat, because having people around them was some kind of defence against blurting out the anger and the pain he was feeling.

Not with her. Never with her. At himself, because Stella had only told him the truth. The thought that she and a child might be dependent on him for their happiness was terrifying. He'd failed the people around him once, and if he failed Stella there would be no coming back from that.

Rob wondered whether she might choose to sleep in the spare room tonight, but she came with him to his bedroom. One last chance. A chance to show her how he felt about her, how much he loved her. But he left the light out as they undressed, and Stella didn't switch it on either. They were a pair of shadows who couldn't find each other in the darkness. When they slipped into opposite sides of the bed, the gulf between them was already too wide to cross. And each moment that he couldn't bring himself to touch her only made it wider.

Stella was right. The solution was the problem. They'd gone into this with their eyes wide open, they both knew what they were getting. Maybe, deep down, they'd both thought the same thing—that they'd spend a few delicious months together, pushing all the boundaries, and then they'd part as friends. But that had all gone horribly wrong when somehow, against all of the odds, their relationship had worked.

He lay awake for a long time, thinking it through and testing out all of the possibilities in his head. Stella was asleep, probably exhausted after a week of uncertainty, and it was comforting to know that at least saying what was on her mind had brought her some kind of respite. But when she stirred, whimpering in her sleep, he couldn't reach for her.

Rob rose early, showering and dressing before Stella was awake. Not knowing what else to do with himself, he went out into the garden, wandering amongst the fruit trees. That had always calmed him before, but this morning he could only see withered branches and decay all waiting to happen.

She joined him an hour later, bleary-eyed but trying to smile. Loving someone made it all too easy to put together the tiny clues that you'd otherwise miss, and something told Rob that Stella had woken up crying.

He had to put a stop to this. If he could bear his own pain, just to spend a few hours longer with her, then he couldn't bear hers. Rob ushered her back inside, switching the coffee machine on.

'I've been thinking about what you said yesterday. Do you still feel that way?' He put her coffee down in front of her and sat at the table.

Stella nodded, taking a sip of the strong brew. 'I have nothing to add, Rob.'

That was it, then, because he couldn't add anything either. He'd thought about it now and the prospect of being responsible for her happiness full-time terrified him. If they had to end, then he'd do it the best way he could. Rob took a deep breath, sucking in the air he'd need to survive this.

'You had the courage to say what we both knew all along. We always knew we weren't right for each other in the long-term, and it's time for us to accept that now. I just want to say that you'll always have a piece of my heart. I'll always be there for you, whenever you need a friend.'

A tear rolled down her cheek. 'I appreciate your honesty. I hope we can be friends too.'

'I couldn't have done what I have in the last few weeks without you. You came here and prised me out of my rut, and showed me that I could move forward again. You deserve every happiness that the future can give you and I have no regrets, Stella.'

Only that he'd caused her pain. That when she left she was

going to take the sunshine of the last few months with her. There was a growing list of the regrets that he'd never tell her about.

'Me neither. This is the right thing…isn't it?'

One last way back. A hint of uncertainty, a last chance. If he took it, it wouldn't change anything; it would just postpone this moment. Once was bad enough, and twice would be unbearable.

'Yeah. I'm sorry, but it is.'

She got to her feet, tearing a sheet from the roll of kitchen towel and blowing her nose on it, her movements suddenly brisk and businesslike. 'You're not going to do anything foolish, are you? Leave your job, I mean…'

Rob had been seriously thinking about it, but Stella's words made that impossible.

'That was one of the things we did together, and I don't want to throw it away. Unless you're uncomfortable with it?'

'No! We hardly see each other during the day, anyway.'

That wasn't entirely true, and maybe it was a hint that he should keep his distance. That was okay. If they both knew that was the score then it would be a lot easier. Rob could keep a low profile in the department and concentrate on his teaching; there was plenty for him to do there.

'And if we do happen to bump into each other, then we'll do what we've been doing all along. Just good friends, eh?'

'Friends. Yes, I'd like that.'

He'd like it too. He didn't see it happening for a while, because parting as friends carried with it the implication that they'd lost nothing. But it would be a workable Plan B, in case Plan A happened to fail and they found themselves thrown together.

Stella was looking at her watch. 'I should go…'

Not yet. He knew that this was coming, but he wanted just

a few moments more. 'You'll stay and have some breakfast, surely. It's a long drive home.'

'I can stop for something on the way. If I get going before nine, then I'll miss most of the traffic at this end of the motorway.'

'Take some coffee at least.' Stella hesitated and he got to his feet. 'You can put the travel cup back in my pigeonhole if you want.'

'Yes. Thanks, some coffee would be nice.'

There were a few moments more, while Rob made the coffee and Stella went upstairs to gather her things. Then he walked her out to her car.

'Goodbye, Stella. Travel safe.' Today, and for the rest of your life. Be happy.

'You travel safe too.' She smiled up at him through the open car window, and he handed her the coffee. She stowed it in the cup holder, fiddling with the clip for a moment, and then drew the seat belt across her. Then it was time for him to step away.

Rob watched from the doorstep as the car started to make its way slowly along the lane and then disappeared amongst the hedgerows. Then he went inside, throwing himself down on the sofa in the sitting room. He felt like a man who had just arranged his own execution.

Sophie stirred from her usual sleeping place in front of the hearth, ambling over to nudge at his arm.

'What is it, Soph?' He spread his hands in the signal that Sophie had been taught to respond to, but she made no effort to point him in the direction of what she'd heard. Instead, she put her paws up onto his legs and nuzzled at his neck in an unusual display of exuberance.

Rob wondered if Sophie somehow knew that Stella had gone, and needed a bit of comfort too. He generally discouraged her from jumping up on the chairs, which wasn't difficult since Sophie had little interest in jumping anywhere these days, but Rob made an exception and lifted her up onto the cushions so that she could sprawl across his legs, leaning her head against his chest.

'Don't worry, Soph. I'm not going anywhere...'

He felt a tear roll down his cheek. Then another. It had been a very long time since he'd cried, and it felt strange. A release from the numb despair that he'd worked himself into three years ago. Stella had made him feel again—the good things and now the bad. This was her last gift to him.

# CHAPTER FIFTEEN

IT WAS ODD. Even though she'd thought that no one knew about her relationship with Rob, everyone seemed to know that it had ended. Stella had done her best to conceal the dark lines under her eyes, and she hadn't cried once at work, leaving that for when she got home. She supposed that it was more difficult to hide the fact that the sunshine that had been following her around recently had now quitted on her.

She hadn't seen Rob in the last two weeks. That was one thing she could be thankful for—that when he promised something he always found a way to deliver. She tried not to think about that too much either, because Rob's promises had always been so delicious.

Stella didn't want to go out, nor did she want to talk to anyone. But she'd told herself that life *did* go on, even if everything seemed to have stopped, and accepted her mother's invitation to Sunday lunch. Maybe the appearance of normality would help burnish the life she'd chosen for herself, because right now it seemed to have lost its shine.

'Darling!' Her father greeted her on the doorstep with a hug. 'We have some news for you.'

'Wait until she gets inside, Edward.' Her mother appeared behind him, wiping her hands on her apron. 'And I'll take a hug too…'

Hugging from two of her favourite people didn't help. Neither did the smell of Sunday lunch, which, if anything, was making Stella feel a little sick.

'What news, Dad?' Since it was highly unlikely that the news would have anything to do with Rob, it would at least take her mind off him for a while.

The usual flurry of organising drinks and deciding whether to sit outside or not ended up with white wine on the patio. Stella twisted the bottle in the ice bucket, inspecting the label.

'This isn't just for Sunday lunch, is it? Are Jamie and Chloe coming?' The wine was her father's favourite, very expensive, and reserved for big occasions.

'They were, but Jamie got a dose of norovirus and Chloe caught it. Then all the kids went down with it.'

That was no surprise. Jamie and his wife lived close to Chloe and her husband and the two families were in and out of each other's houses all the time. If her brother had caught something then it was pretty much a given thing that her sister would have got it, particularly something as easily transmittable as norovirus.

'Are they all right?'

'Yes, your father insisted on them all lining up so he could peer at them on the computer. He was going to go round there, but I told him that they'd already seen a doctor and they didn't need another one.'

'She's right, Dad.' Her father usually acted as if he was the only doctor in the world when his children and grandchildren were concerned. 'And it's the last thing you want to be taking into a hospital.'

'Yes, your mother went through all that. Although I am on holiday at the moment.'

'Really? Aren't you going to Norfolk in September as usual?' Something was clearly going on if her father was taking extra holidays. The thought occurred to Stella that he might be ill. 'Are you okay?'

'Never better. I've been doing some gardening.'

The garden *was* looking very tidy. Rob's fruit trees, and the therapeutic value of watching things grow, floated into her mind and Stella frowned. 'You're sure you're all right? And Mum?'

'You're going to have to tell her, Edward...'

'Tell me what?' Stella was on full alert now, and her father shot her a reproving glance.

'I'm in excellent health for my age, both physically and mentally, Stella. So is your mother; there's nothing for you to worry about in that respect.'

Right. That was a bit more like Dad; she could relax now. Maybe loss had put her on edge and she was overreacting.

'And we're buying a cottage. In Norfolk.' Her mother clearly thought that her father was taking far too long to get around to The News.

'Oh. That's nice. You can go up there with Jamie or Chloe and spend some time with the kids, eh, Mum.'

'*We* can go up there. That's the plan. And of course you can come and join us all, whenever you like. Everyone needs a holiday from time to time. Remember how we all used to spend a month up there when you were little?'

Stella remembered. Days full of sunshine and sandy beaches. Her father would join them for two weeks, which had been the best two weeks of the year. A sudden yearning made her heart almost jump out of her chest, and she wiped a tear from her eye.

Her father was pouring the wine, and Stella resisted the temptation to stop him. Right now, she needed something that she could down in one gulp, and this wine commanded a bit more respect than that. She concentrated on the list of questions that had occurred to her, and asked the one that seemed the least controversial.

'How big is this cottage, Mum?'

Her father smiled, handing out the glasses and then pushing a manila envelope across the table to Stella. Inside was an estate agent's property portfolio, with pictures and floor plans.

'This is huge! And it's gorgeous…' Stella forgot all about respecting the contents of her glass and took a gulp of her wine. The house was a large gabled property, surrounded by wide lawns that led down to the sea. 'This must be five bedrooms at least.'

'Six. With en suite bathrooms.' Her father had always been a stickler for accuracy.

'You're not thinking of moving, are you?' Stella tried to remember if there was a large hospital within easy reach of the area that might attract a respected heart surgeon.

'No, not at the moment. I still have my work to consider.'

This all seemed very impractical. It was a lovely holiday home, but for just two weeks in the year, along with a few visits from Jamie and Chloe, it all seemed a bit over the top.

'I don't understand…'

'The thing is, Stella, I've been thinking a lot over the last couple of years.' Her father turned to her mother. 'We both have, haven't we, Margaret?'

Her mother nodded, smiling, leaving the explanations to her father.

'I spent a lot of time at work when you were little. I missed a very great deal and I regret that now.'

'We knew you were doing important work, Dad. And you were there for the big things.'

'I thought that was enough. But I realise that I should have been there for the little things as well. I *wanted* to be there for the little things. It's too late for that now, but it's not too late to change. I have a wife who's put up with more than she should over the years, three wonderful children and four beautiful grandchildren. I want somewhere that they can all call home.'

'But…do Jamie and Chloe know about this?'

'Yes, it was actually their idea. They were talking about getting a place where both families could go for holidays and weekends, but when they looked into it they couldn't really afford it. Jamie showed me some of the estate agents' leaflets and said that it was going to be a longer-term plan than they'd bargained for. So I asked your mother to run away with me for a long weekend.'

All right. So Mum was in on this personality transplant idea as well.

Her mother was beaming now. 'We had a wonderful time, didn't we, Edward? It was right before Christmas and it was freezing, but we fell in love with the house as soon as we saw it. And your father went down on one knee and proposed on the spot.'

'Is there something you haven't been telling us, Mum?'

Her father chuckled, and her mother rolled her eyes. 'No, of course not. He was quite honest with me when he proposed the first time, and I knew exactly what I was getting. This time, he proposed a different kind of life, and I accepted.' Her mother held out her hand, displaying a new eternity ring on her finger, next to her wedding ring.

'That's gorgeous. Nice one, Dad.'

'We had a little ceremony on the beach, just the two of us. We made some new promises.' Her mother smiled.

'And then we had to go back to our hotel to warm up. I'm not sure whether it was horizontal hailstones or the sea was freezing.'

'It was beautiful, Edward. Just what I wanted.'

There had always been an understanding between her parents, and Stella had never doubted that they loved one another. But this was something new, a bright and different future for them both. Stella felt a tear roll down her cheek, and wiped it away.

'I'm so happy for you both. Truly. And you'll be working less from now on, Dad?'

'I've been in negotiations with the hospital, and we've agreed on thirteen days a month. That'll be enough to allow me to keep up with things, and to pass on my experience to the people who'll be taking over from me when I retire. That's only five years away now. And I hope you'll be able to join us for a few weekends when you have the time. Norfolk's only two hours away by train.'

'I will. I'm still learning though, Dad, you know that.'

'And things are changing from when I was a medical student. I was at a conference only the other week, and I went to a session on work/life balance. There were a number of people there who had very different approaches to their work. One fellow had burned out three years ago, lost his marriage and had to leave his job...'

Stella froze. That would be far too much of a coincidence, although it would be the kind of session that would attract Rob. She didn't dare ask.

'... He spoke very well. Said that it had taken a while, but that he felt he'd recently found his future again, both personally and professionally. He said that he'd learned his lesson the hard way and that he felt that he should have...what was it...found his space.'

Breathe. Say *something*...

'That doesn't work for everyone, Dad. What was his specialty?' She could hardly ask for a name.

Her father shrugged. 'These things are all first names and no one's supposed to say where they come from or what they do. Some tomfoolery about anonymity, although I recognised quite a few faces there. And, frankly, if you can't put your name to your opinions…'

'Don't go on, Edward. No one's ever going to tell you that you're talking rubbish; you're far too senior. That's what I'm here for.'

'Yes, I suppose so. We have to think about the new genera-tion of surgeons, who are still finding their feet.' Her father reached across, taking her mother's hand.

Rob had found his future. He'd said all of the right things to her and she hadn't listened, thinking that it was what he felt he had to say and not what he really wanted. It was just as well that her mother and father were so absorbed in each other, because Stella needed a bit of time to think this through.

'Stella? Darling, what's the matter?' She felt tears on her cheeks, and looked up to see her father staring at her.

'I just… I'm so…'

Her mother walked around the table and plopped herself down next to Stella, giving her a hug. One of those hugs that had been there all her life, whenever she'd skinned her knees or failed at something.

'We didn't mean to upset you, Stella. We just wanted to share this with you.'

'I know. And I'm just happy for you…'

Her father topped up her glass, but Stella ignored the wine and his worried face. 'You've always managed everything so well. But there's no shame in needing a break sometimes.'

Dad had always told her that, and Stella had listened. She'd made sure that she took enough time out, but that had just been because she knew she had to in order to keep working. Maybe she had to take a break for a different reason now.

'I'd love to come and see the house.'

'Of course.' Her mother gave her another hug. 'We signed the contract last week, and it's ours now.'

'Perhaps you'd like to choose your own room?' her father added. When they'd all gone on holiday together, she and Jamie and Chloe had taken it in turns to choose which bedroom they wanted.

'Thanks. I'd really like that.' Stella took the handkerchief that her mother proffered and dried her eyes. Now was the time for one of the biggest decisions of her life and suddenly she felt strong again.

'Mum and Dad. I'd like to propose a toast.' She picked up her glass and her parents followed suit. 'To new beginnings. Wherever we find them.'

Rob knew that things were serious when Phil asked him to the wine bar on Friday evening. Clearly this wasn't something that could be accomplished over an orange juice at lunchtime. When Phil spoke to the barman, indicating one of the bottles that was tucked away to one side, and bought two glasses of single malt Scotch, he knew that he was in for some straight talking.

Rob took a sip of the amber liquid, feeling its warmth at the back of his throat. Then he looked at his watch, in the vain hope that the last train down to Sussex might be leaving sooner than he'd thought.

'Let's find somewhere to sit down.' Phil made a beeline for one of the deep alcoves, each of which contained a table and several easy chairs. Putting his briefcase down on the table and taking off his jacket secured their claim to the booth, and Rob followed reluctantly. No hope that the din in the main bar might preclude any serious conversation, then.

'How are you doing, Rob? I know that you and Stella have broken up, and I haven't seen you around much.'

'It's better to make a clean break.' Rob gave in to the inevitable. 'I have plenty of other places to be, I don't need to loiter around making things awkward. How did you know?'

'Stella told me. You know how meticulous she is about everything, and I suppose she reckoned that having to notify me at the start of a relationship means that it's necessary to notify me at the end of it as well.'

Rob nodded. It was just the kind of thing that Stella would do, and a few weeks ago he'd have smiled at her insistence on order. Now it was just one more thing that he'd lost.

'So, I'll ask again. How are you doing, Rob?'

'I'm okay. We tried but it didn't work.' He took a sip of his Scotch to wash the unpalatable truth from his lips.

'Okay like you were okay three years ago?'

Rob supposed he deserved that. He'd tried so hard to pretend that nothing was wrong three years ago and at the time he'd reckoned he was making a pretty good job of it. Looking back, it must have been obvious that something was going on.

'No. Really okay.'

Phil nodded. 'Because I haven't forgiven myself for going along with you the last time. I let you take some time off from surgery and concentrate on other things because I thought you just needed a break and that you were getting some help. I could have insisted on putting you on sick leave and I didn't.'

Enough. Rob's own guilt was bad enough, and Phil had been a good friend to him. He had nothing to reproach himself for.

'How long do you suppose it would have taken me to get certified fit for work again? I'm a doctor, I know exactly what to say to get myself signed off. And I told you that I was getting help when I wasn't. That's not your fault; it's mine.'

'I suppose there is that to it.' Phil leaned back in his seat. 'But you understand why *okay* isn't really cutting it with me.'

Yes, and it was a challenge. What could he say to make

a friend believe him, when he was saying exactly the same things as he had three years ago? He'd been lying then—why not now?

'Rob…?' Phil had left him to think about it, but he wanted an answer.

'Because I loved her. The things she's marvellous at, and those she's not so great at. Everything in between, including the idiosyncrasies and the things that make you wonder if she's on the same planet as you are.'

Phil looked at him blankly. Clearly, he'd never considered Stella to be on a different planet from anyone else, but she tended not to emphasise the impish side of her nature when she was at work.

'Don't ever tell her I said that, will you.'

'My lips are sealed. Go on, Rob.'

Now that he'd started, it was easier to finish. 'I'm feeling a lot of grief over losing Stella. But that's a real thing, a normal reaction to something that's happened to me. You know as well as I do that clinical depression and anxiety don't work that way, they're medical conditions. I loved her, and I could feel that love. I lost her, and I'm feeling that too, but it's not the same as three years ago. I'm okay, really.'

Phil nodded. 'I get that. I'm sorry to hear it, though.'

'Thanks. And I appreciate your asking.'

They sat in silence for a while, savouring their drinks. Then Phil looked at his watch, prompting Rob to look at his.

'My train…'

Phil smiled. 'Yes. Mine too. If I catch this one, I'll be home in time for supper.'

They were heading in different directions, and outside the wine bar Rob stopped, shaking Phil's hand.

'Good talk.'

Phil looked a little mystified. 'I'm glad it helped. I'll see you next week.'

It had been an excellent talk, and Rob's mind was buzzing as he walked to the station. *Real.* What he'd had with Stella was real. He could feel it still, powering him forward. He'd loved Stella and he'd lost her, and now he could do something about that.

# CHAPTER SIXTEEN

MONDAY HAD BEEN a better day. Not a great day, but a better one, because Stella had begun to feel that she had choices ahead of her, instead of the one path that she'd followed all of her working life. Maybe by Thursday she would have worked up the courage to ask Rob if he'd go for coffee with her.

Thursday was a long way away, and Monday seemed to be keeping hold of her much longer than it should. She arrived home at eight in the evening, wondering if it was too early to go straight to bed.

And then she saw him. Sitting on the steps outside her block, his elbows propped on his knees, looking up and down the road and... Rob had seen her now. He got to his feet, waiting for her.

Too soon. She hadn't worked out what she wanted to say to him yet. Maybe she should send him away, and tell him that she'd meet up with him for coffee on Thursday. But he'd clearly made this unscheduled journey up to London for some reason. Her treacherous hopes were whispering in her ear that maybe Rob had come to see her, and it was impossible to slow her footsteps back to a normal pace as she hurried towards him.

She stopped in front of him, trying not to stare. If he'd come to see her, then presumably he'd worked out something to say, to break the awkward silence.

'I came to talk, Stella. Will you hear me out?'

'Yes.' She hurried up the steps, knowing that he was right behind her. Dropped her keys, and he picked them up, putting them back into her hand without allowing his fingers to touch hers. Good. That was good. If he touched her now, and she had to let him go...

The lift wasn't working, and she made for the stairs, powering herself up them. He was still behind her when she reached her front door and let him in, wondering if everything was as tidy as it should be, and dismissing the thought. Her flat was generally more orderly than Rob's house, where things seemed to move around and get lost of their own accord, and anyway she doubted he'd come to inspect her housekeeping.

She turned to him, still slightly breathless from the stairs. 'Would you like some tea?'

'That would be nice. Thank you.'

So well mannered. They'd never been this polite to each other, even when they'd first met, and right now Stella wanted to engage in something very different with him. Punish him for hurting her, maybe, or just forget about all of that and engage in a little bad-mannered sex.

She dropped her handbag onto the floor and hung her jacket up, draping it carelessly over the hook so that it was left dangling by one sleeve. Rob followed her into the kitchen and she motioned for him to sit down while she made the drinks, throwing the teabags into the cups with unnecessary force. Even though her back was turned, she was aware that he was watching her.

Finally, she could go and sit down at the table, pushing his cup towards him. Now it was all up to Rob.

He reached into his jacket pocket, taking something out, and dropping a small box onto the table between them. A ring box, with the name of one of London's best jewellers in gold on the top.

'What's that, Rob?' She wrapped her hands around her cup, to stop them from inching towards the box.

'You know what it is. And it's non-negotiable. It's the one thing I'm not going to compromise on.'

'Do I have a say in the matter?'

'You always have a say in everything. But it's only fair to let you know where I stand, and that I can't stop loving you, Stella.'

She puffed out a breath. This was the big league. But she was used to high stakes, and she could deal with them. 'What *is* negotiable, Rob?'

'Everything else. I let you go because I was afraid. I've let a lot of people down, and I couldn't trust that I'd changed enough not to let you down. But I'd missed one very important thing. What we had was real. I can't let you down, because it won't allow me to.'

This. Just this was all she wanted. 'I can't stop loving you, Rob. However inconvenient it is.'

He laughed suddenly. 'I'm an inconvenience, am I?'

'No! But I think we both have to admit that we've got very different lives. Please tell me you have a plan…'

'No plan. What we have right now is good enough for the time being. We can spend Thursdays and Fridays together in London, and Saturdays and Sundays in Sussex. We can work from there for a more long-term solution. I could give up my job and come to London.'

'And give up your beautiful house? I won't have that, Rob. It's so much a part of you. Sussex does have hospitals, and hospitals have surgeons.'

'We'll see. There's clearly still some negotiating to do there.' His gaze caught hers, and Stella knew that the most important question was still to come. 'Whether or not we have children—that's got to be your decision. If you decide that you want to be a mother, then maybe I'll get to step up to the ultimate challenge of being a stay-at-home dad.'

'I get to do my share too. You think I'm going to miss out on first steps and scraped knees? Giving them a hug at bedtime and telling them a story...' The look on Rob's face said it all. He wanted a family as much as she did. 'There's some negotiating to do there as well, I suppose.'

'Clearly. I'll share the scraped knees with you, if you share the dirty nappies with me. We'll work it out.'

Stella reached for him, grasping his hands tightly in hers. 'Can we do this, Rob? Can we really do it?'

'We can do it. Just say the word, Stella.' He grinned suddenly. 'On second thoughts, I'm going to say the word...'

He reached for the box, but Stella got there first, opening the lid. Inside, a ring with five sparkling diamonds in a bezel setting, the thin platinum rim snaking elegantly around each stone to protect the sides from snagging.

'Rob, it's beautiful.'

He took the ring from the box, falling to one knee in front of her. Stella was trembling with excitement, hardly able to sit still.

'I can't promise you everything, Stella, but together we can do anything. Will you marry me?'

'Yes, Rob. I love you so much, and I can't wait to find out what that anything is.'

He took her hand, putting the ring onto her finger. Stella flung her arms around his neck, kissing him.

'Can you stay?'

'Yes, I have tomorrow and Wednesday off work. I reckoned that I'd need a couple of days to plot my next move if you sent me away.'

'I couldn't have done that. You're stuck with me now, whatever happens. If things get tough, then we'll work them out together.' Maybe Rob needed to hear that.

'I know. But I love you for saying it.' He kissed her again. 'How do you want to take this, Stella?'

'For starters? I can't work out what I want to do first. Talk and make plans with you or make love...'

'What do you say to going out to eat first, and then we'll have all night to make love? If we're together then the plans will grow on their own.'

'That sounds marvellous. Just beautiful.'

# EPILOGUE

*Two years later*

TODAY WAS A big day. A marquee had been erected outside, and the house was looking its best. All the food was laid out in the kitchen, waiting to be carried outside when the time came. And they were late.

'Did the alarm go off?' Stella sat up in bed, rubbing her eyes.

'Uh? I think it must have done. Why don't you shower first...?'

'What, so you can spend an extra five minutes in bed?'

'Nope. I need a serious man-to-man talk before we leave...' He got out of bed, walking over to the crib to pick Daniel up.

It never got old. Seeing her gorgeous husband and their beautiful six-month-old son together. Rob cradled the baby in his arms and Daniel's blue-grey eyes focused on his father's face, his hands reaching towards him.

'I'll shower and get dressed then. You can go through what Daniel needs to do today with him.'

'Will do...' Rob grinned at her and as she got out of bed she heard him talking to Daniel. 'It's pretty easy really. These old churches really echo, and you'll be surprised at how far your voice will carry. When we give you to Phil to hold, just take a deep breath and give it all you've got.'

'Don't underestimate Phil. Liz told me he was the family baby whisperer when their girls were small.' Stella made for the shower, chuckling at the secret Phil's wife had shared with her.

'Babies are supposed to cry at christenings, aren't they?' Rob called after her.

'He'll do whatever he decides to do, you can't organise that,' Stella shot back at him.

They'd made many plans in the last two years. Several of them had come to nothing. Stella's idea that they might go into general practice together barely saw the sun go down on it, and Rob's idea that they could move to London, and he would take on the renovation of a new house there, shrivelled and died over one idyllic weekend at the Sussex house that they both loved so much.

In the end, the opportunities had presented themselves. Stella's pregnancy had coincided with a job offer to head up the small Reconstructive Surgery unit at a Sussex hospital. The construction of a new hospital on the site was already underway, and her new employers were taking a long-term approach to developing the unit. They'd been open to Stella starting work after the baby was born, and she had already begun the challenge of developing the existing unit in preparation for creating a centre of excellence in the state-of-the-art operating suites that the new building would provide.

Rob spent one day a week in surgery up in London, and the rest of his time was spent on teaching and research. His unconventional approach to both of those tasks gave him a lot of freedom, and much of the preparatory work was done in the butterfly filled conservatory that now contained two desks.

Daniel had his father's eyes and his mother's determination, and he had captained the process of change. He had high standards and many demands, but fulfilling them was the most rewarding task that Stella and Rob had taken on together. Both his mother and father were hands-on parents, and Stella's mum and dad leapt at the chance of caring for their grandson for one day a week. Her father was catching up on what he'd missed when his own children were babies, and Stella loved watching him with Daniel almost as much as her mother did.

It was a busy life, which required organisation and out of the box thinking. But their family times and time for just the two of them were all built into the plan, the bedrock of everything else that they did.

They were almost ready now. Stella was brushing her hair, fixing it up at the back of her head in the soft style that Rob always said he liked so much, trying to think of anything they might have forgotten.

'Christening shawl?' They couldn't turn up without the lacy white shawl that Rob had been christened in and his parents had lent them.

'Done. It's a bit warm for him outside the church, so I've put it in the baby bag and we can take it out as soon as we see my mum on the horizon.'

'Good thought. Order of service?'

'Two copies in your handbag.' Rob grinned. 'Done.'

'Um… Guests?'

'They'll sort themselves out. We've got more than enough food, and a marquee in case it rains.' Rob looked out of the window, checking that the marquee hadn't disappeared during the night.

'That's it, then.' She turned, looking at Rob. 'Your shoes?'

'They're somewhere…' Rob put Daniel down, brushing at the damp patch on the shoulder of his shirt. 'Ah. Got them. Done.'

They tumbled out of the house, taking the footpath that led down to the village. Daniel's christening was an informal affair, most of the guests abandoning their cars on the outskirts of the village and walking the rest of the way to the church in a nod to one of the older traditions of the village.

Stella's parents were waiting for them where the footpath wound around the back of the station, chatting in the sunshine with Rob's two sisters. There was a brief, friendly tug-of-war between Rob and her father, before Rob gave in gracefully, giving Daniel to his grandfather to carry.

When they strolled together along the path to the church they could see Rob's parents approaching from the other direction, the rest of their combined families already waiting in the sunny churchyard. People from the village were appearing from various directions, coming just as they were to welcome little Daniel into their community. Phil and Liz Chamberlain were chatting to Emma, who seemed to be pointing out the main architectural features of the old church.

'Could this be any more perfect?' Rob murmured. Stella glanced towards the crowd of their family and friends and smiled up at him.

'I'm struggling to think how today could have turned out any better.'

'Me too. Only I've given up the struggling part. The funny part of accepting that you can't have everything...'

'Is that suddenly you find you have all that you want?' Stella smiled up at him. They'd discovered that truth in the very early days of their marriage.

He stopped walking, putting his arms around her shoulders and brushing a kiss against her lips. Today was turning out to be everything that Stella had wanted it to be.

'First day of the rest of our lives.' Rob had said that to her

on their wedding day, and at the start of many other days since.
'What do you suppose this one's going to bring?'

The same happiness that had shaped all the others.

'Wait and see, Rob. Let's just wait and see.'

\* \* \* \* \*

# FALLING FOR THE TRAUMA DOC

SUSAN CARLISLE

**MILLS & BOON**

To Ava Grace

I love you dearly

May May

# CHAPTER ONE

CALLEE DOBSON STEPPED to the rail along the back turn of Churchill Downs Racetrack. She inhaled the damp, Louisville, Kentucky, morning air. The smell of dirt, hay and horses filled her nose. These she knew well from childhood. Leaning her arms along the railing, she watched the track in anticipation. The early morning run, the breeze as it was called, when the horses practiced, was the best part of the day. A girl could be taken off the horse farm, but the horse farm couldn't be taken out of the girl.

Having a veterinarian for a father, she loved the animals, but her place was with humans. Her father hadn't taken it well when she'd turned to human medicine just as she had been accepted to veterinary school. Years later he still wouldn't discuss her decision.

As the head of the medical clinic located in the stable area on the Churchill Downs grounds, she had the best of both worlds. Working in what was called the backside, she cared for the people who lived and worked there.

The thunder of hooves grew. She leaned forward. The sound became louder and louder.

Someone came to stand beside her. Callee glanced to her right. It was a man wearing a cowboy hat. She did a double take. Could a man be more out of place? She checked the track again. No horses yet. Covertly she studied the stranger. He wore a collared shirt in light blue with the cuffs rolled up a couple of times over his forearms. Jeans covered his long legs. He lifted a foot and braced it on the bottom rail. She blinked twice. His cowboy boots were dark brown. She grinned. Who was this guy? He must've gotten lost on his way west.

His vivid blue eyes that almost matched his shirt commanded her attention. "Mornin'."

The man's drawl reminded her of thick warm caramel flowing over a hotcake. For a second she came close to licking her lips. She did love a good Southern drawl on a man. Joe had had a drawl when he could speak. Her chest tightened. She didn't want to think about that.

The sound of huffing and puffing, and hooves hitting the ground filled the air. The horses and riders moved into the back stretch. The Thoroughbreds were spectacular in their beauty. She'd almost missed them by the time her attention returned to the track.

Watching the horses disappear in the mist, she looked at the man who reminded her of them, all sleek lines and rippling muscles. She had meteorically flipped over the fence with that thought. Who was he anyway? She looked beyond him to see if he had come with a tour group but saw none.

"That was amazing," the man commented.

"It always is." She turned to go, due at the clinic in three minutes if it was to open on time.

"Do you watch often?" the man persisted.

She said over her shoulder, "Every morning."

"It must be tough on the jockey if one falls at that speed." He stepped up beside her.

"It can be." She needed to get away from this talkative tourist. "Have a good day." Sticking her hands in the back pockets of her jeans, she strolled over to the clinic building.

Located on the second street of the backside of the sprawling Churchill Downs complex, the small white building did not look like much from the outside, but she was proud of it. It had two front windows with a single glass door between them and the title above the door. A smaller building that shared a wall with the clinic held a school room for the jockeys and stable workers. It included a room with computers.

Callee unlocked the front door of the clinic and stepped inside. That area was just as immaculate as she had left it on Friday evening. She took great pride in everything looking just so. Flipping on the lights as she went, Callee headed toward the back where her office was located. She chuckled. It was more like a glorified closet, but it was her private domain. Carl, who handled the waiting area while she saw patients, knew that when her office door was closed not to bother her unless it involved a pouring-blood emergency.

At the sound of the front door opening and closing, she hollered, "Good morning, Carl. I'm back here. I haven't started coffee yet. Would you mind doing so?"

There was no response, but that wasn't unusual, so she continued around her desk and turned on her computer. A few minutes later the smell the coffee brewing reached her.

The thumping sound of boots against the concrete floor brought her brows together. Those footsteps didn't sound like Carl's. She stepped into the hall and jerked to a stop. The man who had been talking to her outside came toward her holding a mug with steam wafting from the top.

He no longer wore his hat. His thick, brown wavy hair looked as if he'd pushed it into some order using his fingers, but a lock still fell over his forehead. He smiled. A sexy one that made her stomach quiver. She took a moment to settle it.

"I brought you a cup of coffee." The Texas twang had her thinking of a warm summer night.

She took the offered cup. He had even gotten her mug correct. Her eyes narrowed. "I'm sorry, but who are you?"

He started back down the hall. "Do you mind if I get a cup before we talk?"

Who was this man? He certainly was bold. Her stranger danger radar was going off. Surely Carl would be coming in soon. Callee followed the man down the hall. She had cared for a number of trainers and horse owners who had been arrogant, but this man might win the prize for being the most self-assured person she had met.

She put a note of firmness in her voice. "Can I help you?"

"No, I'll get it." His reply was causal, and unhurried.

Was he dense on purpose? She had been referring to why he was in her clinic. She waited behind him in the doorway while he poured his coffee. He liked it black. She wasn't surprised. He turned. She had to take a step back for him not to hit her with his cup.

"I'm Langston Watts. You should be expecting me."

Hadn't she read that name somewhere? She studied his face. Yeah, that email from the main office, the one from Dr. Bishop. She half read it before a patient came in. This guy was a doctor doing a study the track was participating in. "Oh, yes, I was."

"You had forgotten about me. That happens." The last two words had an unexpected note. Bitterness?

The man was wrong there. He wasn't someone she would have forgotten. If it wasn't for his hat and boots, then it would have been his drawl or his blue eyes. The man was a shining example of memorable.

Straightening to her five-foot-three-inch height, she didn't intend to let him intimidate her. "You're the doctor who wants to do head trauma evaluations on people who work with the horses."

"Yep, there it is, that's me. Your boss has agreed to let

Valtech, the company I work with, do research on head injuries here. To help us develop more protective headgear."

"That sounds like something useful, but you do know we're coming up on the busiest week of the year around here. There'll be all kinds of people and horses coming and going." She twisted her cup between her hands.

"I realize Derby Week is in a few weeks. That's what makes it such a good time to do my research, because there's so many jockeys and trainers and people who work in the stalls here to study." He shrugged a shoulder. "What better time to get as much information as I can?"

She gave him a pointed look. "Just remember patient care comes first here."

He looked around the waiting area with its handful of chairs. "I'm also here to help with that as needed. I understood the deal with Churchill Downs was I'd also assist you."

She studied him a moment with a skeptical look. What kind of care could a researcher offer? "How much emergency care work have you done?"

"Quite a bit. I'm a trauma physician. I assure you I can handle whatever comes." He took a seat in one of the beat-up plastic chairs and rested his ankle over his knee.

"I certainly hope so." She looked at the door when it opened.

Carl entered. "Hey, boss." He gave Langston a questioning look.

Langston stood and extended his hand. "Dr. Langston Watts. But you can call me Langston."

"Carl." Callee hesitated a moment than said, "Langston is here to do a study. He'll also be helping us with patients as needed."

Carl nodded. "Great. We can use the help. Especially around the Derby."

Langston looked at her. "And may I call you Callee?"

She'd not even had a chance to introduce herself, but he apparently had done his homework. "Sure. We're not formal around here."

"That's good to hear." He took a sip of his coffee and looked at her. "How about showing me around?"

She and Carl looked at each other, smiled. "You've pretty much seen it all, but I'll give you the grand tour if you want."

"I want."

Callee had no doubt he hadn't meant that to sound like an innuendo, but her mind had gone there. What was this reaction she had to him? Since her college boyfriend, she remained cautious and in control about any interest she had in a man. She didn't deserve to have these feelings, yet they were springing up. Why this guy and why now?

At the sound of the clinic door opening, she turned. One of her favorite exercise riders hurried in holding a wrapped hand with blood seeping through his fingers. She rushed to him. "What happened, Jose?"

"The new horse in Barn Seven caught me against the wall while I was cleaning his hoof." He spoke in heavily accented English, and Spanish.

That was her weakness at work. Her Spanish was poor. She'd been trying to improve it by using an online program but wasn't making much progress. She needed to ask medical questions. Not where the nearest diner was located.

Langston spoke rapidly in Spanish to Jose.

She was jealous of his ability having only caught a few words. "Come back to an exam room. Take a seat in the chair."

Jose did as she requested. "I'm going to give this a look. We'll need to make sure it isn't broken."

Langston stood close enough she could feel his body heat.

She slowly unwrapped the rag from Jose's hand. He winced. "I'm being as gentle as I can be."

"I know, Ms. Callee."

She studied the angry, swollen hand already turning blue and purple. He would need stitches and an X-ray.

"You have an X-ray machine?" Langston asked.

"I do."

"Good." Langston shifted as if trying to get a better look.

Not that she needed his approval, but at least after the embarrassing moments over the coffee she felt redeemed. "Jose, we're gonna need to X-ray your hand."

"I not go to hospital. Work." The smaller man looked at her, panic filling his eyes.

Langston spoke to him in Spanish faster than she could follow. Jose nodded.

"I told him that we'd take some pictures to see if it was broken before we decided if he needed to go to the hospital or not." Langston stepped away from her and continued in English. "If we need to send you to the hospital, we'll still get a note for you to give your boss."

Once again, an unsure look came over Jose's face.

Langston repeated what he'd said in Spanish.

Jose nodded.

She touched Jose's arm and pointed to the door. She led the way down the hall to a room across from her office. An old but still reliable X-ray machine stood there. She carefully put a vest over Jose's hand and then set it on his shoulders. Lifting his hand to the table of the machine, she placed the palm down. "Stay right like that and stay still."

Langston stepped out into the hall, and she joined him. Callee clicked a switch and there was a buzz.

"All done," she announced as she reentered the room.

Langston helped Jose off with the vest while she reviewed the X-ray on a screen.

Carl came to the door.

"Carl, please take Jose back to the exam room and give him a couple of over-the-counter painkillers."

To Jose she said, "I'll see you in a minute."

Jose nodded.

She turned back to the X-ray.

Langston came to stand behind her. "Mind if I look too?"

Even if she did, he had already started studying the picture. She didn't see any broken bones, zooming in on each carpal and metacarpal finding nothing that looked damaged. She continued to search for a dark line indicating a fracture. The only sound in the room was that of them breathing. It was too intimate. He had pushed into her personal space. They didn't even know each other. She gave him a slight elbow to the middle. A torso that felt hard and fit. He grunted.

"Sorry. I didn't know you were so close." She stepped away from him.

His gaze met hers. A slight lift to one corner of his mouth implied he didn't believe her.

"Don't you think he needs an orthopedic doctor to have a look?"

She pursed her lips. "He won't go. If he doesn't work, he doesn't get paid. He has a family he sends money to. I'll send this X-ray over to an orthopedic guy who'll look at it. If he sees any problems, I'll talk to the trainer Jose works for and have him insist he go see the doctor."

Langston nodded. "Nice system, Callee. I bet your husband does all sorts of things he doesn't want to do but ends up glad to do it."

"I don't have a husband, and you make it sound like I'm a manipulating woman. I'm not flattered."

He raised a hand in defense. "Hey, I didn't mean to insult you."

"I don't think you meant to flatter me either." She didn't hide the bitter taste in her voice.

He gave her a direct look. "No, I'm impressed."

She narrowed her eyes and clicked off the screen. Jose was waiting. "Surprisingly, it all looks really good."

"I agree."

Callee started toward the door. "I do appreciate the second opinion." She headed straight to Jose's exam room. "Jose, it doesn't look like you've broken anything. I'm going to clean and wrap your hand. No work."

"I must work. I have stalls to clean." Jose looked almost frantic.

"That's not going to happen for you today. We'll see about tomorrow. For today you'll have to get someone else to do it for you. If you need me to write a note, just let me know. I don't think it'll take too much for Ron to see you can't hold a pitchfork. Do you understand?"

The man slowly nodded.

"Now let's get your hand cleaned up and bandaged." Carl had already laid out a bottle of saline and a pan. There was roll of gaze and a tan stretch bandage waiting as well.

Langston stood across the small room watching as she poured the saline over Jose's hand and looked at it closely. "You're lucky not to need any stitches," Callee commented.

Holding Jose's hand carefully, she wrapped the gauze around it, being sure to cover any area with open skin. Over that she applied the stretch bandage. To help with the aching, she put an ice pack on the bandaged wound for twenty minutes.

"Keeping your hand above your heart will also help with the throbbing. I'll give you something for pain as well."

Jose nodded.

"Let me know if you have any problems. Come back tomorrow. I'll call you if the orthopedic doctor thinks he needs to see you. I'll get you an ice pack to take with you." She left the room. As she returned, she heard Langston speaking

Spanish. Even in a different language his voice sounded nice. She could make out enough to know they were talking about being hit in the head.

Soon she sent Jose on his way.

As soon as the man left, she looked at Langston. "Still want that quick tour? Then again, you've already seen most of the place. Afterward we'll go to my office and talk about this study you're doing and how I can help."

Before they had time to walk down the hall another patient entered.

During the morning, Langston had been surprised at how busy the clinic could be. A couple of times Callee had allowed him to do the initial assessment, but she'd been in to see the patient. He might be the physician, but this was her clinic. He wasn't used to working under someone else's direction. His inability to do so had made it difficult in a couple of places he had worked. He might have been right, yet the head of the department didn't like having that pointed out. Langston soon had to move on. That was one thing about his current job—he only took orders from himself.

By the time lunchtime came around, he and Callee had seen sniffles, a rash, and any number of regular everyday aches and pains. Langston had been impressed. Callee had given each one the same amount of attention regardless of how simple their complaint might have been. She treated them all as if they were her friends. She knew each by name and if she didn't, she made sure she introduced herself and practiced using their name. Callee was so personable. He'd seen nothing like it in his work.

He'd gotten the impression she wasn't that pleased to have him around. He couldn't decide if it was because he was encroaching on her territory or because she didn't care for him, or he made her nervous. Whatever it was, he would figure it out. He would be at Churchill Downs six weeks and wanted them to be pleasant. He had a job to do, an important one, then he would move on.

Before agreeing to do head trauma research, he'd worked in a large hospital in the neurological unit with a world-renowned staff. The problem was the head of the department believed there was only one way to care for a particular patient. He and Langston had disagreed, vehemently. Working in the department had become so difficult that Langston had snatched up the opportunity to work with Valtech, the makers of Head Armor. Yet leaving the hospital had taken him away from the personal side of medicine. Working at the clinic that morning he'd found he'd missed it.

"You ready for lunch?" Callee asked after the latest patient went out the door.

"I could eat." His stomach growled. There hadn't been time for even a full cup of coffee that morning.

"Then I'll take you to the best restaurant in town. Where we are going has the best breakfast in Louisville. And the burgers aren't bad. Let me get my money." She started toward her office.

"I'll get your meal for letting me work with you." Langston headed for the front door.

"I can't let you do that." Something about letting him pay felt like a date.

"Sure you can. You can pay the next time. Are we going far? Should I drive?"

"Nope. It's just three barns away." She pushed the door open.

"Really? Three barns, huh."

He sounded amazed by the idea of those directions. "Yep, it's just across the street from the backside so it's where everybody around here eats, and a number of those who have read about it make a point to come in."

Langston pursed his lips. "Interesting. I'm looking forward to the place already."

She called over her shoulder to Carl. "We're going over to the Brown Derby for lunch. You want me to bring you back something?"

"I'll go over when you get back. Maybe it'll have calmed down for the day."

"Okay."

She led the way around the corner of the building and down the road through the barns, waving at a few people as she went.

Langston watched, amazed. "You feel at home here, don't you?"

"Yep. I found where I belong. Despite not having anything major after Jose's hand, we had a busier than normal morning. I appreciate your help. You didn't have to, you know."

"I didn't mind. It was good to see patients again." He hadn't said anything, but he was also anxious to get started on his research.

"You haven't been doing that?" She looked at him in disbelief.

He worked to match his long stride to her shorter ones. "No. Recently I've mostly been reviewing charts."

Callee tsked. "I like paper pushing the least."

"Do you ever handle cases of head injuries involving the horses and riders?" He needed some good solid cases to look into.

"Sure, but not as often as you would think. I act as first responder on those, but the rider is always taken to the hospital. At the minimum put under concussion procedures."

"Gotcha." He looked down the street they crossed to see more barns beyond. At each end of the barns was another street. The barns were painted the same color with occasional colored accents. Someone could easily get lost because every building looked so much like the others.

"Why don't you explain to me more about why you're here so maybe I can help you." Callee stopped to let a truck pulling a horse trailer go by.

"They didn't tell you anything about what I'm doing?"

"The front office isn't known for being clear. They just told me to expect you, which I managed not to do." She grinned.

"I'm studying head traumas over the next six weeks. I also agreed to help out in the clinic since the population on the backside will grow leading up to the Derby."

"How do you plan to do this study?" She waved to a man at the other end of a barn.

"I'll be looking through your files on patients who have come in with head injuries and reviewing them. If they are still working here, I'd like to interview them. I would also be reviewing and interviewing any patients with issues while I'm here. I'd also like to interview all your patients over the next few weeks to see if any of them have experienced head injuries in the past. When patients come in, I want to talk to them about any head injuries they may have experienced in the past, be it a fall from a hayloft or involving a horse."

"I get the obvious connection between the horse-racing industry and technology."

"There are quite a number of head injuries, or opportunities for them in horse racing. I plan to do cognitive tests. I understand that everyone is required to have a yearly checkup or present a report that they have had one. When they come in, I'd like to do additional studies, with their permission, of course."

Their feet crunched on the gravel as they continued down the street.

She gave him a doubtful look. "You think your gonna see everyone working here in six weeks? That's pretty ambitious."

He would try. Failure wasn't a word in his vocabulary. Despite doing so where Emily had been concerned. But he had no intention of letting that happen again. Because he'd never let himself be in a position to care like that. That's why he was known for being good at his job. He focused on it. "Maybe not everyone but as many as I can."

"Have you always done research?"

"No, like I said, my background is in emergency trauma."

"Wow, research and working at my small clinic don't sound like they would be high adrenaline enough for you. What got you out of trauma?"

"I still keep my hand in at the trauma units even when I travel. I do visiting doctor work as well."

"Why head trauma?"

He shrugged. "I slowly became interested in head trauma as I worked with car accident victims and children who had bike accidents and falls. I seemed to gravitate to those cases. I'd be the one called on to care for those patients.

"One particular patient, a cute white-blond little girl came in with a head injury that could have been prevented if the helmet hadn't cracked. I said to myself, *This has to stop.* That's when I agreed to do research on finding a better product to protect children like that little girl. I wanted to make a lasting difference. Not just fix them up to go out there and do it again."

She nodded. Her eyes having turned serious. "What can do I do to help you?"

They came to another cross street. A truck headed their way. He grabbed her elbow to stop her. Her face turned rebellious. He let go. What had gotten into him? He wasn't usually so overprotective. The truck passed in a small cloud of gray dust.

"I need access to the records and for you to encourage your

past and present patients to talk to me. Based on what I've seen so far you know everyone."

"Sounds simple enough. I'll do what I can. It may be tough. This is a close-knit world, and they're suspicious of others."

Langston wouldn't expect less than what he needed. More than one person had told him he was an overachiever. He'd graduated from high school a year earlier than he should have with glowing grades. Medical college fed his hunger for knowledge, and he'd breezed through it. Now he had a number of degrees, had traveled all over the world presenting papers on his work and was considered an authority in the field of head trauma. The only thing he had been accused of was not having a personal life. That, he didn't care anything about having. Hurt lay there.

At one time he had been involved with a girl. He and Emily had planned a life together. He would go to the Peace Corps for two years so he could get Prairie, Texas, the small town they live in, purged from his system. Then he'd return and go to medical school. When Emily finished college, they'd get married. With his fellowship completed he'd start his practice in Dallas, not in a small town where nothing happened.

Instead, he had returned from overseas to learn Emily and his best friend, Mark, had become involved while he was gone. He and Mark had been inseparable when they were kids. Then it had been Langston and Emily as teens. Often Mark joined them. He had even been Langston's college roommate.

Devastated and heartbroken, Langston put all his energy and emotion into his work. He promised himself he'd never open his heart again. To a woman or to a best friend. He'd not only lost his girlfriend but a major part of his life with the loss of Mark. That had been as painful as breaking up with Emily had been.

His entire focus at this point in his life was to gather enough data to improve the quality of helmets in order to save lives.

He and Callee continued walking.

"It looks like the backside is set up on a grid system?"

"Yes. The end of each barn is the corner of a street. They run in front and behind the barns with the exception of a couple of streets where there are grassy areas. The roads have street names, but most people go by the barns' names. Those names are the trainers who lease them."

They came to a main road that was the back boundary of the lot. Callee looked in both directions before crossing. "What do you know about the people who work around a racetrack?"

"I haven't been around horses much. Or racetracks for that matter." Why did he feel a twinge of guilt about that?

She stopped and looked him up and down. "I thought you were a cowboy."

He felt the need to straighten his shoulders. "I'm a Texan who likes hats and boots. That doesn't mean I was raised on a ranch. Sorry to disappoint you."

She chuckled. "If you don't care for horses, you've come to the wrong place."

This small woman wasn't going to intimidate him. "Then I'll need you to help me. I'm a quick learner. I do know how to care for people."

"What exactly do you want to know about people who work with horses?"

"Everything." He did. The more he knew the better the chance of getting the information he needed.

"I don't know if I can give you that, but I can give you some general info." She waved a hand around. "As you know, this is considered the backside. The barns are rented out by trainers. Some barns are held in reserve for the horses that come in for special races."

"Like the Derby."

"Yep." She warmed to her subject.

"If the trainers don't have enough horses for a full barn, they rent stalls out. It's a transit lifestyle for jockeys, trainers and their staff along with the horses."

He liked that idea. It was much like his lifestyle. "You don't mind working where everyone is coming and going?"

"Not really. I just look forward to their return. On the way back I'll show you some points of interest." She grinned. Callee stopped at another cross street and pointed to the right. "See that three-story brick building? That's the workers' dormitory. Some live here year-round. Many need to be close to the horses."

"I had no idea."

"A number of these workers come from all around the world. They're great with horses, but they're not all familiar with the English language. As you saw this morning, it can make it interesting at the clinic."

Spanish came easy to him. "Do you have interpreters?"

A sad look appeared on her face. "Sometimes I can find one. Other times it's more about sign language. Some use translation apps. That can make it interesting."

"I'm sure it does. What time of the day do things get started each morning? I need to plan for my interviews."

"Just before daylight. The breeze is finished early morning before the heat of the day. Then there is cooling down, washing, grooming and feeding of the horses. While that's going on others are cleaning out the stalls. By midday things are settling down." She chuckled. "We're on horse schedule around here."

"Makes sense." He'd adjust. After all, he had done that more than once in his life.

"Now things are different during the month of April. Leading up to the Derby, things get crazier by the day here. By the time Derby Week arrives, we're busy all the time."

"That's a big deal around here." He at least had heard of the Kentucky Derby but never had any real interest in it.

"The biggest. I forgot." She turned in the opposite direction. "Over there's our full-time veterinary clinic." She pointed to the large single-story building. "It stays busy all the time. The horses are constantly checked for various different reasons, including being drug tested."

"Do you handle blood testing for the jockeys?"

"There's a special procedure for them on race weeks, and a special group sometimes uses the clinic for gathering tests. I couldn't handle it all myself. And they are very particular."

He couldn't help but be in awe. The more he knew the more he didn't know. "This really is a world unto itself."

"Yep, a pretty special one."

Langston could already tell that not only was the place special, but Callee was as well.

# CHAPTER TWO

CALLEE ENTERED THE older building with a low ceiling, which had apparently been around for a long time. She glanced over her shoulder to see Langston duck to enter, and grinned. He was a tall one. The door closed behind them, leaving the pair in dim light.

"This reminds me of a good Texas bar." He stood in the doorway looking around.

Square wooden tables and chairs were filled with people in work shirts, jeans and boots. The busy room was noisy, but not deafening.

Callee searched for a table. "Looks like we're at the bar today." She took a seat next to a large man with dirt and dust covering his clothes. "Move over, Macomb. Let me have a seat."

The man looked over his shoulder. "Hell, Callee, you could sit in my pocket."

Callee grinned. "The problem is I want to sit in this chair not your pocket."

She dipped her shoulder, giving him a nudge, and climbed on the stool.

Langston took the empty seat beside her. His knees brushed her from hip to knee, sending an electric current through her. She glanced at him. She certainly wasn't his type. A leggy woman, wearing makeup, nails done and fashionably dressed came to mind. Not the kind who had their hair pulled back, wore T-shirts, jeans and work boots. Like her. Nope she wasn't his type at all.

A man wearing a white apron tied around his waist asked Callee from the other side of the bar, "Hey, what're you having today?"

"A burger and fries," she called without looking at the menu.

The man looked at Langston.

"I'll have the same."

"And two sodas, Fred." Callee flashed a smile.

He nodded and left.

"Hey, Callee, you going to make the game next Wednesday night?" Rick asked as he strolled by.

"Yeah, I'll be there."

"See you then." Rick waved a hand.

"What's that all about?" Langston asked.

She pushed the napkin holder back, making room in front of her. "We have a monthly poker game next door to the clinic at the community center."

"You're very much a part of the family around here."

He said that with an easiness she wouldn't have thought he felt. Something about Langston made her think of stable, safe and sure. Not fly-by-night. "I try to be. For all the reasons I told you earlier, I work to have people trust me. It makes my job easier."

"I've never stayed in one place long enough to have a group to play poker with."

"While you're here you can join us." She picked up the glass Fred had just set in front of her.

Langston looked at her. Really looked at her as if he saw her. "Thanks. I just might do that. You like working here, don't you?"

She smiled. "Yeah. I do."

"How long have you been here?"

Why so much interest in her? "A couple of years."

Their burgers in a basket with fries were placed in front of them.

"What made you decide to do this type of work?"

Callee hoped he didn't notice the sadness filling her eyes before she blinked. She had no intention of telling him that awful story.

"I did my internship while working on getting my physician assistant degree here. The doctor I worked with retired, and I applied for the job. At that time, I really needed to be here." Callee had almost said too much. She ate her burger.

Half an hour later, Langston let the screen door close behind them on their way out of the restaurant. He rubbed his middle. "I have to say that was one of the best burgers I've ever eaten."

"I thought you might like it." She headed across the road. "You should try the breakfast sometime."

"I'll keep that in mind." He walked beside her on the way back to the clinic. She didn't reach his shoulder.

"Hey, Callee." Someone called her name.

Callee looked between the barns. She raised her hand to wave. "Hi, Gina." She looked at Langston. "I need to check on some stitches I put in a few days ago."

He stopped walking. "House call?"

She grinned. "More like a barn call."

"I thought those went the way of the dodo bird." Langston kicked at a rock.

She headed across the grassy area toward Gina, who sprayed water over a horse. "Not when it's your best friend you're checking on."

"Makes sense."

She looked at him. "Can you find your way to the clinic?"

"No problem."

"See you in a few then." She watched those long legs carry him down the road. He was almost as good-looking from behind as he was from the front. She started walking toward Gina.

Callee should have introduced Langston to Gina, but she needed a few minutes away from him. He was too much for her nervous system, and he'd only been there a few hours. Approaching Gina, Callee asked, "How's your hand doing?"

Gina held it up. It was inside a plastic glove.

"Smart idea. You don't need to get it infected."

She and Gina had met just after Callee had come to work at the Downs. They became friends immediately. Gina was on her way to becoming a great trainer. Currently she worked as a groom.

Gina looked beyond Callee to where Langston had just been. "Who was that tall drink of water you were with?"

"New doctor. He's here doing research."

"He could do research on me." Gina wiggled her brows. "Or maybe on you."

"Don't start." Gina knew her secrets. Knew why Callee couldn't go past being a friend with a man. Why she couldn't trust herself to care.

"Callee, you need to give guys a chance. What happened to you with Joe was a fluke. You need to let yourself off the hook."

"I know. I've moved on. I'm working here and have a good life."

Gina rolled her eyes. "Yeah. When was your last date?"

"It has been a while." Callee waved the comment away. "Instead of worrying about my love life you need to be worrying about yours."

"It's more fun to tease you about yours. If you don't want him, can I have him?"

That idea didn't appeal to Callee. "Enough about Langston. Again, how's your hand doing?"

"His name is Langston. I like that. Very sexy."

"Gina, the hand." Callee couldn't help but smile.

"I'm taking care of it." Gina removed the glove and showed Callee. "Someone made me get a tetanus shot. I don't wanna have to do that again."

Callee took Gina's hand, checking for redness or an opening in the incision. "Looks good. Don't forget to stop by and have those stitches out day after tomorrow."

"Can I meet the new guy then?" Gina's eyes twinkled.

Callee laughed. "If we aren't too busy."

"You sure you don't want to keep him to yourself?"

"I'm sure." What would she do if she did have Langston? Callee wouldn't deserve him. She shouldn't be happy after what she let happen to Joe. He was gone and it was all her fault. Callee shook her head. "You're man crazy. See you later."

"Why don't you invite him to poker this month? I could really get to know him."

"I already have." Maybe she should have given that more thought. Callee wasn't sure she wanted Langston to encroach on her private time since he already had so much of her work time. Why it would matter she had no idea. By his own admission he came and went. If she did become interested in a man, it would be one who had the potential to settle down and eventually have a family. That wasn't Langston.

But would it be so bad to flirt with him while he was in town? She harrumphed. What did she know about flirting anymore? It had been a long time since she'd done that.

Twenty minutes later she entered the clinic to find Carl and Langston laughing over something. Both of them looked guilty and quickly hushed.

She looked at Langston. "We should be pretty quiet this afternoon. I'll show you how to access the files."

Langston brought in his legs and stood. "Sounds good."

They walked to her office. Callee put in her passwords. "I saw in the email from the front office that you had clearance to be in the files for head injuries only."

"Yeah." He came to stand beside her.

He had a way of making her too aware of him. Did he mean to? She shook her head. They didn't even know each other. "I have to follow the laws here as well."

"Understood."

The screen opened. "The files you should need are right here. Let me know if you need some help. I'll leave you with it." She bumped him on her way to the door. An electric pulse shot through her.

"Sorry." He shifted out from behind the desk, giving her space to pass.

"I don't know how comfortable you're going to be in here. But it's the best I can do."

Her rolling chair creaked under his weight when he sat. "Don't worry. I'll manage. If you get busy, call me."

"I appreciate it." She saw most of her patients in the mornings and spent the afternoons catching up on paperwork and making phone calls. She planned to share Carl's desk for a while. Earlier in the day she'd heard back from the orthopedist about Jose's hand, which wasn't broken. She needed to call him. If she couldn't get him on the phone, she would go to the barn where he worked and look for him.

By the time Callee walked back from seeing Jose, it was time to close the clinic for the day. She hadn't seen Langston in hours. She went to her office to find him studying the screen with a pen in his hand and a pad on the desk beside him. "Sorry to bother you but it's time to close up for the day."

Langston's head popped up. He leaned back in the chair, put his hands behind his head and stretched. His shirt tightened across his broad chest. She couldn't stop herself from looking.

"I'm sorry. I get so engrossed in this type of stuff I forget what time it is."

"That's what happens when you love what you do." She couldn't help but admire his work ethic.

His look softened. "I'm glad you understand. Quite a few people don't. I've dated women who thought I got a little obsessive."

"We all get obsessive about what we love."

He stood. "It's just nice to meet someone who understands. Let me get my stuff together and I'm on my way out."

A few minutes later they parted company. She watched him walk to a large late model red pickup truck. For a moment she wondered how he spent his evenings. He didn't seem like the kind of person who stayed at home reading a book. Did he go to a hospital to help out or volunteer in a night clinic?

Langston had been busy in Callee's office going through medical files for the last five days. Each day started the same. He met Callee at the track to watch the morning run, then they walked to the clinic.

She saw patients while he worked in her office. A few times she had asked for his help with a patient. He had joined her when Jose had come in to have his hand reexamined. When her friend Gina had stopped by to have her stitches removed, Callee had brought her back to meet him. Langston quickly decide he liked her.

In the afternoon Callee would work up front, and at five she closed the clinic. They'd stroll to their vehicles and say goodbye.

Heaven help him, he was turning into his parents. Living the same old pattern over and over. He shook his head and focused on the screen in front of him. There were only a few more weeks before he would be moving on. Yet something about this place had lulled him into a rut. The sad thing was he didn't seem to mind.

"Langston—" Callee's head popped inside the office "—bring your bag. I need your help."

He shoved out of his chair. "It's in the truck. What's up?"

"I'm needed at one of the barns." She'd already started up the hall. "A groom was kicked and they're afraid to move him. An ambulance is on the way."

Langston hurried after her, going out the front door. He loped to his truck, grabbed his bag. She pulled up in a golf cart. He climbed in. Callee floored the gas.

"How far?"

"Two barns down and one over." He held on as the wheels threw rocks as they went. Callee made a wild turn that almost threw him out of the vehicle. Halfway along the length of the barn she pulled to a jarring stop. People stood outside a stall of a well-kept barn with red doors and ferns hanging along the porch area. A horse stood outside a stall on its lead held by a young woman.

"Move back and let us through," Callee stated with the authority of a seven-foot giant.

The group parted, allowing himself and Callee through. They continued until they reached a concrete floor covered in sawdust. A young Hispanic man lay on the floor with two other men squatting beside him.

Callee didn't hesitate to go down on her knees next to the injured man. "What's your name?"

Langston watched from above.

"Carlos." The word came out as a gurgle. His face twisted with the effort to speak.

"Carlos, can you tell me where it hurts?"

The man lay a hand over his right side.

"Okay, I'm going to look for broken bones. Dr. Watts here," she said, nodding toward Langston, "is going to check you out too."

Carlos's eyelids drooped.

She lightly shook the man's shoulder. "Carlos, we need you to stay wake. I know it hurts, but I need to know where the pain is."

While Langston did vitals, she moved her hands over Carlos's chest. He moaned when she touched his right side. "He has broken ribs."

"Heart rate one-sixty over ninety. BP one-twenty over eighty-seven. Pulse one-forty. Respiration eighty. Labored breathing. He's going into shock." Without another thought, Langston removed his shirt and placed it over the man's chest for warmth. Jerking a horse blanket down off a hanger, he rolled it up and put it under his Carlos' feet to make them higher than his heart.

Callee continued to search for additional injuries.

Langston listened to Carlos's chest. Hearing a sucking of air he said, "He has a punctured lung as well."

Callee took Carlos's hand and studied his nail beds.

Even in the filtered light of the stall's interior, Langston could tell they were a dusky blue.

Langston handed Callee the stethoscope. She listened to Carlos's lungs. "Agreed."

The sound of the ambulance coming, then the abrupt quiet after they turned off the siren said they were close.

"Thank goodness. He needs oxygen ASAP. The ambulance isn't far away. They turn the siren off because it will upset the horses."

Langston nodded. "Makes sense."

Minutes later the emergency medical technicians entered the stall with a stretcher. Callee quickly and succinctly gave a report to the EMTs.

Langston helped lift Carlos onto the stretcher. In no time the injured man and the ambulance had left. He leaned against the wooden wall. "How often is it like this?"

"Seems like more often now that you are around." She picked up his shirt from the floor, studying him. "Very heroic, Dr. Watts."

He grinned. She seemed to like what she saw. "I try." He reached out his hand. "Mind if I get my shirt back."

A sweet pink blush came to Callee's cheeks. She thrust the garment at him. "Uh…no, not at all."

Langston shrugged into his now dirty shirt and buttoned it. He packed his medical bag then stepped out into the bright sunshine behind Callee. A self-satisfied smile covered his lips. Callee could be rattled after all. He looked forward to doing it again sometime.

Callee berated herself for staring at Langston. She shouldn't have been doing that. After all, she was a professional. In her defense there had been a lot to admire. Broad shoulders with defined muscles, with a dusting of hair that included a line leading to a trim waist. It was all well worth viewing. She just wished she hadn't been caught doing so.

Langston grabbed her arm as she started to climb behind

the wheel of the golf cart. "Oh, no. I'm driving. I'm not taking another *Mr. Toad's Wild Ride* back to the clinic."

"But—

"There is no but. Climb in or walk. I'm commandeering your ride."

She let him have his way and took the passenger seat. "I'm only agreeing because I appreciated your help back there."

"Not a problem." Langston made the turn at the end of the barn smoothly.

Callee cocked her ear. Even over the noise of the wheels of the cart she knew that sound. Fear shot through her. "Stop!"

"What's wrong?" Langston pressed on the brakes, jerking them to a skidding stop.

"That horse is wheezing." Her heart raced. She jumped off the golf cart. "They need to get the horse out of here."

She hurried to the man standing by the horse trailer. "Put him back in the trailer now."

"I was told to wait here." The groom looked perplexed about what his actions should be.

She kept her voice low and firm. "The horse has the flu. Get your trainer now."

The groom's eyes widened. He handed the lead off to another groom standing nearby. He nodded and shot off like he was being chased by a wild stallion.

To the man now holding the horse she said, "Don't go any farther than right here." She pointed to the spot at the end of the trailer. "Do not put that horse in the barn. Understood? I'm calling the vet right now."

"What's wrong?" Langston came to stand beside her with a confused look on his face.

"Horse flu. It's highly contiguous. It could shut down the entire Derby. This horse must be quarantined right now."

A man stalked toward her, his face ruby with anger. Behind

him hurried the first groom. "What's going on here?" the man demanded, stepping into her personal space, glaring down his nose at her. "You have no business handling my horse."

Langston moved to where he could get between Callee and the man if needed.

She had to admit she liked having his support. Callee said in a low even voice, "This horse has the flu."

The trainer took a step back, his face turned ashen. "What?"

"I'm going to have to ask you to reload him. Now."

"You have no authority," the man spat, moving toward her again.

"Stay right there," Langston growled.

Callee could handle herself, but it was nice to know she had someone on her side. "No. But I'm calling the vet, who does."

"Get him in the trailer," the trainer barked at the groom.

Callee stepped across the road out of the way. Langston joined her. She watched as the men worked to get the horse back in the trailer. She pulled her phone out and pushed in the number for the Derby Veterinarian Clinic. She raised her voice an octave so it would carry to the men working with the horse. "May I speak to Dr. Dillard?"

The trainer glared at her. Callee raised her chin. She quickly relayed her information.

Finished with her call, she started toward the trainer. Langston didn't miss a step she made. Staying out of reach of the man she said, "Dr. Dillard is expecting you at the clinic."

The trainer turned his back to her.

She and Langston waited until the truck and trailer had turned the corner into the road leading to the vet clinic before she headed back to the golf cart.

"What's the urgency?" Langston asked as he climbed into the cart.

"If the horse comes into contact with any other horses, they

will all be quarantined. As I said, horse flu is highly conta-
gious. In fact, the dirt, all the sawdust where this horse stood
must be removed and burned. All buckets must be sterilized."
Callee took her place in the cart.

Langston started the vehicle. "What you did back there was
impressive and crazy at the same time. Where did you learn
to recognize horse flu? Working around here?"

"No, my father is a veterinarian. I used to go to work with
him all the time."

Langston started down the road. "Really. I'm surprised you
didn't become a veterinarian."

"It wasn't from him not wanting me to." If he had his way,
she would be a veterinarian. She hated she had disappointed
him.

"You make it sound like he wasn't happy when you didn't
become a vet."

Langston was perceptive. She must be careful, or he would
know all her secrets. "He wasn't. He's still disappointed."

"But you would like to make him happy." The statement
held no criticism.

"Yeah. He's my hero. From the time I was a small kid I followed him around. If I wasn't in school, then I was in a barn
caring for an animal or on a call with Dad. In college I had
every intention of going to vet school."

Langston looked at her. "So why didn't you?"

"Because I thought I could make a more important difference if I did human medicine." Now they were getting into a
territory she didn't like to share.

"Something significant must have happened to make you
change your mind."

Her fingers tightened on the support to the top of the golf
cart. Langston was digging where she didn't want him to.
"Yeah. It did."

"Will you tell me about it?"

Callee looked around at the barns, the horse with its head out of the stall, the exercise boy washing a horse nearby. Could she tell the story? How she had failed someone she cared about. What would Langston think of her then?

He didn't say anything and neither did she for a few seconds.

She drew in a breath. "I was in my last year of college. My boyfriend and I were out celebrating my acceptance into vet school with some friends. We rarely went out to have a good time because we studied so much. Joe was planning to be a doctor."

Langston's body tensed as if preparing for what would come next.

"He drank far too much before I knew it. I was so caught up in talking and having a good time myself to be aware of what he had. He wasn't used to it so a little went a long way. I didn't realize how affected he was until Joe staggered to the car. I wouldn't let him drive. He got mad and jerked the keys out of my hand and drove off. I ran back and found a friend who would help me follow Joe. We found him." She went quiet for a moment. "Joe had crashed into a tree. There wasn't anything I could do for him until the EMTs got there. They had to use the Jaws of Life to get him out. He had a massive head injury and spent weeks in the hospital in an unresponsive state."

"You know that wasn't your fault." Langston stopped the golf cart and looked at her.

"That's easy for you to say. You didn't face his parents every day. See the blame in their eyes even when they didn't say it." Her eyes remained on her clasped hands in her lap. "Or worse, be there when they turned off the machine and he was gone. I should have been able to do more. If I had known more human medicine, then I could have done something more. Maybe saved him."

Langston said the words softly as if recognizing their truth. "So you changed to human medicine, thinking you could save others like him."

Callee said nothing. Finally, Langston started driving again. She was grateful when they arrived at the clinic. She needed some time alone. Grabbing her bag, she got off the cart. "Thanks for your help. It was nice to have it."

"Glad I could."

She started for the track.

"Not coming in?" Concern laced his words.

"I will in a few minutes." Callee kept walking. She felt Langston's gaze on her for a long time.

# CHAPTER THREE

By THE SECOND week Langston had been at the clinic, he knew he could find Callee at the track every morning. This one was no different. She stood in her usual position with her foot propped on the bottom rail. Her jeans stretched tight across her bottom. She might be petit, but she sure had curves in all the right places.

Langston couldn't help but smile. Callee had more spunk than he'd given her credit for. As small as she was, she carried a powerful personality. He'd spent most of the last few days in her office on the computer, yet he'd heard her with patients. More than once he had offered to help. She had insisted she didn't need him.

He had quickly learned Callee was a self-sufficient person. It was as if she held herself at a distance, not wanting anybody to really get to know her. He suspected what she'd told him about her past had much to do with it.

He'd looked forward to this assignment, but he'd had no idea how interesting he would find it. Working at the clinic was nothing like what he expected. When this idea had been suggested, he thought it would be rather dull. He'd had no idea when he pulled into the parking spot that first morning and noticed people lined up along the railing, that he'd find himself drawn to it each morning as well. Slowly and unexpectedly he had become one of them.

He'd never guessed there were as many head concussions in horse racing as he was finding. The number was approaching that of football. Every sport would benefit from the information he would gain here. He liked being a doctor, but he wanted to do something bigger and more significant. He would never be satisfied doing what Callee did. Having the same routine day after day in the same place. Like living in Prairie where nothing changed.

Yet when was the last time he had someone he could call a best friend? Or live in a community where his neighbors waved, or he could call them by name? So much of his adult life had been caught up in constant change. But hadn't that been what he'd wanted? To get away from the small-town-going-nowhere life? To see the world. And he had. A couple of times.

Oddly he had found the repetitive mode he'd been in for the past few days settling, reassuring. Almost pleasant. He just might miss the clinic when he left. Or was it Callee who was getting under his skin? He'd never let a woman affect his decisions one way or another again. The one time he had it had been heartbreaking.

The last of the horses ran by. Callee strolled toward the clinic. He fell in beside her. As they approached the building, he saw a group milling around the entrance. "What's going on?"

"It's Wednesday. This weekend they race. They're here for their drug test."

"You didn't say they were going to be doing those here today." If he'd known, he could have been more prepared. To have this many jockeys in one place at the same time was a gold mine of information.

"I didn't know until last night. They don't always give me much notice. The stewards send a crew here to administer the test. Oh, man, I'm sorry." She grabbed his arm. "I should have said something. This is a perfect time for you to talk to most of the jockeys. You don't have to go out and hunt them down for interviews. They have all come to you."

"Yep. My thoughts exactly. I need to get busy. I'll get my notebook. At least I can weed out the ones I don't need to talk to in-depth. Then go find those I do for more of an interview."

She shook her head. "I should have thought."

Callee acted as if she were beating herself up over a simple mistake. "It's good. No worries."

"Sometimes I just don't think." She hung her head.

His brows drew together. Was she thinking about what happened to her boyfriend? That she hadn't stopped him? Couldn't have helped him more? That she'd done something wrong?

One of the jockeys spoke to Callee, and she stepped over to him.

Langston continued inside. The real work was about to begin. A shudder of excitement went through him. He liked the detective work that went into finding the element that made the difference in changing someone's life.

He returned to the front with his notebook and pen in hand. Callee stood at the desk talking to Carl.

"I told them that I'd appreciate it if they'd talk to you," Callee offered. "I'll be out to help after I sign off on the stewards being here and make sure they have everything thing they need. But I wouldn't wait on me. The jockeys won't hang around to answer questions."

He had this. "I think I can handle it."

She smiled. "If you say so."

A man and woman entered. One carried a case. "Mornin', Callee. Sorry we're late."

Callee greeted them by name. "No problem. They're lined up for you out there."

One of the stewards said, "Yep. We'll be ready in a minute, do this thing and be out of your way."

Langston went outside. Intimated for a moment by all the eyes directed toward him. He spoke in Spanish. "Is there anyone here who has hit his head?"

Broad smiles slowly appeared on everyone's faces.

He smiled as well. "Okay, of course you have. Let's go with have you ever been knocked out."

No one moved. Finally, a man looked Langston in the eye and nodded. Then another. He looked beyond Langston.

He turned to see Callee standing nearby. A slight grin on her lips.

To the first jockey he said, "I'd like to ask you some questions about your fall."

Callee came to stand beside him. Langston had to pull the information out of the jockey, starting with his name. He told Langston about the horse throwing him three years earlier.

"Did you have trouble standing, walking, or seeing? Did you see a doctor?" The list of questions went on. Langston continued to quickly ask them until it was that jockey's turn to get his test.

During a pause in the line, Langston turned to see Callee talking to a group of men. He moved on to the next jockey who indicated he'd had a fall. An hour passed quickly. Langston managed to interview five people. Far fewer than the number of jockeys who had shown up for their tests.

"Here you go." Callee handed him a paper. "I found some you can interview."

He looked at the list. There had to be ten names and phone numbers listed. All that time he'd thought she was just socializing. "Uh…thanks. I appreciate it."

"They will have to be tested again before you leave so you can catch those you missed or who have just arrived then."

Langston dipped his chin. "This gives me a good start. I appreciate your support. I realize now I would've had a much harder time getting them to talk if it hadn't been for you."

"Sometimes arrogance doesn't work." She gave him a thin smile.

"I've been accused of that. Something about just because I'm the smartest man in the room I shouldn't tell everyone that."

She started toward the clinic door. "I can see why that would get you in trouble."

"I have a feeling you know just how to keep me in check." Callee cut to the heart of matters. He didn't have to question where he stood.

"I'll take that as a compliment."

"I'm not sure it was meant that way." Langston wasn't sure he liked Callee understanding as well as she did. "How about joining me for dinner this evening."

She cut her eyes at him. "Uh, thanks, but I can't. Tonight's my poker game. I'm a designated dessert bringer. I thought you were coming along."

She wasn't sure if she could handle having him around after-hours, but she'd issued the invitation last week and she'd stand by it. There would be others there, which was much safer than being alone at dinner."

"Who's in on this game anyway?"

"Most of them you've already met." It wasn't like him to act unsure.

"What kind of stakes are we talking about?" He flipped through his notes.

She studied him a moment. Was he looking for a way out of the game. "Mostly penny ante and bragging rights."

"I believe I can handle that. Do I need to bring anything but my wallet?" His face brightened.

"Nope. You're a guest tonight. We start at seven, next door."

* * *

A few hours later Callee knew the moment Langston arrived. Despite having her back to the door, the atmosphere in the room changed. Something about Langston drew her to him. That had to stop. It was unhealthy. Langston moved from place to place like a traveling salesman, but for the first time in a long time a man fascinated her.

She stopped her conversation with Gina to go meet him. As always, he exuded self-assurance. "Hey there. Are you ready for this?"

"I know you said not to bring anything, but I brought some chips and dip anyway."

"Thanks. You can never go wrong with those. Give them here and I'll take care of them." She placed them on the table holding the pizza and drinks.

Gina sashayed up to them. "Hi, there, Langston. I'm so glad you joined us tonight."

"Hi, Gina. How's it going with the horses these days?"

"Great."

"Let's play cards," Rick bellowed. "I have an early morning tomorrow and need to beat you all so I can go to bed."

There was a lot of scoffing and good-natured ribbing in the room while chairs were being pulled to the table.

"Should I sit anywhere special?" Langston asked Callee.

"Everyone has their usual place, but the chair across from me is empty." She would at least enjoy the view tonight.

The group settled into their seats. She quickly introduced Langston. Rick picked up an unopened card deck and broke the seal. "Five card stud is the game tonight, ladies and gents."

She hissed along with a couple of the others. "Rick, you know I prefer Texas Hold 'em."

"When it's your week to call the game, we can play that. Tonight, we're playing straight up poker." Rick shuffled the cards.

Callee looked at Langston to find him watching her. He smiled.

Rick passed out the cards. When everyone had five apiece, he turned the deck upside down on the table.

Calle picked her cards up off the table. Fanning them out, she glanced over at Langston who did the same. Glad she hadn't sat next to him because this way she could see him. She watched his long fingers move the cards around.

Everyone anted up in the center of the table.

Since she sat to the side of Rick, she drew a card and discarded another.

The game came down to two of the eight players. One called the other, and the pot was taken.

When Langston's turn came to deal, he shuffled the cards like an expert and passed them out. His look met hers when he finished. She returned it, her skin heated.

With the first round of play over, Callee pushed back her chair. "I'm hungry. I'm going to sit this next round out."

Langston said, "I'll join you."

Rick murmured, "I'm not surprised."

Gina giggled.

She and Langston picked up a slice of pizza.

"You want a beer with that?" Langston asked, going to the cooler.

"No, thanks. I'll stick with a soft drink." She couldn't trust herself to drink after what happen to Joe.

He nodded and pulled out a can. "I thought after working here all day you'd want to stay away in the evenings."

Callee looked at the table of people laughing and joking with each other. "These are my people."

"Do you do anything else with your time off?"

He made it sound like he thought she might be dull. "I

visit my family. I also have a horse I spend time with on the weekends."

"Do you ever travel?"

"Not really. I'm mostly a homebody. I must be rather uninteresting to you since you've been all over the world." It sort of angered her she'd let him make her feel unsophisticated. Even if she might be.

"The last thing you are is uninteresting. Is there nowhere you would like to visit?" His disbelief rang in every word.

"Sure. A few." She thought of traveling but hadn't had the chance. Still, she didn't deserve that kind of fun either. She and Joe had made plans for vacations. Ones that he never had a chance to experience.

"Like where?"

Why was this so important to Langston?

"Hey, y'all gonna play or not?" Rick called.

"I'm playing." Callee threw the last of her pizza in the trash.

"I want to hear your answer later." Langston brought his beer with him.

"Okay." Her eyes narrowed on the can. She wouldn't let herself spend her poker evening counting others' drinks. Judging others' habits wasn't what she wanted to do.

An hour went by with her watching Langston and him watching her. He had the most amazing eyes. Such a beautiful blue.

"Hey, Callee, when can we have some of those brownies?" Gina asked from where she sat next to Langston.

"Help yourself." Callee tried to concentrate on her cards.

Gina looked at Langston and smiled. "Can't I get you one?"

"Sure."

Gina put her hand on Langston's shoulder and pushed herself to standing. "This is a tight table." She grinned at Callee.

Trying not to react, Callee watched Gina walk away. Her

friend was working to get a response out of her. She had no plans to give one.

Gina returned with a plate filled with brownies. She smiled sweetly at Langston. "I thought we could share."

Rick huffed.

Langston took one of the dark chocolate squares and bit into it. "Mmm. This is really good."

Callee smirked at him. "Don't act so surprised."

"Callee calls it her secret recipe," Gina said, giving her friend a wink.

Langston raised his hand with the brownie in it. "My compliments to the chef."

Heat washed through her.

"Are you two going to make moony eyes at each other or play cards?" Rick sounded disgusted.

Callee pretended to focus on her cards.

"Why wouldn't I want to look at a pretty woman?" Langston quipped.

A rumble of laughs circled the table.

She glanced at Langston. His grin reached his eyes.

"Just play cards," Rick grumbled.

They played another couple of hours before two people at the table pushed back their chairs. "Race day tomorrow. Time to go. The morning will come quick."

"Yeah, it's time I call it a day too." Callee stood and stretched. She started cleaning up; Gina joined her.

"You like him, don't you?" Gina said.

"Who?" Callee tried to sound as if she didn't know what her friend meant.

Gina bumped her shoulder against Callee's. "Come on. It's me you're talking to. Rick isn't the only one who saw all that eye contact."

"There was no eye contact. We're just friends." Callee couldn't start thinking like that.

"I know how friends look at each other. Langston didn't taken his eyes off you all evening. And they weren't 'just friends' looks." Gina threw an empty pizza box away.

Langston had been watching her, but she wasn't going to admit it. "You're nuts."

"I think you need to open your eyes, so to speak. Have a little fun, Callee, you deserve it. You shouldn't punish yourself all your life. Think about it. You never know what you might miss out on." Gina picked up her purse.

Rick called, "Night, Callee."

"Bye, Rick. Better luck next week."

Langston stepped up beside her. "What's the deal with that guy?"

"He's jealous," Gina offered.

Callee gasped. "He is not."

Gina shot back, "He's sweet on you and you know it." She grinned and headed toward the door. "I'd better catch my ride back with the boys."

"If you're ready, Callee, I'll walk you to your car," Langston said. "So you and Rick?"

"That's just Gina talking. You do know I can get to my car on my own without any trouble."

"I'm sure you can, but I want to finish our conversation." He dumped the empty chip bag and leftover dip in the garbage.

"Why does it matter whether I'd like to travel?"

He shrugged. "I don't know. I guess because I don't understand you not being more interested in seeing the world. My father and mother are like that. I never understood it. They're happy in the same old house, in the same old town, with the same old people."

"Is that a bad thing?"

He thought for a moment. "Not bad. More like a sad one."

"Are they unhappy people?" She headed for the door with the glass brownie dish in her hand.

"Well, no." He followed her.

"Everyone has a way they want to live. Apparently, that isn't yours." She pushed the door open.

"Never thought about it like that. I've always seen it as scared to do something different."

What must he think of her lifestyle? "Is that why you stay on the go so much? Because you don't want to be like your parents?"

"I love my parents. They were good ones, but yes, I guess that's it. I just wanted more." He took the dish then waited while she locked up.

A darkness entered his eyes before he answered. Was there more to his running than his parents' lifestyle example? Her words where sharper than she intended. "Or what you believe is more. How many close friends do you have? How often do you see your apartment? Sleep in your own bed?"

Langston raised a hand. "Okay, okay you've made your point."

"I'm sorry. That didn't sound very nice."

He walked beside her. "You don't mind saying what you're thinking, do you?"

"Not usually. But I shouldn't be mean."

Langston walked within touching distance but didn't even brush her arm. "I want to know what you think. Too often women try to tell me what I want to hear."

"I bet they do," she murmured.

"What do you mean by that?"

"Come on. You know you're an attractive man with a good job. You're a real catch in today's dating world." Callee put a little laugh in her voice.

"Thanks. But with those accolades you still don't want me." He made it sound as if he were teasing her, but there was a ring of truth in there too.

"I didn't say that." They had reached her car.

"Because we don't agree on how to live our lives." His statement was matter-of-fact.

She placed a hand on his arm. "Maybe not, but that doesn't mean we can't be friends."

A smile came to his face. "Agreed. That was fun tonight. Thanks for inviting me. It's been a long time since I just hung out with some people."

"You should get another chance before you have to leave." She was becoming too attached to Langston. He would be gone soon. Then what would she have? She took the dish from him and placed it inside her car.

Callee remembered he'd been drinking. She couldn't let him drive home. Would never forgive herself if something happened to him. Like Joe. She wouldn't live though another experience like that. "Hey, Langston. Leave your truck here. I'll drive you home."

He chuckled. "In that clown car? I am well over six feet."

She looked at him. "I guess you would have to ride with your feet over the windshield."

"I probably could, but it doesn't sound like much fun. But I can see that it's a perfect size for you." He gave her a sweeping look she suspected had nothing to do with fitting into her car.

"Then I'll drive your truck," she announced.

He huffed. "Callee, I got this."

"I'd prefer to drive you home. I'm going to insist." She put out her hand for the keys.

"Okay. If that'll make you happy, but it isn't necessary." He handed her his keys.

"It is to me." She started toward his truck. "You coming?"

He slapped his hat against his jean-covered leg. "I'm not sure whether to be disgusted or flattered you care."

"I'm just being a responsible adult." Unlike what she had been years ago.

Understanding washed over his face. "I get it. This has to do with what happen to your boyfriend."

"No. It has to do with not letting friends drive when they've drank too much." Her defense sounded harsher than it should.

"I think you are overreacting, but I'm too tired to argue with you. Can you handle a real vehicle after driving that toy car?"

She grinned. "You just buckle up and watch."

Langston did. And enjoyed the show. Callee had to work to get up into the driver's seat of the high truck. He didn't miss a movement of her twist and turns. This ride home might not be a bad idea after all.

He hurried around the truck and got in on the passenger side. The truck rumbled to life. When Callee grinned at him, he returned it.

The entire evening he had watched her. Rick had been right. Langston had been fixated on her mouth. One minute she was biting her bottom lip, then the next she was sucking on it. All he could think about was how much he wanted to kiss that tender sweet flesh Callee kept worrying.

She backed up, and headed out to the main road. "Which way?"

"I'm over in the Newport area," he said, watching her profile as they went down the road.

She glanced at him. "Wow, high cotton."

"I'm in a corporate apartment." One that looked just like the one before it, and the one before that.

"That sounds better than a hotel."

He nodded. "It is. I've done one of those too often."

"You don't ever get tired of not sleeping in your own bed?" She merged on to the freeway.

"Not so far." How much longer would it be before he did?

"I wouldn't like that. I like my bed."

He imagined her waiting on him in that bed. "Make a right here."

Callee took it a little fast and the tires squealed. She grinned at him. "I need to have some fun."

He leaned back toward the window so he could see her more clearly and draped an arm across the back of the seat. "Go for it."

She grinned. "It's been a long time since I've driven a truck. I forgot how superior it makes you feel."

His brows came together. "Was there a slam on me in there?"

"Depends." Her focus didn't leave the road.

"On what?"

"On your driving. I accuse men in big trucks who drive too fast and tailgate of using their trucks to compensate for their lack of size elsewhere."

"Ouch, that hurts." He dropped his voice into a low stern tone. "I can assure you I don't drive fast or tailgate, and as for the size of my truck…that isn't the case for me."

"I bet that's what they all say," she teased.

He just gave a wry smile, wanting more than anything the opportunity to prove her theory wrong to her.

"The gated community ahead is it. I'm in H building." He pointed toward his building. She drove to where he had instructed her. "Pull into parking spot twenty-three. That's mine."

Callee parked and turned off the engine. She shifted to look at him. Behind the wheel of the large truck, she seemed almost like a child.

"Do you mind if I drive your truck home and pick you up in the morning?"

He unbuckled. "I was wondering if you had thought through how you were going to get home."

"I hadn't but I have a plan now." She looked at his building.

"How about coming in for a cup of coffee? I think I can get one of those together."

Her lips formed a thin line. "Don't tell me you're one of those people who has an empty refrigerator."

"Tread carefully, Callee. You've already insulted my manhood. You don't want to do it twice."

She smiled slightly. "Okay. I'll behave."

"What time should I expect you in the morning?"

"Five."

"Okay. I'll be ready." He climbed out of the truck. Before she could leave the parking space, he walked to her door.

She lowered the window and leaned out. "You forget something?"

"I did. A thank you for caring enough to bring me home."

His mouth brushed hers, oh so softly. Callee's lips were as plush and warm as he had imagined. Could a kiss be any sweeter?

She leaned out the window, returning the touch. "You're welcome. Anytime."

He grinned. "See you in the morning, sweet Callee."

# CHAPTER FOUR

CALLEE WAITED NERVOUSLY the next morning in Langston's truck while he strolled down the sidewalk from his apartment. Unfortunately, she had to pick him up and was forced to sit in a confined space with him so soon after their kiss. Her lips were still tingling and her heart beat faster with just the thought of it.

She'd been kissed before but none had left her reeling at the memory. And it had been only a tiny touch of the lips, but she'd relived that moment all night long. With a mixture of eagerness and reluctance, she looked forward to seeing Langston. To being kissed again.

Callee shouldn't allow another kiss or herself to think like that. She didn't deserve that exhilaration. She hadn't earned that type of happiness.

"Good mornin'," Langston cheerfully said as she scooted over and he climbed behind the wheel of the truck.

"Hi."

He acted so unaffected by their kiss she thought about insulting his manhood to get a reaction. She resisted the urge.

They had a quiet drive to the track. She felt him watching her, but he'd always looked away by the time she could look at him. Langston pulled into his usual parking spot, and they climbed out.

"What's going on today? Something I need to know about?" Langston looked around. "I can't get over all this activity."

Callee stared at him. He was clueless. "It's a race day. We usually race Thursday through Sunday here.

"I assumed they only ran here on Derby Weekend."

"A lot of people think that. Churchill Downs hosts the Kentucky Derby on the first Saturday in May but there are races here almost year-round. The horses have to qualify, so there's races all over the country. Regular race days here are exciting, but they're nothing compared to Derby Weekend."

"I didn't know any of that. I should've done my homework." His tone implied he truly wished he had.

"I suspect the reason why has to do with your work. You don't take notice." She walked toward the track.

"Do you really think I'm that narrow-minded? That I don't appreciate anything but my work?" His voice held a note of disappointment.

She pursed her lips. "It's more like focused."

"You have to work hard to get ahead." He sounded determined.

"That's what's most important to you?" She watched him.

"I would like to make a difference in the world, yes."

Callee stuffed her hands in the front pockets of her jeans. "That's commendable. But the small things add up too."

He appeared to give that some thought.

Callee took her usual place beside the fence. She glanced back at Langston. He stepped up beside her but not too close. She stilled, too aware of his long body. Her look dropped to his lips. Did he remember their kiss like she did? If he kissed her again, what would she do?

She wouldn't let that happen. That needed to remain fixed in her mind.

The horses had just run by when she glanced over her shoulder at the clinic. "Rick!"

She hurried to the clinic where her friend waited in front of the door, his shoulder covered in blood. Inside she led him down the hall toward an exam room. "Come this way, Rick."

Langston had entered the clinic right behind her. He waited in the hallway.

Somehow, she had to get beyond the jitters she had at just the thought of Langston.

"What's going on with Rick?" Langston demanded when she came out into the hall.

"He has a nasty bite on his shoulder." She hurried to the supply closet.

Langston brows rose. "Bite?"

"Horse bite." She placed supplies in his hands when he offered.

"Really?"

"Yeah, it happens more often than you would think." She handed him another box.

"Gold Star is notorious for it." Rick stood in the doorway.

Langston studied the man a moment. "That looks painful." Rick said, "It is."

"Then I think you should sit down." Langston urged Rick back into the examination room by walking toward him.

Callee came in behind them. "Rick, when was the last time you had a tetanus shot?"

The man groaned. "I don't know but I hate needles."

"I'll have Carl check your file. If you need the shot, you'll have to have one ASAP." Callee put the supplies down and faced her patient. "Come on, tough guy. I need to get that shirt off you. Someone who works with animals as large as a horse all day shouldn't be afraid of a little old needle."

"What happened to a woman showing tender loving care,

instead of making fun of a man? If you'd go out with me, you'd find I'm nothing more than a marshmallow."

"Do you mind helping me with this?" She looked at Langston. He wore a frown and glared at Rick.

"Not at all." Langston stepped closer to examine the wound, going into doctor mode.

Callee spoke to Rick. "The skin has been broken so we'll clean it good and see if it needs any stitches. It's pretty mangled."

"This isn't the first time Gold Star has gotten me, but it's the worst." Rick winced as she worked his shirt off.

"I hate to say it, but we're going to need to cut the sleeve off. It's stuck to the wound." Langston picked up the scissors. "We should also do an X-ray of the shoulder socket. There may be damaged to it." Langston lifted Rick's arm, rotating it.

Callee watched Rick's face. He grimaced. She said to Rick, "Come on, big guy." She took his arm. "Let's take a walk down the hall."

Langston didn't follow. "I'll finish getting supplies together."

By the time they had returned, Langston had assembled the saline, suture kit and bandages.

"If you'll pour the saline, I'll hold the pan," Callee said to Langston.

Minutes later they had the site clean.

"Rick, we're going to do some picking around here. We need to make sure the site is absolutely clean. If not, we could just bandage up germs to fester."

Rick released a heavy sigh. "Okay."

Using tweezers, she moved the damaged skin to see beneath it.

Langston stepped closer using his penlight. "Look right there. Isn't that something?"

"Good catch." She smiled at Langston. He returned one that reached his eyes. "It looks like a piece of oat. Rick, we're going to need to do some more washing so don't move."

Langston opened another bottle of saline. She held the pan as he poured. Finished, she studied the site once more. Callee bumped her head against Langston's as she stood. She looked up to find a silly grin on his face. Her heart did a little flip-flop. She liked that one far more than the expression earlier.

"Rick, it looks clean this time. No stitches, but you'll have a nasty scar." She took a tube of ointment and applied it to each mark on Rick's arm.

Langston then applied the gauze bandage, moving around the arm and over the shoulder and back until it was secure.

"All right, you're all done, Rick." Callee stepped back and looked at him. "I'd like to see you back on Monday for a bandage change. No getting in the stall with Gold Star. This must stay clean."

Rick stood. "You know you could keep a closer check on me if you went out with me."

Callee gave him a nudge on his good arm. "Enough of that."

Langston stayed behind to clean up while Callee walked Rick out.

When she returned Langston said, "That guy was hitting on you."

A little thrill went through her. Langston had noticed. "Rick always talks like that. He doesn't mean anything by it."

"You might be surprised. You're an attractive, single woman. What makes you think he's not interested?"

Langston thought she was pretty. She savored that knowledge. "Maybe the fact he hasn't seriously asked me out."

"Would you go?" Langston watched her too closely for her comfort.

"Probably not."

Langston stepped out of the room with a hand full of unused supplies then returned. "Why isn't someone as amazing as you married, or at least have a boyfriend?"

"I could ask you the same thing. Why isn't there a Mrs. Watts or at least a girlfriend?"

"There was to be one. But she decided on another guy. My best friend, Mark."

Callee's eyes widened. She sucked in a breath.

What made him say that? He didn't talk about what happened between him and Emily. And Mark. "Also, because I'm never in one place long enough to have a relationship anymore. That's certainly not your problem. As far as I can tell, your entire world is this place."

What point was he trying to make? "Are you encouraging me to go out with Rick?"

His mouth formed a hard line. "I am not. If anything, I'd like you to go out with me."

Callee hadn't expected that declaration. She looked at him for a moment. "Okay, Wandering Man, I'll call your bluff. I have to attend the Derby Ball week after next."

He grinned. "Then it's a date, Stay Put Woman."

With only two weeks until the Derby, the backside was already busier than it had been when Langston arrived. Trucks pulling trailers filled with horses were arriving daily. The barns were occupied almost to capacity with horses. Trainers were working the horses on the track all day. Exercise boys were busy walking and bathing the horses while grooms and stable hands cleaned the stalls and equipment. All this leading up to Derby Week.

He stepped beside Callee at the track railing early that morning. Speaking in a quiet voice he said, "What's going on? You look nervous."

"Gina is riding this morning. She's super excited."

Langston had started to recognize Callee's moods. He'd never really bothered to do so with anyone else. She was becoming too familiar. He had no idea what he was doing, but just couldn't help himself. He found Callee irresistible. He'd like to call it an impulse to kiss her the other day, but that would be a lie. He'd been thinking about repeating it almost constantly.

He would be leaving in a few weeks, which meant he'd probably never see her again. That idea made him pause. Why did that bother him? He'd dated plenty of women short term and never had a problem. Why couldn't Callee fall into that same category?

In the past he had always been ready to leave when the time came, but the idea bothered him this time for some reason. He had become too attached to the place. Attached to Callee.

Langston grinned. He would have her all to himself at the Derby Ball in another week. It would be nice to get her away from the clinic. That was all she seemed to focus on. Who was he to talk? His work was his life.

Callee's phone rang. Her face blanched. "Don't move her. Call 911. I'm on the way." She looked at him in wide-eyed panic.

"What's wrong?"

"Gina's been thrown while still in the starting gate. She's unconscious." Callee looked as if she didn't know what to do first.

"My bag's in my truck. Let's go." He took her hand, directing her toward his truck.

They ran the short distance and climbed in. As soon as she had closed the door, he started the engine and backed up.

"Take the tunnel under the track. It'll bring us up close to the gates." Callee sat with her hands clutched in her lap.

Langston took a second to place his hand over hers. "She's going to be fine."

Callee stared straight ahead.

His chest tightened. He hoped he had told the truth.

"Turn into the tunnel here." Callee directed him to the left. "Make a right when you come out. Drive along the rail."

"Gotcha."

"Gina was the first person to accept me when I moved here. I needed her to do that. It hadn't been long after Joe's death." She talked more to herself than to him. "She got me to talk about what happened. Just listened and didn't judge. She helped me believe in myself again. She took time to introduce me around. Make me feel a part of this place. Became the friend that I needed. I can't lose her too." The last few words were close to being sobs.

Langston hated he couldn't put an arm around Callee and comfort her. Clearly any head injury she came across immediately conjured in her mind an outcome just like Joe's. Despite Gina's help, Callee had a way to go before completely accepting what happen to her boyfriend.

He drove into the daylight and turned.

She pushed to the edge of the seat, pointed out the window. "Right down there. On the track. Hurry."

Langston drove as fast as he dared. Moments later he pulled to a stop across from the rail where the large metal starting gate sat on the track. Behind it a group of people encircled Gina, who lay on the ground.

Callee was out of the truck before he pulled to a full stop. By the time he reached the rail, she was on the other side and running toward the group. Langston followed with his medical bag in hand.

"What happened?" Callee demanded as she went down on a knee to examine Gina.

"Gold Star was being temperamental this morning. We were having difficulty getting him into the gate. Gina said she could handle him, but the moment the gate opened he reared. Gina was wearing a helmet, but she hit her head so hard on the back gate the helmet split."

That horse again. First Rick and now Gina. When did a trainer say the horse was too dangerous?

Langston asked, "Has 911 been called?"

Someone in the crowd yelled, "Yes. An ambulance is on the way."

Langston dropped to his knees across from Callee. He made a mental note that one of the policies for all track personal should be training on emergency care of head injuries. "We need a blanket here."

He glanced at Callee. Her eyes swam with tears. As the most experienced with this type of injury and the expert here, he should take the lead. In a stern voice he said, "Callee, I have this. This is my area of expertise. Go hold Gina's feet up to prevent shock while someone gets something for them to rest on." He barked out an order to a nearby man.

She looked at him a second. Finally, her eyes focused. She then stood and did as he had told her.

Pulling the penlight out of his pocket, he lifted Gina's eyelids. They were fixed and dilated. He set the helmet to the side, and said to no one in particular, "This needs to go to the hospital with her."

Then Langston pulled a neck brace out of his go-bag. Gently he worked it around Gina's neck. Someone put a blanket within his eyesight, and he placed it over Gina's chest. With his fingertips he carefully examined the back of her head, looking for bumps or indentions.

A man hurried forward with a low step and handed it to Callee. She slipped it under Gina's feet, then returned to Langston's side. She said in a controlled voice, "I'll do vitals."

"I can use your help." Langston was proud of her strength. He moved his hands along Gina's shoulders and arms, looking for any breaks.

Callee checked her heart, blood pressure and other vitals.

"Don't move her legs," Langston snapped to a man near Gina. "She might have a spinal injury."

The sound of an ambulance pierced the air. Moments later it quietly entered the space between the stands and the track fence, then stopped at the open gate. The EMTs rolled a stretcher over the red clay surface.

"Callee, give the report." That would give her something to focus on instead of worrying about Gina. "I'll be going with Gina."

"Okay." Her eyes still looked watery.

He wanted to take her into his arms, but his focus needed to stay on Gina.

With a straight back, Callee went to meet the EMTs.

Quickly they had Gina on the stretcher and headed to the ambulance. Langston gathered his bag and hurried toward his truck. Callee was right beside him.

He climbed in. She stopped him from closing the door with a hand on his arm. "You'll keep me posted on what's going on. How she is."

He took her hand and squeezed it. "Of course, I will."

"I can't leave the clinic." Agony filled her eyes.

He nodded. "I'll let you know everything I know. You can get a ride back?"

"Don't worry about that. I'll get one of those guys to take me. Go take care of Gina."

"Consider it done." Langston gave her a reassuring smile. He intended to keep his promise.

Callee arrived at the hospital as soon after the clinic closed as she could. Langston had kept her posted on how Gina was progressing. He had been as good as his word. He'd texted almost hourly. By the time Langston had arrived at the hospital, Gina had regained consciousness.

He instructed Callee to text him when she got to the hospital, and he would meet her. She had never been so glad to see someone as she had when Langston stalked toward her in the hospital lobby. He opened his arms and she walked into them. Those strong arms pulled her close. She wrapped hers around his waist. She pressed her ear against his chest and listened to the steady reassuring beat of his heart.

Langston kissed the top of her head. "She should be fine. They're going to keep her in ICU for observation for tonight."

"I was so scared."

"I know, honey."

"I wasn't much help. What kind of medical person am I if I can't even help my best friend?"

"The best kind. You have a big heart. Now clear up that face. Gina is expecting you. Her parents should be here soon." He released her and took her hand. It felt right there. "This way."

"That was my first time handling a head injury since Joe."

"I thought it must be by your reaction. You do know that not every head injury ends in a bad result?"

"The ones I'm familiar with do. Joe was in a coma, he never regained consciousness. His parents had to make the decision to take him off life support."

"That is tough." He squeezed her shoulders.

"They blamed me. Wouldn't let me see him. Even to say goodbye."

"People don't always act nice when their emotions are involved."

"I needed training then. I need more now."

"I made a note that the track needs more training for everyone." He led her to the elevators. "Too many times people with no knowledge are the ones on the scene first. The right helmets are important too."

"Thank goodness Gina was wearing one."

The door opened and they stepped onto the elevator. "Yeah, but it wasn't one of ours and it split. That shouldn't have happened."

They arrived at ICU to learn they had taken Gina down for an MRI. Langston directed Callee to a small waiting room. The nurse had said she would come get them when Gina returned.

"I'm glad you were here when she woke. Someone she knew. Her family lives in California. She doesn't really have anybody but me around here. Thank you."

Langston took her hand again. She liked having hers in his. It felt strong and secure. As he spoke, he played with her fingers. "Hey, that wasn't a problem. Hopefully Gina will see us in a little bit."

"I'm glad they're keeping her in the hospital overnight. They need to make sure she's okay."

"I thought it was for the best."

Callee looked at him in surprise. "You're her doctor?"

He nodded. "I'm one of them."

"You have privileges here?" She continued to watch him.

"I told you I fill in some when I travel. I have temporary privileges in one hospital in every city I'm living in. It makes it easier if something like this happens. I also do research in hospitals. Or in this case have my own patient."

"That makes sense. I'm impressed."

He grinned. "I'm glad to hear it. I wasn't sure I could impress you. Just the other day you were mad at me."

"Yeah, but you shouldn't—"

Langston gave her a quick kiss. "I shouldn't have brought it up."

"Are you going to kiss me every time I mention it to shut me up?"

"I might. I'll just have to see."

She would be disappointed if he didn't.

A nurse walked toward them. "Dr. Watts, she's back. The test results you wanted are posted as well."

Langston rose and offered Callee a hand. She placed hers in his, and he helped her to her feet.

"I'm going to check those results. The nurse will show you to Gina. I'll meet you there."

Callee joined the nurse.

"Your friend has one of the best trauma doctors in the country. He's brilliant. We're honored to have him in our department even for a short time."

Callee had no idea. Langston had played down his credentials.

"Here you go. She's right here. I know she's anxious to see you." The nurse showed her to a corner room.

Callee entered the glass-enclosed room to find Gina sitting up in bed but looking pale. Callee hurried to the bed. "Hey, how are you doing? You're not looking too much worse for wear."

Gina offered a weak smile. "I don't feel too bad. Just a little unsteady when they let me walk. Which isn't often."

"Then I suggest you don't walk. Take advantage of the help around here." Callee touched Gina's hand. "You scared me."

"Sorry. I didn't intend to. I've had a lot of attention today. Especially Langston's. Did you know he was such a rock star in the medical world?"

"No, he never mentioned it." Why hadn't he?

"I'll admit he was pretty nice to wake up to. The problem is he only wants to talk about you." Gina smirked as she watched her friend closely.

Callee blushed. "I seriously doubt that."

"Is there something going on that I should know about?"

"Nothing other than we're going to the Derby Ball together." Callee looked at the floor not wanting to meet Gina's look.

She grinned. "I think there's more than that."

There were those few quick kisses. But so brief they couldn't have meant anything. "Believe what you like. Enough about me. How does your head feel?"

"Pretty good. I'm not sure why they're making me stay here overnight, but Langston insisted."

Callee wasn't surprised. "He has a habit of getting his way."

"Callee, he's a good guy."

"Yeah, he kind of proved his worth today." Callee appreciated Langston's steady hand when she'd been so shaken. She couldn't have survived the loss of another friend.

"Thanks," Langston's deep voice said from behind her. "I'm glad I came in when I did."

"Don't let your ego get carried away," Callee quipped.

He stepped up beside her. "Watch it. My feelings can be hurt."

Callee looked at him. "All you have to do is step out in the hall and the nurses are all agog."

"Excuse me, patient here." Gina pointed to herself.

"Yes, you are." Langston looked at her. "Do you still have a headache?"

"Yes." Gina touched her head.

"It should get better slowly. If it gets worse, I want you to let the nurse know immediately."

"I will." Gina looked at Callee. "Instead of hovering over me, why don't you two go out to dinner? I'll be right here when you get back."

"I think I need to stay here with you." Even injured Gina was busy matchmaking.

"My parents will be here soon. Anyway, they're going to kick you out soon. Go on. I'd like to take a nap."

Callee pointed a finger at her. "Okay, but I'm going to have the nurse call me if you don't do exactly what they say."

She and Langston walked down the hall toward the elevators. "Do you mind if we get takeout? I don't generally do that when I take a lady out, but I am hungry and not up to waiting at a restaurant."

"We don't have to go to dinner together. That's just Gina trying to matchmake."

"As far as I'm concerned, she's wasting her efforts." He pushed the button for the elevator.

A sadness washed over Callee. She'd been right. Those kisses had meant nothing.

Langston gaze met hers. "Because I'm already interested."

Callee swallowed the lump that had formed in her throat. She smiled.

"Now that's settled, how about some food." He named a local chain.

"Sure." She would agree to almost anything Langston said this evening. He'd cared for her best friend and said some sweet words to her.

"Then I'll drive. I'll take you home and pick you up in the

morning. We can check on Gina before going to the clinic. Do you think you can miss a breeze?"

"I can for Gina."

He led her out of the hospital to his truck.

As he drove out of the parking lot, Callee said, "I appreciate you being there for Gina today. Staying all day. I hate that I couldn't help more."

"I'm glad I could be here." He made a lane change.

"One of the nurses said you're a big deal in the head trauma world. Why didn't you tell me?"

"How was I supposed to say that without sounding insufferable? That certainly wouldn't have been the way to get your cooperation. Or earn your respect."

"Still, you could have said something." She studied his profile.

He glanced at her. "Would it have made a difference?"

"Probably not."

"I hate that Gina got hurt, but she sure did give me a nice case study. One from start to finish. As I mentioned, she wasn't wearing one of our helmets. I'm all about making one stronger, better fitting and light. But people have to wear them."

"At least she had something on. If she hadn't, she would have been sanctioned for it. Could even have lost her job. The racetrack promotes safety in every aspect. For both people and the horses."

Langston glanced at her. "You know I'll have to report all the details of the accident."

"I understand. Gina is going to be okay?"

He reached across the seat and took her hand. "I believe so. So far there haven't been any indications that there's any brain malfunctions. Other than that knot on the back of her head and being unconscious for a while, Gina doesn't appear to have any lingering issues. All the tests have come back normal."

"That's a relief." Callee rested her head against the back of the seat and closed her eyes. She took a moment to memorize the feel of her hand in Langston's. There might not be many more of those. Somewhere during the day she had decided she would take all she could get from him as long as he was around to give it.

# CHAPTER FIVE

CALLEE RELAXED AS Langston pulled into the drive-through of the agreed upon hamburger place. It made her happy being with him. He placed their order and drove around the building to pick it up. A female teen gave him a broad smile when he said thanks.

"Do all the females you meet fawn over you?"

"All of them but you." He placed their food between them on the seat. "With you I've had to work at it. But it makes it so much sweeter when you earn something you've had to worked for."

"I won't ever fawn over you." She refused to.

His gaze met hers. "That's not really what I want."

"What do you want?" He had her attention now.

He didn't immediately answer. "I want you to want me as much as I do you."

"Oh."

"Does that shock you?" He stopped for a red light and looked at her. "You should know as well as I do that there's been something between us since day one."

"I don't know about that." Liar.

"Then you're fooling yourself," he said. "Gina sees it. Rick too."

She sat straighter. "Rick?"

"Yeah, he did all that talking about going out with him

because he could see the electricity between us." The light changed and Langston drove on.

"I don't believe you." But she was afraid he told the truth.

"About the electricity or Rick?"

This conversation had turned uncomfortable. "Both."

"Closing your mind to it doesn't mean it isn't so. I know you're scared. That your last real relationship ended sadly, but that doesn't mean you shouldn't be happy ever again."

Thank goodness they were almost to her house. This frank discussion made her nervous. "You need to turn left at the next light. Then take the next right. I'm the third house on the right. There's a horse on the mailbox."

"Why am I not surprised."

"Don't you like horses?" She couldn't imagine life without her horse PG.

"It's not that I don't like them, it's that I don't have any experience with them." Langston pulled into her driveway.

"You don't ride?"

He turned off the truck. "No. Never had a reason to learn."

"Then you need to learn. It's like swimming, everyone needs to know how."

His chin lowered and his face turned unsure. "I don't know."

"Now who's scared?" Callee gathered the food and climbed out of the truck.

Langston met her with the drinks in hand. "It's not being scared. It's more about not having the opportunity."

"Maybe I can take you out to the farm and teach you. Between now and the Derby, I have to be at the clinic. But when things settle down we'll try." She unlocked the front door and entered.

Langston followed. "Maybe."

Callee turned on a lamp then walked into the kitchen.

"Come on back here to the kitchen table. I hate eating in my lap."

He had lagged behind her. Stepping into the kitchen, he stopped. "Wow, this isn't what I expected."

Callee looked at him from where she pulled food out of the bag at the table.

"It's so, uh…feminine." Disbelief hung in the air.

She grinned. "I am a girl."

"Yeah, I've noticed. But I've never seen you in anything but practical shirts, jeans and boots to walk in on floral pillows, cushy furniture and pastel colors. I'm just a little surprised. And this kitchen looks like a chef lives here."

She laughed. "I'm not sure if I should be hurt or pleased. And I like to cook."

Langston placed the drinks beside the food and took her hand, looking into her eyes. "I'd never hurt you intentionally. A man likes a woman to surprise him every once in a while."

A shot of warmth went thought her. Langston was charming her, and she liked it too much. She pulled her hand back. "I thought you were hungry. Let's eat."

He ran a finger over the tablecloth with such care she wished he'd been touching her. "On this pretty cloth?"

Callee mentally shook herself. "I'll get us some plates and something to drink." She hurried to the cabinet and returned, setting a plate in front of him and one at her usual spot. She returned to the table. "Have a seat."

Langston took the chair to the right of her. His knees hit hers as he pushed under the table. She moved her feet so that there was room for his long legs. They passed out the food and started eating.

Callee sat back. "Where are you going after you leave here?"

Langston finished his bite. "I'm head back to Houston to

compile my notes from the places I've been studying. I also have a head trauma conference to attend."

"Will you be presenting at the conference?"

"I will." He continued eating.

"Do you like to do that sort of thing?" She fingered the napkin in her lap.

He shrugged. "I like knowing that what I've learned and shared can save someone's life."

She caught his gaze. "You're a good guy, Langston Watts."

His smile reached his eyes. "Thank you. That's nice to hear."

They continued to eat. The silence wasn't uncomfortable, instead a companionable one. When they'd finished, they cleaned the table.

He looked toward the kitchen area. "You wouldn't happen to have some of those brownies around like the ones you made the other night?"

"No, but I have some chocolate chip cookies. Would you like some?"

He grinned, looking like an eager kid. "I sure would."

She went to the cookie jar. Would he make a comment about it looking like a bouquet? She opened the top and offered the cookies. He peered inside, smiled and looked at her. "May I have more than one?"

"Sure you can."

He grabbed a handful.

Callee put the container on the counter. "Let's go sit in the cushy chairs."

"You're not going to let me forget that are you?"

She grinned, shaking her head. "Probably not."

Langston took a bite of a cookie. "Mmm. These might be the best thing I've ever eaten."

She laughed. "Now you are exaggerating."

Langston eased into the love seat. "I am not. I could fall in love with you over these."

Callee knew he was kidding, but just the thought of enjoying time with a man who appreciated her and said so would be nice. She moved to sit in one of the chairs.

He patted the cushion. "Come sit beside me and I'll share my cookies with you."

She moved to the corner putting as much distance between them as possible. Not because she didn't trust him, but herself. "I only want one."

"Good. Because I didn't really want to share." He grinned as he protected the cookies against his chest.

"There are plenty."

He gave her a serious look. "Who taught you to cook?"

She gave him a direct look. "I bake."

"Bake then."

She took a bite of the cookie he offered her. "Mostly myself by trial and error."

"Not your mother?"

She shook her head. "She tried to keep me in the kitchen, but I liked the animals too much. I was always off with my father. There was no time or energy for anything more."

"You enjoyed that time."

"I loved it. I like what I do, but I also loved working with the animals." Even she heard the wistfulness in her voice.

"Or maybe it was more about the time you were spending with your father."

She never thought about it like that. "Maybe it was."

"Is there anything you don't do well? You're great with patients, horses and cooking."

"A lot. I don't speak Spanish like I wish I could."

He devoured another cookie. "I could teach you."

"What? A crash course before you go?"

He shrugged. "That and maybe some over the phone lessons. We'll start now." He picked up her hand and placed it on his head. "*El cabeza*. Say it after me."

"*El cabeza*. Head."

"*Pierna*." He took her hand and lay it on his thigh.

Her fingers itched to massage the hard muscles beneath the jean material. "Leg."

The air around her thickened. She forced out the word. "*Pierna*."

"Good. Now, *el corazón*." He placed her hand beneath his over his heart. "Heart."

She repeated the word while feeling the heavy beats of his heart.

"You just have to practice them now." He abruptly let go of her hand. "Tomorrow, I'll give you a few more to work on. By the time I leave you should have a nice vocabulary."

He watched her for a long moment before he stood. "I better go."

"Uh, okay." Why the sudden change in him? She walked him to the door. "Thanks for going above the call of duty for Gina today. It means a lot to me. It was really nice to know you were there for her when I couldn't be." On an impulse gave him a kiss on the cheek.

"No problem. But I think you can do better than that little peck on the cheek." He took a step closer. "Will you please kiss me, Callee? Like you mean it."

She met his deep look, one of hope and desire. She took a step forward, reached around his neck and went up on her toes. Her lips met his. The sugar and chocolate from the cookies mingled with the taste of Langston, which made the experience heady.

Seconds later Langston's arms wrapped her waist and pulled her against his hard body.

Callee eased the kiss. Langston made a grumble of complaint before she nipped at his bottom lip then caressed it with the tip of her tongue. She asked and gained entrance to his mouth. He was eagerly waiting. His arms tightened, taking over the kisses.

Callee was immediately transported to a sphere of sensation she'd never experienced. One she didn't just want to visit but bask in. Langston's desire was a hard bulge pressed against her.

He released her mouth and put the smallest amount of space between them. "As much as I'd enjoy taking this further, it has been a long emotional day for both of us. I think I better go before I can't. Walk me to the truck."

Callee's knees were weak, but she made it to the truck. There she stopped and looked at him. She had become far too attached to a man who would be gone in a few weeks. She poked the fire of heartache. Langston was a wandering soul. He wouldn't be happy in the same place. She'd never live like a vagabond. How could they ever have more than what they had right now? Still, the man made her feel sweet things she wanted for as long as she could have them.

"Until next time." He gave her a quick kiss on the lips.

"You're mighty sure of yourself."

He grinned. "I am."

The next morning, they stopped by the hospital early.

Langston held the door for her to exit the elevator behind someone in a wheelchair. "Do you mind hanging around while I interview Gina if she is up to it? I need to ask her some questions while what happened is fresh on her mind. She is an excellent test case."

"No, I don't mind. I'd like to hear what she says too."

"Good. I've got to check her chart beforehand." Langston started down the long, tiled hallway, his boots making a thumping sound. "Then I'll meet you in her room."

Langston stopped at the nurses' station while Callee continued on to Gina's room. She knocked on the door then pushed it open. Sticking her head in, she said, "Hey there.'

"Hey. I knew you would be here early." Gina sat up in the bed as the sun began to shine through the windows of the room.

"Langston and I wanted to check on you before we went to work."

"I'm fine. You can stop worrying about me now."

"Gina, you could have really been hurt." That Callee knew too well. Head injuries she didn't take lightly.

Gina smoothed the sheet across her lap. "Yes, but I wasn't. I'm good. And I'm ready to go back to work."

"That will be up to your doctor, who thinks you need to take a few days off." Langston had entered without them hearing him.

"And my doctor needs to make more noise when he's coming in my room." Gina glared at him.

Langston appeared unaffected as he grinned at her. "If I promise to be noisier, would you be willing to answer a few questions for my research?"

"Sure. What do you want to know?"

"I'll get to that. First I'd like to examine you." He adjusted the stethoscope hanging around his neck.

Callee sat on the edge of the plastic-covered chair on the other side of the room, well out of the way. She watched as Langston listened to Gina's heart and lungs.

He pulled out a penlight from his shirt's front pocket. "Gina, I want you to look just over my right shoulder. Focus on a spot. I'm going to check your eyes. Now, look up, down, left then right. Blink. Good. Is your vision blurry?"

All this time he spoke low and encouragingly to Gina. His bedside manner must be a large part of his success. Callee sat enthralled and she wasn't even his patient.

"No," Gina said.

"Good to hear. Now I would like to check your reflexes. Will you hang your feet off the side of the bed?"

Gina pushed away the covers and twisted until she was in the right position. Langston then went through the routine of tapping on her joints and watching her muscular reaction.

"Okay. Now I'd like to ask you a few questions." Langston let Gina settle under the covers once more. He took the other chair in the room, crossed one ankle over a knee and pulled out a small notepad from his pocket. "Now, tell me what you remember about the accident."

Gina went through how the horse wouldn't settle, that she knew he was raising his feet and the next thing she knew Langston was looking down at her at the hospital.

"When you woke, was your vision clear or blurry, or narrowed?"

"A little blurry."

Langston nodded. "I know I asked you to move your fingers, and you could, but did they hurt, hesitate, tingle?"

"None of that."

"Good. How about your head? Did it hurt then? Does it hurt now?"

"I have a little bit of a headache. Not bad, just an odd feeling that it's not right."

Langston jotted down a note. "I'd like to examine your head as well. All I'll do is run my fingers over your scalp. You tell me if any spot hurts while I check for bumps or indentions."

Over the next few minutes he slowly felt Gina's head. Callee sat amazed at how gentle and thorough he was.

At Gina's wince he looked at her face. "How bad does it hurt?"

"Not too bad."

"I'm going to order an MRI before you go home." He stepped back and looked at her. "Your parents are here?"

Gina pursed her lips obviously not pleased with the turn of events. "Yes. They got in late last night."

"Good. I want someone with you for a few days or you stay in here."

Callee had no doubt from the firmness in his tone Langston wouldn't change his mind.

Fifteen minutes later she and Langston were on their way to Churchill Downs.

"What will you do with all that information you got from Gina?"

"I'll compare it to other people's I've interviewed. Right now, I'm particularly interested in the area of the head that the subjects have hit."

"Are you seeing signs of it being the same place?"

Langston grinned. "You are quick. Yes. And it would make sense to make helmets thicker and stronger there. In Gina's case even angling it farther down the neck. I will input my findings and suggestions then the engineers will go to work. It's a slow process but a rewarding one."

"So you've asked all those other people you interviewed the same questions."

"Mostly. Some are more in-depth because of what happened than others. Being kicked in the head by a horse is hard to prepare against. It's so unpredictable."

"What you are doing is more impressive than I first gave you credit for."

He chuckled. "I am glad I've gone up in your estimation."

Callee wouldn't tell him how much. She'd come to really like Langston. Too much.

"I appreciate you taking such good care of Gina."

He found her hand and squeezed it. "That's what I do."

Langston came to stand beside Callee at the rail every morning of the next week. It had become a ritual for him to bring her a coffee and meet her at the track. An occurrence he looked forward to. Oddly he'd never had a habit he shared with anyone, much less a woman.

Since their too hot kiss at her house, he'd kept his distance unless they were in public. He didn't trust himself alone with Callee. The more he learned about her, the more his desire for her had grown. Yet he shouldn't lead her to believe he might stay around. That wasn't in his DNA. It had been once, but he'd moved beyond that. Nothing about him was forever.

"Good mornin'." He handed her the cup of steaming brew.

"Hey." She smiled. "It's Derby Week. It's all hands on deck."

"That probably puts an end to the plans I had for this week."

"How's that?"

"I was going to the barns to see if I could interview some of the jockeys."

Callee's lips thinned. She shook her head. "Yeah, that probably is dead in the water. They will be too busy to talk."

"I have some other work I need to do anyway. Are you usually busy on these days?"

"It just depends."

A stable worker came running toward them. "Hey, Callee, come right now. Henry got his hand stuck in a trailer."

"Stuck in a trailer?" Langston looked from the young man to Callee.

"No telling what that means." Callee said. "Let me grab my bag. I'm on my way. Which barn?"

"Turner," the young man responded.

"Got it."

Langston grabbed his bag from the truck and climbed in the golf cart. Callee got in beside him. "You don't mind if I go too?"

"No, I can probably use your help."

Langston liked the fact Callee valued having him around. At first he wasn't sure she felt that way.

"Turner barn. Down on the right?"

"Yes. A couple of streets over and to the left. Barn seven."

Langston took off. Soon he pulled up to a group of people standing around a large horse trailer.

The trailer rattled with the stomping of horse's hooves against metal.

"So what's the problem?" Callee asked.

Langston looked around for someone hurt.

A man pointed. "Henry's inside."

"Is he hurt?" Langston asked in rapid Spanish.

The man nodded.

"We need to get this horse out so we can get to him," Callee announced. "Let's get the horse settled down and out of here."

"He won't settle," one of the men close by said.

"Then get his trainer here with a restraint." Callee walked to the side of the trailer.

Langston joined her. She looked through the metal bars. Langston did as well. He could see a man standing in an awkward position.

"Henry, are you hurting?"

There was a groan and the man moved slightly.

"Are you bleeding?" Langston asked.

"*Sí.*"

"Where?" Callee called.

"Arm. Broken maybe." The man forced the words out.

"Okay." She stepped back from the trailer. "It looks like he's hung on the latch that divides the trailer for two horses and is in the section with the horse."

Agitated, the horse shook the trailer again as it shifted positions.

"We need to get this temperamental horse out of here." She went to the side door and opened it, looking in at the wild-eyed animal.

Langston grabbed her arm. "What're you doing? Let these guys see about the horse. We don't need you getting hurt."

She glared over her shoulder. "I got this."

The horse jerked against the lead tied to the other side of the trailer.

Langston couldn't stand by and watch Callee get hurt. "I'm not letting you go in there."

Callee faced him, fury on her face. "I can handle it."

"Let one of these guys go in there." He nodded toward the men standing around.

"No. They can't touch a horse they don't work with."

Langston pointed. "What about the guy in there?"

"He works for the trainer."

Langston still didn't feel good about this. "Are you sure you know what you're doing?"

"I'm positive. You be prepared to go in and get the guy out while I see about the horse."

Langston shook his head. "I don't like it—"

Callee didn't wait for him to finish. "Stand back where the horse can't see you."

He shifted back two steps, but he refused to give another inch. If she needed him, he'd know it. He would be able to see her.

"Hey, boy." Callee's voice had dropped to a soft sultry level.

The sound rippled over Langston's skin. Did she use the

same tone when making love? He'd like to be on the receiving end of that attention. Apparently, the horse did as well. He looked at her. She reached out her hand.

"Easy, boy. I'm not here to hurt you."

Langston's chest tightened. He had to stand there and watch while someone he cared about walked into danger. He didn't normally stay around long enough for that to happen. Somehow Callee had gotten under her skin quickly.

"It's okay, boy." She continued to beseech the animal. Callee held the large horse's attention. She had Langston's as well. Slowly she walked to the horse with her hand outstretched. The animal lowered his head and jerked it up almost hitting Callee. In a reflex action, Langston stepped forward.

Callee spoke to him in a low tight voice that was a little more than a hiss through her teeth. "Don't move."

Langston had no doubt she spoke to him. He did as instructed, watching with his heart pounding. The hulking animal could run over Callee.

She continued to speak evenly to the horse. "All I want to do is help you."

The wildness ebbed from the horse's eyes. He lowered his head.

"Okay, boy, I'm going to reach out and touch you."

Langston questioned if she said that more for his sake than the horse's.

Callee touched the end of the horse's nose with the back of her hand. It shook its head, snorting. She waited patiently. After the horse settled she tried again. This time she slipped her hand under the halter. The horse jerked his head almost pulling Callee's feet off the floor, but she hung on.

Langston shifted.

"Not one step or sound."

This time Langston knew for a fact she spoke to him.

"Okay, boy. Let's go out and get some sun." She very carefully untied his lead and gave him a nudge forward. The horse resisted at first before it walked with her.

As she passed Langston, she said softly, "See about Henry."

Breathing a sigh of relief that Callee would be safe enough now that the horse was outside, he hurried into the trailer.

The man remained conscious. He still stood in a corner of the trailer with his arm in an awkward angle and above his head. As Langston approached, he could see his hand was caught in the latch between two sections of the trailer. "How did you manage to get into this situation?"

"The gate latch was stuck. I climbed up to kick it free. Then fell and my arm got hung."

"We'll have you out soon." Langston's attention went to the blood dripping on the wooden slat floor. He had to stop that flow right away.

"Henry, I'm Langston. A doctor. I need to see where this blood is coming from. It may hurt but I'll be as gentle as I can."

"Okay," he groaned.

Callee stepped into the trailer. "What have we got here?"

"Possible broken arm, bleeding from the biceps area, but not life threatening. What I need the most is a couple of guys to help me lift him up."

"I'll get them."

Two minutes later Callee, followed by two men, entered the trailer.

"I need one of y'all on the right side of me and the other on the left. Callee, I want you to call out what's happening with the arm and maneuver it out from between the bars as we lower him. On three everyone. One, two, three."

Langston grunted along with the other men as they lifted the awkwardly positioned Henry.

Callee called, "Hold. Let me work the arm out."

Langston watched with one eye as Callee carefully eased Henry's arm to freedom. "Okay, lower him." A moment went by. Callee said to Henry, "You're almost down."

"Put him on the floor," Langston told the two men.

Callee immediately placed her hand over where the blood flowed from Henry's upper arm. "I need my bag."

Langston pushed it to her then grabbed his own, going to his knees across from Callee.

"Let's get the bleeding under control then we can take him to the clinic." With one hand Callee dug into her bag for a pack of four-by-four gauze squares.

"Give it to me." Langston took the package and opened it, handing it back to her.

She applied the square to Henry's arm and pressed. "There's a roll of gauze in my bag."

"Here you go." Langston handed her a roll he'd pulled out of his bag.

Callee nodded. Evidently, she wasn't the only one who kept their bag prepared. "Okay, Henry, we're going to head up to the clinic and get you cleaned up." Callee stuffed things back into her bag. "We're going to help you outside. Do you think you can stand?"

"*Sí.*"

"Good. Here we go." With Langston's help Callee got Henry to his feet. They walked with him between them out of the trailer. Someone had pulled the golf cart close.

She directed them. "Langston, if you'd drive, Henry and I'll sit in the back."

Langston took her bag and set it beside his in the front seat. Callee settled Henry and took her seat.

"Ready?" Langston asked.

"Go slowly."

"Got it." Langston took off with as small a jerk as possible, but Henry still moaned.

Callee told him, "We'll be at the clinic soon. I can give you something for the pain there."

Not soon enough for Henry, she was sure, Langston stopped in front of the clinic. Between the two of them they got him inside and settled in an exam room.

"You want me to get supplies or see about getting his shirt off?" Langston asked.

"Shirt." Callee stepped out in the hall for a moment to calm her temper. She had kept it contained while they worked with Henry, but it had started to bubble over. Langston had over-stepped while she tried to get the horse out of the trailer.

Taking a deep breath, she went to the supply closet. When they were alone, she and Langston would have a few words. Her more than him. She returned to the examination room with her hands full.

Langston looked at her. His eyes widened a fraction in question. "You okay?"

"Yes. We'll talk about it later," she snapped.

His brows rose, but he returned his attention to their patient.

Despite the tension between them, they worked together to clean Henry's wound, which was nothing more than a large flesh wound. Then their focus went to his arm. After X-rays it was agreed that it wasn't broken just twisted badly. They placed Henry's arm in a sling.

"Henry, you're going to be on light duty for a few days. I want to see you back here in a week just for a check." Callee wrote him a prescription. "Take this for any pain."

"Thanks for helping me." He looked at her and then Langston. "I hear you're asking questions about people who have been hit in the head. I wasn't going to volunteer before today, but you're okay. I've been knocked out. I'll talk to you."

Langston put out his hand. "Thanks, Henry. I appreciate that. I'll come find you one day soon. Right now, you need to rest."

"I'll tell the others too." Henry smiled.

Langston returned it. "That would be a great help. Thanks."

"Carl's going to give you a ride back to the dorm." Callee led him out of the room toward the front door. It was time for her and Langston to talk. Her jaw tightened.

She returned to where Langston was straightening the room.

He faced her when she entered the room. "Is something bothering you?"

Callee glared at him. "Yes, it is."

"Having to do with me?" He wore an innocent look.

That fueled her anger. Langston had no idea what he had done. "Don't you ever try to stop me from doing my job again."

"What? When did I do that?" He looked perplexed.

"While I was trying to get to Henry."

"You mean when you were handling that enraged breast?"

"Yes. I knew what I was doing." She stomped to within arm's length of Langston. "I'm the lead person here. In a couple of weeks you'll be gone."

He bent to her eye level. "If you're ever in harm's way, I'll always say something or stop you."

She leaned toward him with her hands on her hips. "You have no say over me."

"I may not, but I can't and won't stand by while you do something dangerous. I didn't need two patients to care for."

"I knew what I was doing." She moved closer.

"I didn't care. I needed to know you'd be safe." His nose almost touched hers.

Callee glared. "Don't ever question or stop me when I'm trying to get to a patient ever again."

"Getting that horse out of the trailer wasn't your job. And the horse was upset. You could've been hurt."

"It wasn't your place—"

Her words were cut off by Langston's mouth. His arms encircled her, crushing her to him from head to foot. She went up on her toes as he lifted her. Her hands held on to his shoulders while his tongue traced the seam of her mouth. On their own her lips opened to the sweet invader. Heat washed through her, pooling at her center. Her arms went around his neck and tightened as she took all he would offer.

She dipped her tongue inside his mouth. Langston groaned. One of his large hands traveled along her spine to cup her right butt cheek, bringing her securely in contact with his long thick manhood bulging between them.

In slow motion he lowered her. She had no choice but be aware of his desire.

He whispered in her ear. "Never doubt that when I fear for your well-being, I'll step in."

"But—"

He gave her a quick kiss. "There'll be no buts. It'll always be a fact. Now, do you have more excitement planned for today? Because I'd like to be prepared. Otherwise, I'm going out to see if I can conduct some interviews."

Callee rocked on her heels when he let her go and walked out the door.

Langston tugged at his collar behind the black bow tie of his tuxedo. He now remembered why it had been so long since he'd been to a formal affair. Oddly he hadn't flinched before agreeing to go with Callee.

After the scare she had put into him dealing with the horse, their argument and then that kiss that had him staying up at night, he'd been a mess for the last few days. His anticipation of this evening had only grown. At least tonight he would have Callee to himself with the safety net of them being among people. He could hold her in his arms while they danced. Maybe steal a kiss.

He walked toward Callee's front door. She had wanted to meet him at the ball, fearing she might be late because of last minute patients at the clinic. He'd insisted on picking her up. He had given her an irritated look then stated, "No, we agreed this was a date. I pick my dates up. They don't meet me places. Are you trying to get out of going with me?"

"I'm not," she had assured him. "I was just trying to make it easier on you."

"You don't need to worry about me."

He rang the doorbell and waited. Was she nervous about seeing him?

Langston's finger lay on the doorbell button to ring it again when Callee opened the door. His heart did a flip-flop and burst into a fast gallop at the sight of her. She was gorgeous. She'd been pretty before but with her hair pulled back in a wild little bun, her eyes made up to accent their size and the lines of her dress hugging her curves she was breathtaking.

In slow motion she studied him from the top of his head to the tips of his shiny black shoes pinching his feet. A slow smile came to her lips. "No boots."

Heat warmed him at her appraisal. He grinned. "I left my dress boots in Texas."

Their gazes met.

He said, "You have to be the most gorgeous thing I've ever seen."

"Thank you. You look quite dashing yourself."

"There's no way you won't be the most beautiful woman at the ball. I'll be proud to have you on my arm."

She turned away to gather her purse. "You keep that kind of talk up, and I might start to believe you."

As she joined him, he said, "You should because it's true. Come, your chariot awaits." He offered her his arm and escorted her along the sidewalk.

The driver hopped out of the car, came around and opened the back passenger door for them.

"You got a driver for tonight," Callee said in awe.

"I thought I'd enjoy sitting in the back with you. I didn't think my truck was what we needed to roll up in."

"You didn't have to do this, but I have to admit it's wonderful." Pleasure filled her voice.

Langston helped her into the car then climbed in beside her. She giggled when he had to work his long legs into the space.

"Are you laughing at me?"

"No, never." But her eyes twinkled with mischief.

He grinned. At least she was releasing some of her nervous energy.

Soon they were rolling away from the curb and toward downtown Louisville.

"By the way. I like your hair. I hadn't expected that hairdo."

Callee touched her bun. "Yeah, it was Gina's idea. She said you've been checking on her every day."

"I want to make sure she's recovering well."

"And get a few study notes." She watched him.

"That too but mostly making sure she doesn't have any residual problems."

Callee shifted into the seat, getting comfortable. "She seems like her old self, but she still hasn't returned to work."

"I'm glad to know you haven't noticed anything amiss. The ones closest usually see it first."

"Some people don't." Sadness washed over her face. The smile that had been there faded.

Langston wished he hadn't said anything. He was confident her thoughts had gone straight to her old boyfriend. He took her hand. "Nothing but fun thoughts tonight. You're on a date with me, and I want you to have a good time. Tell me about the ball."

"All the bigwigs of Churchill Downs will be there, including my boss. But you know him. Also many of the horse owners and some of the famous trainers attend. This is the first time I've ever been. I'm not sure why I was invited."

"Don't sell yourself short. You're an important part of keeping things going on the backside."

"Maybe so but these people are out of my league."

It was more like she was out of theirs. Callee had built a pig puddle of guilt around her she couldn't see past to the amazing person beyond. "Looking like you do, they're nowhere near your league."

"You are too kind."

"I tell the truth." He took her hand and squeezed it then released it.

The closer they came to downtown Louisville the more Callee clasped and unclasped her hands. She was afraid. Langston had been convinced she feared nothing. "Callee, settle down. There's no reason to be so nervous."

She looked at him with tight lips. "I bet you do this sort of thing all the time."

More often than he liked but not regularly. "I don't."

"Yeah, but I bet when you do go it's by choice, rather than feeling you have to." She looked out the window as if judging whether to hop out at the next light or not.

"That part might be true."

"These are your kind of people not mine. I don't even know what they're talking about half the time. I'm just a physician assistant who happens to work at the clinic."

"You're lovely and intelligent, and you have nothing to worry about. They're just people like you and me."

She studied him a moment. "Nobody's like you." She ran her hand down his lapel. "You are very handsome."

"Thank you. I like hearing that from you."

Their driver pulled into the line behind the other cars waiting to unload in front of the modern large hotel in downtown Louisville. Their turn came. Langston slipped out of the car and offered Callee his hand. She didn't hesitate to place hers in his. He helped her out.

He shouldn't be so taken by a woman. Or even care about her feelings to the point he would protect her. Yet Callee had him doing just that against his better judgment. "Remember tonight we're just a couple on a date. We'll just pretend no one else is around and enjoy each other."

She smiled. One that reached her eyes. "That I can do."

# CHAPTER SIX

CALLEE HADN'T BEEN able to help being jittery with excitement during the past week. She had tried to pretend it was everything to do with Derby Week and nothing to do with going to the ball with Langston. But she knew better. She was looking forward to spending time with him. If he hadn't agreed to go with her she probably would have found an excuse not to attend. Balls weren't her type of thing. Give her a barn, a horse and she was happy.

Derby Week was always an exhilarating time, but this year it was over the top. As the time for the ball drew near, she became thankful for the steady stream of patients to keep her mind settled. If left with too much time to think, she would turn into a bundle of nerves.

She couldn't remember the last time she had been so concerned about her looks. Working around the backside, what she wore mattered little as long as it was functional. Regardless, the last thing she wanted was to embarrass herself or Langston.

One evening she'd managed to find a dress. Fortunately, she'd found one quickly. A dusky rose color with simple lines and a flowing skirt. It was an extravagant expense on her income, but the look on Langston's face had made it worth it.

She had been too busy to take time off to have her hair done. So Gina had insisted that Callee go to her house and let her do it. Callee had relented, even agreeing to something modern yet traditional. Later she had spent extra time on her makeup, something she rarely wore.

She was glad she had after seeing Langston's expression. He looked so handsome in his black tux with the white pleats across his chest and the black skinny bow tie. The shiny black strip running along his slacks side seam make his legs appear longer. Everything about Langston made her heart race. Callee thought she might melt right there in front of him when she had seen him.

When he'd complimented her, she'd felt it all the way to her toes. The man had a way of making her feel beautiful. She couldn't help but appreciate the possessiveness that filled his voice. It had been so long since someone claimed her as theirs. She liked the sound of it. She would have the best-looking person in the room as her date.

Tonight, she would forget the past and enjoy.

Langston ushered her into the revolving door of the hotel. Stepping out, she put her hands under her wrap and ran them over the silky material of her dress.

He took her hand and whispered close to her ear, "You look beautiful. Smile. No scowling tonight."

"I'm not scowling."

"Sometimes you do." He grinned.

"Only when you're making me really mad."

They continued down the hall. "Tonight the idea is for you to be really happy. Let's go enjoy. I'm looking forward to dancing with you."

She hesitated. Dance. "I don't dance."

"I hope you will with me. Don't worry, I'll take care of you." That was the second time he had said that. Something about his tone made her believe he would be there for her as he promised. She'd never considered herself the type of person who needed someone to take care of her, yet she liked the idea of being under Langston's watchful eyes.

They strolled down the long corridor with other couples. Callee looked at each man, but none of them measured up to Langston's strong presence. She shook herself mentally. Langston had her head tangled up with emotions.

She could hear the sounds of a party not far away. After showing their invitation, they entered the ballroom to the soft sound of the band and the chattering of people. A number of them were in groups.

Langston took her elbow. "Let's see if we can find a place to sit."

They circled around the room until they found available seats at a table where only one other couple sat. Langston made the introductions.

A waiter came around to ask if they would like to have a drink. He carried highball glasses with a finger of dark liquid in them. There were also silver tumblers with a mint sprig sticking out of the top. Langston accepted bourbon in the highball glass.

He looked at her. "Don't worry. I won't overindulge."

Callee's chest tightened. "I know you think I'm being silly."

"No, I think you had a traumatic experience that you're having a difficult time getting beyond. We all can say that on some level."

"Thanks. Did you know that a mint julep is the traditional drink of the Kentucky Derby?"

"I'm not surprised since this state is the bourbon capital of the world."

She relaxed. "Maybe I could have one mint julep. It has been a long time."

"You don't have to do that to make me happy."

"I trust you to be responsible. Therefore, I should trust myself as well. I know I shouldn't be such a prude about it. But it scares me." She suddenly wanted to let go of the past. To accept she couldn't have done any more for Joe than she had. If only she could believe that.

"You don't owe me any explanations. I like you just the way you are."

Her heart opened to him. "Thank you for that."

Langston took a swallow of his drink. "I'm not in this area often, so it's hard for me to pass up fine bourbon especially since so much of it is made here."

The waiter made another trip around. This time Callee accepted a mint julep.

Langston raised his glass and she tapped hers against his.

She took a sip. "I forgot that it was more lemonade with a lot of crushed ice than bourbon."

"Good?" Langston watched her.

She smiled. "Good."

"Tell me what will happen tomorrow." He leaned in closer.

Would he kiss her? When he didn't she said, "Tomorrow is the Kentucky Oaks race. It's for the three-year-old fillies. There will be thirteen races. Many of the women spectators, and the men too, wear pink to bring awareness to breast cancer and ovarian cancer. Everyone comes as well-dressed for tomorrow's races as they will be on Saturday. The Oaks race is the eleventh one of the day. A blanket of pink lilies is presented to the winner."

"Will we get to see any of this?" He took a sip of his drink.

"Nope. All that happens on the other side of the track at the grandstands."

"Really? None of it?"

"I usually catch some of the races on the monitor in the clinic waiting room. What we do see is some of the horses headed for their race. Saturday is Derby Day, and there are fourteen races. For the people attending, it's all about the three-year-old males running. The winning horse receives a blanket of red roses. The men and the women are well-dressed. Many of the women wear the most amazing hats. People watching is a real thing."

"Except you are stuck in the clinic." He pursed his lips.

She shrugged. "It's my job."

"I know but wouldn't it be nice to attend one race?"

"It would." She had another sip of her drink. "I had forgotten how good one of these is."

"Watching the races on TV doesn't sound like it's the same as being there."

"It isn't, but you can still feel the excitement in the backside. The horses are coming and going for their run in the greatest two minutes in sports. They are calmly walking and fifteen minutes later they running as if for their life. They barrel around the track with the jockey urging them on. How can you not find a thrill in that?"

"I can see your point." Langston smiled. "It does sound exciting."

"Horse racing is an extremely expensive sport. It requires a major investment. People to train the horse, care for it, vet bills, barn costs and it goes on and on. All just for that moment their horse crosses the finish line first. To win the Triple Crown is almost impossible."

He raised his brows. "Triple Crown?"

"Are you sure you don't know all this?"

"Maybe I do, maybe I don't. Either way I enjoy listening to you. You get very animated about the subject."

She studied his handsome features and recognized the twinkle in his eyes. "Are you making fun of me?"

"I would never do that." He grinned. One that gave her a bird in flight feeling in her middle. "So what's the Triple Crown?"

"It's when the horse wins the Kentucky Derby, Preakness Stakes and the Belmont Stakes. All in the same year. If they do that, their racing career is over."

Concern filled his voice. "At three years old?"

"Yep." She grinned. "They get a new job. They put them out to stud."

He leaned close, giving her a wolfish grin. "Now that's a career I could get behind."

Her center tingled. She bet he would be good at it too. "I thought you might."

"Did you go to the Derby when you were growing up?"

"No, that was too adult an event. My parents felt like the liquor was too free-flowing and people sometimes behaved badly. Plus it is expensive to get tickets. We did watch it on TV like some people watch the Super Bowl."

The band began playing again. Langston stood and offered his hand. "Would you care to dance with me?"

Callee hesitated a moment. She had little experience with dancing, but she couldn't pass up a chance on being in Langston's arms. Taking his hand she said, "I will, but it needs to be slow and easy and not too many fancy steps."

"I promise to take care of you."

She didn't doubt he meant it. Langston was the type of man who took care of those he cared about.

He held her hand as they walked to the dance floor. There he wrapped an arm around her, bringing her close. He was so much taller than Callee, but her high heels helped. Her head almost reached his shoulder. They slowly moved around the floor along with the other dancers. It was wonderful, dazzling and disturbing at the same time. She enjoyed being in Langston's arms too much.

She pressed her cheek against his chest. He tightened his arms. They swayed to the music. She relaxed listening to the steady reassuring beat of Langston's heart. Was it wrong to wish it could last forever?

Langston had not prepared to relish holding Callee as much as he did. It had been too long since he'd last had her in his arms. It felt so right having her next to him. He enjoyed it more than he should have. Despite their height difference they fit. He led her around the dance floor with little effort, pressing her close.

Callee was a strong, vibrant woman who knew her own mind, yet she carried insecurities. Her past dictated her future. The accident with her college boyfriend had frozen her in time. An irrational guilt lay heavy on her. Just seeing him pick up a drink sent her spinning into what could happen.

Her small hand drifted down the breast of his jacket, pushing all other thoughts but of touching her from his mind. She smiled and his middle constricted.

He kissed the top of her head. "You take my breath away."

Their dancing turned from less about moving around the floor to more about touching each other. He could get used to this. Too easily. He had his next job to think about. A long-distance relationship rarely worked out. He knew from experience. It wouldn't be fair for Callee to always be waiting on him to return. If she did. Emily hadn't. Or had he been unrealistic to think she would? But Callee was different. Stronger, more confident in her abilities. Still, she deserved better than to spend her days waiting on him. Could he leave her alone? She pulled at him just as gravity pulled at the earth. To break away might send him spinning into nothingness. The music ended. They looked at the band.

A man stepped to the microphone and said, "Dinner is served." Maybe it was just as well they had to take a break. He might have touched her more freely, and she wouldn't want her bosses to notice.

They lined up with the others at the buffet. Callee faced the table. "This is unreal. Look at that ice sculpture of horses racing. And all this food. I'm out of my league."

He leaned close and said for her only, "You are far beyond everyone here."

Her soft smile grabbed his heart and squeezed. They filled their plates, returning to their table. By this time two more couples had joined them. During their meal, they had a lively discussion about past Derby Weekends and the number of times they had experienced it. They all poked fun at him because he'd never attended.

Callee squeezed his knee then stepped in to defend him. "I've lived within two hours of here all my life and I've never sat in the grandstands before."

The eyes of the other couples widened in disbelief. "Really?"

Langston sat straighter having her support. That was something he could get used to.

With dinner completed they returned to the dance floor. Callee said, "I hope they weren't too hard on you back there."

He lifted a shoulder. "I'm pretty thick-skinned, but it was nice to have you defend me. I found it very sexy."

Callee hesitated a beat and Langston stepped on her foot. He looked at her with concern. "I'm sorry. Is your foot, okay?"

"My fault. I just saw Dr. Bishop."

Langston recognized the man as being her boss. He was also the person who Langston had discussed his project with four weeks ago.

"I should speak to him so he'll know I attended." She didn't sound like she really wanted to, but he guided her off the dance floor. As they approached the older gentleman, his gray eyebrows rose. He looked between the two of them, then at Langston's hand resting at her waist.

"Hi, Dr. Bishop. I wanted to say thank you for the invitation to the ball."

"I'm glad you could attend. And bring Dr. Watts with you. I realize this is a busy time for you with very little chance to appreciate the Derby festivities."

Langston shook hands with the older man. "You're right, she doesn't take much time for herself."

Dr. Bishop studied him a moment. "I understand you two make a good team. We hear things from the backside all the way to the front office."

"We have had a couple of interesting cases since Langston arrived, but things will settle down again after the Derby. He's been a lot of help." She looked at Langston and smiled.

"I hope you've had a chance to do your research as well."

"I have. I've gotten a lot of excellent data," Langston assured him.

He nodded. "Good to hear."

Two overweight gentlemen with highball glasses in their hands joined them.

"Bob," one said to Dr. Bishop, "are these the two people you were telling us about?"

"It is." Dr. Bishop made the introductions of Dr. Mitchell, and Mr. Sorensen, the CEO at Churchill Downs.

"Dr. Watts, your reputation precedes you. Nice to meet you," Dr. Mitchell said, shaking Langston's hand, followed by Mr. Sorensen.

Langston turned to Callee. "This is Callee Dobson. She's the brilliant PA who runs the clinic." He sensed more than saw her anxiety at the arrival of the two men.

"It's a pleasure to meet you, Mr. Sorensen. I've heard a lot about you. Dr. Mitchell, it's a pleasure to meet you as well."

Dr. Mitchell said, "Aw, just the person I was hoping to speak to. I hear you're almost as good with horses as caring for people. I'm looking at starting a new program that works with the jockeys and horses. You'd care for the jockeys but also study their interactions with the horses. I need people who understand both groups. It's a rare person who has skills and qualifications on the human side and an understanding and appreciation of horses too. I heard about how you handled the situation with the man who had been caught in the horse trailer."

Callee raised her chin. "Thank you, sir. My father is a veterinarian."

Dr. Mitchell said, "I'd like you to consider coming to work with me. Possibly progress to the head of the program in a couple of years. Would you consider it?"

Callee glanced at Dr. Bishop. He said, "You'd go with my blessing. We already discussed your qualifications. I'd hate to see you go, but you'd have my wholehearted support if you did. Apparently, many of your talents are wasted with us."

Callee shifted. "Dr. Mitchell, I don't know what to say. I'm happy where I am."

"I can appreciate that, but please think about what I've said. If you change your mind, Dr. Bishop knows how to get in touch with me."

Mr. Sorensen said, "Callee, I'd like to offer my thanks for your quick and sure actions regarding the situation with the horse with the flu. If it hadn't been for your actions, the Derby might not be running this year. If there is ever anything you need, please let me know."

"Thank you, sir, but I'm sure somebody else would have recognized it…"

The older man said, "They may have, but it also might have been too late."

"I'm glad I was there at the time," Callee said. A woman with a neck encircled by jewels called Mr. Sorensen's name and waved him toward her. He said his goodbyes and left. The other two men did as well. Langston gave her a gentle squeeze. "You must be proud of yourself. That was a nice job offer. I'm glad for you. It's well deserved."

Callee's eyes filled with shadows. "I haven't thought about another job."

"It would give you a chance to work with people and their medical needs along with using your practical experience from working with horses and your father. You are in the unique position of understanding the horse and rider. It would be the best of both worlds. Perfect for you."

"It would but my place is at the clinic." She looked overwhelmed.

Not wanting to upset Callee tonight, Langston kept his opinion of how she hid at the clinic because she felt guilty about what happen to her boyfriend. That she hadn't been able to save his life. Mentioning it would only start an argument. Something he wasn't doing this evening. "All I'll say about it now is you have so much to offer any place you work."

"Thank you. That's a nice thing to say." That wiped the shadows from her eyes.

"It's easy to say nice things to you. You're nice. Would you like to have a few more dances then slip out of here?"

He tightened his hold, bringing her against him for a second.

"That sounds good to me. I have to be at the clinic early."

"In that case I'll need to be there too." He escorted her to the dance floor and with a flourish brought her into his arms.

Callee giggled and smiled at him. This dreamy feeling must be what heaven felt like. She stepped closer. The arm at her waist tightened. Langston had started to become part of what made her happy. They danced to a fast song, then he brought her to him again for the slower one. He held her tight, her hips cradled against him. His hand lay low on the curve of her back. Hot heat of want filled her. His body brushed hers with his every movement. The song ended. Langston whispered, "Let's get out of here."

"I'm ready." For more than leaving the party. She was ready to have Langston to herself. They returned to their table and said their goodbyes. Langston helped her with her wrap. His hands caressed her shoulders for a moment as he smoothed the material into place. Taking her hand, he walked toward the door matching his pace to hers, yet there was a determination to his movements.

She tightened her hand around his. "Is there some hurry I don't know about?"

"I'm sorry, sweetheart." He stopped giving her a look of concern. "I didn't mean to drag you along. I'm just anxious to kiss you."

Her heart revved like a motor. "Oh. Then let's go."

His lips formed a vivid smile. Soon they were climbing in the back seat of the car. It had hardly moved off when Langston took her in his arms. His kiss made her blood heat and speed throughout her body. Callee clung to him as he ravaged her mouth. She returned his need. Making a half turn, she faced him. Her fingers plowed through his hair as she held his head to hers.

His hand ran up her leg bringing her dress with it. She moaned. His lips released hers. She blinked coming out of the Langston created daze. He nipped at her earlobe. "Not here. Soon." Horrified she had come close to letting him undress her in the back seat of a car with another man not feet away. She scooted away and straightened her dress.

Langston grinned and leaned in close, giving her a light kiss. "Don't go too far." He gave her hand a tug, encouraging her to move closer. She did so, leaning her head on the upper part of his arm. They didn't say much as they finished the ride. Finally the driver pulled alongside the curb in front of her house.

After climbing out, Langston then helped her. He pulled her hand through his arm and rested his hand over that one. They strolled to the front door. Taking her keys, he opened the door.

Was she just going to let him go? She didn't want that. "Would you like to come in for a cup of coffee?"

He looked at her for a long moment. "Callee, if I come in it won't be for a cup of coffee."

Unable to stop herself she said, "I don't want a cup of coffee either."

"You need to be sure."

With complete confidence she said, "I'm sure."

# CHAPTER SEVEN

CALLEE LEFT THE door open while Langston returned to speak to the driver. She dropped her purse and wrap on a living room chair, then kicked off her shoes beside it as she passed. She stood in the kitchen filling the coffeepot with water when she heard the door close. She called, "I'm in here."

She felt the moment Langston entered the room and faced him. "I thought you might change your mind."

Langston removed his suit jacket and hung it on a chair at the table. He watched her a moment with predatory eyes before walking toward her. He stopped in front of Callee, leaving her plenty of room to step around him. "I haven't changed my mind. About coffee. I'm more interested in this."

He kissed her but never placed his hands on her. She fisted his shirt in her hands to steady herself against the onslaught of emotions flooding her. Langston had her quivering all over.

She'd questioned her boldness of asking him to stay, but there was only so much time left before Langston would be gone. She'd decided the moment he kissed her in the car she wanted one night to remember. She had never felt like this about another man. It had been so long since she'd let herself care about someone at this level. She had a difficult time letting go of the barriers she'd created to protect herself. Langston had slowly pulled that wall down brick by brick, kiss by kiss.

He backed her to the counter away from the coffee maker.

Placed his hands against the counter, boxing her in yet she didn't feel threatened. She was right where she wanted to be. Callee reached her hands around his neck, playing with the silky hair at his nape.

His lips met hers with a demand that heated her core. Their tongues danced and mated.

He lifted her onto the counter then returned to kissing her neck. His fingers found the hem of her dress. His hands branded the skin of her calves before he ran them along the outside of her legs, pushing the material higher to gather across her thighs. He stepped between her legs.

Her hands ran across the ridge of his shoulder kneading his taut muscles. He lifted her hips. Tugging on her dress, she bunched it around her waist.

Langston stepped closer as he continued to caress the outside of her legs. He kissed her shoulder then found the dip below her neck. Her nipples hardened, pushing against the fabric of her dress.

Callee murmured her pleasure. Her head lolled back against the cabinet door. She closed her eyes while she soaked in Langston's heated desire.

"You feel so good." His fingers feather-brushed each vertebra as he lowered the dress's zipper down her back to her hips. With each touch the throbbing at her center grew stronger. Her breathing slowed, held with anticipation.

Langston hooked a finger beneath the shoulder strap of her dress and pushed it down inch by inch. He kissed her neck, to her shoulder then across and back before he moved to the hollow of her neck again. There the tip of his tongue flicked out to taste her.

She squirmed. He held her secure on the counter. His hands brushed the straps to her elbows revealing her breasts. She moved to cover herself, but Langston stopped her.

"Such beauty should never be covered."

Callee heated inside and outside as Langston looked at her. Using his lips, he touched the top curve of a breast and moved down. His tongue circled her nipple. Pulling away in a gradual motion, he gave her a gentle tug. "So sweet. So responsive."

Langston continued to explore and tease her breasts. Her center ached while her breaths turned heavy, and short.

She wanted Langston. All of him. Desperately.

He stepped back, lifting her breasts. "Watch me, Callee. See how I adore you."

Doing as he demanded, she raised her head and saw him lift her breasts as if testing their weight. His tongue darted out to taste a nipple before he sucked and then did the same to the other.

Callee's center contracted. She squirmed. She held his mouth to her while he teased, tortured and tested her reaction. His tongue twirled around her nipple, tugging. She savored the feeling along with his attention. Her breasts grew heavier, her center wet.

His gaze met hers. "You're everything I dreamed you'd be."

She blinked. He'd been dreaming of her. Callee cupped his cheeks and brought his mouth to hers, kissing him deeply.

His hands ran up her legs to clasp her hips, slid up her butt. He lifted her to the edge of the counter. His manhood pressed into her center. She flexed into him.

"Sweetheart, too much of that and it'll all be over too soon." Desire had darkened his blue eyes to storm cloud gray.

Holding her gaze, he let his finger trace the top of her panty line causing her middle to quiver. Her fingertips bit into his shoulders as his finger slipped under the elastic to brush between her legs. Her center beat like a drum. Langston's look bore into hers. He continued to hold her look as his finger slid between her legs. Callee widened her legs involuntarily to give him better advantage.

Langston growled. "I need to touch you. Lift your hips."

She didn't hesitate. Pressing her palms against the counter, she lifted her hips.

Seconds later Langston had stripped off her underwear. He dropped them to the floor without a backward glance. His look captured hers. He stepped between her legs once more. His hands lay on her thighs.

Callee's breathing grew faster in anticipation. Her hands gripped his biceps. His thumbs unhurriedly stroked the sensitive skin between her legs, moving closer to where her body begged for his touch. Still his eyes didn't waver.

"Tell me what you want?"

Could she?

"Tell me." His eyes demanded. His tone demanded. His hands gave her thighs a gentle squeeze.

"Touch me." The words were little more than a whisper.

The pad of his thumbs swept her center.

She shuddered.

"I love how you react to my touch." His mouth found hers in a hot, wet, sensual kiss.

His finger entered her. Callee's body flexed, clasped around him. Her legs widened giving Langston all the space she could. His touch had her holding on to him to keep from spinning off. She wanted more. Ached for it.

Langston removed his finger.

She moaned her disappointment.

His tongue simulated the same as his finger reentering her, moving faster.

A tightness grew, intensified, spun and built on itself until it exploded. She threw her head back and shook as she wailed her gratification. Thrown into a world she'd not experienced before, she hung there in the bliss and floated back to reality. Panting, her head fell forward to rest on Langston's shoulder. She shivered.

Langston's arms circled her, pulling her close. "Bedroom."

"End of the hall."

With an arm around her waist and the other behind her knees, he lifted her against his chest.

Callee held on to Langston's neck as he worked his way down the hall to the open door at the end. Taking three long steps, he stood beside the bed. He gently laid her in the center. She held her dress over her chest.

"I don't know why you're clutching that dress over those beautiful pieces of womanhood when I was feasting on them a few minutes ago." He bent a knee and leaned over her.

She stopped him with a hand on his chest. "Maybe because I expect equal time."

He grinned. "Not a problem."

Callee watched with rapt attention, not missing a movement of Langston undressing. His long nimble fingers, which she knew so well, now released each button from its hole in rapid succession on his shirt. Callee appreciated the slow sexy reveal of Langston's chest. Unlike when they were in the stall, she got to enjoy the muscles flexing and contracting across his chest as he worked. Finished with the buttons, he shrugged out of the shirt and let it drop to the floor.

He sat on the edge of the bed and removed his shoes.

She took advantage of the opportunity to run her hands over his back valuing the muscle and strength there. She kissed his shoulders and nape. Her arms encircled his neck. She pressed her breasts against his back as her hands explored his chest, enjoyed the dusting of hair there.

"You keep this up and I might undress for you again." He turned to kiss her.

"I would enjoy that." She kissed across his shoulder.

Langston groaned. "Mmm. I like that."

She nipped the top of his shoulder.

Langston jerked to his feet and shucked his pants. His black biking shorts quickly followed.

Callee admired his trim waist, firm butt and steady thighs. The man was as gorgeous from the back as he was from the front. She enjoyed the private showing.

Langston reached for his pants and pulled out his wallet, removing a couple of packages of protection. He placed them on the bedside table. Turning to her, he asked, "May I help you remove your dress?"

Callee smiled. So formal sounding. Langston stood there in all his magnificent glory. His manhood tall and thick. "I was wrong about your truck."

"What?" His eyes held confusion.

"In your case I was wrong about the size of your truck being a reflection of your inadequacies."

Langston gave her a wolfish grinned. "Compliment taken."

He reached for the hem of her dress. "Okay?"

"Yes." She let go of her dress as he tugged it over her head, slowly revealing her legs, her stomach and with a shoosh of material, all of her.

Langston dropped the dress in a rose-color pile beside his formal clothes with no regard for care. His focus remained on her. His eyes burned with need. "Honey, I desire you like I have no other."

Callee felt the same. Want made her body tense, jittery and hot. She watched in fascination as he opened a package and rolled on the protection.

Langston came down beside her, bringing her close. He nuzzled her neck. His knee moved between her legs. Callee gave no resistance. She wanted this. Running a hand to her breasts, he fondled them. She enjoyed the feel of being in his large, gentle hands. Her nipples rose to greet him. He accepted the call, giving them both equal attention with his mouth. Sliding over Callee, he settled between her legs. His tip lay just outside her entrance, waiting.

She raised her knees cradling him in her heat and dampness.

Langston met and held her gaze. "You're sure about this? I want no regrets in the morning."

"I've never been surer. I want you inside me," Callee said with confidence she felt down into her soul.

His lips found hers.

Her heartbeat increased in anticipation. Blood rushed to her center.

Langston rose on his hands. Slowly, exquisitely so, he entered her, settled deep. He didn't move as if he were savoring the experience. His jaw tightened. He pulled away and pushed in once again then increased the rhythm.

Callee flexed to meet him. He increased the tempo. She squirmed, begging for more. She clutched at Langston, holding him. He didn't slow. The sensation built, swirled, curled, expanded, climbed higher and crashed.

He continued to plunge into her.

"Langston…" she crooned as she floated to an ecstasy she had never known. She returned to earth shattered and weak, and complete.

Renewing his efforts, Langston drove into her. Callee wrapped her arms around him. He stiffened. With eyes shut, he made long strokes. With a groan that sounded forced from him, he found release, shuttered and collapsed.

His weight pressed her into the mattress. Callee ran her hands over his back, loving the feel of the strong man beneath her fingers. She liked touching him. So much.

Just before she would have to complain about his weight

he rolled to her side. Langston's hands encircled her waist and pulled her close. He hauled the edge of the bedspread over them.

Callee closed her eyes and snuggled against his warmth.

He murmured, "I like it when you scream my name."

Callee reached for the offending alarm clock and shut it off. It couldn't be time to get up.

She wiggled into the warmth at her back. Hadn't she just gone to sleep?

A firm long arm wrapped around her waist and pulled her back against a sturdy chest. Mmm… Langston.

His mouth nuzzled her neck. One of his hands covered her bare breast. "Let's chuck it all and stay here."

That sleep-roughed voice made her skin ripple, sending heat to her core. "People who go from one part of the country to the next don't have to worry about showing up for work. Those of us who go in regularly do. It's Derby Weekend. The busiest we have. I have to work."

"You had a job offer last night," he murmured against the top of her head.

An offer she hadn't much time to think about that. All she had been concerned with was Langston and his touch. She smiled. It had felt delicious last night just as it did now.

Langston's hand slipped to the V of her legs.

Her center throbbed. "We don't have time."

He nipped at her ear. "We can save time by showering together."

Would she ever get enough of this man?

She rolled to face him. His lips found hers. Her arms went around his neck. Langston rolled to his back. Her legs straddled his hips. His hands rested at her hips. She leaned down to kiss him. He lifted her so his manhood easily slipped inside her. She settled on him. This she could get used to having all the time.

But she dared not. Yet she would enjoy it while it lasted.

Half an hour later Callee lay basking in the feeling of being well loved. Her entire body felt like warm putty Langston had played with. She glanced at the clock and despite her desire to remain where she lay, she sat straight up. "I've got to get going. You're a bad influence."

"You can't blame me. You were in control this morning."

She had been. And loved it. Langston was a generous lover. "You complaining?"

"Hell, no." He grinned as if he'd just won the Derby.

"I'm going to get a quick shower, then I'm headed out. If you want a ride, you'd better be thinking about getting out of that bed." She snatched jeans out of the closet and found a T-shirt in the chest of drawers. "If you want to call a service to pick you up, you're welcome to stay. I'll see you at the clinic later."

"I definitely need to go by my place. I don't think showing up in my tux is a good idea."

"You'd be the best dressed doctor there today."

"Yeah, but I miss my boots."

She grinned. "And you might need that big red truck."

He chuckled, rose and stalked toward her. "Are you besmirching my manhood again?"

She gave him a wicked look then dashed into the bathroom. "What if I am?"

"Then I'll need to prove you wrong. Again."

Callee giggled as she stepped under the warm spray of the shower. The morning after should have been uncomfortable but with Langston it all seemed so natural, easy.

"Don't hog the water." Langston gave her a little pop on the butt and stepped in with her. "I'll wash you if you'll wash me."

"I don't think this is a good idea."

"Come on, Callee. Where is that adventurous spirit of yours?" He took her in his arms.

Bathing with a man wasn't something she had done. She and Joe had been kids. Langston was a man with different wants and needs. She couldn't help but touch his water-slicked body.

Langston growled. "You keep that up and we'll be having our own race. To the bed."

Only five minutes late, Callee pulled into her parking spot. There were many more vehicles in the area than usual, as it was Kentucky Oaks day. The place was teaming with people and horses.

There would be no breeze that morning, so she headed straight to the clinic.

Two people were already standing outside the clinic door waiting on her. And it wasn't even daylight yet. The grandstands across the track had no one in them yet. They would fill up later that morning. Right now, all the activity was on her side of the track.

Unlocking the door, she let her patients inside. She had seen one of them before. The woman had a simple cut on her hand. Even that had to be taken care of when working around animals. An infection could so easily set in. Callee cleaned and bandaged it, writing out instructions to wear a glove and come back to see her in three days.

Fifteen minutes later Langston arrived. She heard him speaking to Carl and then to the man waiting. At the sound of footsteps, she looked away from her patient to see Langston leading the man to an exam room. She liked having his help and support. Liked having him around far more than she should.

They sent their patients out as the same time.

"Callee, I need to ask you about a file in your office." Langston started down the hall.

"I need to clean up the room then I'll be along."

Langston gave her a pointed look then strolled on.

Her brows drew together. What was that about? Was he regretting their night together already? She quickly put things in the exam room away and hurried to her office. "What's up?"

Langston stood and closed the door behind her. "I missed you."

"You just saw me."

"Yeah, but I didn't get a kiss."

She liked silly, befuddled Langston. The day they met she'd thought him a stuffed shirt. He had an air of superiority. Then, he started to let his hair down. She had a chance to see the man beneath.

"Then we need to fix that." Feeling a little off center herself, her hands went behind his head and pulled his lips down to hers. She gave him a kiss that had them both hot.

They broke contact. Langston rested his forehead against hers. "You keep kissing me like that, and I'm not gonna be able to see patients."

"Then you better watch out."

Langston concluded he'd made a mistake of a lifetime. But no way would he have done anything different. He'd let himself become involved with Callee. She'd started to really matter in his life. His heart moved closer to becoming involved. He cared for Callee more than he should for a man leaving town in a few weeks.

He'd never felt like this before. With anyone. Not even Emily. He wanted to run, but then he didn't. What made it worse was he didn't want to share these emotions with anyone but Callee. Yet he couldn't stay. Would she consider going with him? He had a job to do. One that was important and mattered.

He couldn't call what he had in Texas a home. He was rarely there. It was more like an expensive storage room or glorified hotel. He dropped things off and then left again. Callee's place was a home. It looked and felt like who she was. It had life in it. What did he expect? For her to leave that to follow him around the world?

Callee loved what she was doing. The people she worked with. Knew them, shared her life so much that she didn't even want to consider taking a different job, one that was tailor-made made for her.

He had no one he could call a best friend. Not since Mark. Hadn't he found that again here at Churchill Downs? People spoke to him when he went by. Came up to him to ask questions. Had accepted him as part of the culture. All because of Callee. What was he thinking? He wasn't staying here. Or making a commitment to Callee. He would leave in a few weeks and not look back. So why did the idea make his chest tightened?

He had a job to do. Starting Monday, he had to finish up the interviews he had been doing and start wrapping up his research. At this point, he had to keep his eyes on the prize instead of worrying about his emotional attachment to Callee. There would be another woman in another town. What he feared was there wouldn't be another like Callee.

He kept an ear open during the day for Callee if she needed help. She'd been busy but not excessively so. A couple of times he stuck his head out to see if she needed him, but each time she'd waved him away.

At lunchtime he wandered up to the front of the clinic. She and Carl stood facing the TV.

"What race is it?"

"Fourth," they said in unison without looking at him. He moved to stand behind Callee. Tempted to touch, he resisted because Carl was nearby. She wouldn't like to appear unprofessional.

The horses left the starting gate. They ran in a group and slowly spread out, a few getting ahead of the others. Halfway around the track one horse took the lead. Another moved around three horses and came in behind the leader. The roar of the crowd, not very far away, seeped into the clinic. Dirt flew as the horses ran. They circled the turn closest to the clinic.

Callee backed into him. He didn't move. She trembled. Sadly, he didn't think it was because of him. Her attention remained totally on the race.

The horses continue down the backstretch then around the last turn and headed for the finish line.

Callee, along with Carl, started to shout for the lead horse.

Langston found himself caught up in the race, eager to see who would win as the horses raced side by side. He could see the splendor in the event as well.

When the second horse pulled ahead of the others and won the race, Callee turned around and threw her arms around his neck and jumped up and down. Right then, he believed he could become a fan of horse racing. "I have to admit it's easy to get caught up in a race."

Callee grinned. "I told you so." She stepped away from him. "With any luck we'll go out to the track to see the Oaks race."

"Which one is that?" Langston teased. He had listened and remembered what Callee said about the races. It was important to him that he be interested in what she was interested in.

Carl shook his head and walked back to his desk.

"You know which one it is. It's the one with the largest purse and the best horses." Her tone implied exaggerated patience.

Five hours later Callee popped her head into the office. "Hey."

He jumped.

"Sorry, I didn't mean to startle you. I don't have any patients right now. You want to watch the Oaks?"

"Okay, sure." He didn't care anything about the race, but he would go along.

"Then come on. It's about to start." She didn't wait on him.

He hopped up from the chair and hurried after her. She pulled the door open and kept going until she reached a spot near her usual one at the track fence. Others stood along beside them. People filled the center of the track. In the distance, he could make out the filled stands under the twin spires of Churchill Downs.

The air pulsated with excitement. Attuned to Callee he could feel her tremble beside him.

The track announcer said over the loudspeaker, "The horses are in the gate, and they're off!"

Those around them went quiet. Callee took his hand. Seconds later the horses thundered by them and out of sight. He had to admit it was enthralling for those few moments to see the jockeys in their bright colors and the power of the horses. "That's much better than watching it on TV."

"Just think what it's like from the grandstands. To see the entire field." The wistfulness got to him.

"Isn't it about time to close up for the day?" he asked.

"It is." She turned back to the clinic.

Carl joined them, stopping Langston from asking Callee about their plans for the evening. If they had any. He didn't want to assume there would be a continuation of their morning. He wanted Callee to ask him.

Back at the clinic Langston returned to the office to close out his work.

Callee entered a few minutes later. She pulled her purse from the drawer then hesitated, giving him an unsure look. "Uh… I'm headed home."

Langston reached for her hand and tugged her into his lap, giving her a tender kiss. "I've been thinking about doing that all day."

Her arm snaked around his neck. "You have?"

Langston kissed her again. "I have. I wondered if you'd like me to pick up some takeout. Maybe I could come to your place for dinner."

She smiled. "I'd like that."

He nudged her out of his lap and stood. "Good. How does lasagna, bread and salad sound?"

"Delicious."

"Then I'll pick it up at the Italian restaurant near me on my way to your place."

He kissed her again. She softened against him. How would he ever give this up? But he would somehow. He must in order to achieve what he wanted. Callee wasn't part of his life plan.

"You know for such a small woman you sure have a big weapon with your kisses. I'll do almost anything to have one."

She searched his face. "Is that a good thing or bad thing?"

Heaven help him, he feared it was the latter. "I'm not sure yet."

# CHAPTER EIGHT

CALLEE FEARED WHAT was happening to her. She'd thought her and Langston's night together would be it. She should have known better. Here she was inviting him into her house once again and looking forward to the possibility of another night together.

She had spent the day working in a daze of memories, anticipation and fatigue. She was exhausted, but she couldn't fault the reason. A night with Langston was worth it. He had been tender, considerate as well as encouraging and demanding. Everything she wanted in a lover. Even more.

The way he had stood so close to her during the races, his body heat melding with hers, and the hot kisses left her with little doubt he still wanted her as much as she wanted him. The heady feeling of being desired by Langston made her nerves tingle.

She had taken a shower and pulled on a T-shirt and a pair of cutoff jean shorts by the time Langston rang the doorbell. She hurried to the door.

He stood there holding two large white bags.

"Let me have one of those. Did you buy enough for an army?"

He winked. "I thought we might need to keep our strength up."

Despite him having seen and touched all of her, heat still washed to her cheeks and turned them hot.

"I've got this." He headed toward the kitchen.

Langston had changed into something comfortable. He looked super sexy in his tight-knit shirt, well-worn jeans, and boots. How could the man wear something so simple and turn her on just by coming in the door?

"Callee, are you coming? I am starving."

"On my way." She entered the kitchen to see him unpacking the bags on the kitchen counter. Something about the picture made her pull up short. How easily they had slipped into being a couple. In two weeks she would be alone again. Wasn't she opening herself up to pain?

"I got us some cheesecake too. The lasagna is still hot. Let's eat before it gets cold."

"I'll get the plates," she murmured stepping around him.

Langston caught her by the waist. He studied her a moment. "Hey, you okay? If you don't want me here, just say so."

"I want you here, I do. It just seems like we're playing house pretty easily."

He let go of her. "I should go."

She placed her hand on his arm. "Please don't. I'm just tired. It has been a long day."

He gave her another long look. "Okay, I'll stay awhile."

"Good. I like company with my meals." She went to the cabinet and removed two plates and handed them to him. While he served portions of lasagna onto their plates, she filled glasses with ice and tea, gathered tableware and napkins.

They ate their meal in polite quietness. She hadn't meant to create this uncomfortable silence. "It's all very good."

"Mama Marzetti is a good cook. She has taken care of me more than a few nights since I've been here." He dug into the lasagna.

Callee took a sip of her tea. "It figures you'd know her

personally. Here I was wondering what you were doing in the evenings."

Langston forked another mouthful. "If you go in regularly, they get to know people."

"Somewhere in there I feel a little sorry for you."

He stopped eating and looked at her.

She shook her head. "You had to eat alone every night. I should have invited you to dinner. And you eat out so much that a restaurant owner has become a friend. I'm sorry."

"No need to feel guilty. I'm used to it."

She pursed her lips. "That's sad on a whole different level. I'm sorry that didn't sound very nice."

"No problem. It might be true."

"Anyway, I'm glad you met Mama Marzetti because I'm enjoying her food. I'll have to try the restaurant."

"Tell her you know me and I'm sure she'll give you a deal."

What he left off was, when he was gone. Why had she made it weird between them a few minutes ago? Because she was scared. Afraid he would carry her heart with him when he left.

Langston picked up a piece of bread. "Thanks for encouraging me to watch the races today. I found them interesting and exciting. I can't believe I've not seen one before."

"I just wish we could see the Derby race. But the clinic comes first. As soon as I left, someone would need medical attention."

"It usually happens that way." But her comment gave him an idea. A few minutes later Langston pushed back from the table. "I better go. I know you must be tired." He stood and picked up his plate. He took her empty one as well.

*Do something. Say something.* Callee swallowed. "Langston."

"Yeah?" He looked over his shoulder while placing the dishes in the sink.

"Don't go."

"Callee, it's okay. I'm good. I understand. I shouldn't have assumed anything."

"You didn't. I've just had a taste of what it would be like to have you all the time and I liked it."

Langston cleaned his hands and came to her. "I'm still leaving in a couple of weeks."

"I know. You never said different."

He cupped her cheek. "Can't we just enjoy each other while we can?"

She would rather have that than nothing at all. Somehow, she would figure how to survive after he left.

Langston groaned at the shrill sound of Callee's alarm clock going off. It was morning already.

Callee's head rested on his chest. She turned so he could see her face. "It's morning."

"Yep. It seems like we just went to sleep." His fingertips traced over her waist.

She yawned. "It wasn't but a couple of hours ago since we did. Someone kept waking me up."

"You started it."

Callee ran a hand over his chest. "Maybe I did, but you didn't fight very hard. Or at all, in fact."

He grinned. "I'm glad I didn't."

Callee kissed his chin. "I better get going. I have another long day ahead."

"I wish we could stay here for the day." He grabbed her hand and played with her fingers.

She looked back at him. "How about we make plans for that tomorrow?"

Langston kissed the tips of her fingers. "I'll hold you to it."

"I hope you do." She pulled her hand away and crawled out of bed. "Come on, it's time to meet the morning."

He groaned and pulled the covers up.

She nudged him. "Have you ever heard the saying you can't stay up with the turkeys if you want to soar with eagles?"

"Where did you get that one?"

"It's an old saying my dad uses meaning that you can't stay up all night and get up and be at your best the next morning." She went to the dresser.

He threw the covers back and got out of bed. "Whose fault is that?"

"You're blaming me? You're the one who woke me in the middle of the night." Callee looked at him in feigned shock.

"It wasn't my fault. You pushed that delectable bottom against me," he teased.

She put her hands on her waist. "I was only trying to get warm."

He grinned, standing straighter with his chin high. "I warmed you up, didn't I?"

She huffed and started toward the bathroom. "I'll accept half the guilt. The other is yours."

Langston chuckled. Everyone should be as lucky to wake to such stimulating conversation with a beautiful woman.

Callee looked up from the charts she had been working on when Langston said, "I have a surprise planned for you. I hope you like it. If not, we don't have to do it."

"What're you talking about?"

For the last two days, excitement and expectations hung in the air. The horses shifted in the stables, trainers, grooms and barn workers seemed to walk faster and talk excitedly. Langston continued his work on his interviews. Yet he would stop without hesitation to help her if there was a need. In a few hours that would be over. Derby Day would have come and gone.

"I've made arrangements for us to attend the last couple of races today."

"What? How?"

"I asked Dr. Bishop for permission. He agreed to send another doctor over so we could enjoy part of the day."

Carl came to the door. "Callee, there's someone here to see you."

"That must be Dr. Lawson, your replacement." Langston followed her up the hall. "I hope you don't think I've been too high-handed. I just wanted you to have a nice surprise."

Callee wasn't sure how she felt yet.

Langston stepped around her in the waiting area. "Hello, you must be Dr. Lawson. Thank you for coming. This is Callee Dobson who runs the clinic."

The white-haired doctor shook her hand.

Langston spoke to Callee. "We're just swapping places with Dr. Lawson. He was working in the stands. I thought it was a shame for me to be this close to a famous horse racing track and not even see a horse race. And you certainly should get to see it. Even Cinderella got to go to the ball."

Callee wasn't sure how she felt about this. Her gaze landed on Carl. He smiled and nodded. "Go."

"I can't go wearing jeans and a T-shirt. All those people in their hats and dresses."

"I fixed that as well. Again, I hope you don't mind. I ordered you a dress and hat. It should be here in a few minutes."

As if planned to the minute, the door opened and a deliveryman entered carrying a hatbox and a large square box. "I'm looking for Callee Dobson."

Langston walked over to him and took the boxes.

Carl said, "Come on, Dr. Lawson. I'll show you around. Hopefully things will be quiet until closing time."

The deliveryman left, and Langston offered the boxes to Callee. "If you don't want to go, we won't. But if you do you, have no excuse not to go. I'll abide by your decision."

"I don't know what to say." She wanted to see the Derby race, but Langston had done too much.

"Don't say anything just get ready to go." He gave her a nudge toward the hall. "You know you want to."

"But the clinic—"

"Dr. Lawson will handle it."

She looked at the boxes. "Okay, but I don't know about this dress. Where did it come from?"

"I ordered it from a boutique this morning. The saleswoman said it was just what you needed. That it easily fits a number of sizes. There's a hat to match. I understand you must have a hat to be completely dressed." He gave her another nudge. "Now go to your office and get changed. I have a golf cart waiting to take us over to the other side. I need to change too."

"You have clothes?" The man had thought of everything.

"I picked them up when I went by my apartment this morning. They're in the truck. Now stop asking questions and get dressed. I'll meet you right here in—" he looked at his watch "—twenty minutes."

"I'm going to agree this time, but don't make this type of thing a habit."

Langston grinned. "You have my word."

She carried the boxes to the office, placing them on her desk. She opened the larger one and pulled out a floral dress with large flowers in pink, yellow and green. The flowing material of the wrap dress had a ruffle neckline that crossed between her breasts and tied at her waist. She smiled. It was pretty and very feminine. She loved it. Beneath the dress were a pair of sensible pumps.

Callee then opened the hatbox. Inside she found a wide-brimmed white hat with flowers of the same colors as her dress around the rim of the hat. They matched perfectly.

"I hope they fit." Callee quickly removed her clothes. Minutes later she adjusted the tie at her waist. She moved one way then the other, letting the material flow around her. The dress was perfect for a spring evening at the races. She had never worn a hat, certainly not like the one Langston had given her. She pushed her hair behind her ears then placed the hat on her head. It looked wonderful as well.

With a smile on her face, she walked down the hall to meet Langston.

Langston felt like a king, seeing the look on Callee's face. She looked lovely enough to be queen of the Kentucky Derby. He smiled back at her, wishing he could always bring a smile to her lips like the one she wore now.

"I'm ready."

"Yes, you are." If Carl and Dr. Lawson hadn't been there along with a patient, Langston would have said more. He resisted the urge to kiss her. "Then let's go." He held the door for her to exit.

They settled in the waiting golf cart. As soon as they were seated, the driver took off.

Callee touched Langston's knee. "Thanks for doing this for me. What a nice surprise."

"You said you wanted to go. I thought it was something I could give you to remember me by."

She leaned against his side for a second. "As if I would forget you."

He swallowed hard. Maybe this was a bad idea. It would

be a memory for him as well. "I thought we'd enjoy seeing the race together since we've never seen the Derby race in person before."

"Thanks. This is amazing. It's one of the nicest gifts I've ever received. How did you work all of it out?"

"This morning I spoke to Dr. Bishop and he gave his permission for you to go and found Dr. Lawson to cover for you. He also said that Mr. Sorensen has two extra seats in his box that he's willing to give us. We'll be right on the finish line. How does that sound?"

"Amazing." She wrapped her arm around his waist and squeezed.

"I like you in the hat. You look like a true Southern belle."

Callee batted her eyelids. "Well, thank you, kind sir."

The golf cart deposited them in the parking lot outside the grandstands.

"I hope you know where we need to go." Langston looked lost.

"If we're going to the main boxes, they're this way." Callee led him inside the grand old building. "Part of this building has been around for over one hundred years. The Derby is older than that."

They walked through and around the crowd.

Callee stopped and looked at the digital race board. "There's still plenty of time before the next race. Do you mind if we go by the paddock on our way? I'd like to see the horses up close."

"Sure. Whatever you like." Langston would give her whatever she wished except for him to stay.

Callee smiled. "This way."

She didn't stop until she'd worked her way up to the paddock fence. Langston stayed right behind her. She was so small, he was afraid he might lose her.

Callee looked at him. "Aren't they beautiful?"

He looked into her glowing face. "Yes, they are."

She turned back to watch the jockeys mount with the help of a groom supporting their leg.

He needed to leave soon. The more he was around Callee the deeper his emotions went. If he wasn't careful, he'd hurt her and possibly himself. In fact, he possibly passed that point already. But for today he would enjoy the time he had with her.

Callee led him under the stands. "We need to get to the elevator and ride up to the Spires Terrace & Suites floor. That's where Mr. Sorensen's box is."

They rode the packed elevator up then walked a flight higher. Along the way, Callee grabbed a booklet from a kiosk.

"What's that?" Langston looked over her shoulder.

"A program. It tells you all about the horses. How many races they've won. Their number. The jockey. How to place a bet. It's almost too much to absorb." She kept walking.

"Are we planning to bet?"

She shook her head. "I'm not. I could be fired for that. I work too close to the jockeys and the horses, but I like pretending I can."

"When we sit down, will you show me how to read it?" He took her elbow, directing her around a group of people ahead of them.

"I sure will. We need to hurry. The next race will be starting in a few minutes."

They picked up their pace along a hallway going past an area with a buffet spread out, with people filling their plates. They continued on out to a terrace where people were lining the rail overlooking the finish line.

Langston stepped up behind her. "I thought we were sitting in a box?"

"No time to be social. The race is about to start."

Langston grinned. She had her race face on. He'd had more

fun with Callee than he'd had in a long time. He placed his arm around her waist as the horses took off. He felt the excitement of the horses thundering past them and moving out of sight around the turn. They became a small pack of dots on the back stretch and far turn. They ran full-out as they came in front of the stands. The crowd roared as the pack closed in on the finish line.

Callee jumped up and down shouting as the race ended.

She would never leave this. The people, the horses, the excitement was too much in her blood to travel from place to place with him even if he would ask her. The realization saddened him. They just didn't want the same things in life. Yet, the idea of being a part of this made him long... No, that time had passed years ago.

"We can go find our seats now. There's about a thirty-minute wait until the next race. The Derby race won't start until six fifty-seven. We'll have quite a wait on that."

Callee led him to the hallway where the box seats were located. She stopped at the door where a security officer had been stationed. "I'm Callee Dobson and this is Dr. Langston Watts. Mr. Sorensen is expecting us."

The guard entered the room and soon returned. "You may go in."

Mr. Sorensen was there to greet them. "Glad you could join us."

"Thanks for having us," Langston said, shaking the man's hand.

Their host introduced them to the others there then said, "You're welcome to any empty seats and the buffet outside. Let the waiter know if he can get you anything."

Langston directed Callee to seats in the back of the very swanky box. It had glass windows that looked out onto the track and the large racing board with the lineup of horses for the next race. The seats were cushioned and comfortable and the floor carpeted. Langston knew that other sports had something similar but had no idea that horse racing did as well. If he thought about it, he should have realized. As Callee had once said, horse racing was a big money business.

"This is nice, isn't it?" Callee whispered close to his ear. She settled into a chair.

He liked the brush of her lips against his skin. "It is. How about explaining the program to me before the next race. I'd like to pick one to pull for."

She grinned. "You're starting to get into this."

"You know the saying when in Rome…"

Callee opened the paper booklet and leaned in close to him. She ran her finger across a column, pointing out different aspects of a horse and the jockey information. "This horse is a long shot. See how high the odds are?"

"So who do we pull for?" He studied the program. "I'm going with Mo' Money."

"I'm going with Texas Tall," she said without hesitation.

"I'm honored." For some reason her choice touched him. As if he were the one Callee would be pulling for.

"Do you mind if we go back to the Terrace to watch the race? I like the open air and the crowd."

"Whatever you like. This is for you." He stood.

"I do like my surprise."

"I'm glad. I hoped you would."

Callee led the way out of the door. They worked their way to the Terrace and found a spot on the railing. "I like to watch them loading the horses in the gate."

Once again, he stood behind her out on the Terrace.

Among the crowd was a boisterous man who was large in both height and bulk. He was dressed in a bright red blazer. His cheeks were a ruddy color almost as deep as his coat.

He raised his arm above everyone with his glass in his hand, sloshing the liquid on those too close. He declared, "I put it all on Texas Tall."

Those around him cheered.

"He might have had too much of a good time," Langston commented, shifting Callee away as much as the crowd would allow.

Soon the horses were circling the track. When Callee's horse took the lead on the back stretch, she started jumping.

The man in the red coat became more animated.

Langston couldn't help but grin at her enthusiasm. He glanced at the man jumping around as well. With Callee against him, Langston felt the exhilaration and anticipation in her movements.

She grabbed his arm as she continued to bounce while yelling. She screamed, "Go, Texas Tall. Go!"

With the thunder of hooves, the horses came toward them. Callee's grip tightened on his arm. She continued to yell as Texas Tall crossed the finish line.

"He won. He won."

To Langston's surprise, she put her arms around his neck and gave him a smack on the lips.

He returned her kiss. "I could stand for you to win regularly."

Callee stepped back and looked around as if remembering her professional position. She smiled. "It had everything to do with the name."

"I don't know about that, but it did make the race fun to watch." If asked if his life was fun before today, he wasn't sure he could have answered positively. Callee had a way of making him enjoy whatever they were doing together.

"But I'm not as excited as that man."

Langston followed her look to the man in the red jacket. He

hopped around holding a ticket high in one hand and a glass in the other. "I won. I won."

Seconds later the glass dropped to the concrete floor with a crash. People scattered. The man clutched his chest, groaned and fell with a hard thump.

A woman shouted, "Help. We need help here. We need a doctor!"

Langston didn't hesitate. He had no doubt Callee was right behind him as he fought his way through the crowd. "I'm a doctor."

Callee's hand remained on his back as he went.

The man lay on his back surrounded by broken glass.

"Everyone, please step back. Someone call 911." Using his foot, Langston quickly swiped away the larger pieces of glass so he could go down on his knees.

The man's face had been bright red moments earlier but had washed white. Blood ran from the back of his head.

Langston put his cheek to his mouth. A shallow breath came out of the man. Placing two fingers on the man's neck Langston checked for a pulse. None.

Callee moved across from him.

"Watch for the glass."

She brushed the floor with her foot before she got down to her knees.

"He's had a heart attack," Langston announced. He quickly shrugged out of his suit coat.

Someone behind him helped him remove it.

"Callee, see about his head while I start chest compressions. Use my jacket to stabilize his head. He had a hard fall," Langston told her. "Someone get the portable defibrillator. There's one inside on the wall."

He placed a palm of one hand on top of the other. Using

the heel of his bottom hand, he applied pressure to the man's chest. Keeping count, he pushed down with a steady rhythm.

While he worked, he was aware of Callee checking the man's pulse, his respirations.

Someone above them said, "He'd been drinking heavy all day."

Langston sensed more than saw Callee tense. Was she thinking about what had happened before? He glanced at her but didn't have time to reassure her. Determined he wouldn't let her experience that loss again, he renewed his efforts. He would see this man recovered.

Callee called, "I need a cloth here. Something to stop the bleeding." A waiter handed her a few cloth napkins. Callee placed a napkin to the back of the man's head. She then tied two napkin corners together creating a bandage long enough to wrap securely around the man's head, and tied it in place.

She returned to checking vitals. "I've got no pulse."

The portable defibrillator appeared at Langston's right side. He opened the man's shirt not sparing the buttons. Callee had removed the lead package and was preparing them for placement. She handed the first one to him.

"Clear," he called, and applied the charge.

Langston leaned back on his heels to watch the man. His eyelids flickered open.

"Lay still, mister. The EMTs will be here in just a few minutes. You'll be fine."

Langston picked up the man's wrist and placed two fingers, checking his pulse.

Callee adjusted the bandage.

"Make way. Give us room," someone from behind them said.

Moments later two medical personnel broke through the crowd surrounding them. The group shifted. An EMT crouched in front of the patient. Beside Langston, another man took the same position.

"I'm Dr. Randell. We've got this now. You've saved this man's life."

Langston stood and watched as an EMT place an oxygen cannula under the man's nose. He stepped beside Callee who now stood at the man's head.

He squeezed her hand. "You okay?"

She smiled. "I'm better than okay."

"We make a good team."

"Yes, we do."

Too much so for his contentment.

They watched the EMTs load their patient onto a gurney and wheel him away with his family beside him.

Callee tugged at her dress, adjusting it. A large circle of blood stained it near the hem. "I'm afraid my beautiful dress is ruined."

"Callee, you're bleeding." Horror filled him. "The glass."

"I'm fine. It's just a little cut. I'm more concerned about my hat."

A woman handed it to Callee with a sad smile. The crown had been crushed.

"Oh, my poor hat." Callee popped the crown out, but there was a hole in the straw. She looked at him. "I know in comparison to saving a man's life my hat doesn't matter. It just makes me sad you gave it to me and now it's messed up."

"I'll buy you a new one. But right now we're going to see about your knee. I want to make sure there's no glass in it." Langston picked up his jacket. It was completely ruined. Blood and footprints were all over it.

"So much for my jacket." He stepped to the nearest trash can and stuffed the coat in it. "Let's go find a first-aid station and get your knee seen to. Then find a bathroom so we can get cleaned up." He took her elbow.

"We can leave if you want," Callee suggested.

"You don't want to see the Derby race?" He led her inside the building.

"I don't want you to feel like we have stay." She turned to the right.

"Honey, I want what you want."

She raised her chin. "Then let's clean up the best we can, have dinner and watch a great race."

Langston nodded. "Consider it done. First the first-aid station."

A staff member headed their way. Langston asked him for the nearest first-aid station or first-aid box. The man pointed to a bar across the room. There Langston got a box.

"Let's find a restroom where I can clean and patch you up." He looked around.

"You do know that you're making more of a deal out of this than it is."

He gave her a pointed look. "And you could learn to let someone care for you."

Callee cringed. Was she really that bad about letting someone do something for her?

"Now, let's find the restroom. We have a race to watch." Langston helped her up.

They found a single restroom. Langston went down on one knee to wash and clean the wound. His actions were gentle and caring. Each movement was tender.

"I'm not hurting you, am I?" He glanced at her.

"No." Callee watched his head bow over her knee.

"This might hurt." Langston ran a damp paper towel over the area.

"Ouch." She moved her leg.

Langston looked at the towel then showed it to her. "There was a piece of glass in there." He returned to cleaning the wound. Looking through the first-aid box he brought out antiseptic spray. "This may sting."

"I can handle it."

He gave the can a squirt. The spray covered the injured area. Callee sucked in a breath, held it. Langston waved cool air across the wound, cooling the sting.

"It's been a long time since someone did that for me. My mom used to when I was a little girl." The pain eased. "It feels better now."

"Good. I'm sorry I hurt you." Langston quickly applied a perfect bandage. He kissed her on the thigh just above the covering.

Callee's heart swelled. Would she be able to let him go?

An hour later Langston escorted Callee back to the terrace to wait for the Derby race to begin. He listened to Callee sing "My Old Kentucky Home" at the top of her voice along with thousands of others in the stands. Some of her excitement of earlier had died with the adrenaline rush of an emergency, but the song returned it. They had agreed on a horse to cheer for with good odds but not the favorite.

During the race Callee yelled for their horse, which came in second.

Langston was happy either way. Because she was having such a good time. "We were close."

She smiled. "Yes, we were."

People hung around even though it had been the last race. "Why aren't people leaving?"

"They're waiting to see the ceremony in the winner's circle." She pointed across the track toward the race boards to a U-shaped area.

A number of people including the winning jockey and horse gathered there.

"That's the owner getting the silver trophy," Callee said. "That's the blanket of roses going across the horse's neck. That's why the Derby race is called the Run for the Roses."

"For someone who has never been to the Derby you sure know a lot about it."

"But because of you I can now say I have attended." Her eyes glowed with happiness. "If you're ready to go, I am too."

"I'm ready. You lead."

He and Callee worked their way around and through the crowd to where the golf cart had left them. One waited.

"How did you manage this?" Her expression was one of astonishment.

He winked. "I have my ways."

"I'm impressed."

"That's what I like to hear." He helped her into the cart.

They returned to the backside through the tunnel and were deposited at the clinic. Carl had already closed up. Despite the business of the day, the barn area was quieting for the evening.

"I need to go in and get my purse and clothes." Callee unlocked the door.

"I'll wait while you get those. Make sure you're safe." He stayed in the front.

"You don't have to do that. Until you came I handled it alone all the time."

Was she trying to get rid of him? Or remind him that he would soon be leaving? "Haven't we already established you don't have to feel responsible for everything? I'll wait."

Callee wasn't gone long, but she had taken the time to change her clothes. She carried the boxes out with her.

He took the boxes from her. "I don't want to take it for granted, so I'm going to ask if I may come over tonight?"

"I hoped you would." She started toward her car.

His second of insecurity fled. Complete confidence was his middle name, so how did Callee always manage to keep him guessing?

Twenty minutes later she pulled into her drive and Langston parked behind her. He followed her into the house.

"I'm going to soak this dress and hope I can get all the stains out." She took the boxes from him.

"Hey."

She looked at him.

Langston dropped the boxes into a chair and opened his arms. She walked into them. "I've been wanting to do this all day. You were amazing today."

Callee tightened her arms around his waist and pressed her cheek into his chest.

He held her close, then kissed her. Could life get any better than this?

# CHAPTER NINE

THROUGH THE NEXT week Langston settled into a routine he wouldn't have believed he'd have agreed to much less enjoyed. Or would have allowed to happen. He and Callee made love and showered together each morning. They then had coffee in her kitchen as they made breakfast and headed off to work. In the evening Callee cooked or he stopped for takeout. After their meal they watched TV, read, or played cards but mostly they fell into bed together, which he always found satisfying.

He taught her some Spanish words by kissing the parts of her body as he named them. She would repeat them by returning those kisses on his. He looked forward to those lessons all day long. He found living with Callee far too satisfying for his comfort. It baffled him how well he'd taken to the domestic life.

This had never happened before during one of his trips. There had been women he'd seen during those times but none who had him feeling so settled. On all the other jobs when it had become time for him to leave he had been ready. This occasion he dreaded having to tell Callee goodbye.

Just before they were going to bed on Saturday evening his phone buzzed. Looking at it he sighed. "I better get this."

By the time he'd finished his conversation, he found Callee in bed sound asleep. It was just as well. That phone call hadn't been one she would like hearing about. He was needed back in Dallas for new tests Valtech was running on a plastic he'd helped develop. It was unlike him, but he had asked to stay the amount of time he had originally planned. He was told no, he had to leave on Tuesday to make his meeting.

Now he had to figure out how to tell Callee.

He showered and slipped under the covers next to her warm soft body. He pulled her to him. She sighed softly. This was almost as good as having sex.

He was in trouble.

The next day Callee woke and stretched in the afternoon sunlight streaming through her bedroom window. She touched the hard, heated body lying next to her. She and Langston had slept late, made love and shared breakfast in bed to sleep once again.

What she would do when he left, she couldn't fathom. She would be lost. Yet, she would have to keep going somehow. Hadn't she done so when Joe had his accident, then died? She had moved on with her life. Or had she? She would survive the hurt of loss again somehow. At least she had another week or so to enjoy with Langston.

Langston nuzzled her neck. "Good morning."

She loved the sound of his low sexy voice. "It's afternoon."

He gave her a wolfish grin. "It goes fast when you're having fun."

"What do you have planned for today?"

Langston fluffed the pillow and placed it behind his back and leaned against the headboard. "I thought we'd stay in bed all day. Why? Do you have something else in mind?"

Too aware of the fact he would be gone soon she wanted to make the most of their time together. "I do have something I need to do this afternoon for a few hours."

Using his palm, he rubbed her stomach. "Want to tell me what it is?"

"Let's just say it's a surprise."

"I like surprises." His hand dipped lower. He kissed her.

An hour later they were in Langston's truck traveling down a narrow tree-lined road toward Thompsons' farm.

"There sure is a lot of nice fencing in this area," Langston commented as they passed one horse farm after another.

"That's because it's all about the horses here. Barbed wire isn't used because that can damage the horse's coat. So as far as you can see there's nothing but wooden fencing."

"Impressive."

She directed Langston off the main highway for a couple of miles then told him to turn onto another country road. He drove down a pebbled drive lined by a white wooden fence that led to a house. They forded a running creek with trees hanging over it and kept going.

The two-story red brick Federal-style house she loved so much sat among large oak trees surrounded by pasture. The trim had been painted white. Ferns hung from hangers on the porch. The grass had been mowed to look like a golf green.

"What a nice place," Langston commented.

"Most people around here take great pride in the appearance of their farms. Mr. and Mrs. Thompson certainly do, but they're getting too old to handle it all. In fact, they've been talking about selling. If I had the money, this would be mine in a heartbeat."

"It's a beautiful part of the world."

She sighed. "Go past the house to the barn out back. You can park there."

He followed her instructions, stopping in a lingering cloud of dust outside the large red barn's doors. He lowered his chin and narrowed his eyes. "This isn't what I think it is, is it?"

She gave him a cheeky grin "And what do you think it is?"

"I think you're planning to get me up on a horse."

She tapped the end of her nose with her index finger. "You're so smart."

He looked unsure. "I don't know about that. And the Thompsons are what to you?"

"Landlords. Now friends. I needed a place to board my horse and I found them. They live closer than my parents." She climbed out and came around to meet him on his side of the truck.

He joined her. "So this is where you spend your weekends. I wondered. I had no idea."

"There's a lot of things about me you don't know." She wished he was staying around to learn them.

Langston stepped close so she was sandwiched between him and the truck door. He leaned close. His voice turned low and suggestive. "I know the important things. Like how sweet you taste." He gave her a quick kiss.

Disappointment filled her because there wasn't more.

"And how your skin quivers when I run my tongue over your hip bone." His hands went to her waist, the pads of his thumbs resting in the spot he just mentioned.

Heat shot through her.

His lips nuzzled her ear. "And best of all I know how you sound when you scream my name as you come."

Her center pulsed with want.

Someone cleared their throat.

Callee jerked away from Langston with embarrassment making her stumble. Langston steadied her. She pulled at her shirt adjusting it where Langston's hands had worked above her pant line. "Oh, Mr. Thompson. I didn't hear you come up."

"Understandable." His eyes twinkled. "You were busy."

Her cheeks burned. "Uh… I'd like you to meet my friend, Dr. Langston Watts."

Langston reached out a hand. "Just Langston. It's nice to meet you, Mr. Thompson. You have a beautiful place here."

"It has been a good home for fifty years." The older man looked around with pride. "I don't want to keep you. I just wanted to say hi and let you know that Mrs. Thompson expects you to stop in for tea and cookies before you head back to town."

"We'll be sure to do that. We're going for a little ride this afternoon." She touched Langston's arm. "He's never ridden a horse so do you mind if we take Maribel?"

"Not at all. I'm sure she'll appreciate the outing. I'll leave you to it." Mr. Thompson started back toward the house.

Callee took Langston's hand. "Come. I'll introduce you to Maribel and PG."

"PG?"

"Pride and Glory. He's a descendent of Man o' War. One of the great horses in racing so PG was given a fancy name. I shortened it when Daddy gave him to me. PG missed the great running gene, but he's been a great friend. Especially after what happened to Joe."

Langston gave her a quick hug.

She tugged him toward the barn doors. "Come on. It's time for you to learn some horsemanship."

"Let's think about this for a minute." He didn't move.

"Langston, for a man who deals with the type of stuff you do all the time I can't believe you're scared of a horse. I promise you Maribel will be gentle with you. She would never hurt a fly."

Callee went to a stall and brought a horse out.

He looked appalled. "You're going to put me on Maribel? My feet will drag the ground."

"Would you rather ride Rebel? That big black stud over there." She pointed to the horse in the stall ahead of them.

"Maribel sounds like a lovely lady." He came toward her. "I'm sure I'll be able to ride her."

"I'm sure you've ridden a lot of things," Callee said with a cheeky grin.

His voice went deep. "I've let you ride me a couple of times today already."

Heat washed over Callee. She swatted his arm. "No more of that talk around the horses."

Over the next thirty minutes, Callee showed Langston how to approach and walk around Mirabel by putting his hand on her rump, so she always knew where he was, which really wasn't a problem since Langston stood a head taller than the horse. She then instructed him in the proper way of putting a bridle on, adding a saddle blanket and cinching the saddle.

"Now I want you to stand there and get to know Maribel. She likes to be scratched behind the ears and talked to. I'm going to get PG out of the stall and saddle him."

"Are you sure about leaving us alone together?" Langston sounded doubtful.

Callee shook her head, grinning. "You'll be fine. I'll just be right over here. Maribel doesn't kiss on the first ride."

Langston gave the horse's lips a dubious look. "Good to know."

Callee saddled PG. When they were ready to go, she dropped the reins of PG confident the horse would stay where he was. She returned to Langston. "I'm going to show you how to mount. Hold the reins, put your left foot in the stirrup and swing your leg over."

"I know those basics. I've watched western movies."

Callee dipped her chin. "Excuse me."

Langston followed her instructions, easily mounting the horse.

"Good. Well done, Maribel." Callee patted her neck.

"What about me?" Langston asked?

She patted his thigh. "You did good too."

"Thanks. Maribel and I both work well with praise."

"I'll keep that in mind." She returned to PG. "Do I need to tell you how to go and stop or have you got that covered from watching a movie too?"

Langston smirked. "Why don't you give me a refresher just in case I missed something."

"Take the reins in one hand. Nudge Maribel to go by touching her with your heels. Not too hard, she's a sensitive old soul."

"I'll keep that in mind."

Callee continued. "To stop pull back on the reins. Mostly she should follow PG with no problem at all."

"You sound very confident of that." Langston wasn't.

"Either way I'm right here beside you." She mounted PG.

Langston liked the sound of that. Callee meant while riding horses, but she was the type of person who stood beside the ones she loved. The kind who would wait no matter how long she had to wait. Her promises would mean something. But at the time Emily had meant hers. Yet, while he'd been gone she'd changed. And then, he'd changed.

Because he'd been so caught up in her betrayal with his best friend of all people. Why couldn't he see that before now?

He would never put Callee under those same restrictions. It hadn't been fair to Emily to leave and ask her to wait for him, and it certainly wouldn't be fair to Callee. Even now he couldn't bring himself to tell her he was leaving sooner than expected. He would find the right moment. Sometime. Today he wanted to give them at least a little while longer to enjoy their time together.

He secured the reins in his hand and gave the horse a bump

with his heels, following Callee out of the dim light of the barn into the bright sunshine.

"We have a pretty day for a ride." Callee placed a hand on PG's rump and turned to look at him.

"Where're we going?" He wasn't sure he wanted to go far.

"We're going around the field. I usually check the fences for Mr. Thompson when I'm out for a ride. Then we'll follow the creek and come back to the barn."

The horses walked slow and close enough together that he could touch Callee. She rode with complete confidence, straight with shoulders back.

He tried to relax but couldn't completely let go of the saddle horn. Despite the amount of travel he had done and the different places he had been, this was a new experience on a different level. He had moved out of his comfort zone. He was learning he didn't always have to move around to experience life. Callee had led him into a whole other realm. He would've never thought doing a research project would have turned into such an enjoyable time. It was all because of her.

They rode through a copse of trees and came out on the other side to a small pasture area. They crossed it and arrived at the edge of a babbling brook.

"Is this the one I drove through?" Langston asked.

"It is. We're going to stop here and let the horses drink and have a rest. This is how you dismount." Callee grabbed the horn of the saddle, slung a leg over and came down on one foot. She brought the reins over PG's head. "Now you do the same. Remember it's important to hold on to the reins because if you don't and have a lively horse, it could get away from you. That's the last thing you need."

Langston climbed off the horse with a wobble at the end.

"That needs a little more practice, but you have the basics."

"Thank you, ma'am." Langston lifted the reins over Maribel's head. He had finally gained some confidence.

"Now we're going to lead them over to the water and let them drink. We don't want to overwater them especially if they're really hot."

Afterward they tied the horses to a tree. Callee took his hand and led him to a large rock by the water.

He sat and brought her down between his legs. Her back to his chest. Wrapping his arms around her waist, he rested his chin on top of her head. "It's gorgeous here."

"Like no other place on earth." A dreamy tone hung in her voice.

"That's how my parents feel about where they live in Texas too."

"That's not a bad thing. Oh, yeah, it's a restrictive thing as far as you're concerned. You know it doesn't have to be all or none. You can have roots and still see the world. People do it all the time. Life can be good with both."

"I realize that, but it hasn't really worked out that way for me."

"Have you tried it? Or even want to?"

This conversation had taken a turn he hadn't wanted to make. Was she leading him into promising something he couldn't or didn't want? On a pretty Sunday, by a babbling creek, in the warm sunshine, with the trees hanging over them and Callee in his arms, he might say something he would regret. He gave her a light push. "Shouldn't we be going?"

She stood. Clouds of hurt filled her eyes before she blinked them away.

He and Callee were going to have to talk about his departure. Soon.

Leaving this time would be more difficult, but he would do so on Tuesday. They could remain friends. He might even visit if he was in town again. He'd let his feelings make decisions before. Feelings couldn't be trusted. His heart had controlled his brain then. Langston would no longer allow that to happen, as he was determined feelings would not dictate his life decisions.

They continued to walk the horses along the creek bank. He and Callee kept their thoughts to themselves, talking very little. When they arrived at the drive, they crossed it and stayed along the fence line until the barn came into view. They started toward the building, dismounting outside it.

"You're starting to look like a natural," Callee said, smiling.

He lifted the reins over Maribel's head. "That's what happens when you have a good teacher."

Callee proceeded to show him how to remove the saddle and bridle then where to store them. "After a ride a horse always needs to be groomed." She showed him how to do that as well. With that done, they put the horses back in their stalls. Callee washed her hands in the rain barrel beside the barn. "It's getting late. We need to go see Mrs. Thompson."

She waited while he cleaned his hands. They walked to the back door of the house. Callee knocked.

Mrs. Thompson opened the door. She smiled at them. "Hello, Callee. It's good to see you." She looked at Langston. "I heard you had a young man with you."

Callee made introductions.

Mrs. Thompson backed out of the doorway. "Come in, come in. I've got cookies made. We'll have a cup of tea."

Callee climbed the steps. "We can't stay long."

"You have time for a cookie and tea, I'm sure. Have a seat at the table. Nothing fancy here."

Callee took a chair, and Langston sat at the one next to her.

He looked around the relaxing room. If he was the settling down type, it was just the kind of place he'd like. A brick fireplace, a large wooden table and a country sink spoke of home. Even the big heavy stove looked wonderful. There was wooden wainscoting on the walls with warm yellow paint above. Everything about the place said people who lived here were happy. Before coming to Louisville and meeting Callee, would he have even noticed that?

"You and Mr. Thompson have a beautiful place."

"We have enjoyed living here. Raised our family here." She placed a plate of cookies on the table.

"The house is over a hundred and twenty years old. It's seen a lot in its time." The older woman turned back to the counter.

"Richard," she said, raising her voice, "Callee is here. Tea is ready."

Mrs. Thompson brought them cups and saucers.

"Can I help you?" Callee moved to stand.

Mrs. Thompson placed a hand on the younger woman's shoulder. "You just be a guest for once. So Langston, I can hear a Texas drawl in your voice. I'm guessing that's where you're from."

"I'm from a small town just outside of Dallas."

"What brings you to Kentucky?" Mrs. Thompson set the milk and creamer on the table.

Langston told her about his research.

Bringing a steaming teapot to the table, she poured them a cup. "That sounds like important work. I'm sure Callee has been very helpful."

"It's more like he has helped me. Langston is an excellent doctor." She looked at him. "I'm not sure what I'm going to do without him."

His chest tightened. Callee was making it harder for him to leave without looking back.

Mr. Thompson entered and joined them at the table. "I'm sorry. I was right in the middle of a newspaper article."

Over the next half an hour they enjoyed polite conversation.

"We should go." Callee stood and Langston did as well. "All the fences look good, Mr. Thompson."

"Thanks for checking them. They'll need to be in good shape when we sell."

"I'm going to call a Realtor in the next of couple weeks. I hate to do this to you, Callee, but you're gonna need to start looking for a place for PG. The family next door is going to take Mirabel."

She looked at her teacup as she turned it one way then the other. "I wish I could buy this place and keep Maribel, but it's just not possible. I've looked at the numbers and I can't swing it."

"I wish we could stay, but it has become too difficult to climb upstairs to the bedrooms. We need something all on one floor," Mr. Thompson said.

"I'm looking forward to moving closer to our children," Mrs. Thompson said.

Langston glanced at Callee. Her eyes held the same look of sadness that they had at the creek. He'd do anything to make that look disappear.

"I knew it was coming. I just didn't expect it to be so soon," Callee told them. "And I'll miss you both."

Mrs. Thompson took Callee's hand. "We'll miss you too, sweetie."

He and Callee walked to the door.

Mr. Thompson said, "I'll be in touch if something happens about the place. I'll give you as much time as I can to make arrangements for PG."

"I appreciate that. If all else fails, I can take him home to Mom and Dad. I'd sure hate to do that. They're so far away."

She gave the older couple a hug. Langston shook their hands.

As Callee went out the door she said, "Mrs. Thompson, tea was lovely, thank you for having us."

"You're welcome, hon." She looked at Langston for a long moment then nodded. "Remember, young man, a good thing doesn't come our way often. Don't let it get away."

# CHAPTER TEN

THROUGH THE REST of the evening and throughout the hours before dawn, Langston had thought often about Mrs. Thompson's parting remark. What had she meant? That remained an insignificant question compared to how to tell Callee he had to leave sooner than she thought.

Of course, he could stay. Maybe work it out so Louisville would be his home base. Yet, the idea of that scared him to death. What if it didn't work out with Callee just as it hadn't with Emily?

He would still have to travel. Would Callee wait on him to return? He couldn't take the chance he'd return to her and there would be another man in her bed. That devastation he couldn't survive again. But it had been his decision to leave before. It was his decision to do so this time. Shouldn't he bear some of the blame? If he'd been there for Emily, she might not have turned to Mark. Couldn't the same be said for leaving Callee?

But if what had happened with himself and Emily hadn't happened, then there would never have been a Callee. He couldn't imagine not having her in his life.

And what if they decided they didn't work? He couldn't bring himself to even think about that hurt or hurting Callee. It would be best if they just parted and that was it. A clean sharp pain was always better than a long lingering ache.

Langston pulled Callee into his body. He would miss this

until his dying day. If he stayed, he could have this every day. No, he couldn't think like that.

The alarm went off. Time for them to get up. He couldn't put it off any longer. The time had come to tell her. He jiggled Callee, using the arm around her waist. "We need to get moving."

"I know but I don't want to." She rolled to face him, burying her face in his neck and holding him tight.

Their lovemaking had been sweet and poignant the night before. As if Callee were marking him as hers. He feared she'd accomplished that mission.

"It would be nice to stay here, but we can't. Work calls."

Maybe he could just stay through the week. He couldn't if he must bein Dallas on Wednesday for the tests on the plastic. As it was he would cutting close with such a long drive ahead of him. If he stayed any longer it would just prolong the agony. They would call each other for a while, then they would get busy with their lives, and it would fizzle out to nothing. It's better and easier in the long run to cut it off and have a sharp pain instead of a lingering one.

"Callee, I've been trying to figure out how to tell you this since Saturday night. I guess there's no good time and it can't wait any longer."

"What?" she murmured against his chin as she kissed it.

He backed away so he could see her face. "I have to leave tomorrow. That's what the call was about the other night."

Callee didn't say anything for a long time. She just squeezed him. With a burst of energy, she flipped the covers back and climbed out of bed.

Langston soaked in the view. A beautiful one he would think about every morning.

"Why didn't you say something sooner?" She grabbed her clothes.

"I didn't want to ruin a beautiful day yesterday or our time together last night." He gave her a pleading look. This was exactly what he hadn't wanted to happen.

"Or you didn't have the guts to tell me."

He grimaced as he put his feet over the side of the bed. "A little of both."

She glared at him. "You know it doesn't have to be this way."

"What're you talking about?"

"I'm talking about you leaving." She moved to the bathroom door.

"I don't know what you mean. You know I have work to do. That's what I've been called back to Dallas to do."

"No, I think you're running. You do know it's okay to stay in one place. There are plenty of places close by where you could get data. Or you could travel out and return. You don't always have to be running."

"What brought this on?"

She took a moment before she answered. "I like you. A lot. I haven't let anyone into my life in a long time. Certainly not into my bed. I think we might have something special, but I don't know that we can do it long distance."

He started picking up his clothes. "I'm not doing long distance. I've been there done that."

She took a step toward him. "Yeah, but that wasn't with me."

"No, but I won't take that chance. You'd get tired of waiting around on me."

Callee came closer, a pleading look on her face. "You don't have much faith in me. Just because one girl didn't remain true doesn't mean I won't. You're just scared to try."

"That's not true." Or was it?

"Sure it is. You're just afraid if you care too much you'll get hurt, be disappointed. I think you're past that."

"This is our last day together. Let's not have an argument. Why can't we just part as friends?"

Her lips formed a line. "We can't have this discussion tomorrow because you'll be gone. The problem is you won't stay around to argue. You'd rather ignore the issue. Maybe that is the issue. You left before and because you did, your girlfriend found someone else. Could the problem really be that you don't want to take any responsibility for what happened? Has it ever occurred to you that just maybe you and your girlfriend wanted different things out of life?"

"Leave Emily out of this. You don't know what you are talking about!"

"Really? If you had been there, would things have been different? Maybe. Maybe not. But at least you would have known. It's easy to blame others when it should be ourselves we're looking at."

He took a step forward, glaring at her. "You're one to be talking. You've lived your childhood around your father and what he wanted then you changed your mind because of a sad accident you had nothing to do with. One you feel guilty over and refuse to deal with. Now you live your life for a man who is dead. You've found a place, the clinic, where you can do good to make up for something that wasn't even your fault to begin with, and you stay because it's comfortable and you're sure you can always handle the problem."

"You don't know what you're talking about." She turned and went into the bathroom.

He followed her to the door. "Then I'll give you an example. You're offered a job that's perfect for you, but you won't even consider it. Why? Because you're afraid you'll make a mistake in judgment. You're scared to step out of your comfort zone. Broaden your horizons, seize new opportunities."

"You seem to be well-informed about my life. I think you

should spend some time on yours. Like eventually you'll have to give up your Peter Pan lifestyle. You'll have to go home and face your past so you can move into your future. When is the last time you saw your family? Or faced Emily? Or even Mark? What's the plan? Dodge them forever? Those are people you were supposed to love and care about."

"I have a job that keeps me moving. An important one. I have work to do."

She dumped her clothes on the counter and turned on the shower. "All excuses."

Disgusted he said, "This conversation isn't going anywhere. I'm going to my apartment. I have packing to do."

"With that you have a lot of experience," Callee spat.

He snarled at her. He picked up his duffel bag and stuffed the items he had kept at Callee's into it. "I'm sorry we couldn't have parted on a friendlier note."

"Yeah, it was fun while it lasted."

"Yep, right down to when it wasn't." He stalked out of the room down the hall and slammed the front door on his way out. With a roar of the truck engine and a satisfactory squeal of tires, he drove off. The very idea of Callee telling him he had a problem when hers dwarfed his by a long shot!

At his apartment he finished packing by cramming everything into his large bag. He looked at the bag and small duffel sitting beside the front door. Almost his entire life fit into them. For once he found that sad.

Langston made a few calls arranging to check out of the apartment. He let the hospital know he was leaving. The only thing left to do was to go to the clinic and wrap up his research papers. There were also three interviews he needed to complete. Two he would do today and the other tomorrow morning first thing, then he was out of town.

He drove to the clinic and pulled up beside Callee's car just as he had every day. A surge of grief overwhelmed him. He put his arms on the steering wheel and his forehead on his hands.

He didn't want to leave things between him and Callee in such an ugly mess. He cared about her, more than he had ever cared for a woman. Even Emily. But he couldn't let that affect his decisions. He had done that before and what had it gotten him. Nothing but a broken heart. He couldn't take the chance on it happening again. He wasn't ready to give what Callee demanded and needed.

Climbing out of his truck, he squared his shoulders and walked to the clinic. Maybe Callee had settled down some. He entered the building. She was talking to Carl. She didn't look at him before she ended the conversation and walked down the hall.

Was she not even going to talk to him again? How quickly things had gone from blissfully happy to complete devastation.

He wished Carl, who had a perplexed look on his face, good morning and went to the office. He passed an exam room where Callee fiddled with some supplies. He knew full well she was dodging him.

Langston spent the morning organizing his research then went out after lunch to find the two jockeys he needed to interview. He returned to learn from Carl that Callee had left to check on Gina, who had returned to work. Langston explained to Carl he was leaving in the morning, that he would be coming by to do one more interview and he would then leave for Dallas.

That evening he drove to his apartment, the empty, sterile one with no light and happiness in it, for the night. The entire day had been tense, drawn out and miserable. Callee had treated him like he never existed.

The night was worse than the day. He couldn't sleep. Finally giving up on the bed, he moved to the sofa with no luck.

He ended up watching TV until it was time to go to the clinic. With his two bags in the back of the pickup truck, he was ready to drive away as soon as he finished the interview.

Langston finished his interview and examination of the jockey in one of the exam rooms. Once he'd left, Langston went in search of Callee. He would not leave without telling her goodbye. He found her in the office. "Callee, can we talk?"

"I think we've already done that." She looked at the computer instead of him.

"I have more I want to say, ask really. If I asked, would you come with me? I'm sure my company could find a place for you."

"Please don't. Anyway, it really wouldn't make a difference. You don't want me following you around, and I don't want to be one of those women."

"What do you want? For us to call each other daily, which would go to every other day, to once a week, until we're too busy to speak to each other. Maybe I could stop in every once in a while, but even that would get old. It's better to cut it off clean. It won't hurt as much, I promise."

"That's right, you've done all this before."

The bite to her words hurt. He had, but with Callee it was much harder. The pull to stay stronger. But it would do her no good, or him either if he stayed. In the end he would still leave.

He sighed. "Then I'll say thanks for sharing your clinic with me. I'll be leaving now. Walk me to my truck?"

Her sad gaze met his. She shook her head. "I'd rather not. I hope you have a good life."

Disappointment flooded him.

She turned her attention back to the computer.

Langston headed up the hallway his shoulders heavy with remorse. He didn't like leaving this way. Maybe it was just as well. It would be better to just leave and not hang on to their relationship than to later watch it slowly die.

At his truck, he had opened the driver's door when a golf cart flew to the front of the clinic and jerked to a stop. A man, scraped and bleeding, sat in the back seat. He held his arm as if it were broken.

Langston loped back to the clinic. Callee would need his help.

Regardless of Callee's best intentions, she followed Langston up the hall. She stood at the door, watching him walk to his truck. She wouldn't cry. It would only make it harder to let him go. She would be strong. The last thing she wanted Langston to remember was her sobbing. Or begging him not to go. She was better than that.

Callee didn't want a man who didn't want her. She wanted one who would be there in the morning, every morning. She'd already lost one relationship. She didn't want to lose another.

A golf cart stopped in front of the clinic doors, drawing her attention. She hurried to the bloody man in the back seat. Helping him to stand she said, "Come on, let's get you inside and taken care of."

The driver went to his other side and between the two of them they managed to get the man inside.

Carl had left early for an appointment so she would have to handle this herself.

"Callee?"

Langston was back. How many times was she supposed to live through him leaving? Why hadn't he kept walking?

Seconds later he entered the small room, making it feel smaller. "What happen here?"

"Bike accident."

He shook his head. "It must have been some accident. What can I do to help?"

"I thought you needed to leave." She didn't like her own bitter tone.

Langston gave her a hard look. "You need my help."

Callee's disappointment ebbed away. He would always come if she needed him. Langston moved to one side of the man and she to the other. "We need to get him on the exam table."

They helped the injured man up. There were very few visible areas that didn't have a scratch or a gash. Mangled was the only way to describe him. The misery in his eyes matched his damages.

"I'm Callee and this is Langston. And you are?"

"Rodriguez."

"Sorry we have to meet this way." Langston was in the process of cutting the man's shirt off him. "What happened, Rodriguez?"

"I was riding a bike. A truck pulling a trailer hit me. Knocked me into a barn then to the gravel."

Langston shook his head. "All this from a bike accident."

Callee gathered supplies and brought them into the room. "Bikes are a good mode of transportation around here, but this happens so often."

"That's a shame."

"Rodriguez, we'll—" she looked beyond the man to Langston, meeting his gaze "—have you cleaned up and bandaged in no time." She tried for a positive smile.

Langston nodded and went back to putting scissors to their patient's shirt while she set up the saline, bandages and instruments on a tray.

"I never saw anybody with quite so many superficial cuts and scrapes," Langston said in wonder. "They are shallow but everywhere."

The man winced and jerked his arm. "Sorry."

Together she and Langston finished removing the shirt. The man stiffened.

"Sorry about that, Rodriguez. We'll soon get you straightened out. Just as quick as we can."

"I have to get back to work." Rodriguez looked toward the door.

"I'm afraid this isn't going to happen for a while, but right now we need to exam you and see if you need any stitches." Callee worked to reassure the patient.

"I'll take care of vitals. Mind if I borrow your stethoscope?" Langston asked.

She pulled it from around her neck. Their fingers brushed as she handed it to him. That same shot of awareness raced through her. Would that ever change? Heartache quickly followed.

"You got to cut my pants?" Rodriguez asked.

"If you are up to removing them yourself, then we won't have to."

Rodriguez nodded. "I can handle it."

"Then Langston will help you while I get you something to wear." She stepped out of the room, sensing the young man wanted privacy. "I'll be right back."

Callee returned to find Rodriguez sitting on the exam table with a hospital gown on. She went to work examining him. "There were many abrasions and scrapes, but it doesn't look like you'll need any stitches, which is good. In fact, the only ones we will bandage are the larger ones. The others will remain uncovered. But I will want you back here to check for infection every other day."

"May I check out your head?" Langston asked.

Rodriguez nodded.

Langston stepped in front of him and pulled out his penlight. Shining it into his eyes he said, "Please follow the light. Good. Now look at a spot over my left shoulder. Don't move. Good."

Pulling on examination gloves Langston said, "Now I'm going to run my hands over your head. Let me know if anything hurts." Slowly he worked his fingers over Rodriguez's skull.

The man flinched.

"It hurts right here?" Langston looked closer at Rodriguez's head.

"Yes."

"Okay. There's a knot. It's coming out so that's good. If you have any headaches, eye bleariness or trouble walking, come see Callee right away." He met Rodriguez's look. "Do not wait. Understand? You should go for a head scan at the hospital. You took a real tumble. Callee will help you with that."

"I understand."

Callee would miss this Langston too. The one who truly cared about his patients. His abilities were wasted on nothing but research. He was too good with people.

Over the next hour she and Langston cleaned and bandaged the wounds needing their attention.

When they'd finished, Rodriquez gave them a weak smile. "I look like a mummy."

She grinned. "You sure do. You need to keep the bandages clean and dry. Come see me before the weekend."

"I need to work."

Callee shook her head. "Not in a barn."

When Rodriquez started to say something, she stopped him. "I know, but you're gonna need to let somebody else handle the hay and grain. The airborne stuff can cause infections. You'll have to take a few days off and then be only outside. No mucking."

She caught Langston checking his watch. "I appreciate your help."

"I'm sorry I have to go." His eyes held shadows of concern.

"I understand."

Langston said, "Rodriguez, take care of yourself. Be careful on a bike."

Langston gave her another searching look before he touched her on the shoulder then went out the door.

# CHAPTER ELEVEN

THE DRIVE FROM Louisville to Dallas was long and lonely, giving Langston plenty of time to think. Not what he really wanted to do. His chest felt tight since he pulled out of the parking lot of the backside hours ago. He didn't like the way he and Callee had parted. Yet he feared if he'd allowed them to continue seeing each other, he'd never be able to leave her. Even now he wasn't sure he could survive without her.

He replayed their conversations, over and over. Was he running? Not taking some of the blame for what happened with Emily. And Mark. He had accused Callee of hiding but wasn't he just as guilty? Staying on the road and not facing his past? He made it an art form to stay away from the town where parents and Emily and Mark lived. He'd taken all those jobs because he didn't want to face the past and his hurt.

The farther he drove away from Callee the tighter his chest became. He would learn to live with the ache. Surely it would go away in a few days.

Tired and emotionally drained, he stayed in a hotel for the night believing he would get a good night's sleep. Instead, he tossed and turned, and was miserable. Another night of sleep missed. He blamed it on being in a different bed, but he knew better. It was because Callee wasn't there. Too many times he had reached out to pull her to him and been disappointed to find nothing but a cold pillow beside him.

* * *

The late heat of Dallas made sweat pop out on his brow. He already missed the spring breeze and green trees of Kentucky. Wednesday evening after the meeting he just made in time, he entered his apartment and went stock-still. He dropped his bags with a thump.

The place looked as sterile as an operating room. There was no life in it. None of the warmth of pillows, soft lighting, or the colors of Callee's home. Nothing about it looked welcoming or lived in. Or even cared for. It was completely the opposite of Callee's place. And his heart felt just as cold and empty as this place.

Langston turned around and walked out, unsure of what to do. In his truck again, he started to drive. To his surprise he ended up in Prairie. At the welcome sign posted at the town limits, he pulled over and looked at it. It had been years since he'd returned. He'd made excuses not to. His parents visited him when they came to Dallas, or he met them somewhere for dinner but he hadn't been to town since Emily and Mark had told him they were getting married.

The town had been a good place to live. He'd grown up happy there. But he'd let bitterness control his life. Because of that he'd punished his family by not visiting them. He'd let that pain overshadow all the good of his childhood.

That happiness he'd had so long ago had returned while being with Callee. It was the first time since childhood he'd felt he belonged. Even had a sense of being a member of the backside family. If he wanted that feeling back he had work to do. He had to face his past. That meant he needed talk to Mark and Emily. His mother had once told him Mark and Emily had moved into Mark's parents' house after they'd moved to the coast.

He pulled in front of the house with the white picket fence.

Emily had always talked about wanting one. He'd always thought they were a sign of being settled, as a restriction. Yet he hadn't seen the white fence around the Thompsons' farm like that. There he'd seen the fence as protection of something of value.

The idea of being fenced in with Callee didn't make him want to run now. Somehow the idea made him feel secure. As if he'd found the place he belonged, where someone would always be waiting on him to return and would be happy to see him. Had Callee been right about him and Emily wanting different things out of life back then? Were they just not meant to be?

Langston parked on the road in front of the house. He walked to the front door and knocked. Would they be glad to see him or close the door in his face?

Mark answered the door. He looked older and settled. He'd always been the home body of the two of them. His temples were graying. giving him a distinguished look.

Mark's eyes widened. His face paled in disbelief. "Langston."

"Hi, Mark. I'm sorry I didn't call first, but I didn't have your number." Langston heard sounds of children playing in the backyard. "I was wondering if we could talk for a few minutes. I won't take a lot of your time."

Mark looked behind him, concern etching his features. "Come in. Emily's in the backyard with the kids. We're getting ready to grill hamburgers."

"I didn't mean to interrupt your mealtime. I can come back later."

"No, no. Now is fine. I know Emily will be glad to see you. I certainly am." Mark led him down a hallway to the back of the house.

"I won't stay long."

"How have you been? When I see your mother or father in town they proudly tell me where you have been and everything you have been doing. I'm not ever surprised. You were always an achiever and eager to leave this town."

Langston looked at the house as they walked through it. He remembered the 1960s layout, but Emily had made a number of changes, along with the very lived-in space that included shoes, book bags and toys. The feelings were the same ones he got at Callee's minus the children's paraphernalia. As if the people who lived here loved each other.

They continued out the glass back doors to the patio. A boy and a girl played on a wooden swing set. Emily stood nearby watching them.

"Emily," Mark called.

She turned, and her mouth dropped open as a look of astonishment covered her face moments before a smile formed on her lips. "Langston!" She started toward him. "Louise and Willy, come here. I'd like you to meet a friend of ours."

Langston returned the smile, felt it ease the tension that had filled him.

"What a nice surprise. It's good to see you."

Emily looked just as she had before with a few more lines around her eyes but still a cheerful mild mannered person. Nothing like the strong, self-assured, sassy Callee.

The boy and girl came up and stood beside their father. "Kids, I would like for you to meet one of our friends. This is Dr. Langston Watts."

Langston went down on his heels, meeting them at eye level. "It's nice to meet you. Your mother and dad and I used to be great friends."

The girl the obvious elder of the two said, "We know who you are. Mom and Dad talk about you. You are the doctor."

Langston glanced at Emily and then Mark.

"They tell stories about all the fun things you did around town growing up. They laugh about them even when it isn't funny."

That touched Langston's heart. Why had he waited so long to do this? They did share wonderful memories of living in a small town where they wandered around not having to always be on guard. Where they knew everybody, and everyone knew them. He'd let the bitterness of what had happened between Emily and him overshadow everything. Including his relationship with his parents and how they'd chosen to live their lives.

"Yeah," the boy said. "They tell me to study hard if I want to be a great doctor like you. That you help people."

Langston's heart warmed. Emily and Mark had used him as an example to their kids. Wow, that was high praise. Too high after the way Langston had acted. "You do have to study, but it's all right to have fun sometimes too."

Emily spoke to the children. "Go play while the grown-ups talk. We'll eat in a few minutes." She then led him over to a picnic table with Mark, where Mark and Emily sat beside each other.

They looked like they belong together. Someone at the ball had said he and Callee looked like they belonged together.

"Thanks for letting me in."

"I have to admit I was a little more than surprised to see you." Mark took Emily's hand and gave it a squeeze.

"I didn't exactly plan this."

"So why after all this time are you here?" Mark asked.

Langston looked from Mark to Emily and back again. "Because I owe you both an apology."

It was the couple's turn to look at each other.

"I acted poorly. I've carried a grudge." He looked at Emily. "At first, I was mad you didn't wait on me. But the truth is I left you behind." His focus went to Mark. "For too long I believed you took Emily away from me. But I can see now y'all belong together. I finally see what you saw. We wanted different things. I just wanted to apologize for being such a jerk and staying away so long. I've missed your friendship."

"Your reaction was natural. We've been hoping that you would change your mind and at least speak to us. Thank goodness you have. You needed to go, and I needed to stay." Emily glanced at her children.

"What made you change your mind?" Mark asked.

Emily smiled and spoke before he did. "He's met someone."

"I did." But would she have him back? After he left her, just as he had Emily?

"I've been telling Mark for years that all it would take is for you to find the right one and you would understand, forgive us." She looked pleased with herself. "It's finally happened. So tell us all about her."

"Callee's the PA at Churchill Downs' backside clinic. She smiles all the time. Knows everyone. Can handle horses. Looks great in a ball gown." And was perfect for him. Why hadn't he realized that before now?

"I found the right man for me and apparently you've found the right girl for you." Emily leaned her shoulder against Mark. "I'm glad."

"Would you like to stay and have supper with us?" Mark asked.

Langston stood. "I better not. I still have to see my parents. May I take a rain check?"

Emily nodded. "Only if you promise to bring Callee by to meet us."

"You have my word." That's if he could get her to forgive him.

Fifteen minutes later he knocked on the kitchen door of

his parents' home. Before his mother could get there to open it, he walked in.

"Langston!" his mother squealed, and dropped the knife she'd been using to peel an apple.

"Hi, Mom."

His father came in from the other room. "Dad."

His mother rushed to bring him into a hug. Tears filled her eyes. Guilt washed through him. He should have made it a point to see his parents more often.

Langston's mother let him go seconds before his father hugged him, slapping him on the back. "This is a wonderful surprise."

"A real nice surprise." His mother continued to touch his arm as if she feared he wasn't real.

"Sit down and I'll get you a cup of coffee. Have you eaten yet?"

"No, Mom, but I'd like to take you guys out for a meal."

His mother shook her head. "No, no. I was working on an apple pie and your father requested pork chops. There's plenty for us all."

"She's still the best cook in town." His father looked at his mother with such love.

It was similar to those Callee gave him. Why hadn't he seen it before? Because he didn't want to believe it. Didn't want to examine his own feelings.

His mother brought the coffee, filling his cup.

"Mom and Dad, I owe you an apology." He was saying that a lot lately.

"For what, honey?" His mother looked concerned.

"For not coming home as often as I should."

"We understand that your work is important." His father picked up his mug.

"Not more important than the ones I love. I let my feelings

about Emily and Mark affect my actions. You didn't deserve that. I'm sorry. I was so wrong."

"You were hurt. We understood that." His mother's fingers clutched the back of one of the kitchen chairs.

"Still, that was no excuse. I went to see Emily and Mark."

"How did that go?" his father asked.

"We are good."

"I'm glad to hear that." His mother's voice held such relief.

"Mom, Dad, I could use your help with something."

Langston told them about Callee and how he'd left things between them. Since having a taste of the warmth and the feeling of belonging that he had with Callee, he realized what he'd been missing in life. He wanted it back. He wanted Callee.

At times Callee hadn't been confident she would survive the week after Langston left. She had looked for him at every turn, then had hoped he would return, while crying herself to sleep each night. She had already lost too much sleep in her life over something she couldn't change. Joe. Now she was doing so again over Langston.

He had broken her heart. And she'd let him.

Not even after Joe's accident had she been this devastated. Only in the last few weeks since Langston had come to town had she'd been able to talk about Joe without being shackled by guilt. Because of Langston she'd started living again. Finally accepting she couldn't have done any more for Joe than what she had done. It felt good being released from those bonds.

But the crying had to stop. Langston wasn't coming back. Thank goodness she'd been too busy to watch him drive away. She would have been a blubbering mess. He wouldn't have liked that, and she wouldn't have either. Instead, she'd gone home and fallen apart.

It had been difficult for her to function at work without

sleep. She disliked mopey people and she had become one of them. She kept one foot in front of the other. Barely.

Callee now understood why she'd kept other men at arm's length for so long. This pain was excruciating. She hadn't allowed her other relationships to move past the friend stage on purpose, stuck in her pain and her guilt, but Langston had pushed that barrier out of the way.

It was time for her to pick herself up. She had been through loss before. She could, she would survive this one.

Dr. Bishop had stopped by one day to ask her how it was going and how things had been with Langston helping out. Callee shared that everything had gone smoothly. For a brief second, he studied her a little closer than she would've liked. Had he noticed their closeness at the ball or the tightness around her mouth? Could he see the gaping hole where her heart had been?

More than once she'd noticed the concern in Carl's eyes too. It took him to midweek after Langston left before he asked, "Have you heard from Langston?"

"No."

"I sure liked having him around. Good doctor," he said causally as he watched her too closely.

"Yes, he is."

"Do you think he'll come back?"

She snapped, "No."

"I'm sorry, Callee. It's his loss."

She hated the sympathy in his voice. Hated that she cared. They were the last things she wanted. Her eyes watered. She turned and headed to her office.

After that Carl said no more about Langston.

Determined to snap out of the Langston-induced funk, she tried to keep her regular schedule, which was to go visit her parents the next weekend, but she couldn't bring herself to do anything more than go to work and then crawl into bed. She did manage to call. After all, she needed to make arrangements for PG to go home until she could find another place to board him closer to her.

Her mother's voice was a balm to Callee's soul. "It's so good to hear from you. It's been too long."

"I know, Mama. There was Derby Week. And you know how that is and then other things came up. Sorry. I'll be out to see you soon."

"I'm just glad to hear from you."

Emotion filled Callee's throat. She was too. "Is Dad around? Can I speak to him?"

"He's on a run. He should be home soon."

Callee looked around her bedroom. "He always seems to be on a run. He needs help."

"Yeah. But he can't seem to find someone he trusts."

"I let him down, didn't I? He'd planned on me helping him." Callee used to go with him. She loved every minute of the time they spent together.

Her mother sighed. "You didn't let him down. It was more like disappointing him. But you know how your father is when he makes up his mind about something. It's hard to change it." Her mother paused. "You want to tell me what's going on?"

Callee fiddled with the edge of the blanket on the bed, bringing it to her nose. It smelled of Langston. "Just the same old stuff. Nothing special."

"I can hear in your voice something is wrong."

Was Callee's unhappiness that obvious? "Why do you say that?"

"Because I am your mother and I know you."

Callee blinked to control the moisture threatening leak from her eyes.

"Telling me about it, honey."

That was all it took for Callee to let her emotions spill out to her mother about Langston. Before she finished Callee's words were gasps. "I haven't heard from Langston since he left. We had a big fight. He said a lot of things about me and my life that I didn't want to hear."

"Such as?"

"That I can't talk to Dad about my feelings and that I've let the situation with Joe control my life."

Her mother's voice softened. "Honey, I have to agree. I think you've carried responsibility for Joe's accident and death for far too long.

"Your father's home. Let me take the phone to him. You two need to talk. You should tell him how you feel."

That didn't sound like fun to Callee.

"After you do that, I suggest you think long and hard about what you want out of life. What you want it to look like. Only you can decide that. Here's your dad."

Callee's palms started to sweat. She sat up on the edge of the bed.

"Hey, Callee girl. How are you?" Her father's voice said he was pleased to hear from her.

Had he always greeted her like that? Why hadn't she noticed before? Did her concern over disappointing him color her view of her father? Maybe she was the one who needed to see things differently. "Hi, Dad."

"It's been a while since I've been home. Your job must be keeping you busy. We miss you around here."

"I'm sorry about that, Daddy. I'll be home soon. What kind of case did you have today?"

"An old mare with a cyst on her neck."

She heard the bang of the storage door on the side of the truck. Her father was putting equipment away. "I always loved going with you on your runs."

"Yep, then you turned to human medicine."

"But I learned so much from you that I use every day on people, like compassion, talking softly when they've shared, to how do I get them to do what I need them to do. All that I learned from you."

There was a pause as if he were thinking about that. Now was the time to say it. "I know I disappointed you when I changed to human medicine. I'm sorry for that but I'm where I belong."

"I was disappointed. I let myself have big plans for sharing my practice with you. But I was thinking about me and not you."

"I had thought at one time I would join you too."

"I resented you for changing after Joe. I guess I thought in a way he took you away from me. Then I saw you blossom when you talked about your work. The passion you had for it that was beyond even that which you showed for animals."

It had been that way. She had fallen in love with caring for people. It had fed a part of her that she hadn't even explored because she had been so caught up in thinking about being a veterinarian.

"I heard what happened with the horse in the trailer. Also, the horse with the flu."

"You did?"

"We vets talk. Especially when my daughter is involved."

She heard the pride in his voice. The cold she had been feeling started to warm up a bit. "Small world."

"I am proud of you. I'm proud of the quality work you do. Along with the person you are."

"Thanks, Daddy. I needed to hear that."

"I also heard you had a big deal doctor working with you for a few weeks."

Langston. She wasn't sure she could talk about him with her

father. It had been all she could do to discuss Langston with her mother. "Yes. I didn't realize what a big deal he was." In more ways than one. "But he's gone now."

"Will he be coming back?"

She looked out the window to the sunny day beyond. "I doubt it."

"Sounds like you might have liked him."

"Yeah, but he's gone now." Gone. She didn't like the sound of that. "I've been offered a new job."

"You have?"

"It's working with the jockeys and the horses. Studying their interactions. It's a new program that Churchill Downs is supporting where I'd do the care for the jockeys, but I'd also be in on their work with the horses. It would be the best of both worlds for me. I wasn't going to take it but I'm rethinking that. Dr. Bishop is encouraging me to do it. A Dr. Mitchell would be one of the lead people on the program. In a few years I might have the opportunity to run the program."

"Sounds like it would utilize your skills."

"But I like where I'm working." She did. So much she couldn't see beyond it.

"It's easy to stay where you're comfortable. It's much harder to stretch yourself."

"Someone else said the same thing to me the other day." Langston.

"I think you can do anything you put your mind to. You need to think about what you want and what uses your skill set." Her father's voice had turned firm.

"Now you sound like my mother."

His tone held warmth when he said, "Your mom's a smart woman."

Her parents had been together since they were teenagers.

They had a home and raised their family, but they still loved each other. What could she do to have that?

Callee's tears had cleared during her conversation with her parents. It was time for action, change. To move toward, to go after what she wanted.

Langston had been right. She'd been using the clinic to hide, had created a cocoon where she didn't let herself make mistakes. She didn't take chances out of fear. She would look into the job opportunity. See what it involved.

It was past time for her to pick herself up and move on.

Langston pulled through the stone gateposts into the drive of the Thompsons' farm. Since it was Sunday afternoon, Callee would be there to see PG. Would she be glad to see him? He hoped so. His happiness and life plans depended on it. It had been a long emotional week since he'd last spoken to her. He couldn't complain; he was the one who said it would be best to cut it off clean. His words had come back to bite him like a rabid dog.

He'd promised not to contact her, and he'd kept his word but it almost killed him. The number of times he picked up his phone with her in mind went into the hundreds.

Would she hear him out? Was she still angry with him? Would she be as excited to see him as he was her? Had he spent too much time reorganizing his life when he should have been begging her to take him back? The questions ricocheted around in his head.

His heart beat faster the closer he drove to the house. His palms sweated against the steering wheel as he drove past the house and pulled up next to Callee's car parked outside the barn. Relief washed over him. She was here. Mrs. Thompson had told him to hang on to a good thing. He hadn't listened at the time. Now he knew exactly what she had meant. If Callee would have him, he'd hold on tight this time.

After returning from Prairie, the first call he made was to Valtech headquarters to propose opening a permanent location in the Louisville area. He volunteered to start the program along with creating an affiliation with the University of Louisville to further study sport safety. That took some persuasion, but he managed an agreement. He also contacted the hospital in Louisville for permanent privileges. The board eagerly agreed to let him be on staff.

His last and final call had been to the Thompsons asking if they would hold off on the selling of their home until he could talk to Callee. If she agreed, he hoped they could make it their home. The Thompsons had agreed to wait.

He hoped his plans didn't backfire. All that had to happen was for Callee to turn him away.

Climbing out of his truck, he took a deep breath and rolled his shoulders. He walked into the dim light of the barn more nervous than he'd ever been.

Callee was halfway down the hall. PG stood between them so she couldn't see Langston coming. While she brushed the horse, she talked to him. "It's time to move on, ole boy. For both of us. We both need a change."

She leaned down toward the horse's belly, paused and popped up. Stepping around PG's head, she stopped. Even in the dappled light Langston could tell her eyes had widened.

"Langston." His name was a little more than a whisper.

"Hi, Callee." He stepped closer.

"What're you doing here?" His reception was cooler than he'd hoped.

"I came to see you."

"Just passing through, I guess." She was thinner than she'd

been when he left. What had he done to her? It made him heart sick.

"A little more than that."

She patted PG's nose. "I thought you'd be off in India or someplace by now."

Callee wasn't giving him an inch. What had he expected, a warm welcome? He'd hurt her. It was time for some fast talking. "Can we talk?"

"I'm busy here." She picked up the brush. "I thought we said all there was to say before you left."

"Yeah, but I've accepted something while I was gone that has changed things."

"And that would be?" She started brushing PG once more.

He stepped closer. "Callee, do you think you could look at me?"

"No."

The word was so soft he almost missed it. "Why not?"

"Because it's too hard." There was a catch in her voice.

Was she crying? His chest tightened.

"Why'd you come back here anyway? You said to cut it off so it wouldn't hurt."

"I'm trying to tell you why I'm here."

She spun around and glared at him. "Then tell me."

"Because I love you."

Callee blinked. Her eyes brightened and a smile flashed across her face. She dropped the brush and started toward him. He opened his arms and she jumped into them, wrapping her arms around his neck and holding him tight.

Her mouth found his in a smacking kiss that rocked his world. Callee was his world.

"I love you too." She kissed his eyes, his cheek, his temple and nibbled at his ear.

He kissed her long and tenderly with all the love in his heart.

Finally, he let her slip along his body until her feet touched the sawdust floor.

"Wait here." She took PG to a stall and closed him in.

"Callee, we still need to talk."

"I have something I want to tell you too." She took his hand. "Come with me." She led him outside to a bench resting against the side of the barn. They sat.

Langston twisted until he faced her. He pulled a piece of hay out of her hair. "Do you think the Thompsons are wondering what we are doing?"

"They're off hunting a new house." She kissed him. "They'll be gone all afternoon. May I talk first?"

"You keep that up and you can have anything you want." He returned a kiss.

She held him back when he would have gone further. "I want to tell you my news."

"That is?"

"I talked to my father." She beamed. "He said he was proud of me. All is good between us. I should have told him how I felt sooner."

"That's wonderful. I know that makes you very happy."

Callee sat straighter, with her shoulders back. "I'm going to resign from the clinic. I'm going to take that job with Dr. Mitchell."

"So you decided to do that. That's wonderful. I think it's tailor-made for you."

"I believe it is too. I never would have considered it if it hadn't been for you and what you said. You were right. I have been hiding and paying my guilt penitence for Joe. You made me see that. Thank you." She gave him a quick kiss. "The best part is I'll have the freedom to travel with you or visit you or however you want to work this out between us. All I know is I want you in my life."

"About that…"

* * *

Callee's heart lodged in her throat. She dared not guess what he would say next. Fearing he wouldn't want her traveling with him or worse not to even try long distance.

"I'm coming to Louisville to start a Valtech office here. I'll still be doing research but in affiliation with the university. I'm also going to be on the staff at the hospital. There'll still be some travel but not as much as I've been doing."

"You're moving here?" Callee looked at Langston in disbelief. Was her dream really coming true? She shook her head. "No, I can't let you do that for me. You'll hate it, then you'll start resenting me. I want you to be happy."

"Sweetheart," he said, kissing her quiet. "I'll be happy anywhere you are."

She cupped his whisker-roughened cheeks and kissed him like he was the most wonderful man she knew, and he was. She pulled away. "Are you sure?"

"I'm sure. You aren't the only one who listened to some truths. I thought about what you said to me too. I went to Prairie. Visited Mark and Emily."

Callee's mouth formed an O. "That must have been hard for you."

"It was but therapeutic as well. I think I was hurt on two fronts. By Emily, but also by losing my best friend as well. I hope we'll find our way back to some of what we had. They want to meet you."

"You told them about me?"

"I sure did." He brushed her hair away from her face. "Emily knew right away I was in love."

"Did you see your parents?" She hoped it went well.

"I did. It was nice. I've hurt them, but they love me so they'll give me a chance to do better. They helped me come up with my plan."

"Your plan for what?"

"For my new jobs, coming here to see you and one more thing."

"I still don't understand." Callee remained completely confused.

"I'm sorry. I think I'm going about this a little backward. I love you and I want you in my life forever." He scooted off the bench and went to one knee, taking her left hand. "I'm totally under your spell, Callee Dobson. Yours forever."

Callee's heart fluttered. This couldn't be… She'd dreamed it but never imagined Langston would…

"Will you marry me?"

"Yes. A thousand times yes." She launched herself at him making him fall to the ground. He grabbed her around the waist and held her tight. She kissed him with all the love in her heart. Minutes later her legs straddled his hips as she looked into his beautiful eyes, which returned her admiration and love. "I love you so much, Langston. I want you to be happy."

"I am when I'm with you."

A few minutes later she helped Langston up and they dusted themselves off. "Well, I was thinking that if I was going to have a wife—" he smiled at her "—that we should have a place where we could raise our children and keep her horse. Maybe some place like this, if she liked it."

Callee looked at him in disbelief. "You're not thinking of buying the farm, are you?"

He shrugged. "Only if it is what you want."

Her eyes widened. "I can't believe it. You would really want to live here?"

"If it would make you happy, it would make me happy."

Callee smiled. "It sounds perfect to me. You know I love this farm, but the most important thing is you'll be living here with me. All I've ever really wanted is your cowboy boots beside my bed—forever."

"Honey, this man is finished wandering. I've found my home. You."

* * * * *

# MILLS & BOON MODERN IS
# HAVING A MAKEOVER!

The same great stories you love,
a stylish new look!

Look out for our brand new look
## COMING JUNE 2024

MILLS & BOON

# COMING SOON!

We really hope you enjoyed reading this book.
If you're looking for more romance
be sure to head to the shops when
new books are available on

## Thursday 23rd
## May

To see which titles are coming soon, please visit
**millsandboon.co.uk/nextmonth**

MILLS & BOON

# MILLS & BOON®

Coming next month

## UNBUTTONING THE BACHELOR DOC
### Deanna Anders

'Dance with me,' Sky said, her blue eyes dancing with a fevered excitement that flowed over onto him.

He knew he shouldn't. This wasn't a date. They were there purely as professional colleagues. Nothing more.

But as her arms wrapped around his neck, his own arms found their way around her waist, pulling her closer. And when she laid her head against him, he let himself relax against her. What could it hurt to share one dance?

It only took a minute for his body to answer that question. It was as if a fire had been lit inside him as his body reacted to the feel of Sky against him. His muscles tightened and he went stone hard. He tried to keep his breathing as even as possible as they swayed to the music, her body rubbing against him with each movement. He glanced down and their eyes met. As she drew in a breath that appeared as labored as his, his eyes went to her lips, the same lips that had teased him for months. For a moment he considered tasting them. Would they be soft and supple? Or would they be firm and needy? He had just started to lean down when the couple next to them bumped into him, breaking whatever spell he'd been under.

What could one dance hurt? It could destroy his whole reputation if he let himself lose control on the dance floor.

He pulled himself back from the brink of doing something that would scandalize the whole room with a willpower he hadn't known he possessed. But when the song ended and she stepped away from him, his arms felt empty. It had only been one dance. The fact that her body had molded so perfectly to his didn't mean a thing. But he'd danced with many women before Sky and he'd never felt anything like this before.

'We should go,' he said, though his traitorous feet refused to take a step away from her.

'Why? Do we have plans?' she asked, her voice soft and breathy. His body responded as once more she stepped toward him.

He wanted to pull her back into his arms, to kiss that mouth that had teased him for the last six months. Only he couldn't kiss her now any more than he could have kissed her all those other times. He had to step away from her now just like he'd done over and over when she had tempted him. He needed to put things back to the way they'd been before that dance. Before he'd felt how right her body felt against his.

It should be simple. One step. Just take one step and walk away. But this was Sky. Nothing about the woman was simple.

*Continue reading*
**UNBUTTONING THE BACHELOR DOC**
Deanne Anders

*Available next month*
millsandboon.co.uk

afterglow BOOKS

From showing up to glowing up, Afterglow Books features authentic and relatable stories, characters you can't help but fall in love with and plenty of spice!

## OUT NOW

To discover more visit:
**Afterglowbooks.co.uk**

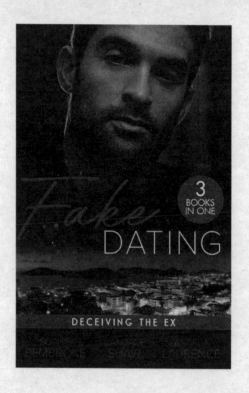

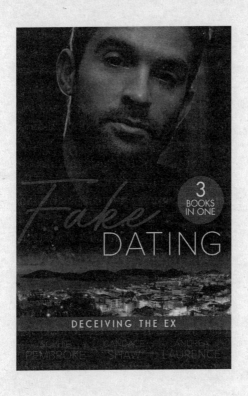

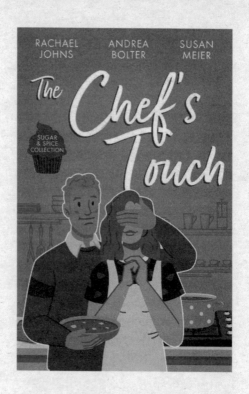

LET'S TALK

# Romance

For exclusive extracts, competitions
and special offers, find us online:

f MillsandBoon

𝕏 @MillsandBoon

⊡ @MillsandBoonUK

♪ @MillsandBoonUK

Get in touch on 01413 063 232

# MILLS & BOON

## THE HEART OF ROMANCE

---

## A ROMANCE FOR EVERY READER

---

### MODERN

Prepare to be swept off your feet by sophisticated, sexy and seductive heroes, in some of the world's most glamourous and romantic locations, where power and passion collide.

### HISTORICAL

Escape with historical heroes from time gone by. Whether your passion is for wicked Regency Rakes, muscled Vikings or rugged Highlanders, awaken the romance of the past.

### MEDICAL

Set your pulse racing with dedicated, delectable doctors in the high-pressure world of medicine, where emotions run high and passion, comfort and love are the best medicine.

### *True Love*

Celebrate true love with tender stories of heartfelt romance, from the rush of falling in love to the joy a new baby can bring, and a focus on the emotional heart of a relationship.

### HEROES

The excitement of a gripping thriller, with intense romance at its heart. Resourceful, true-to-life women and strong, fearless men face danger and desire - a killer combination!

###

From showing up to glowing up, these characters are on the path to leading their best lives and finding romance along the way – with plenty of sizzling spice!

To see which titles are coming soon, please visit

## millsandboon.co.uk/nextmonth